Also by Margaret Kaine
from Hodder & Stoughton

Ring of Clay
Rosemary
A Girl Of Her Time
Friends and Families
Roses for Rebecca
Ribbon of Moonlight

About the author

Born and educated in Stoke-on-Trent, Margaret Kaine now lives in Eastbourne. Her first novel, Ring of Clay, won the 2002 Romantic Novelists' Association/Reader's Digest Of Love and Life New Writer's Award and the 2003 Society of Authors' Sagittarius Prize.

Find out more at www.margaretkaine.com.

Margaret Kaine

Friends and Families

HODDER

First published in Great Britain in 2005 by Hodder & Stoughton
An Hachette UK company

This paperback edition published in 2018

1

First published by Poolbeg Press Limited (Dublin) 2005

A CIP catalogue record for this title is available from the British Library

Paperback ISBN 978 1 473 67864 4

Typeset in Plantin Light by Palimpsest Book Production Limited,
Falkirk, Stirlingshire
Printed and bound by CPI Group (UK) Ltd, Croydon CR0 4YY

Hodder & Stoughton policy is to use papers that are natural,
renewable and recyclable products and made from wood grown
in sustainable forests. The logging and manufacturing processes
are expected to conform to the environmental regulations
of the country of origin.

Hodder & Stoughton Ltd
Carmelite House
50 Victoria Embankment
London EC4Y 0DZ

www.hodder.co.uk

Acknowledgements

As always, my gratitude to the wonderful writers'
workshop I join each Wednesday morning at
the Adult Education Centre in Leicester.
And again to my friend, Biddy Nelson,
who so generously reads my draft chapters,
and shares her own writing experience.

To my brother, Graham Inskip, for his help
with technical details of the ceramics industry.
To my sister-in-law, Philippa Kaine, who
patiently answers my phone calls to
confirm my local knowledge.

But most of all, to my husband,
for his love and support.

For my daughter, Jo

"Happy is the house that shelters a friend."
EMERSON

Chapter 1

Georgina Hawkins lived in the 'Big House'. At least that was what the neighbouring children called it. Her father, William Hawkins, had built his home in the middle of one of many rows of terraces belonging to him. True, it was a superior street, situated as it was at the top of a hill, with views over the industrial landscape of pottery kilns and factories. But to his wife's bitter chagrin, it was not an address in keeping with what she regarded as their 'proper social status'.

William, however, had other views. It pleased him to be living in a detached, square redbrick house, with its gleaming bay windows and impeccably kept lawns. What pleased him even more was the contrast between his own imposing home and the cramped houses surrounding it. The tall yew hedge around his property dominated the street, and the sight of envious stares through the black iron gates at the impressive frontage gave him a welcome sense of importance. He was a self-made man, a man who had built his own small empire. But his achievement had spawned a sense of power, of dominance, which sustained him, but alienated his wife and frightened his

1

daughter. William Hawkins had married late in life to acquire a son, and when his wife presented him with a puny female infant, and tearfully informed him that she could never bear another, he didn't bother to even look at the child.

Alice Hawkins, when told that the mewling blood-covered baby lying between her legs was a girl, had merely turned her exhausted face to the wall. As the mother of William's longed-for son, his heir, her standing in their marriage would have been enhanced; it would have given her a weapon against him. For it might be 1949, but William's outlook on life, and especially his view of the role of women, was exactly the same as that of his father and grandfather before him.

"I don't want to go!" Georgina hung her head.

"Nonsense!" Alice told her

"Why can't I go to school here? Why not?" Georgina persisted.

Alice looked at her in exasperation. "Because your father thinks you'll get a better education at boarding school." This was a lie. William wasn't in the least interested in what was best for Georgina. But Alice was fully aware of his calculating ambition. In a few years his daughter would become an asset. A successful marriage could bring useful contacts, increased prosperity. And for that, she needed to mix with the right people, move in the right circles. An expensive, well-regarded school would be an investment.

"Well, I don't want to!" Greatly daring,

Georgina stood her ground. It wasn't so much the thought of going away. Although she often felt lonely, at least here she could get away from it all, merge into the background, retreat into her books. But in a public domain like boarding school there would be nowhere to hide, no refuge.

Georgina often agonised over why she couldn't be outgoing like the other girls at the private junior school she attended. She longed to be like them, laughing, boisterous, unafraid of the strict teachers. Sitting by herself at a single desk in the classroom, standing alone in the playground, she would try to pluck up the courage to join in, but even as she hesitated the moment would pass.

"Don't I have any say in it?" Georgina appealed to her mother, but already knew there was little likelihood that her face, with its mask of expensive make-up, would soften.

"You could always try arguing with your father," Alice suggested, then felt a fleeting compunction as her daughter's face whitened. "No, I thought not," she added grimly.

The uniform, when it arrived, was hideous. A grey gym slip and watery blue blouse, to be covered by a grey, fine wool cardigan. Just the colours to wash me out, Georgina thought miserably. With lank fair hair and a long nose, she had no illusions about her looks. She would have loved to have arresting eyes, blue perhaps, deep pools of mystery like the heroine in her current book. But no, her own eyes were a funny sort of green, boring in her opinion – just as she was. She hated her life,

3

hated living in the Big House. She was never allowed to play with the other children in the street. Once, when she was younger, she had crept out of the house, and with a guilty backward look, gone to watch some girls skipping in the road. Standing on the pavement, she listened to them chanting, "All in together, girls," as two held each end of a rope, while the others skipped through as their names were called. Eventually one, a wiry girl with black curly hair jerked her head, calling, "Come on!" and Georgina had ducked under the rope and for the next half hour felt happier and more alive than she'd ever done in her short life. The pace was fast, leaving little time to talk, but then suddenly the game was ruined when an older girl sauntered up and, with one swift lunge, grabbed the length of clothes-line the younger children were using.

"Mum wants to hang some washing out," she snapped, and then her glance darted to Georgina. "What are you playing with *her* for?"

"She's not doing anything!" the black-haired girl protested.

"We don't mix with her sort, Josie Ford – you never know what tales she'll tell!"

"I wouldn't!" protested Georgina.

"Oh yeah? Come to slum it, 'ave yer? You and yer private school! Georgina! What sort of poncy name is that? Go on, clear off!" She gave Georgina a violent shove which made her fall backwards and collide with a wall.

Josie's face crimsoned with anger. "What did

4

yer do that for?" she yelled. "You're nothing but a bully, Muriel Machin. That's what you are!"

"And what are *you* going to do about it?"

Incensed, Josie rushed at the bigger girl, head-butting her in the stomach, and they both went down, to roll on the ground, scratching and pulling each other's hair. Shrieking encouragement for Josie, the others crowded round as Georgina struggled to her feet, and stood to watch in horrified fascination. So involved was she, that not even the sound of a car's engine warned her, until the blast of its horn caused the two fighting girls to draw apart and, with a last slap at each other, scramble to their feet. Georgina looked up, saw the familiar Hillman Minx, and her throat closed in terror as she met the appalled glare of her father. For one split second William stared at her, his eyes bulging with fury, before he blasted his horn again and began to edge through the crowd of girls.

Georgina turned and ran. Ran as fast as she could, frantic to get inside the gate, through the front door and up to her bedroom.

A few seconds later, his strident voice echoed through the house. "Alice! Alice!"

Georgina heard her mother's conciliatory voice, her father's angry tones, and then there were sharp footsteps on the stairs, and the door to her room was flung open.

"Get downstairs!"

Georgina cowered back. "I didn't do anything," she gabbled. "I only went down the street . . ."

Alice seized her shoulder. "How many times

5

have I told you not to go out on your own. How dare you disobey me! Do you know what you've done? It's me who'll get the blame, not you!" She dragged Georgina towards the staircase. "Now, get downstairs!"

With her mother behind her, Georgina stumbled down the wide richly carpeted stairs and, her heart hammering in her chest, stood in fear in the doorway of her father's study.

"And what have you to say for yourself!" he thundered. "Don't stand in the doorway – come here and answer me!"

Georgina forced her trembling legs to move forward.

"Cat got your tongue, or what?"

"I – I . . ." she began to stammer, "I only went out to play."

"Play? You call that playing? Standing watching those little guttersnipes brawling in the middle of the road?"

William's harsh voice seemed to lash at her very insides, and Georgina, sick with nerves, felt her eyes fill with tears. How she wanted to shout back at him, but no-one argued with William Hawkins.

"I was playing skipping," she managed at last.

"Well, you can skip in your own garden in future. And," he added, his face thrust against hers, "there'll be no more sneaking out, do you hear me? Do you?"

Georgina raised her eyes to her father's bristling grey moustache and mottled bulbous nose.

"Speak up!" he shouted.

"Yes."

"Right, now get out of my sight!"

Georgina left in tears, only to be confronted by Alice. "He'll expect me to punish you," she snapped. "So, there'll be no sweets for a fortnight!"

The threat was a severe blow. Sweets were still on ration, and although she was careful with her coupons, Georgina had a craving for chocolate. Crunchie bars were her favourites, and she would nibble at the milk chocolate casing, and then put in her tongue to dissolve the delicious honeycomb sweetness.

Since that episode, Georgina had never strayed again. When travelling in the car, she often saw the other children, and would look furtively for her champion, which was how she always thought of Josie. Occasionally their gaze would meet, but all too soon her father would snap, "Eyes in front, Georgina," and mutely she would turn her head away to stare blankly ahead. But even her father couldn't control her thoughts, her feelings. Georgina only knew that she envied Josie Ford and her friends. They might be poor, and, as her mother described them, 'rough' but not a day passed that Georgina didn't daydream of how much happier life must be inside the small terraced houses that lined each side of the street.

Chapter 2

Josie Ford was born as an afterthought – or, as her mother always said, as the result of a bet. The bet came into the equation because her husband Sid, not known for his willpower, had succumbed to a challenge. It hadn't mattered that the man in question was a stranger in the pub, an establishment Sid regarded as his second home. When he cast aspersions on a beer-drinker's ability to handle spirits, Sid had considered it not only a slur on his character, but a matter of honour to prove otherwise. It must have been a good malt whisky, Lily Ford told anyone who would listen, furious to find herself pregnant again.

"I'll tell you all something for nothing," she said. "There'll never be another bottle of the stuff in *our* house. Not if there's a chance of Sid getting his hands on it!"

But when Josie was born, Lily was entranced, feeling a surge of protectiveness and love for this unsought-for child she'd never felt for her other three. As for Sid, he just couldn't believe that in his late forties he'd fathered another baby, a girl at that, one who stared at him with piercing blue eyes, her little barrel chest proclaiming her arrival in the world.

At twelve, their eldest boy Dennis had been appalled when he realised there was to be an addition to their family.

"You'd think they'd have finished with all that at their age," he muttered. "Makes you want to throw up!"

John, two years younger, was a boy who lived in a world of his own. He didn't know what 'all that' meant. Totally absorbed in lining up his collection of bottle tops, he hadn't shown much interest.

Peter, who was nearly eight, just hoped the baby wouldn't cry a lot or have smelly nappies.

But again, Josie charmed them all. They would take turns to hold her, wondering at her daintiness, finding within them a gentleness they hadn't known existed. At least that was what happened inside the house. Outside, of course, Dennis and Peter had to be tough. "A flaming girl," Dennis announced, while young Peter complained loudly that she'd never be able to play football! John, however, surprised them all by being fascinated by the tiny baby, even offering to push her pram around the local park.

So Josie grew up in danger of being 'spoiled rotten', as neighbours would say. But that didn't happen, couldn't happen, not in a house where self-denial was as regular as breathing. Sid Ford worked as a labourer in a pottery factory, or potbank as they were more widely known. The work was arduous, the wage low, but it was the best he was capable of. 'Broad of shoulder, strong of back and not much upstairs,' was how Lily's father had described him, and she'd known it was true. But Sid had a teasing way that caught at her heart, and although he was older, his good looks had made him the most attractive prospect in the area. So, Lily had married him, and it was only sometimes, as she stood at the copper manhandling steamy sheets or stared in frustration at the sparse larder shelves, that she wondered if she could have done better for herself.

But Josie loved her dad. He tickled her, and slipped her a three-penny bit when her mum wasn't looking. Then she could go to the corner shop, and drool for ages over such delights as sherbet dips, Kali crystals to dip her finger in and suck, long-lasting gobstoppers, and liquorice root. Sweet rationing didn't affect the Ford children: their pocket money was so limited, it rationed them anyway.

Growing up with three brothers had made Josie more than capable of standing up for herself. A staunch friend, she was also a girl with a strong sense of fair play, an attribute many a younger child in the playground had cause to be grateful for.

"She's a belter when it comes to a scrap!" Peter would boast, although Sid wasn't too happy about that. His "little princess", as he liked to call his daughter, was growing up; she should be acting more like a lady, and he told her so.

Josie giggled. "Me, going all ladylike! Did you hear him, Mum?"

"Yes, I heard him," Lily snapped. "And what have I told you about sitting with your legs all sprawled out? Put your knees together – you're a big girl now."

Josie sulked. She didn't want to be a big girl. Particularly now she knew first-hand what that entailed. Monthly misery, that's all it was, and messy with it.

But the Fords struggled by, and despite the shabbiness of the house, and the constant effort to make ends meet, they were happy enough. Eventually, Dennis got married and went to live in Fenton, one of the six Potteries towns. "I won't be far, Mum," he said. "Me and Mavis'll come over often, you'll see." Mavis, a plump, sensible girl, was a paintress at the Tuscan Pottery in Longton, where they both worked. Sid and Lily liked her, and as the young couple were expecting their first child, were looking forward to becoming grandparents.

But Lily worried about John, who constantly had difficulty holding down a job. "He's not trying hard enough," Lily said one night to Sid. "Well, I'm not standing for it. I can't be doing with a grown man hanging around the house."

Sid glanced at her with a frown. "This last time, it wasn't all his fault, you know. Old Hawkins is a difficult bugger to work for."

"Maybe. But we all have to put up with things we don't want to."

"You're too hard on him, Lily. He'll get something, you'll see."

"It might help if he took a bit more interest in other people's doings," Lily said tartly. "He's forever absorbed in what interests him, but, as we all know, having a proper conversation with him is nigh on impossible.

"Aye, well, we are as we're made," Sid said, "and I doubt if he'll change now."

Peter was in the Royal Navy, having dreamed of going to sea since he was a small boy. After completing his National Service, he'd signed on as a regular, and although Lily worried about him picking up infections in foreign parts, not to mention, she muttered darkly to Sid, bad habits, they were both proud of him.

Josie caused them no anxieties. She was bright at school, sailing blithely through her lessons. She'd been bitterly disappointed when, after passing the scholarship, she hadn't been able to go to high school. Privately, Lily thought they could have managed the extra money, now that two of the boys had left home, but Sid didn't think it was necessary, not for a girl.

"I can't see the point of us scrimping and saving. She'll only go and get married and have kids," he'd argued. "It would have been different if it had been one of the lads."

But John had bitterly opposed their decision. "You should let her go," he insisted, and they had both stared at him in amazement. It was unheard of for their middle son to express an opinion about anything.

12

"And why's that?" Sid had demanded.

"Because she's special, that's why." John, his normally pale face flushed, had stood his ground. "And none of us boys were clever enough. She is – so she should have her chance."

Well done, lad, Lily thought, knowing what an effort such a speech must have been for him.

However, Sid was adamant. "I'm sorry, John. We just can't afford it."

But gradually, as she entered her teens, Josie's spirit began to rebel at 'doing without', as Lily would call it. But her discontent was transient as she came to realise that it was just the same for all the other girls she knew.

Then, several months after her thirteenth birthday, Josie, having with reluctance accepted her lowly station in life, changed her mind. The weather was freezing, one of those days when you could play breathing clouds into the air, and Josie had escaped from a quarrel between her parents. Even as she left the house she could hear them.

"It's not my fault the woman died!"

"It wasn't mine either," Lily snapped. "I was the one who cleaned for her for ten years! But it means I haven't got a job, and until I get another, we're going to have to make sacrifices. Or do you think losing my wages won't have any effect?"

"Don't talk daft! But you can't expect a man not to have a pint!"

"You can't expect your family to go hungry either!"

"Aw, come off it, Lily. It's not that bad!"

"Not at the moment, no. But cleaning jobs don't grow on trees, you know! And what if I can't get another one? And there's a rumour old Hawkins is going to put the rents up. I'm just saying it wouldn't hurt you to cut down a bit on the beer and fags."

Sid glared at her. Didn't she realise it was a matter of pride that a man should have his 'spends'? He'd be a laughing-stock down the pub, if he couldn't stand his round. "I'll think about it," he said abruptly.

Lily sighed. "All right, bury your head in the sand as usual." But her anger was spent, and wearily she pushed back her greying brown hair. She'd ask around again tomorrow, but what she needed now was a cup of tea, and she knew just who was going to have to make it! Of course, Lily mused, as she filled the kettle, now that there was only Josie at school, she could try and get a full-time job on one of the potbanks, but Sid had always been set against the idea, and refused to change his mind. Part-time work he'd allow, but as far as he was concerned, a woman's place was in the home.

Josie, who'd hoisted herself to the top of a nearby high wall, dug her hands deeper into her brown threadbare tweed coat. She was just deciding to go and see if one of her friends would ask her in, when suddenly she heard the sound of a motor car, and looking round saw William Hawkins' car, being driven slowly because of the icy conditions. As the car drew level Josie was able, from her vantage point, to stare straight into the interior.

But for once she wasn't interested in trying to make eye contact with Georgina. Her gaze had fastened on the blue fur muff on the other girl's lap, and she tried to imagine the bliss of slipping her cold hands into its warmth and softness. Then as the car began to draw away, she looked up into Georgina's eyes. The other girl smiled, but Josie, transfixed with envy, just stared stonily at her.

She'd never been in a motor car. What must it be like to sit enclosed in its warmth, being driven to wherever you wanted to go? Not to have to trudge through the snow, or in the summer have to walk miles in the sultry heat? How wonderful life must be, she thought wistfully, to live in the Big House. She'd heard it was beautiful inside, with thick Axminster carpets, and that they used real silver cutlery. As an only child, Georgina must live a magical existence, cosseted and spoiled. I bet *she* never wears scuffed shoes, Josie thought, jumping down from the wall and aiming a kick at a stone on the pavement. Stamping her numb feet, she decided to walk back up the street and 'have a stare'. She stood before the black iron gates, looking at the formal lawns frosted with ice, at the pristine drive and huge oak door. Taking her hands out of her pockets, she stared down at her square capable fingers, at her fingers so blue with cold that they hurt. One day, she told them, *you'll* be snuggled inside a fur muff, I promise. And, Josie vowed, as she turned away with a flounce, I might even have a matching coat and hat as well!

Chapter 3

It was Sissy Whalley who told Lily about the job. She'd got it from her sister who lived next door to the gardener at the Big House. Funny, Lily thought, how nobody referred to it by its proper name, even though gold letters on the gate proclaimed *Rosemount*, for all to see.

"Cross my heart and hope to die," Sissy said. "Emmie Pott's leaving. She's going to live with her sister, up Tunstall way."

"Would you believe that," breathed Lily. "She's cleaned for the Hawkinses for as long as I can remember."

"Aye, and it's a good job. That's if you can put up with Lady Muck's airs and graces." Sissy pulled a face. "I'd have put in for it meself if it wasn't for me bad back."

Lily smiled to herself. Sissy's bad back was legendary. "Thanks, Sissy, you're a pal. I'll get myself up there straightaway."

"Good luck!" Sissy shouted after her.

Once home, Lily hurried upstairs and stood before her sparse wardrobe, wondering what to wear. Then, thinking of the status of her prospective employer, decided to wear her best frock.

16

Although seven years old, it was still a decent serviceable navy serge, tailored with a square neckline and long sleeves. Fumbling in her haste, she fastened the clasp on her simulated pearl necklace and combed her hair, pinching her cheeks to bring out the colour. She had rouge in her drawer, but decided a plain, submissive appearance would appeal more to Alice Hawkins. Lily had often seen her drive by, beautifully made up and expensively dressed, and a woman like that wouldn't welcome glamour in another. Lily didn't believe in false modesty. She knew she was a handsome woman for her age. Thankful that she'd shampooed her hair only a few days before, she applied a touch of lipstick, and brushed her tweed winter coat. It had seen better days, but that couldn't be helped.

The recent cold spell had eased and the welcome sight of a blue sky lifted her spirits as she walked briskly along the pavement. This job would be ideal; it couldn't be more convenient! As she opened one half of the tall black iron gates it swung easily on its oiled hinges, and closing it carefully behind her she straightened her shoulders and marched along the drive to the front entrance. Then she paused, with the uneasy feeling that to knock on that imposing oak door would be a mistake. Tentatively, feeling suddenly nervous, Lily went to the side of the house and made her way round to the back door.

Much to her relief, Emmie, whose thin face was a creased map of worry lines, opened it. "I can guess why you've come," she said. "News travels fast!"

"Yes, well, old Mrs Adams died, as you probably know."

"Yes, I did hear." Emmie looked at her with speculation. "That's a few weeks past – things must be tight."

"We're managing," Lily said, lifting her chin.

"Mrs Hawkins has been asking whether I knew anyone suitable. I'd got you in mind." Emmie pursed her lips and warned, "She's a bit particular like."

"Well, she'll not find much wrong with *my* work," Lily said.

That was true, Emmie thought. No-one had ever seen the Ford children go to school scruffy, and Lily's front step and net curtains were an example to them all.

"She's not so bad," she said. "As long as you keep your place and don't gossip. He's the one to watch out for. It's a different house when he's at home, but that isn't often, thank God!"

"I can imagine," Lily said, then anxious to get the ordeal over, asked, "Do you think she'll see me?"

"I don't see why not. You wait there, and I'll go and ask her."

As Emmie left, Lily gazed around the kitchen. Compared to her tiny scullery, it seemed huge and was much bigger than her previous employer's. But then, the reason Mrs Adams had needed a daily help was because she was crippled with rheumatics, not because she had money to spare for non-essentials. How the rich live, mused Lily – able to pay someone else to cushion life for them. But then, she reminded herself, what would ordinary people like me do without the jobs they provide? It was no use being envious, or discontented; Lily believed that people should accept their lot in life. Reaching for the moon brought nothing but unhappiness, that's what her mother had instilled into her.

But she couldn't help a pang of envy as she saw the gleaming copper pans, the large scrubbed table in the centre of the room, the warm fire in the grate. The quarry tiled floor gleamed with Cardinal polish, and there was a warm rug before the sinks. Sinks! Heavens above, the woman had two sinks! But where was the copper? Lily looked around, then seeing two doors decided one must be the larder – but the other? She sidled over and opening the first peeped through. It was an indoor washroom, with one of those new-fangled washing machines with a mangle on the top. There was yet another sink, and an overhead clothes-dryer on a pulley. Just fancy having all the wet laundry out of the way! They probably had a walk-in airing cupboard upstairs as well. At home, Sid was always complaining about the clothes-horse being in front of the fire.

"I can't feel the heat," he would complain.

"Maybe, but it's better than getting a chill from clothes which aren't aired," was Lily's stock answer.

She closed the door and returned to her position, waiting with apprehension as the minutes ticked by. And then Emmie was back.

"She'll see you now."

Lily, her stomach hollow with apprehension, followed her. After they left the kitchen, she gained an impression of a spacious hall with a fringed circular Indian carpet covering a parquet floor, and then Emmie was tapping on a large mahogany door.

"Mrs Ford to see you, Mrs Hawkins."

Lily moved forward, was aware of the door closing behind her, and stared into the cool eyes of the woman who everyone knew had married William Hawkins for his money.

"Must have done," was the local opinion. "No-one would marry that miserable old bugger for love!"

Well, it had certainly paid off, was Lily's first irrelevant thought. Alice Hawkins was immaculately dressed, her fine woollen frock making Lily acutely conscious of the cheap quality of her own. It was one she'd been proud to wear the past few years, but now, the contrast between the two fabrics was so striking, that she knew she'd never feel smart in it again. It was stiflingly warm in the large, heavily furnished room, and she longed to take off her coat, but instead stood waiting for Alice to speak.

"Mrs Potts tells me you were, until recently, regularly employed." Alice's voice was cool, distant.

"Yes, I worked for Mrs Adams, in Cobden Close, for six years, until she passed away."

"And that was?"

"Four weeks ago."

"Hmm . . . So you won't be able to provide references?" Alice frowned. William always insisted on references for anyone who came to work at the house.

But Lily was prepared. "I'm sure the vicar, the Reverend Powell, would give me a reference. He was a regular visitor there."

Alice nodded. Even William couldn't find fault with a recommendation from a man of the cloth. This all seemed eminently satisfactory, and would save her a lot of inconvenience. Everyone was complaining that since the War it was becoming difficult to find reliable help in the house. Most women, now they'd experienced working in the munitions factories, preferred a job with more company.

"I would need you to do four hours every morning," she said. "Nine until one. Would that suit?"

Suit? Lily almost went dizzy at the prospect. She'd only 'done' for Mrs Adams for two hours a day. But then it had been a much smaller house.

"The work would entail cleaning, of course," Alice continued, "but also laundry. Are you a good ironer?"

Lily thought quickly. Was she? Not her favourite job by any means, and she tended to rush it a bit, but she could be more careful . . .

"Yes, I quite enjoy it."

"I pay an hourly rate of . . ." she named a figure

which Lily knew was fair, if not generous. "Would that be satisfactory to you?"

"Certainly, Mrs Hawkins."

Alice looked at the woman standing before her, who was wearing neat but shabby and outdated clothes, and decided she wouldn't do any better.

"Good. Perhaps you could ask the vicar for a reference, and subject to that I suggest we give it a month's trial. Mrs Potts has recommended you, and she has always given satisfaction." Alice stood up to indicate the interview was at an end, and as an afterthought added, "Perhaps it would be best if you came in one day before Mrs Potts leaves, to learn the ropes, so to speak. I would pay you, of course."

A few seconds later, Lily went back into the kitchen, the huge grin on her face telling Emmie all she needed to know.

"I can't thank you enough," Lily said. "I'll send Josie along with a couple of bottles of milk stout."

Emmie beamed. "That's very good of you, and much appreciated."

"So," Lily said, anxious to know, "when are you leaving?"

"I promised I'd stay until she'd got a replacement." Emmie thought for a moment. "I'd need another week, I think, if that's all right with you."

"Perfect."

"Oh, there's just one thing." Emmie said. "She's fussy about appearances, is Mrs Hawkins – so, no slippers. She thinks they're sloppy. Mind you, if she had to be on her feet as much as we do, she'd think different!"

"I'll remember. She wants me to come in one day before you go, so shall I come next Friday?"

As Emmie nodded, Lily looked at the hard-working woman before her. Emmie Potts hadn't had much luck in life. Her only son had been reported 'missing in action', and her husband had recently died from pneumonia. "I hope you'll be happy, living with your sister," Lily said.

"Well, we're both on our own now and her house is bigger, so it makes sense. In any case, we'll need extra space if ever . . ." Emmie's voice trailed off, and Lily knew she would never give up hope that her missing son would, one day, knock on the door. There must be hundreds of women like this, she thought, clinging to the possibility that their son, husband or brother, could still be alive. Perhaps it was preferable, although that was a terrible word to use in such circumstances, to receive a telegram saying "killed in action". At least then their families knew, and could mourn their loved ones.

As she returned home, Lily felt sobered by the misery she'd fleetingly seen in Emmie's eyes. What must it be like to lose your husband and son? She thought of Sid, of his cheery presence, how he would tease her out of a bad mood. Of Dennis and, to her surprise, of how much she missed him now he'd left home, her first to 'fly the nest'. Of John, who she found difficult to get close to or even understand, and of Peter, living his life so

23

far away. Yet with guilt, Lily knew that Josie was her favourite, had been right from the moment she was born. Now, she wondered whether she'd shown her sons enough love, enough affection. I hope they think I've been a good mother, she thought, and then pushed out such negative thoughts. This was no time for getting maudlin!

As soon as she got in, Lily changed back into her old skirt and jumper, and then put on her flowered pinafore. She couldn't wait to see Sid's face when she told him – not even the thought of tackling a pile of ironing could dampen her spirits.

Chapter 4

There were signs of spring everywhere, as Georgina, sitting in the passenger seat beside her mother, was driven home for the Easter holidays. Looking out over grey dry-stone walls, she could see green buds on the trees, glimpse bright daffodils in cottage gardens, and even early tulips sheltering beneath trees. She loved the Peak District with a passion, loved all of Derbyshire, in fact. The beauty and grandeur of the landscape with its hills and limestone dales seemed to answer a need in her heart, and whereas she knew the other girls were looking forward to the 'hols' with excitement, Georgina would have preferred to remain where she was. The dreaded boarding school had become her refuge.

It hadn't happened immediately; her first term had been a nightmare of loneliness and misery. Homesick for her own bedroom, and privacy, she'd spent most of her time in despondency, believing that to be popular at this school meant being good at games. And Georgina was not only hopeless at any form of gym, she loathed every minute of it. Her slight frame seemed to lack strength, and she suffered agonies of humiliation when she couldn't climb the ropes, or got stuck halfway across the vaulting horse. She hated most games, and the very thought of playing lacrosse made her shudder. At first, she stayed in the background, remaining quiet, intimidated by the self-confidence of the others. But this was a different environment from her previous small school, and her housemistress was a woman of sharp observation. To her amazement, Georgina was made a prefect, a responsibility that meant she *had* to mix with the other girls, and gradually she began to relax, to smile, to laugh at their jokes. After a while, she became friends with a couple of other girls who were also dismal at sport.

June, whose weight was her problem, was scornful of the other girls' grins of derision as she lumbered around the gym. "I'm used to it," she declared. "It doesn't bother me." But her bravado was belied by the hurt in her eyes, and Georgina, not for the first time, wondered why people had to be so cruel.

Her other friend was Fiona, a languid redhead who came from Edinburgh.

Her mother was English, and was an old girl of the school. Fiona had the ability to be good at games, but she just couldn't be bothered to make the effort. "I can't see any point in charging around a cold, muddy field," she declared. "But just you wait until you see me on the tennis courts in the summer. Now that's more to my liking – prancing around in a white tennis dress!"

Georgina agreed with her. She quite enjoyed

26

playing tennis, even if she did have a rotten backhand.

And over the months that followed, Georgina had come to feel that she belonged, was part of a group. She was, for the first time in her life, happy.

Now, sitting in the passenger seat next to her mother, Georgina wondered why on earth she hadn't accepted Fiona's invitation to stay with her over Easter. Why did she have this forlorn hope that when she saw her mother this time, it would be different? But no, it had been just the same – a cool, distant kiss on the cheek, no enthusiasm, no affection. Yet while waiting for her mother to arrive, Georgina had watched other girls collected, seen the delight with which they were greeted, swept up into hugs, had watched them depart amidst laughter.

"How are your lessons going?" Alice thought she had better say something, or they would spend the whole journey in silence.

"Fine." Georgina racked her brains for something to add. "I got an A plus for my essay last week."

"Good." Alice stifled a yawn with a pang of guilt.

She found parenting an onerous task. But then, she hadn't exactly had a role model. Left a widow in her early thirties, her own mother had promptly decided that life was too short to be stuck at home. During her formative years, Alice had been left with a succession of indifferent nannies, while her fun-loving mother had, in her own words, 'lived life to the full'. So much so, that when she fell overboard while sailing on a private yacht, it had surprised no-one. "Fond of the sauce, darling," one of her friends had told Alice, who, left without the means to support herself, had married the first wealthy man who proposed, namely William Hawkins.

Now, the prospect of having Georgina home for a whole three weeks filled her with dread. What on earth was she to do with the girl?

"Is Father well?"

"Yes, he's fine." Alice thought she should probably say he was looking forward to seeing his daughter, but that would be a lie. Until she'd reminded him at breakfast that morning, he'd even forgotten she was coming home. "Are you looking forward to the break?" she said instead.

"Yes, very much, thank you." Besides good manners, one thing boarding school had taught her was that that you could hide your true feelings behind politeness and a masked expression.

"Good."

Little more was said as the miles sped by, until at last Alice pulled up outside the gates of Rosemount. Georgina got out of the car and opened them to enable her mother to drive through, and then followed along the short drive to stand by the boot, waiting for it to be unlocked.

"I can manage," she said, taking out her suitcase.

Alice looked at her in surprise, realising just

how much she'd grown. She's going to be tall, she thought, taller than me – more like her father. She studied her for a moment, and then said, "I went to see the film *Rebecca* last week. You know, you're beginning to have a look of Joan Fontaine about you."

"Really?" Georgina felt a surge of pleasure at the compliment, and followed her mother into the large square hall.

"Yes, she's tall and pale, just like you."

Georgina said, "When I'm old enough to wear make-up, I'll be able to remedy that – the paleness, I mean."

For a moment Alice was stunned. The maturity of Georgina's words revealed just how quickly she was growing up. How old was she now – almost fourteen? It was a sobering thought that within a few years her daughter would be a young woman.

"We'll see," she said shortly.

Once inside the house, Georgina carried her suitcase up to her bedroom, and dumped it on her silk-covered eiderdown. She glanced around and then went to the window to look out at the rear garden. It was at its loveliest in the summer, when the formal beds of roses were in bloom, but still there was colour at this time of year, with plantings of spring-flowering pansies and hyacinths. Eager to change out of her uniform, she went to the wardrobe and selected a pleated skirt and her favourite pink twin set. It was lovely to be able to choose what you were going to wear. She wondered what was for lunch; she was always

29

hungry these days. At least now she was home, she'd be able to stuff herself. The food at school wasn't bad, but it was plain and boring, and for someone with a healthy appetite like hers, only just adequate.

But when, after unpacking, she went down to the kitchen, it was to see her mother frowning at a casserole dish.

"I put this in the oven before I left," she said crossly, "and told her to switch the oven on. She's obviously forgotten."

"That's not like Mrs Potts."

"Mrs Potts has left," Alice said. "I'll just have to do us beans on toast instead. I need to save the eggs. You did bring your Ration Book?"

Georgina nodded. "Why did Mrs Potts leave? She's been with us for years." She'd also been a part of her childhood, someone who could be relied on for a kind word, a cheery smile.

"She went to live with her sister, in Tunstall. We've got Mrs Ford, now."

Georgina forgot about her hunger. "Mrs Ford? Does she live down the street?"

Alice glanced at her. "Yes, she does. How do you know her?"

Georgina shook her head, her mind in a whirl. It must be Josie's mother! Josie Ford's mother was actually working in their house! She couldn't believe it, and a warm glow of excitement began to spread through her body. "I'm sure she didn't mean to forget," she said, anxious to placate her mother.

"Yes, well I have to admit that so far she's doing very well. But these people should be reliable," Alice snapped. "That's what they get paid for."

Lily remembered about the Hawkins' casserole that evening, just as she was about to dish up her own. Well, she called it a stew, but it was the same thing really.

"Damn!" she said.

"What's up?" Sid looked hungrily at the appetising chunks of rabbit nestling in the rich gravy. He'd had to skin it; Lily wasn't keen on the job. But Sid got a rabbit whenever he could, to help to stretch out their meat ration, and Lily never asked where it came from, just added a few cubes of shin beef and some sage.

"The oven!" she said, one horrified hand going to her mouth. "I forgot to switch the oven on. Mrs Hawkins had gone to fetch Georgina from boarding school, and she'd made a casserole, ready for when they got back."

Seeing she was looking worried and distracted, Sid asked, "How did you come to forget?"

To his relief, Lily carried on ladling out the stew, while she answered. "It was that telephone. The dratted thing rang after she'd gone. It got me right flummoxed – I didn't know whether I was supposed to answer it or not. She's always been there before."

"Who has?" Josie strolled into the back room. "Mmm, that smells nice!"

"Come and sit down," Lily instructed. "You

31

know I don't like you being late for your meals."

"Sorry, I was practising my spellings."

"Do you want me to test you on them?" John said.

Josie flashed him a smile, knowing how much he hated anything to do with learning. "Thanks, that would be a big help."

The whole family was on tenterhooks, as Josie, now she was thirteen, had the chance to go to a technical school. Even Sid couldn't argue with the practical aspect of this, because, as Lily pointed out, they had her extra wages coming in now. So, the decision had been taken – all Josie had to do was to pass the examination.

"Mrs Hawkins, I'm talking about," Lily told Josie, as she handed a plate to John. He glanced up, and she smiled at him, but as usual her difficult son avoided eye contact, merely bending his dark head over his food.

"Why, what about her?"

"She went to fetch Georgina home for Easter, so she wasn't in when the phone rang."

Josie sat up straight. Ever since her mum had announced she'd be working at the Big House, Josie had been waiting for Georgina to come home.

"But we don't break up until next week," she frowned.

"Oh, private schools are a law unto themselves," sniffed Lily. "It wouldn't do for them to be like the rest of us."

With relish, Josie tucked into her stew. Somehow, she was going to have to find a way of meeting Georgina again, of getting a look inside that house. If she was going to be rich one day, which she had decided she definitely was, then she needed to know how such people lived.

And she was lucky – because her chance came two days after she began her own Easter holidays. Lily had left for work, with instructions that Josie was not to 'mooch about wasting time', as the inside windows needed cleaning. Disgruntled, Josie wrung out the chamois leather in vinegar and warm water, and began to do her allocated job. The sooner it was out of the way the better, as far as she was concerned.

It was then that she saw the shoes. Lily kept a pair especially for work, and always took them with her in her shopping bag. She must have put them out to be polished, and forgotten them. Her dad regularly polished all their shoes – he had a box full of tins of blacking, brown polish and shoe brushes. Josie knew her mother had gone out in her fleecy-lined bootees – Mrs Hawkins wouldn't be happy to have *them* tramped all over her bedroom carpets! Oh, yes, Josie knew that Georgina had a proper carpet in her bedroom, and often fantasised about what it would be like to walk around on a soft warm floor. In the Ford house, there was only lino, much of it old and cracked, and it struck bitterly cold to bare feet in the winter. She had a pegged rug at the side of her bed, of course, but she hated it. Lily had made it out of worn-out clothes during the War, and although she'd done her best, the fading colours were hardly pretty.

But now – this was the opportunity she'd been waiting for! Chafing at the delay, Josie finished cleaning the windows, knowing it was no use missing the corners – her mum would only make her do them again. Then, task completed, she rushed upstairs to change – this adventure called for more than her old grey skirt.

Within minutes, hair freshly brushed, although no amount of brushing could control the spring of her black curls, and carrying the shoes, she walked sedately up the street.

Her heart beating with excitement, she opened the gate to Rosemount.

Once inside, she paused for a moment, over-awed that she was actually on the other side, inside the grounds so to speak. The main entrance with its Georgian pillars looked forbidding, and Josie paused, wondering whether she should go round to the back, but almost immediately the front door opened, and she halted, her cheeks flaming. For a moment she almost fled, and when Mrs Hawkins appeared, followed by Georgina, Josie felt herself rooted to the spot – like a trespasser.

Alice stopped abruptly. "Yes?" she called in a sharp tone. "What do you want?"

Josie's anger flared. She hadn't done anything *wrong*; she was only bringing her mum's shoes, for heaven's sake!

But there was no doubt as to Georgina's reaction. Her face wreathed in smiles, she was already walking towards her. "Hello, Josie. It's Mrs Ford's daughter," she said over her shoulder.

"Oh." Alice looked at the two girls, so similar in age, and frowned. "You'd better go round to the back," she said. "Your mother's in the kitchen."

Josie found her voice. "Thank you." She found the use of her legs too, and walked forward. "Only, she left her shoes."

Alice looked at the shoes dangling in Josie's hands, remembering the sight of Lily in those awful, brown suede bootees. "All right, take them round to her."

With a quick glance at Georgina, Josie began to hurry round the side of the house.

Watching her go, Georgina suddenly pleaded, "Couldn't she stay for a bit? You know I'll just be in the way at your coffee morning."

Her words had a ring of truth. Alice was taking her because it salved her conscience – the girl was being left on her own far too much. But William would be livid if he found Georgina playing with one of the girls from the street. Yet the daunting prospect of the next couple of weeks made Alice hesitate. Although she tended to think of the neighbouring children as 'local urchins', she had to admit that this girl had seemed polite, and she was neatly dressed. It was all very well for William to refuse to countenance his daughter inviting a school-friend to stay – he wasn't the one who had to entertain her all the time. And at the moment, the last thing Alice wanted was to have her own freedom curtailed. If the two girls were to become friends . . .

Eventually she frowned, and said, "What would your father say?"

Georgina, who'd been waiting with trepidation as she watched her mother actually consider her impulsive request, blurted out, "We needn't tell him!" She clapped a hand to her mouth in horror at what she'd said, but to her surprise her mother didn't reprimand her.

Alice was wondering whether she could turn the situation to her advantage. Could she trust Georgina? The girl wasn't a blabbermouth, but if William ever found out . . . She gazed thoughtfully at her daughter. "You knew her name. Have you met before?"

Georgina nodded. "Years ago, that time when I played skipping in the street."

Alice remembered the occasion. She also remembered William's fury at the time. Was it worth the risk? But then, lately she'd grown in confidence, deciding she was sick of living her life under William's old-fashioned dominance. She was a woman in her prime and this was the early fifties, for heaven's sake! Surely she was allowed to make *some* independent decisions?

Chapter 5

Hardly able to contain her excitement, Georgina hurried back into the house. It was only when she was about to open the door leading to the kitchen that she had an awful thought – what if Josie didn't want to stay? Not that Georgina would blame her. It was ridiculous the way her parents had kept her apart from the other children in the neighbourhood. What were they afraid of – that she'd catch impetigo or something?

She pushed open the door. Lily, having unzipped her bootees, was in the process of tying the laces on her comfy shoes. Josie, her gaze raking around the kitchen even as she talked, was saying, "You should have seen her face when she saw me inside the gate . . ." She stopped as Georgina entered. "Oh . . ."

As the room fell silent, Georgina looked at their surprised faces, and feeling the heat rise in her cheeks, said, "I decided to stay in, after all." She hesitated. "I was wondering? Would Josie like to stay for a while? That's if," she turned to Josie, "you haven't already made other arrangements."

Both stared at her. Josie, with a rush of adrenalin,

37

felt her face break into a stupid grin. Did she want to stay for a while? You bet!

Lily was taken aback. "I'm not sure," she began to say. "Have you asked your mother?"

Georgina said eagerly. "Yes and she agreed."

"Did she now?" Lily looked at Josie. "Well," she said, wanting to give her daughter an excuse if she needed one, "*have* you made other arrangements?"

Josie shook her head with vigour. "No, I haven't."

"So," Lily said, "do you want to stay, or not?" As she looked at the two girls, Lily thought how different they were, one so fair and pale, the other dark and bristling with energy.

"Yes, I'd like to!" Josie's answer came out louder than she intended, and reddening she looked away in embarrassment.

Georgina, relieved and happy, didn't notice. "Come on," she said. "Let's go up to my room."

"Wipe your feet again," Lily told her daughter, and watched them go with a sense of unease. But then her more practical side took over. If her daughter was to get on, perhaps even work in an office, then she could learn a lot from Georgina Hawkins. Lily had never seen a girl with such beautiful manners, and the way she talked! She could be on the BBC, that one. But nevertheless, over the past week, Lily had found compassion in her heart for the Hawkins' only daughter. She wandered around this great house like a lost soul. Still, Lily thought, as she dragged out the heavy upright Hoover, it will be interesting to see how they get on together.

Josie, trying to hide her curiosity, tried not to stare around too much as she followed Georgina into the hall. Cripes, it was bigger than their sitting-room! Then she saw the wide staircase with its oak-panelled balustrade and red carpet, and gave herself up to the novel experience of feeling her feet sink into the rich pile. Her mum hadn't told them much about Rosemount, apart from saying they had carpets everywhere. Mrs Hawkins had made her promise not to gossip. But this house was just like the ones she saw at the pictures, and for a moment Josie had an image of herself, looking uncannily like Margaret Lockwood, sweeping down the staircase in a ball-gown.

"My room is this way," Georgina said, as the stairs divided.

Josie gaped. The Hawkins had *two landings*! She didn't know people could have two landings. Their own was so small and narrow that she could jump across it. Then Georgina was opening a wide door and ushering her into her bedroom. It was absolutely gorgeous. Alice Hawkins might not have much love for her only child, but she did love her house. And on this issue, William acknowledged her good taste, and within reason, indulged it. The bedroom carpet was ivory with a pattern of pink roses, while in the bay window that overlooked the garden stood a kidney-shaped dressing-table. It had a glass top, and a frilled skirt to match the pink and gold striped curtains. There was even a matching stool. Josie was dumbfounded.

Georgina, mistaking her silence for nervousness, said, "Do you like books?"

She went to a set of bookshelves, crammed with titles, and Josie breathed a sigh of relief – this was one thing they did have in common.

Josie literally haunted the tiny local library. Situated in a church hall, its few shelves lined one dusty wooden-floored room. The librarian, a plump fair-haired woman, knew Josie by name, and often teased her, saying, "You'll go cross-eyed if you read any more!" But Josie read anything and everything. She simply ran her finger along the shelves, and took out any book from the limited stock that she hadn't borrowed before. In the evenings the library took on a different character, with shutters over its shelves, when chattering little girls came in to learn ballet and tap. Cubs learned how to tie knots, and Brownies how to earn their badges and to sing around an imaginary campfire. Their use of the library left a distinctive lingering odour, combined with a pungent 'woody' scent from the cheap wooden boxes which housed the groups' differing equipment.

Now, realising Georgina was waiting for an answer, Josie replied, "Yes, I'm always getting teased about being a bookworm."

"What sort of thing do you like?"

Josie glanced at some of the titles. "Oh, I used to love these." She took out a copy of Noel

Streatfeild's *Ballet Shoes*. "I've read the whole series."

"Me too."

"And I've read all the *Chalet* books." Josie looked sideways at Georgina. "Of course, you'll know what it's really like – boarding school, I mean. Do you have midnight feasts and things? Do you have to sleep in a dormitory with lots of other girls?"

Georgina grinned. "Yes, all of that. Mind you, I hated it at first, but I love it now."

"Don't you miss your mum and dad?" Josie couldn't imagine spending one night away from home, never mind months.

Georgina's expression became guarded. "You get used to it." She sat on the pristine rose-pink eiderdown, and after a moment's hesitation, Josie sat gingerly beside her, feeling a bit awkward. She glanced again at the bookshelves, noticing there were sets of the classics.

"What would you recommend?" she said abruptly. She wanted to read the right things, and it was becoming difficult to choose now that she'd grown out of the books aimed at schoolgirls. "Among the classics, I mean. We've done *Great Expectations* at school, but that's the only one I've read."

Georgina's face lit up with enthusiasm. "Oh, but you must read Jane Austen. *Pride and Prejudice* is a good one to begin with. Miss Proctor says it's worth persevering to read good literature, as it extends your vocabulary."

Josie stared at her. She'd never heard anyone

of her age using such long words. But what the other girl said made sense, and she tucked the information away in her brain, realising she could learn a lot from Georgina Hawkins. She wasn't at all 'snobby', either, if you ignored the posh way she talked.

"Can *you* recommend anything?" Georgina said, remembering that one should always show an interest in the other person's views. Not that she needed reminding – she was fascinated by everything about Josie who seemed to have brought vitality into the room, a sort of restless energy.

Josie considered for a moment. "I've been reading *The Scarlet Pimpernel*, you know, by Baroness Orczy."

"Oh, I haven't read that – I'll get it next time I'm in town."

Just like that, Josie thought. Fancy being able to buy books whenever you wanted to!

"How old are you?" Georgina suddenly asked.

"Nearly fourteen."

"Same as me! When's your birthday?"

"The seventh of June."

"Mine's in June as well," Georgina said. "The fifteenth." She grinned at Josie, delighted that the other girl seemed to like being there. "What shall we do? Do you want to draw? " Going over to a side table, she opened a drawer and took out a couple of sketch pads and a selection of pencils. "We could practise our perspectives, if you like."

Josie remembered their art teacher going on

about perspectives. Not that she'd taken that much interest; he was the most boring person she'd ever met. "Yeah, fine."

Georgina went to the bookshelves and came back with a large book on sketching. "Here," she said. "Choose something you'd like to draw – I'll find another chair."

She left the room, and Josie looked around again, still amazed at the size of the dreamy bedroom. She hadn't got room for an orange box, never mind a lovely polished table to work on. Trying to suppress a sharp pang of envy, Josie opened the book and began to skim through the pages. She soon found her subject – a graceful manor house in a leafy setting. Lots of perspectives there, she decided.

Meantime Lily, having put the Hoover away, was 'doing out' the china cabinet. Carefully, as instructed by her employer, she dusted each piece of valuable china. It was all Staffordshire pottery, of course.

"Mr Hawkins," Alice told her, "doesn't believe in buying foreign goods. He holds the view that we can't expect our country to prosper if we don't support local industry."

Lily, her hands caressing a delicate Royal Doulton figurine, was of the opinion that the people of the Potteries were the best workers in the world. I mean, she thought, looking at a Spode china tea service, who could want anything better than that? But even as she worked, she couldn't help wondering how the two girls were getting on.

"It was a right turn-up for the books," she said to Sid later. "Who'd have thought it, our Josie hobnobbing with the likes of Georgina Hawkins!"

And the two girls did get on well, finding they had more in common than they would have imagined. Neither had any cousins, nor did they have any living grandparents.

"My Granny Ford was lovely," Josie said. "Although she did have this big whisker sprouting on her chin. I asked her once why she didn't cut it off, but she said it would only grow thicker, and if she pulled it out it would be painful and leave a hole in her face."

Georgina couldn't help giggling. "I saw an old lady once with a moustache! I mean, can you imagine? But," she continued, "I never knew any of my grandparents. I know my Grandfather Hawkins died in an accident at the Shelton Iron and Steel Works when a girder fell on him. My grandmother died before I was born. As for the other side," she shrugged, "my mother never talks about them."

When it was time for Lily to leave and the two girls came back down to the kitchen, their ease with each other was apparent.

"Your mother should be back any minute," Lily said with a relieved smile. "She's usually here before I leave."

"That's all right, Mrs Ford. I can easily fend for myself."

44

"Are you ready, Josie?" Lily was changing her shoes for the warm bootees. "What do you say to Georgina?"

Josie rolled her eyes. How old did her mother think she was – six? She looked at Georgina, saw the amusement in her eyes, and said in a child's high voice: "Thank you for having me!"

Both girls burst out laughing, and Lily looked from one to another, and then had to smile herself. "All right, all right," she conceded, "I know. Sometimes I forget how old you are." And it was true, she did forget. But in that one instant, as she looked at the two girls before her, Lily could see the promise in both of them. Georgina so tall, fair and elegant; Josie, with her vivid colouring, like an exotic bird. They're going to be beautiful women, she thought suddenly, and her emotions were mixed as she picked up her bag before they left. Part envy of their youth, their clear skin and shining eyes, part fear and apprehension of what the future might hold. It wasn't an easy world, particularly for women.

Chapter 6

Lily told Josie not to mention her visit to Rosemount. "It might just be a one-off. And you don't want to cause jealousy among your friends."

"No, it's not," Josie protested. "A one-off, I mean. She's asked me to go again, only she's got to check what her mother's got planned."

"Mmm." Alice Hawkins' way of life was a mystery to Lily. Her employer was always going out, not only to coffee mornings, but also to 'lunch', which Lily assumed meant dinner. She would waft past in her fur coat, heavily made up, and leaving a delicate cloud of perfumed air behind her. Normally, Lily wasn't keen on what she called 'scent'. Sometimes she would dab on a drop of Eau de Cologne if she had a headache, but it was just something she'd never bothered with. But she had to admit that Alice Hawkins smelled wonderful, not at all like some of the women she sat next to on the bus at times. Then, it could be so overpowering it was enough to make you feel ill. I suppose it's like everything else, she mused as she filled a galvanised bucket with hot water; you get what you pay for!

"Don't you get fed up with cleaning?" Josie asked, watching her mother prepare to swill out their backyard.

"Why should I?" Lily said tartly. "It's what I was put on this earth for, to clean up after other people! What do you think?"

"Sorry, I was wondering whether you really minded, or just accepted it. I mean, you've been on all morning, and now look at you."

"What choice do I have? We need the money, that's why I go to Rosemount. And as for here, you wouldn't want to live in a dirty house, now would you? And you can just go and finish that ironing, if you don't mind!"

Josie knew that the last few words were more of an order than a question, and got up to fetch the basket of washing. "I'm coming back a boy next time," she grumbled. "Women have to do all the housework."

"It's women's work so far as men are concerned," Lily told her. "Always has been."

"Doesn't mean it's right!"

"Maybe not, but you'll learn to accept things as you get older. Anyway, remember what I said. Keep mum about Georgina, at least for the time being."

And that was exactly the decision taken at Rosemount. When Georgina said that she would like Josie to come again, Alice felt a gleam of satisfaction. The arrangement would suit her very well, very well indeed. In fact, it was almost as if fate was playing into her hands.

47

"As long as you both remain in the house," she said, "and as long as Josie understands that she's not to broadcast it."

Georgina frowned. She didn't want Josie to feel she was ashamed of being her friend. "Could you explain that to her mother?" she said.

"Yes, I'll have a word with Mrs Ford. But I want you to stress it to Josie. Understood?"

The following morning, Alice tackled Lily.

"Mrs Ford," she said. "About Josie."

Lily looked up from where she was polishing the silver. "Yes, Mrs Hawkins?"

"The two girls seem to have taken a liking to each other, and I'm perfectly happy about Josie coming here, except . . ."

Lily waited, apprehensive.

"It's a little bit awkward, Mrs Ford. I'm sure you know that Mr Hawkins is a man of very rigid views." Alice hesitated; she didn't want to hurt the woman's feelings, but how else could she say it? "To put it bluntly, he wouldn't approve . . ."

Lily flushed. "Are saying you don't want her coming again?"

"No, not at all," Alice said quickly. "The opposite. I just meant . . ." again she hesitated, "do you think we could keep it to ourselves?"

"Oh, that!" Lily said with relief. "I've already told Josie not to mention it to anyone. I'm not being funny, Mrs Hawkins, but she's got to live here when Georgina goes back to boarding school. She'll need her other friends then, and you know what these girls can be like."

48

"Exactly." Alice gave a smile of relief. That was all right then, another obstacle overcome. "So, we'll leave it to the girls, shall we? You know, to organise things?"

"It's fine with me." Lily watched the younger woman leave the kitchen. Wouldn't approve indeed! In other circumstances she might have taken offence, but there were too many advantages to be gained. It was no use cutting off her nose to spite her own face, so to speak. In any case, it only confirmed what she already knew: William Hawkins was an awkward bugger all round. Give her Sid any day, even if she did have to go out cleaning!

Georgina had agonised over what to say to Josie. In the end, she'd decided to tell her the truth. Disloyal it might be, but as the years had passed, her childish terror of her father had gradually lessened, to be replaced by dislike and bitterness. Distance had helped, enabling her to see him for what he was, not an all-powerful figure, but a man who regarded his wife and child as property rather than as people. She still feared him but, by avoidance, she ensured that she saw as little of her father as possible.

On that second morning, when Josie arrived with her mother – they'd decided to say she was helping with the ironing – Georgina simply said, "I'm sorry about all this secrecy, Josie. But it's my father – he's a colossal snob. It's nothing to do with me."

"Don't worry about it," Josie said carelessly.

Not even to her mother had she admitted how much she minded. I'm just as good as them, she thought fiercely, and one day I'll prove it. But nothing kept Josie down for long, and with her eyes brimming with laughter, she added, "It will make it more exciting, like a clandestine rendezvous."

"The nearest we'll get," laughed Georgina.

"Ah, but just give us a couple of years!"

They both giggled. Then Georgina opened a drawer in her dressing-table and took out a box. She unlocked it and Josie saw it was full of make-up.

She put a hand to her mouth. "You never do!"

"No, of course not, at least not in public. But it's fun experimenting. And we'll be fifteen next year. Why wait until then to learn how to put it on? Do you want to have a go?"

"You bet!" Eagerly, Josie picked up a crimson lipstick and, leaning forward to look in the mirror, outlined her lips in a perfect Cupid's bow.

"Mum never lets me touch hers," she said. "She always says it's too dear to waste."

"You can have some of mine. I've got loads." Georgina grinned at Josie. "Don't look so worried – I get it free. My friend June – you know, I told you about her? Well, her mother owns a cosmetics firm."

"Crikey!"

"Look, you sit there, and I'll make you up, and then you can do me."

And that was how the rest of the summer holiday

went. Three mornings a week, Josie would go with Lily to Rosemount, telling her friends she went to help with the ironing. Lily told Sid, of course, knowing he would keep it to himself. "Not a word to our lads, mind," she said. "It would only take one stray word, and it'd get straight back to old Hawkins. You know how it is around here."

Sid thought it was all women's chatter. He didn't read too much into it himself, two lasses spending time together. And their John hardly talked to them, never mind anyone else. Still, if that was what Lily wanted, it was fine with him. He'd got more important things on his mind.

"Can you lend me ten bob?" he asked.

"Ten shillings? What do you want that for?"

"It's our Josie's birthday coming up in June. One of the blokes at work says he could get me a silver bracelet."

"Oh, yes. Where from – off the back of a lorry?"

"No," Sid protested, "nothing like that. His sister's got a stall on the market – he says she can order me one wholesale, like."

Lily softened. "You'll give it me back – the money, I mean?"

"I always do, don't I?"

It was true, she thought as she fetched her purse. Sid might go short at times – she suspected he was betting on the horses – but he always paid her back when he got his wages. "Here you are." She handed him a note and then ruffled his hair and kissed him on the cheek.

"What have I done to deserve that?"

"You're a good dad, that's what."

There's more warmth in these four walls, cramped though they are, she thought, than ever there is at Rosemount. The beautiful house seemed like a shell somehow, and when William Hawkins was at home, which thank God wasn't often, there was enough nervous tension in the air to cut with a knife. It would do Georgina good to mix with their Josie, Lily thought. Give her a taste of what normal life is like. Not that she could ever imagine Mrs Hawkins agreeing to her daughter visiting Josie's home. But, she mused, perhaps that's just as well. We'd never keep their friendship quiet then.

By the time Georgina returned to Derbyshire, the two girls had become firm friends. Although Georgina had worried at first that Josie might be ill at ease at Rosemount, to her surprise and admiration she soon realised that nothing much fazed Josie Ford.

"We'll have all the summer holidays, Josie," she said before she left. "You could come more often. After all," she grinned, "there's bound to be more ironing to do when I'm at home. You'll just have to tell everyone I'm terribly spoilt, and insist on changing my clothes twice a day."

"Oh yeah! And how about the ironing money I'm supposed to be earning? I can hardly spend something that doesn't exist!"

Georgina considered. "I know – you can pretend to be nauseatingly moral, and say you gave it to your mother to help with your new school uniform, or something."

"I haven't passed the exam yet," Josie said glumly.

"No, but you will."

"I wish I had your confidence."

"You'll pass. Trust me, I know these things. And Josie?"

"Yes?" Josie looked up from where she was trying on Georgina's pearl necklace.

"If there are any books you want to borrow, just stick a bit of paper in them now so your mum will be able to see it. Then she can take them home for you, one at a time."

And Lily did just that. Once Josie had finished with a book, Lily simply concealed it inside a large yellow duster. Then, when it was her day for dusting Georgina's room, she would search for the next book which had a torn-off slip of paper tucked inside, and exchange it. Normally, Lily hated deceit, but if it would help her daughter to achieve the potential she undoubtedly had, then she felt her action was fully justified. Not, she thought wryly, that Alice Hawkins would notice if she walked around the house with a grenade in her duster – lately she seemed to be in a different world altogether.

Chapter 7

Alice, with Georgina safely away at school and William immersed in plans to expand his business, had for over a year now been free to come and go as she chose. And Alice chose, oh yes, she chose. It had taken her a long time to realise that as an attractive woman, particularly one who could afford to make the best of herself, there was another life outside Rosemount. Not that it had been easy; she'd had to convince William that to do otherwise would affect not only his social status, but his ambitions.

She chose her time carefully, waiting with increasing impatience until the right opportunity presented itself. Her chance came when William, arriving home in a genial mood, having completed a take-over of a rival building firm, had opened a bottle of his finest claret. Alice knew he wouldn't be able to resist finishing it off, and, by the end of the meal, he was mellow and unusually sociable. Closing her mind to the 'bedroom stuff' she knew was bound to come later, she made her move.

"I've noticed," she said, "that very often prominent businessmen get involved in local charities."

William gazed at her thoughtfully. He'd never

admitted to anyone that his ultimate ambition was to be the city's Lord Mayor. Had she guessed? Then he shrugged. Who knew what went on in women's minds? But he didn't say anything, and Alice pressed on.

"Of course, you're far too busy to attend committee meetings, but if I became involved, I could be an ambassador for you. Mrs Emery," she said, naming the wife of an even larger builder than William, "she's a member of several committees."

"Is she now?" William looked up, his keen eyes sweeping his wife's face.

"I'd be happy to do it," she said, "particularly with Georgina away, but . . ." She picked up her napkin and began to roll it.

"But what?"

Alice inserted her napkin into its silver ring. "As you know, people judge a successful man by how he can afford to dress his wife." She had used this ploy to her advantage in the past. "If you wished me to – help to promote your profile, so to speak – I'd need an increase in my allowance."

William frowned. "How much?"

Alice mentioned a sum she knew to be extortionate.

"Don't be ridiculous, woman!" he snapped. "Who do you think I am, Rockefeller?" He thought for a moment, then asked brusquely, "You know, do you? That you could get on one of these committees?"

"Absolutely, more than one. I just wasn't sure

you would approve." Alice, as was her custom, kept her expression bland. The subterfuge came easily to her; she'd had plenty of practice. In certain moods, even the wrong expression could bring forth a burst of temper.

"I'll give you half that amount," he decided. "Take it or leave it."

He might have been talking to an employee, Alice thought bitterly, but then, wasn't that how he'd always treated her? But she was past caring; she just took from him as much as she could get. And half the amount was exactly what she needed.

And so, Alice became a useful and prominent member of the community.

What she lacked in compassion for the causes she purported to serve, she compensated for with efficiency. For, away from William's domineering influence, Alice discovered she had an aptitude for organisation, and making decisions, an ability she realised had never been put to the test. With this knowledge came confidence, and with that, an increasing awareness of her femininity. That side of her nature had never been uppermost in Alice's mind. She was vain enough to want to dress well, enjoyed wearing fur and expensive silks, but so far as men and certainly sex were concerned, they were just a necessary evil if a woman wanted to be supported. But during the last year, Alice had found her gaze wandering over the features of men she met, wondering whether they found her attractive, whether, in fact, she was attracted to them. Alice Hawkins was ripe for romance, and she knew it. Not, she assured herself, that she would ever *do* anything. She hadn't suffered sixteen years of marriage with William Hawkins to risk losing the luxurious home she loved. No man was worth that. But she enjoyed occasional moments of discreet flirtation, a glance from beneath her eyelashes, a half smile, the feeling of power it gave her. As for William, he was 'bothering' her less as he got older, which suited her very well.

They'd always had their own bedrooms, William regarding the sharing of a double bed as a working-class habit. His attitude was ridiculous when one remembered his origins – he was the son of a bricklayer, for heaven's sake! It was pathetic really, the way he aped the upper classes, she thought, as if by copying their way of life, that would somehow enhance his sense of super-iority. But for Alice, life in her forties was very good indeed.

Lily too, was finding life more pleasurable. The extra money she earned at Rosemount, was, as time went on, enabling her to buy things for the house. Sid couldn't understand why it made her so happy.

"They're only new curtains," he teased, watching how Lily would touch them and stroke them. "Not the crown jewels."

"But look at the flowers, the colours!" Lily admired the floral pattern. "It's like bringing a garden into the room."

Sid smiled at her. "You've got a right way with

words, Lil – I can see where our Josie gets it from."

"I'm so proud of her, Sid, passing that exam."

"Aye." He looked at her with a sheepish grin. "It was a damn good bottle of whisky that started *her* off!"

"Oh, get on with you!" Lily threw a cushion at him and he caught both it and her, pulling her down on his knee.

"Just look at the pair of you, like a couple of kids," Josie said, as she came through the door. "Anyone want a cuppa?"

"Yes, please, love." Lily got up, slightly embarrassed, and smoothed her hair.

"It's no use even asking you, Dad. You're ready for one, any time."

"Ha ha! And Josie?"

"I know, strong with two sugars!"

"I can't stand weak tea," he grumbled.

"No, you like to be able to stand your spoon in it," Lily said laughingly. "You'd even drink it from an enamel mug if I'd let you, like you do at work."

"Tastes better," Sid said, surreptitiously turning to the racing pages of his newspaper. If he hurried, he'd just have time to get a bet on. "Where's John?"

"Not out spending his wages, that's for sure, seeing he's not working again." Lily looked at him. "What are we going to do with him, Sid? I've never been able to get inside that head of his. Is he just lazy, or what?"

Sid shook his head. "No, no. I'd have knocked that out of him years ago, if it was that. He just doesn't seem able to get on with people." He glanced away in discomfort. "They say he's a bit odd, like."

Lily sat down. "He's a bit slow, Sid, as we've said before. And I've always wondered whether he's happy, even when he was a child. He seems to live in a world of his own." And it was in a different way than his father, she thought. Sid might not be the brainiest person, but he was willing, and easy-going. He'd held down the same job since leaving school. But John – well, she just couldn't fathom him.

Josie brought the tea in.

"I'll have a biscuit as well, love," Sid said.

Bringing in the biscuit tin, Josie sat at the table, and munched one thoughtfully. "I heard what you were saying, about our John. He might be slow in some things, but just look how good he is at his model-making! Anyway, I know what would suit our John. A window-cleaning round."

They both stared at her.

"Well, think about it. He'd be working on his own all day. He wouldn't have to take orders from other people or be sociable. And as John only talks about things *he's* interested in, he certainly wouldn't miss the company."

"You know, Josie, you might have hit on something," Sid said. "I'll mention it to him when he comes in, see what he thinks."

"He's all right, you know – our John," Josie said.

59

"I heard what you said, Dad, about him being a bit odd. He isn't really – people don't understand him, that's all."

"And you do?" Lily said.

"He just wants to be left alone. He's happy enough, as long as there aren't too many demands made on him. John will get by, you'll see."

Later, when his tall, ungainly son came in from his solitary walk, Sid told him of their idea.

"I'm not sure," John said slowly. "I've never been up a ladder."

"You're not afraid of heights, though, are you, love?" Lily had now convinced herself that the job would suit him perfectly.

"I don't think so," but his tone was still hesitant.

"It was actually Josie who suggested it," Lily said.

John gave her one of his rare direct looks. "Honestly? She thinks it's a good idea?"

Lily nodded. "We all do."

John thought for a moment, then said, "Okay, then, I'll give it a go."

"Leave it with me," Sid said. "I'll ask about a bit."

And, as if Josie had ordained it, within a few days, Sid heard of a window-cleaner who was looking for someone to help him out. To Lily's amazement, John took to the work with alacrity. Bert, the other man, was a terse individual of few words, and John liked being out in the fresh air, and away from people giving him orders. Josie

60

suspected that his problem had been understanding what he was expected to do.

"He's learning a trade," Sid told Lily, "and maybe as time goes on, he'll be able to get a round of his own."

And so Lily thought all was well with her world. And for several weeks it was. The whole street was in a state of excitement about the Coronation, and Mrs Fisher, the next-door neighbour, persuaded her husband to rent a television set. They were all fascinated by the small screen flickering in the corner and, as Sid said, how so many people could crowd into one small living-room was beyond him. Josie, who from a small child had collected pictures of the young princesses, was enthralled. Lily just felt privileged, conscious they were the first commoners to be able to see the historic ceremony. Although, everyone agreed that it was such a pity it rained.

Then one Saturday morning, there came an unexpected knock at the front door.

Josie answered, and then called out, her voice high-pitched and strained.

"Mum?"

Lily bustled through, cross at having to leave her baking, and then when she saw the uniform, her face became as white as the flour on her hands.

"Yes?" The word came out as a whisper.

"Mrs Ford?"

"That's right."

"May I come in?" The policeman was stolid,

61

his expression carefully composed, but Josie looked at his eyes, and knew something terrible had happened.

Lily stood aside, her hand fluttering to her throat, her mind full of panic. What was it? Could it be Peter? Oh my God, she thought, is it Dennis? Please no, it can't be. There's a baby coming! John?

Sid was out in the backyard, squatting down to oil his bike, and hurriedly Josie went to fetch him.

"Dad! There's a policeman here!"

Sid got awkwardly to his feet and, wiping his hands on a rag, felt his heart hammer painfully as he went into the house. Josie followed.

The policeman took off his helmet, and stood awkwardly in the middle of the square sitting-room. They all waited.

"I'm sorry, but it's bad news," he said. "You have a son who's a window-cleaner?"

Lily, her throat suddenly dry with anxiety, nodded. "Our John," she whispered. "What's happened to him?"

"His ladder slipped, at least that's what we think. But he was unlucky. It was fully extended and he came straight down on to a rockery, striking his head on a large boulder."

The policeman hesitated, struggling to find the right words. It was Josie who found the courage to ask in a hoarse whisper, "Is he . . .?"

"I'm afraid so . . . I'm very sorry."

Lily felt her legs collapse beneath her and Josie caught hold of her, helping her into a chair. Sid stood and stared at the policeman as if he couldn't take in the words he was saying.

Josie looked at them both, seeing suddenly in their stricken faces an image of how they would look in old age. "Where is he?" she said quietly.

"At the Infirmary. But there was nothing anyone could do."

Lily remained with her head bowed, as tears swam into her eyes and she said brokenly, "Can we see him?"

"Of course. We'll need a formal identification, anyway. We'll send a car round."

Sid stepped forward. "I'll do that." He turned to Lily. "You stay here, with Josie. There'll be plenty of time to see him after . . ." He looked at the policeman and their eyes met. Sid had seen active service; he knew how gruesome, how shocking, injuries could be, particularly head wounds. And if John had smashed his face in . . . Sid shuddered – he didn't want his womenfolk remembering John like that.

Lily didn't speak. She couldn't. She was hardly aware of her husband sitting near her with his head in his hands, or of the cup of tea that Josie placed by her side. She could only feel a terrible guilt. For only Lily knew that she had loved John less than her other children. Even as a small boy, he'd irritated her. He just wasn't like the other children. Always alone, with hardly any friends, at times she had despaired. Life seemed such a struggle for him, and now, just when he seemed to have found his niche, and was happier than she'd ever known him, it had all been taken away. As for herself – what sort of mother had she been to him? Overcome with grief and shame, Lily could only think that when she'd first seen the policeman, poor John had even come at the end of the list.

Josie was devastated. If her quiet brother had loved anyone, Josie knew it had been his sister. Even as a tiny child, his rare smiles had been for her. Now, conscience-stricken, she blamed herself. It was all her fault! She was the one who'd suggested a window-cleaning round. If she'd kept her mouth shut, this wouldn't have happened. John was only twenty-four.

No one should die at twenty-four! But how could it happen? How could someone go out of the door in the morning, and never come back? Why?

It was the staves. Sid, after identifying the body, had gone to see Bert, who was in a terrible state. "I told him," he said. "I told him always to check the staves!"

"That's what caused it?"

Bert nodded. "According to the police. John had my old ladder, you see – I got a new one when I took him on. Not that there was anything wrong with the old one," he hurriedly added. "Just, you know, how you pass things down."

"And the staves?" Sid's face was grim.

"They seemed fine then, but any ladder-user should always do a regular check – it's a routine thing." He looked at Sid, his regret and sadness etched on his lined face. "I'm sorry, mate. He was a good worker, had no fear of heights at all. This should never have happened."

"No need to blame yourself," Sid said gruffly, and before he left shook Bert's hand, knowing that the man would always feel partly responsible. As he trudged home, he kicked aimlessly at a stone on the pavement, and watched it roll into the gutter. It wasn't right, your son dying before you. And it was so futile. Just down to carelessness – and whose fault was that? John's, or his? As his father, shouldn't he have foreseen this danger, instilled into his son the necessity of being safety-conscious? But he hadn't thought! He'd just assumed that having worked on and off since he was fourteen, John would have been aware of such things. Or had he and Lily expected too much of the lad? After all, they'd always known he was different – he hadn't talked until he was nearly four – but lots of families had a child who was a bit 'slow'. People just accepted it. With a grimace, Sid remembered how he himself had been regarded as such at one time. Yet he'd always been in work, had brought up a fine family. And at that word, he had to turn his head away, as people began to stare at the working man in his cap, blinded by tears streaming down his face.

Dennis too, was full of regrets. Sid had caught a bus to Fenton to tell him the terrible news and now, having brought his father home on the motor-bike, he sat in the parlour talking in a low voice to Josie. How many times, he thought miserably, had he been impatient with his younger brother, cuffing him when they were boys, calling him stupid when he didn't understand jokes, even ignoring him at times.

"I feel awful about it," he told Josie. "Kids can be so cruel, can't they? I just wish I'd tried to understand him more."

With hearts full of sorrow and guilt, John's family buried him in the small churchyard at the bottom of the hill. Dennis, there alone, as his wife had given birth to a son that morning.

Peter, the youngest of the three brothers, could have been granted compassionate leave, but unfortunately, was too far away to make it in time.

And so, Lily thought, as they walked back among the graves, some neglected, some cared for and colourful with flowers, life goes on. With a death had come a birth, a new life, and she knew she would thank God for it. But not yet – she was too bruised, too sore. Her mother always used to say that time was a great healer, and Lily could only cling to that.

Josie, following with Dennis's arm around her shoulders, hated it all – the smell of damp earth, the weeping, and sadness. She lifted her face to the sky, feeling the warm breeze with a hint of the summer to come, and made a vow. I'm going to enjoy my life. I'm going to live each day as it comes. I'm going to make the most of whatever brains I was born with. For some reason, I was given John's share as well as my own. And the best way I can remember him is not to let them go to waste.

Chapter 8

Georgina, when she came home for the summer holidays, could only kiss Josie on the cheek and say, "I was so sorry to hear about your brother."

"You heard then?" Josie removed herself from the embrace, feeling embarrassed. None of her other friends would ever dream of kissing each other. That was reserved for close family.

Georgina sensed Josie's withdrawal, and her face reddened. She'd acted without thinking – after all, everyone at school greeted each other in this way. And, according to what she'd heard, people on the Continent were not content with kissing one cheek when they greeted each other, but both! Perhaps it was a class thing.

"Yes," she said. "My mother wrote and told me." Her face closed. Alice had, indeed, scribbled a note on the back of her birthday card. But although, as the school rules dictated, Georgina wrote home each week, it was rare that she received a reply. "So," she said, "tell me – did you pass?"

"Of course I did!" Josie grinned.

"I told you it would be okay." Georgina crossed over to the window.

It was a lovely summer's day, and the rose gardens were in full bloom, a delight of rich crimson, bright pink, creamy white and yellow. She could see their gardener, Cyril, toiling in the vegetable garden. "He'll be finished soon," she said. "He comes early, often before we're up. He says it's the best time of the day."

"Who?"

"Cyril." She turned to Josie. "You know, it's ridiculous, all this secrecy. We can hardly stay stuffed in here all the summer. Can you play tennis?"

Josie shook her head. "I haven't got a racquet. I've had a go with one though, just hitting the ball across the street."

"Right." Georgina went to her wardrobe. "You can borrow this. I got a new one for my birthday." She took out a racquet and began to unscrew the press.

"But we can hardly go up the park," Josie objected. "Someone's bound to see us."

"No need." Georgina's eyes widened. "We've got our own court. Didn't you know?"

"Yer never!" Josie pressed her lips together. She was trying so hard to talk properly, but sometimes the words just popped out.

"Yes. Right at the end of the garden, further down than the vegetables. Look," she beckoned Josie to join her at the window, "see those oak trees?"

"Yes."

"Behind those. You can't see it from the house,

or the street. We can play there in complete privacy." With delight, Georgina began to rummage in a drawer. "Here, try this on."

Josie picked it up dubiously. "It's a tennis dress," she said.

"Course it is, silly."

"But I'm wearing navy-blue knickers."

"Oh! You'll just have to borrow these." She threw over a pair of her own, and, disconcerted, Josie stared at them. She couldn't possibly change her knickers, with Georgina standing there! "Thanks," she mumbled, and grabbing them, together with the dress, went off to the bathroom. Within minutes, she returned, dressed all in white, with only one discordant note. Her black pumps.

"What size are you?" Georgina frowned.

"Five."

"Bother, I'm a six. Still, what does it matter? You look great! The dress is actually better on you – it's a bit short on me. What do you think?"

Josie looked at herself in the ivory cheval mirror. If you ignored the black pumps, she looked just like one of those girls on the films, the sort who attended country house parties. Meantime, Georgina quickly got changed, picked up a box of balls, and then struck an exaggerated pose. "Anyone for tennis?"

Josie giggled, and they ran down the stairs only to stop short before they fell over Lily, who was on her hands and knees, polishing the balustrade.

"My God, just look at you," she said, glancing up to see her daughter.

69

"I'm going to teach Josie how to play tennis, Mrs Ford," Georgina told her. "Has Cyril gone?"

"Just." Lily said wryly, and watched the girls go out into the bright morning, before returning with a sigh to her task. Sometimes she wondered if she'd ever been young and light-hearted. Smearing more lavender wax polish on to her duster, Lily began to rub vigorously. Every time she got fed up of cleaning, she just reminded herself that financially things were better than they'd ever been.

And over that summer, Josie's visits increased to four and sometimes five mornings a week. "I polish the silver as well as iron," she told her friends. "It's a sort of holiday job."

As for tennis, with her wiry frame and boundless energy, Josie soon became the better player, much to Georgina's shame. "I feel awful," she wailed. "Here's me, been playing for years, and you come along and beat me!"

"You've either got it or you haven't!" Josie ducked as Georgina threw a silk cushion at her. "Anyway, you look much more elegant on the court than I do!"

The two girls were sitting on the bed, playing Monopoly, and waiting for Cyril to leave. "This can't last, you know," Georgina said, "this hole-and-corner stuff."

"Your dad can't keep you locked inside your ivory tower for ever," Josie pointed out.

"Maybe not. But what if he found out and your mum lost her job?"

70

"He wouldn't!" Josie sat bolt upright.

Georgina turned away. Josie looked at her downcast face, and felt a surge of pity for her new friend. She was glad William Hawkins wasn't *her* father, even if it meant she couldn't live in this lovely house. And Georgina was rapidly becoming almost her *best* friend. While still envying the other girl her wealth, Josie genuinely liked her and as the weeks passed the bond between them deepened.

"It'll be ages before we see each other again," Georgina said at the end of the summer vacation. "You'll make lots of other friends though, at your new school."

"Hope so," Josie grinned. "I can't become a hermit, just because you've swanned off. Anyway, I'll see you at half-term."

"I'm not coming. Fiona's invited me to go up to Edinburgh."

"Oh." Disappointed, Josie felt a swift pang of jealousy. "You'll have to put up with being called George again, then."

Georgina pulled a face. "Don't *you* ever start. It's bad enough at school – you know I hate it." But Josie had no intention of calling her George. She rather liked having a friend with an unusual name like Georgina. Although she always threatened to flatten anyone who used her own full name. After all, who wanted to put up with stupid boys chanting, *"Not tonight, Josephine!"*

Minutes later, she was walking home, and with

an effort turned her mind to the next few months and to her new school.

Josie was determined to do well. "I'm going to learn all I can," she muttered, as she let herself in through the front door. Georgina will have to, she thought, I don't suppose you have much choice when you live in the same building as your teachers. And I don't want her to do better than me. I want us to be equals – in the brains department, if nothing else. In any case, I owe it to John.

But now, Josie's main priority was to get her mum something to eat, knowing that she'd be ready for it when she came home in half an hour. Honestly, she never seemed to stop in that house. Josie felt a bit ashamed as she sliced cheese very thinly, and then, getting out the bread knife, began to cut a loaf. What had *she* done all morning, except enjoy herself? We all take Mum for granted, she thought, and then, thankful that bread, at least, was now off ration, cut an extra slice. Lily loved grilled cheese on toast, and as a special treat deserved to have the lion's share of their allowance.

As time went on, Josie settled quickly into her new school, and by working hard, did well in most of the subjects. She and Georgina met in the school holidays and played tennis whenever they could.

"I can't believe these last two years have gone so fast," Georgina said, lounging by her bedroom window, leafing through a *Woman's Own*. "Gosh, it's going to be hot today."

Josie was lacing up her new tennis shoes. "Is Cyril still there?"

"Just tidying up. He won't be long."

Georgina held out a picture of a glamorous model with a short hairstyle, combed into a DA at the back. "Do you think that would suit me?"

Josie giggled. "You know what DA stands for, don't you? Duck's Anatomy! Or, even worse!"

Georgina grinned. "If it's good enough for Doris Day . . ."

"Your mum would have a fit. Anyway, your hair's nice like that." With a touch of envy, Josie looked at Georgina's fine blonde hair. She was wearing it in a pageboy bob, and the shorter length gave it more fullness. "I can't do a thing with mine," she grumbled, running her fingers through her dark curls. The only style she'd ever had was a sort of elfin cut, which she thought made her look like a boy.

"You could wear it long," Georgina suggested. "A bit wild, like Jennifer Jones – you know, in *Gone to Earth*."

"Do you reckon?" Josie crossed over to the mirror – maybe that wasn't a bad idea. At least it would make her look a bit more grown up.

Just sixteen, both girls were obsessed with their appearance. They were also obsessed with boys. In Georgina's case, it was all theory, as she hardly knew any – in fact, the only member of the opposite sex under fifty to have crossed her path so far was Fiona's brother, and he was only fourteen! Even her teachers were all female.

Josie, on the other hand, had been going to the local Youth Club for the past year, where, on Saturday nights, a dance was held. "It's supposed to be romantic," she told Georgina, "but don't you believe it! They've either got sweaty hands which leave a mark on the back of your dress, spots, or bad breath."

"Haven't you met anyone you're . . ."

"Keen on?" Josie shook her head with vigour. "Not me, I'm fussy."

"Maybe, but at least you've been kissed!" Georgina protested. "Look at me! Talk about a vestal virgin – untouched by human hand, that's what I am!"

"Oh yeah, but that was just Postman's Knock," Josie said. "Believe me, it was nothing like you see on the films. Anyway, you still haven't told me – what are you going to do? Stay on at boarding school?"

"I can stay on only if I intend to go to Teacher Training College, or train to be a nurse. Apparently," she said with bitterness, "those are the only careers my father thinks are 'suitable'. I mean, have you ever heard of anything so ridiculous?" Georgina hesitated, one finger plucking at a loose thread on the eiderdown. "The trouble is, I definitely don't want to be a teacher, and I can't stand the sight of blood! But I'm just not clever enough for university."

"You're good at English, though, like me. What about a secretarial course?"

"I don't suppose they'd let me come on the same one as you?"

Josie grimaced. "Pigs might fly! You'd have to mix with the peasants, and that would never do!"

Georgina winced. "I hate it, you know," she said suddenly. "All this snobbery."

"Try being on the other end," Josie said wryly.

The two girls had been lucky. Not once during the past two years had William Hawkins had a day off sick, and Josie's supposed part-time job had proved the perfect cover. Alice Hawkins didn't seem to object to her presence at all. That didn't mean that she made any effort to be friendly, and she took no interest at all in how the two girls occupied themselves. When she *was* at home, which wasn't often, she spent most of her time in her bedroom, "titivating", as Georgina called it.

"Look," Georgina said, "the coast's clear." She picked up her racquet, and warned, "Don't think you'll beat me so easily this time. Fiona's been giving me some coaching."

William Hawkins was finding the late morning heat oppressive, and driving back from a meeting, found he was longing for a cool drink. And once the thought entered his head, he realised he was only minutes away from home, whereas it would take another twenty minutes to get to the office. Iced home-made lemonade was what he needed, none of this fizzy commercial pop in bottles. So, breaking the habit of a lifetime, William arrived at Rosemount in the middle of the day.

As soon as he entered the hall, he could hear the sound of a vacuum cleaner upstairs, and swore to himself. Damn, Mrs Ford was still here! Then a few seconds later, he realised that Alice wasn't. Feeling oddly disappointed, William took off his jacket, and his thirst having reached desperation point, went into the kitchen and opened the door of the huge Kelvinator refrigerator. In triumph he saw the glass jug on the top shelf. I suppose I'm lucky, he thought, pouring a generous amount and adding ice. Not many men in the Potteries will be drinking something like this. But then, not many would have a refrigerator. He'd done well, he had to give himself that. The cold, slightly tart drink was immensely satisfying, but the noise of the Hoover irritated him, so William wandered into the garden, welcoming the shade provided by the trees overhanging the path. Cyril does a good job, he mused, unable to find fault with the well-kept lawns and immaculate flowerbeds. Maybe he should do this more often, take time to enjoy his home – after all, he was the one who earned the brass to pay for it.

Then suddenly the silence was broken by the sound of a ball on gut, a clear young voice calling, "Sorry!" and he realised that Georgina must be on the tennis court. William felt pleased, as at times he wondered whether the court was a bit of a 'white elephant'. He didn't play himself, had always considered the game to be the province of 'toffs', but Alice sometimes gave Georgina a game, although she wasn't a keen player. He recalled suggesting they should join a Tennis Club, but Alice hadn't seemed keen, and Georgina was away most of the time. Now he found it gave him pleasure to hear sounds of activity in his garden, to know that his wife and daughter were at home. It never occurred to him that anyone else would be on the court, as William didn't approve of visitors to his house – being firmly of the opinion that if suppliers found out how wealthy he was, they'd be less inclined to knock down their prices.

Still holding his now almost empty glass of lemonade, William strolled past the vegetable garden, and rounded the corner of the screening trees.

The two girls, oblivious at first of his presence, had just begun a prolonged and fiercely fought volley. Eventually, Georgina struggled to reach a long ball, and managed to get it back over the net, whereupon Josie immediately hit it to Georgina's weak backhand.

"Oh, damn! Your game!" Georgina said, laughing and mopping her brow with the sweatband on her wrist. "What's the matter?" She squinted at Josie, who was making weird gestures with her head. "What?" Mystified, Georgina turned round and saw her father.

William Hawkins stared at them both. And the uppermost thought in his mind wasn't curiosity about the other girl. It was of the pleasing scene he'd just witnessed of the two young girls in white tennis dresses, with their lightly tanned bodies portraying health and vitality. It was a shock to realise that one was his own daughter, that nondescript figure who sat at his dinner table in meek silence!

Was this the same girl, her face lit with determination and enthusiasm, with an easy confident laugh? Even as the question occurred to him, he saw Georgina's face change. It was as though a light had been turned off, and once again he saw the blank expression he'd become accustomed to. Frowning, William switched his attention to the other girl.

"Who's this?" he barked.

Panic rising, for one wild moment, Georgina sought for an excuse, a fabrication as she raised her eyes to meet those of her father, his face flushed with the heat, his bushy eyebrows drawn together in a frown. But the decision was made for her, as Josie walked swiftly around the end of the net and came towards them.

"I'm Josie Ford, Mr Hawkins."

William stared at the slim girl, at the challenge in her blue eyes, and realised that this young chit wasn't in the least afraid of him.

"Josie Ford?" His brows drew together. "Are you any relation to . . ." He jerked his head towards the house.

"I'm her daughter," Josie said, her voice clear. She lifted her chin and met his gaze in defiance. Why should *I* 'kowtow' to him, she thought with bitterness. I don't work for him! And how dare he refer to my mum with an insulting jerk of the head!

Georgina, who knew Josie well enough to recognise that her temper was up, found the courage to intervene. "Josie's a good tennis player, father. You know how you're always saying the court doesn't get enough use?"

William looked at them, seeing anxiety in one pair of eyes, resentment in the other. "Where's your mother?"

"She's gone to a committee meeting in Stoke," Georgina said.

"I see." William walked to a shady seat at the side of the court. "Go on, then," he ordered, waving an imperious hand in the direction of the court. "Let's see you play!"

"You let me win on purpose," accused Georgina an hour later. The two girls had taken their cold drinks up to her bedroom, and hot and exhausted, collapsed on to her bed.

"I couldn't show you up in front of *him*, could I," Josie retorted. "It was awful, trying to play with your father watching." She shuddered, remembering the heavily built oppressive figure, so incongruous in the heat in his blue serge waistcoat and trousers. "Still, at least things are out in the open now."

"Not quite," Georgina said. "He knows you come to play tennis, but not the rest."

"Ah, but it's a foot in the door. Did you see Mum's face when we came in!"

"I wonder if he said anything to her?" Georgina worried, twisting a length of her hair around her finger. "He came in several minutes before us."

"I'll soon find out. If he did, she wouldn't say anything in front of you. And you'd better tell your mother."

"Yes, and before he does," Georgina said grimly.

But William Hawkins wasn't seething with rage

as the girls imagined. He was shaken, yes, but not by the discovery of Josie Ford in his garden. He was a hard man, was proud of being so, but it had shocked him to see how the sunlight vanished from Georgina's expression when she saw him. A shutter had come down, and with uneasiness, William faced the painful knowledge that he hardly knew his daughter – someone he'd long dismissed as being colourless. But seeing her face alive with vitality, the attractive picture she portrayed on the court, had made him realise that not only was the girl a stranger to him, but that she was a daughter to be proud of. The concept was strange and unexpected. Staring down at his large-knuckled fingers, William admitted to himself that he'd always blamed and resented Georgina for not being the son he'd so longed for. As a man who believed that to apologise or admit a mistake was a form of weakness, he normally paid scant attention to matters of conscience. Yet now he recognised that the heaviness within him was one of both guilt and bitter regret. His discipline had been too harsh, even though he'd only treated the girl in the same way as his employees. William Hawkins was not given to introspection, yet even though he heard Josie's step on the stairs, her voice talking to her mother as they both left, he didn't move from his chair in his study. While the sunlight filtered beneath the curtains – drawn against the sun to protect the heavy mahogany furniture – he remained where he was, deep in thought.

Chapter 9

Alice Hawkins, at the time that her husband was on his journey of self-discovery, was in a state of suspended excitement. As the man sitting beside her moved his suede shoe to lightly touch her own, she felt the heat rise in her cheeks, as it had risen several times already that morning – and it wasn't due to the warm atmosphere in the room. Neil Maxwell had only recently joined the committee devoted to care of the elderly, but from the first moment she saw him, Alice scented danger. His gaze had rested on her within seconds of his arrival, and each time they met the sexual tension between them hung in the air and grew ever more powerful, as did her awareness that soon there would be a line to cross. And Alice was unsure that she could resist the temptation. Neil, with his saturnine good looks and narrow moustache, had aroused a sensuality she now realised had lain dormant for far too long.

"Meet me afterwards," he whispered.

"I can't. I have to get back for lunch." Alice darted a quick look around the large boardroom table, and bent her head over her notepad.

Neil scribbled on his own pad. *"Next time, let*

me take you to lunch," and slid it towards her.

Alice became very still. This was it: this was the line. To agree to meet him for a meal, even in a public place, would be a tacit admission, if not of an actual affair, then of an intention to have one. Panic swept over her only to be superseded by a heady exhilaration, every nerve-end tingling at the prospect of an intimate relationship with such a fascinating man. And she wasn't the only one who found him attractive, Alice knew that Neil Maxwell could have his pick of women. And surely the fact that he too was married would be some form of security. As a well-known solicitor, it would be in his interests, as well as hers, that they were discreet. Because Alice knew that lunch would be merely the prelude. A man like Neil would make love with finesse – he was a professional man, a man of culture in the way that William Hawkins could never be. Alice closed her eyes for a moment, remembering how for years she'd endured her husband's brusque fumbling; always in the dark, always beneath the blankets. She glanced down at Neil's wrist resting on the table, at the slight dusting of dark hairs on hands, at his manicured nails. Then almost without her conscious decision, the words appeared on her notepad: "_I'll look forward to it._"

When Alice arrived home the first thing she noticed was William's new car in the drive. This was so unusual during a working day that she was full of apprehension as she parked her own car, closed the gates and hurried to the front door.

"William?" she called his name as soon as she entered the hall. "Is anything wrong?"

Georgina came running down the stairs, and with a jerk of her head, went into the kitchen. Alice followed her.

"He just turned up," Georgina whispered, "a couple of hours ago. We were playing tennis!"

Alice caught her breath. Damn! There was bound to be a scene, and she was too distracted and hot to cope with one. "Did you tell him who Josie was?" she hissed.

"She told him. He didn't say a word, just asked us to carry on playing."

"And?"

Georgina shrugged. "He sat at the side and watched. He's been in his study ever since."

Alice thought quickly. "I'd better get some lunch. And a sandwich won't do for your father! We'll have the rest of that cold chicken. There's some apple-pie left as well, and there's always the Stilton . . ." While Alice began to rinse lettuce, and prepare a salad, Georgina set the table in the dining-room. William Hawkins never ate in the kitchen.

Alice turned as she came back in, "There's potato salad," she said, "and, for heaven's sake, cut the bread and butter thin!"

Fifteen minutes later, the meal was ready.

Alice tapped on the study door.

"William . . .?" She went inside to see him sitting in his winged leather chair, staring into space. "Are you all right? Has something happened at work?"

He turned. "Work? No, of course not."

"It's just that it's so unusual for you to come home during the day."

He heaved himself out of the chair. "I was close by, and fancied a glass of your lemonade, that's all."

"Oh. Well, lunch is ready."

"Good."

Alice began to feel uneasy. Where was anger, the bullying tone, an accusation that she'd gone behind his back?

But if Alice felt uneasy, Georgina felt bewildered, because as she took her place at the table, instead of ignoring her as he usually did, her father turned to her and smiled. And for once, his smile reached his eyes. Georgina was uncertain whether to smile back. But her father then broke another habit. He asked her a question, and in a tone of voice she'd never heard before: not a bullying tone, but an *interested* one.

"Did you enjoy your morning's tennis?"

"Yes, very much." Georgina waited for the inevitable sarcasm, the biting comment.

"You play well," he said. "And so does the other girl."

"Josie!" Georgina said stiffly.

"Ah yes." William turned to Alice, "A good idea that. I like to think of the court getting more use."

Georgina looked pleadingly across the table at her mother, raising her eyebrows and trying to communicate by widening her eyes. Didn't she see that this was the ideal opportunity? Tell him – she sent thought-messages – tell him how well we get on, that we're friends!

But Alice, relieved at her husband's good mood, merely began picking at her food.

"We get on very well," Georgina said, raising her voice to make an impact.

William drew his eyebrows together, and shot Georgina a suspicious glance. It was obvious she was making a point. If the girl *was* to leave boarding school, which seemed likely, then obviously she would need local friends. It just seemed a pity she had to scrape the barrel with the cleaner's girl!

Georgina, having found her courage, decided to go the whole way. What had she got to lose? "In fact," she said, "I was wondering whether I could do the same as Josie – take a secretarial course at the College of Commerce in Burslem. Apparently, they do a one-year intensive one, open only to students with O levels."

At this, Alice came out of her reverie and began to pay attention. Georgina at home all the time? Travelling through the towns all the way to Burslem? What if, at some time in the future, she saw her with Neil?

"Oh, I'm not sure about that," she interjected. "I would have thought a private college some-where would be more suitable." As soon as she spoke, she knew she'd made a mistake. William didn't like anyone to dismiss a suggestion until he'd expressed his own opinion.

And in this she was right, because he turned to her with his accustomed aggression.

"I can't see what's wrong with the idea. After all, the girl should get to know her home town. She's been away long enough."

"To her advantage," Alice pointed out. "You can't deny that she's grown in confidence since she's been at boarding school." And *you* got a lucrative contract, she thought, but this time was wise enough to remain silent. It was true; William's firm had renovated a large warehouse in Derby, owned by the father of one of Georgina's school-friends.

"Is that what you really want to do?" William asked, ignoring his wife's comment. "A secretarial course?"

Georgina, astounded that her opinion was actually being sought, said promptly, "Yes, it is. Everyone says that being able to do shorthand and typing opens a lot of doors." With a calculating look at her father, she added, "Perhaps eventually to management."

William, wondering why he'd ever thought her a dimwit, frowned and took a sip of water. Alice realised that this impromptu lunch was the nearest thing approaching family life they had ever experienced.

"But if we agree to a secretarial course, are you sure this is the best option?" she demurred. Turning to William she added, "I heard Gloria Emery praising a private college in Oxford once. Apparently her daughter went to it."

Georgina groaned inwardly. The Emerys were a very prominent family in the area. Why did her parents have to be so impressed by such things?

But William was recalling a determined young face. He recognised guts when he saw it, and young Josie Ford had it in abundance. Now if a bit of her strength could rub off on his daughter . . .

"You say you get on with this girl?" he demanded.

Startled, Georgina said, "Josie? Yes, very well!"

Could her father possibly be considering letting her go? Anxiously Georgina waited, watching the brooding expression on his face. Once she darted a glance at Alice, thinking she would be pleased if all the subterfuge came to an end, only to see a strange expression on her face. Why was her mother looking so apprehensive? Georgina turned her attention back to her father. He was eating slowly, methodically, chewing each mouthful as he deliberated. Her own meal finished, she waited in an agony of impatience.

William put down his knife and fork, and wiped his mouth on his napkin.

"You'd have to go on the bus," he said. "You couldn't expect your mother to take you every day."

"Of course not," Georgina said quickly. "I can travel with Josie." She tried to think what would impress him. "I'll meet other girls from good schools. Probably from St Dominic's, Thistley Hough, or the other grammar schools – the College of Commerce has a very high reputation."

Alice looked from her husband to her daughter. "I think . . ." she began, and then paused. What did she think? Would Georgina's presence really be a danger? After all, forewarned would be fore-armed – she and Neil would just have to take care. Realising they were both waiting for her to continue speaking, Alice looked at her daughter and felt an unusual stab of compunction. Why not let the girl have her own way for once? "I think," she repeated, "that we ought to let Georgina decide. She's old enough to know what she wants."

Her face lighting up with gratitude, Georgina turned with trepidation to her father. Would he agree?

William sat with his face closed, his fingers drumming on the table. Georgina, from long expe-rience, knew better than to disturb his thoughts. "All right. I agree," he said finally. "That's settled then." Glancing at his watch, he pushed back his chair. "I'd better be off."

Leaving Georgina sitting in a state of euphoria, Alice followed him to open the front door, and dutifully kiss his cheek.

William looked down at her, thinking how smart she looked in her muted blue Hebe suit. A fine-looking woman was his wife. He was thoughtful as he unlocked his car, and stood for a minute to stare at the impressive frontage of his home. This was a house in which a child had grown up into a girl who obviously had little affection for him. But then, what affection had he ever shown her? Even her name was a constant reminder of the boy she should have been. The child had been like a frightened rabbit, and that had always nettled him. Now if she had been more like Josie Ford, things might have been different. He couldn't see that girl being scared of anyone! And with the comforting thought that the problem wasn't entirely his fault, William decided he'd wasted enough of the day on personal issues. It was time to get back to his business. He couldn't afford to be absent for long, not if he wanted a full day's work out of his employees.

Chapter 10

"*Carriage return . . .*" the deep male voice boomed out from the record-player, and with a clang, ten girls returned the long carriages on their manual typewriters. In time to the rhythm of the *William Tell Overture*, their fingers hit the blank keys, as the class, proud to display their touch-typing skills, copied the exercises from a large textbook propped on a stand before them. It was Friday afternoon, and this was the one session they all looked forward to.

"Once more, I think." Miss Jameson, their form tutor, lifted the needle ready to play the record again. "Ready? Backs straight and eyes on the text!" She turned to walk between the desks as the girls typed, her keen gaze making sure that no-one committed the cardinal sin of looking at their keys. This was a good group, one of the best she'd ever had, and she had high hopes for the examination results that year. Academically, there had been no problems; they were keen to do well and worked hard. Although it hadn't been easy at first; it had taken some time for the group to knit together. But then, with strong personalities like Josie Ford and Marlene Walters in a class, what could you expect?

Georgina, if she could have read Miss Jameson's mind, would have agreed. The term had only just started, when she heard Josie in a fierce argument with Marlene.

"You can take that back!" The two girls were standing in a corridor. Although dress was a personal choice, both wore grey pencil skirts with a split at the back, and cotton blouses with detachable white collars and cuffs.

"Georgina's *not* a stuck-up bitch who thinks she's better than the rest of us!" Josie's voice was stiff with anger.

Marlene, who everyone swore applied her make-up with a trowel, snapped, "Oh yes? Who else around here says 'baaaath', or 'daaaance'!"

"Okay, so she uses the long 'a', so what?"

Georgina stepped forward. Grateful though she was to Josie, she was no longer a timid eight-year-old. Your role as my champion became redundant a long time ago, she thought, and strolled up to join them.

"Hello, you two," she said. "I couldn't help hearing that, Marlene. Silly, isn't it, the difference in the way people pronounce their vowels. What we learn as children stays with us all our lives. Actually, I feel embarrassed at times, but I can't seem to help it."

Josie watched in amazement as Marlene's expression changed from spite to eagerness as, almost stammering, she hurried to reassure the tall, blonde girl who was smiling so appealingly at her. "Sorry, Georgina, I didn't mean anything by it."

91

"Good. Now, shall we all go and face the dreaded shorthand test?" Georgina linked arms with them both, and Josie thought wryly – there's another lesson you've learned! So this is how the middle classes deal with things; they turn on the charm!

She was finding it fascinating to watch Georgina in class, to see how poised and self-assured she was, how her good manners impressed the tutors – knowing beneath that polished exterior lay a sensitive and somewhat shy nature. It was only when Josie noticed that Georgina was watching *her*, she realised with a jolt that she herself was also under scrutiny. It was understandable really. After all, their friendship had taken place entirely in isolation – they were both seeing 'another side of each other', as Lily would say.

And Lily had said plenty. When Josie told her that William Hawkins now knew that she and his daughter were friends, and had agreed to let Georgina go to the College of Commerce, Lily had been both surprised and pleased. She'd never liked all the secrecy. However, much to Josie's disappointment, she'd laid down two strict ground rules. On the first, she was adamant. Georgina was not to visit the Fords' house.

"You know I've always made your friends welcome," she said. "But in this case it's different. It just wouldn't do for the landlord's daughter to be nipping in and out. Before we knew where we were, the neighbours would be resenting us. I want to live in peace, thank you very much."

"But—" protested Josie.

"No buts!" Lily looked at her daughter's indignant face, and sighed. Injustice had always riled her only daughter. "Look, love, I've been in this world longer than you. Folk can get very jealous. You'll find that out, particularly if you get on. How would it look, me working every day at Rosemount, and Georgina along here all the time? We'd be accused of being in old Hawkins' pocket. No, it wouldn't do at all."

"Oh – people!" Josie complained. "They cause all the problems in the world."

"Yes, and the world's full of them, so just remember that. There's no point in looking for trouble."

The second rule took the form of advice. "Try not to neglect your other friends," Lily warned. "The ones you've grown up with." Lily worried that Georgina would eventually be drawn into an exclusive social circle, one with a similar background to her own. Wasn't that what these people always did, mix with their own kind? There would be no place for Josie there. Much as she liked Georgina, Lily's advice to Josie was: "Don't put all your eggs in one basket."

But at the moment, there were no such clouds. Both girls were enjoying the course, particularly being members of such a small group. The College of Commerce was an old Victorian building, with no facilities for refreshment, so at lunch-time the girls would stream out into Burslem, past the Market Place and the impressive old Town Hall with its famous Golden Angel on top. Then they would commandeer a large table in a cosy café in the main street. Here, they would order beans on toast with a poached egg on top, or Welsh rarebit, always turning each time the door opened in case their current heart-throb, a Port Vale footballer, should come in. It had only happened once, but that didn't stop them all dreaming!

"This is ridiculous," pronounced Josie, one wet Wednesday. "What we all need is the real thing, a proper boyfriend."

"I'd rather have an improper one, myself," Marlene grinned, tossing her hair which everyone suspected her of bleaching.

"You would," Josie said shortly. She was "fast", was Marlene, you could tell.

"But I *have* got a boyfriend," said Heather, a girl who had an unfortunate tendency to spit when she spoke. "What about my Sam?" Her gaze challenged them all, and she looked uncomfortable when they burst out laughing.

"You can't count him!" Marlene said.

"Why not?"

"Well, you've been going out with him for six months, and he's never tried anything on yet! At least that's what you say."

"He respects me too much," Heather said.

"Hasn't got it in him, you mean!" Marlene was always trying to needle Heather.

"What difference does it make? I wouldn't let him anyway."

"That's not the point," Josie said. "The impor-

94

tant thing is that you should be inflaming him with desire. If you're not, then it doesn't count."

Heather stirred her hot chocolate, with a sulky expression. "You're hardly an expert, Josie. How many boyfriends have *you* had?"

"Ah, that would be telling," Josie said. "But if you lot ever want to know about kissing techniques, just ask me." She winked at Georgina.

Georgina, remembering Josie confessing that she'd 'gone outside' with one of the boys at the Youth Club Dance, grinned back at her. "I just wanted to experiment," Josie had told her, a bit shamefaced. "And he seemed as good a bet as any. He was a good kisser, I'll give him that. Mind you, once I'd satisfied my curiosity, I was off. Besides that wall was digging in my back!"

"Oh, yeah?" Marlene now scoffed. "Pull the other one!"

Josie glared at her, while Georgina said hurriedly, "Anyway, there'll be lots of talent at Trentham ballroom. And not just from Stoke-on-Trent – people come from miles around."

"And what's wrong with Stoke-on-Trent talent?" a voice enquired, and they looked up to see a young man grinning at them.

"Who was talking to you?" Josie said. Cheeky devil, butting in like that!

"No-one. But an overheard conversation is always the best sort!"

"Eavesdropping, you mean." Josie's tone was tart, but Georgina leaned forward and smiled. She thought he was good-looking, but then, as Josie

95

kept telling her, she'd find anyone in trousers attractive. "Stands to reason," she pointed out. "After the way you've been living, among a load of women. I'm going to have to watch you don't fall for the first bloke you meet!"

But Georgina liked what she saw. And she also saw that he was smiling back at her. He was dark, with laughing brown eyes. Her gaze quickly summed up his appearance. Good clothes, obviously worked in an office somewhere, probably in his early twenties. So, reasonably well educated then. Suddenly she realised what she was doing – evaluating someone at first glance! And using her parents' values to do so. A sense of shame swept over her. Did she want to turn out a snob?

"Okay, okay, just trying to uphold our honour!" He gave a slight shrug, then moved on to find a table in the corner.

"I think you've made a conquest," teased Heather. With light brown hair, and nondescript features, she was what Lily would term "a thoroughly nice girl". A peacemaker, she was always trying to smooth over any friction within the group. Privately, Josie found her irritating, although that could be because Heather always did her shorthand homework, enabling her to be top of the class in the frequent theory tests.

"Right," Josie said, draining the last of her tea and putting down the cup with a flourish, "I'm off to buy some new nylons. Coming, Georgina?"

"I'll see you back at the College," Georgina said. "I fancy one of those cakes."

Josie shot her a suspicious glance, noticing Georgina's heightened colour, and the way she was studying the checked tablecloth, then shrugged and left.

From where he was sitting, Dominic Hargreaves' gaze, when he looked up, was in direct line with Georgina's, and their eyes met once or twice as he ate his sandwich. He watched her as she got up and went to the counter to buy an Eccles cake, and another cup of tea. The other girls began to rise from the table, with much collecting of gloves, bags, and fumbling for coins to leave as a tip.

"Don't be late," instructed Heather. "We've got Commerce, and you know what old Vickers is like."

Georgina smiled. "He's a sweetie, really."

"He still doesn't like us being late."

Thoughtfully, Dominic watched them leave, and then studied the fair girl who was now sitting alone. She was lovely, and tall too. He normally went for petite girls, but all that had happened so far was that his 6 ft frame began to develop a stoop, a fact sharply pointed out by his parents. Should he go over? Was it even worth bothering in his present circumstances? But then Georgina looked up, her glance quickening his pulse, and suddenly the decision was made for him. Picking up his rapidly cooling tea, Dominic went over to her table.

"Is it okay if I join you?"

Georgina felt herself redden. "Of course," she said through a mouthful of flaky pastry.

"Are you at the College?"

She nodded, and wiped her mouth free of crumbs. "Doing a secretarial course. And you?"

"I work in Burslem."

"What as?" Georgina was finding him more attractive with every second.

"I work for my father." A shadow came over his face, and then he grimaced. "Family firm and all that."

"What sort of firm?" Georgina became alert – surely not the building trade? No, that would be too much of a coincidence.

"Nothing too glamorous, I'm afraid." Dominic hesitated, and then decided there was no point in trying to hide the truth. "We're wholesale slaughterers, you know, for the butchery trade. I work in the offices." He looked anxiously at her. "I don't have anything to do with, well, you know, the abattoirs, or anything."

Georgina concealed a shudder as the word 'abattoir' brought with it an image of spring lambs and bloody carcasses.

"See," he said, "it's put you off." His tone was bitter. "I just wish I could say I was a doctor or something! My name's Dominic, by the way."

"Georgina." She held out her hand and he shook it briefly.

"Georgina! That's unusual."

She smiled. "My parents were hoping for a boy."

"Well, I'm glad you weren't." His eyes met hers and held her gaze, until Georgina, feeling slightly embarrassed, looked away, and began fiddling with her teaspoon.

"Where are you from?" he asked.

"Dreston."

"Oh, 'neck-end' way," he teased, referring to the local idiom for Longton, the town where the potbanks specialised in earthenware.

"That's me," she laughed. She finished her tea and glanced at her watch.

"I'll have to be off."

"Did I hear you and your friends mention Trentham on Saturday?"

"Yes, they'll be there."

"Will you?"

"I'm hoping so." Georgina pushed back her chair and gave him a quick smile. "Bye."

Dominic watched her go, admiring her poise and long, slim legs. She was so intriguing – he'd never met anyone like her. Look at the way she spoke for instance, and when she smiled . . . He hadn't planned to go to Trentham or indeed anywhere on Saturday night; in the circumstances there hadn't seemed much point, but he suddenly realised that now nothing would stop him. Despite everything, he *had* to see her again . . .

Chapter 11

"**Y**uk!" Josie stared at Georgina in disbelief.

"It's not his fault," Georgina said. "He can't help what his father does."

"He could opt out! Ugh, just think of all that blood! And you'd never know where his hands had been!"

"Dominic has nothing to do with that end of the business – he works in the offices," Georgina said defensively.

"It's such a brutal trade!" Josie shuddered at the very thought.

"I haven't heard of you refusing your roast beef on a Sunday," Georgina snapped. "Nor meat and potato pie. Someone has to do the job."

Josie looked shamefaced. "I know. It's just . . ." Then she grinned. "All right, I'll back off." But she looked thoughtfully at her friend. Georgina was such a trusting soul – it came of being locked away from the real world. Now if she'd had to cope with the rough and tumble of a mixed playground, she'd have a more realistic view of the opposite sex!

Georgina was more concerned about persuading her parents to let her go dancing. But in that, she had an unexpected ally.

"Mrs Hawkins," Lily broached one morning, "is your Georgina going to Trentham Ballroom on Saturday?"

Alice looked vaguely at her. She was immersed in *Vogue*, while Lily cleaned the sitting-room windows.

"I can't recall her mentioning it."

"Only, Josie wants to go, and I'd feel happier if there were two of them. There are other girls going from the course, but they don't live this end, and although there's a late bus, I don't want her travelling on her own."

Alice closed the pages of her magazine and got up to leave the room. "I'll have a word with Mr Hawkins and let you know. When you've finished that, would you give the fender a polish?"

"Of course." Lily glanced at her watch. Just half an hour to go, then she could go home, have a sandwich and put her feet up while she listened to the wireless. Maybe, she mused, she could even have forty winks. She seemed to get so tired lately. Still, it was only to be expected at her age. She'd found the change very difficult, was still getting over it. Who'd be a woman, she thought. There was no doubt in her mind who had the easier life – men, every time!

"Did you ask her?" Josie demanded when she got home from college. It was raining heavily, and she was soaked. "We had to wait ages for a bus when we got to Longton bus station," she grumbled. "We'd just missed one."

"Never mind. Get those wet things off. I've got

some nice belly pork for tea. That'll soon warm you up."

"Great! Well," Josie asked again, as she rolled down her wet stockings and took them off, "did you?"

"I did, and she said she'll ask His Nibs. Although why Georgina couldn't bring it up herself, I don't know."

To Alice's surprise, William had calmly agreed, and even offered to take the two girls and to pick them up at 1 am. "I don't want Georgina travelling by public transport at night," he told her.

Alice stared numbly at him. Fetch the girls – William? Like any normal father? Bewildered, she wondered what had happened to change his attitude to his daughter so much. It all dated back to last summer, when she'd found him unexpectedly at home in the middle of the day. Talk about a Jekyll and Hyde, she thought. It's a good job he hasn't got a laboratory in the cellar, or I really would be worried!

But Alice's thoughts soon drifted away from Rosemount and its inhabitants. Sometimes she thought her life, her real life, began only when she closed those black wrought-iron gates behind her. The gold-painted sign of the home she loved so much seemed to mock her as she drove through, but she didn't care. The past few months with Neil Maxwell had been the most exhilarating of her life. Even the secrecy gave her a thrill. The illicit meetings at secluded country hotels, the elaborate arrangements Neil made to conceal their liaison, all combined to make her feel unique, important, that she was living a life of glamour, of passion. And passion there was, for Alice had discovered that sex wasn't all about 'lying back and thinking of England', but could be an intense physical experience. Sometimes, as she and Neil sat up and leaned back on the pillows to smoke their cigarettes, she wondered why she had no conscience about it. After all, they both had families. And then Alice would remember her mother, her promiscuity, love of excitement and, she'd found out later, weakness for dubious characters. I must get it from her, she thought. What do they say – 'blood will out'? Alice was under no illusions about Neil. Theirs wasn't a great love affair – in fact she doubted he even loved her. But he desired her, as she did him, and Alice often wondered whether that was the key to its success. There was no emotional involvement, neither did they make any demands on each other. Neil showed no curiosity about her personal life; he'd never even asked how old she was, and Alice suspected that her lover was younger. She'd seen what an older man's body looked like – she was married to one. And Neil's flat stomach and firm biceps belied his somewhat 'lived-in' handsome face – although that was probably due to the amount he smoked and drank. Certainly he was a man who believed in indulging his whims. But whatever his faults, their relationship had made her happier than she had ever been. Not for me, she thought, a life like that of Lily Ford. Good, honest, hardworking Lily. And where had it got her? There wasn't any fun in being respectable, not from what she'd seen of life.

Lily, however, was perfectly content or would have been but for the sadness about John's death which was always with her. If she thought about her role in life at all, it was purely on a practical level. As long as she could keep her home clean and tidy, her man under control, and be proud of her children, then she asked for nothing else. And now she had another role – she was a grandmother. Both she and Sid doted on Dennis's little boy. He and his wife had called him John.

"Seemed only right," Dennis had said. "Seeing as how he was born on the day we buried our John."

Lily had been deeply touched, and told him so. Yes, she was proud of Dennis. He'd grown into a fine young man. Not one who would ever make a stir in the world, mind. Ordinary was their Dennis, someone you'd hardly notice in a crowd. But he was hardworking – his steady job as a warehouseman proved that. And Lily got on well with his wife. Mavis had given up her job now she had little Johnny, and every Wednesday afternoon brought the toddler up to visit. Lily looked forward to that. It had become a highlight in the week, even if she did worry about that blasted motorbike and sidecar when Dennis came to have his tea and collect them.

"Catch me getting into one of those things,"

she would grumble at Sid.

"Maybe. But it's transport, isn't it? Better than relying on buses."

"Yes," she retorted. "Well, if you did those pools right, we could all have cars!"

But all that Josie and Georgina could think about was what to wear on Saturday night. After several changes of mind, the decision was made. Josie was to wear her blue pinafore dress. In fine needle-cord velvet, it was cut in a princess style, with a full skirt. And, as she pointed out to Georgina, it made her bust look at least a size bigger.

"Are you sure people don't dress up more – in long dresses, for instance?"

Josie looked pityingly at her. "It isn't a New Year's Eve formal affair. We don't need to be all bare shoulders. People are going to be doing this new rock and roll, as well as the foxtrot!"

"Okay, I'll wear this then." Georgina held up a pretty crepe flowered dress.

"Oh, no, you won't!" Josie was horrified. "That's much too ladylike!" Searching through Georgina's wardrobe she said, "The trouble with you is you've got too much to choose from. Now with me, it's either one or the other. Here . . ." she held out a black shot-taffeta circular skirt, and white blouse. "Perfect. When did you get this?"

"End-of-year party at school. I've only worn it once."

"Have you got a stiff petti?"

"Sure."

"That's it, then, and you could wear your black patent shoes."

"Do you think he'll come?" Georgina's expression, to Josie's disgust, went all dreamy.

"If you mean the Bloody Butcher, how would I know?"

"I wish you wouldn't call him that!" Georgina snapped.

Josie bit her lip. Still, there would be lots of other young men for Georgina to meet at Trentham. Wholesale butchers indeed!

Chapter 12

When Saturday night arrived, Josie walked along to Rosemount. And the fact that she could now legitimately knock on the front door never failed to give her a sense of satisfaction. How many years was it since she'd first come through those gates carrying her mum's shoes? Only three, but it seemed far more. And now look at her, about to ride in William Hawkins' car, although not the same one that had so often interrupted their street games. His had been the only car then, but now there were others. Tommy Siddaway had a Ford 10, and at the other end of the street, Mick Shaunessy had just bought an old Austin. His wife was already complaining that he spent more time tinkering with that than tinkering with her!

But even before Josie lifted the knocker, the door opened and Georgina, looking slightly flustered, came out with her father. William nodded at Josie, opened the garage door, and started the car. The girls stood to one side in the drive as he reversed it and then Georgina opened the back door for Josie to climb in, closed it, and got into the passenger seat.

It was the first time Josie had ever been in a car, and slightly awed by the leather seats and the feeling of luxury, she gazed out of the window at the familiar houses as William drove along the street. It seemed strange to be going by her own home, and she gave a half-embarrassed wave when she saw Lily hovering behind the net curtains.

"It's very kind of you to give me a lift, Mr Hawkins," she said, as much to break the silence as anything else. Georgina hadn't spoken a word so far.

"It's my pleasure," William said.

In fact, he was quite enjoying having the two girls in the car. He could sense their excitement although he thought they'd both overdone the perfume a bit. He glanced at Georgina, who was studiously looking out of her side window. He'd tried hard these past months to get closer to her, but it was proving more difficult than he'd antici-pated. The barrier she'd erected between them was ever-present, although at least now they were managing to communicate.

Georgina, however, wasn't thinking about her father. She was too busy looking forward to the evening ahead. She loved dancing, had learned how to at school, but this would be the first time she'd actually been to a public dance. I've led far too sheltered a life, she thought. Mixing with the other girls at the college had shown her just how limited her experience was. She might have learned independence, she'd certainly received a good education, but she was well aware that she was regarded as 'different' in some way. Was this one of the reasons why people of her class – how she hated that word – usually moved exclusively in their own social circle? The trouble with me, she thought, is that I want to be part of both worlds.

Josie, although enjoying the ride, was just fidgety. She couldn't wait to reach their destination and climbed out of the car at the gates to Trentham Gardens as soon as William drew to a halt.

The two girls were full of excited anticipation, fuelled by glimpses of the illuminated ballroom through its large windows as they joined others walking along the drive to the main entrance. The night air was crisp, the atmosphere already infectious. Georgina, hoping and praying that Dominic would be there, turned to smile at her friend.

"Are we set?"

"You bet."

With the strains of 'Mambo Italiano' in the distance, they queued to check in their coats. Then in the small square cloakroom, they joined several girls who were crowding before the mirror, spraying perfume, dabbing at their noses with Crème Puff, and applying lipstick. Others peered over their heads, trying to attain the sophisticated image they craved. Josie fluffed out her dark curls, Georgina smoothed her blonde bob, and with one accord they turned.

"Here we go," Josie breathed.

"I can't wait!" Georgina followed her into the

ballroom where the noise was deafening. The large band was playing a jazz number now, while people crowded around the front of the stage, swaying to the beat. Josie nudged Georgina. "You're the tallest," she hissed. "See if you can see the others."

Obediently, Georgina craned her neck over the dancers, and eventually spotted Marlene over the other side of the room. "Follow me," she said over her shoulder, and in single file they made their way around the edge of the dance floor.

Relieved to see their friends had a table, Josie's eyes widened when she saw Marlene's dress. She glanced at Georgina and their eyes signalled the same scandalised message: just look at that cleavage! Heather wasn't able to come – her boyfriend didn't like dancing, and he disapproved of her going anywhere without him. But two other girls from their class were there. Hazel, a dark-haired girl who was rather shy, and Sue, a pert blonde.

"Have you seen 'em?" Sue jerked her head in Marlene's direction.

"Could hardly miss!" Josie retorted.

"If you've got 'em, flaunt 'em, that's what I say," Marlene grinned, not at all dismayed by the five disapproving faces surrounding her. She bent down to adjust the strap on her evening sandal, and Josie averted her eyes. Honestly, you could see right down to her toes! Still, if Marlene wanted to attract the wrong type, it was up to her!

"Right," Josie said. "Have you seen any talent?"

"Loads!" Sue was wearing red, with white daisy

earrings to match her waspie belt. "We haven't been on the floor yet though. We've only just got here."

"Speak for yourself," breathed Marlene, as a burly young man approached. The other girls watched as he swept her away in a quickstep.

"Looks like a boxer," pronounced Josie. "And let's hope he doesn't look down – the shock could kill him!"

Georgina wasn't paying attention. Her gaze was searching the crowded ballroom for Dominic, but without success. Then she turned as a touch came on her shoulder, and a fair-haired youth of about eighteen stood there. His blue, slightly prominent eyes bored into hers and, with sweat beading his forehead, he said, "May I have this dance?"

Georgina, feeling unaccountably nervous, nodded, and followed him on to the dance floor. Josie grinned as she saw him immediately tread on Georgina's toes, but within seconds was on the dance-floor herself. Her partner, much to her disgust, was short and fat. If it hadn't been for hurting his feelings, she would have refused. But Josie remembered Peter telling her how dreadful it felt if a girl refused an offer to dance.

"I've known some blokes when it's taken them months to pluck up the courage again," he'd said. He was due on leave soon, and Josie couldn't wait to see him. The house was always livened up by Peter's presence.

Georgina was finding it difficult to follow her partner. At school she'd only ever danced with

111

other girls, and now the hand on the back of her waist was so hesitant that she had no idea which way he was going to turn. Wistfully, she looked at other couples, twirling and dancing with panache. All *she* felt like was an awkward schoolgirl stumbling around with a schoolboy, an unattractive one at that! As soon as the music stopped, he escorted her back to her table without a word, and she looked ruefully at the hole rapidly appearing in the toe of her nylons. At that moment Josie re-appeared, but with another girl in tow.

"This is Pauline," she announced, "an old friend of mine. The girl she was supposed to meet hasn't turned up, so I told her she could join us. That okay?" Without waiting for a reply, Josie moved a chair from an adjoining table and drew Pauline down beside her. "Georgina, Marlene, Sue, Hazel," she said.

Once the other girls were talking together, Pauline nudged Josie.

"Is that who I think it is?" she whispered, indicating Georgina.

"Sure is. Hey, Georgina?"

She turned. "You remember Pauline?" Josie said. "Only this time their Muriel isn't here to spoil the fun."

Georgina frowned, and then light dawned. "It was your rope we were skipping with! You're Muriel's younger sister!"

"Well done, Sherlock," Josie laughed.

"Lovely to meet you again, Pauline." Georgina looked with interest at the girl she remembered having protruding teeth and pigtails. The teeth were now only slightly prominent, and Pauline wore her brown hair in a pageboy style made popular by the film star, June Allyson.

"Pauline's working," Josie said.

The others immediately paid attention. Working? That meant earning money, money that could be spent on records, make-up and clothes.

"Lucky devil," complained Sue. "It'll be months before we can get some cash. What do you do?"

"I'm a lithographer," Pauline told them. "On a potbank."

Georgina wrinkled her forehead, puzzled for a moment. "Oh, you mean a pottery factory! Sorry to seem ignorant, but what exactly does a lithographer do?"

"I size the plates," Pauline told her. "Then I put the transfers on, and when they're ready I sponge them off! After that, the ware goes to be fired."

"My mum used to work on a potbank," Marlene said, "but she had to leave."

Curious, Josie leaned forward. "Why?"

"She was having an affair with the foreman. Only his wife worked there as well. When she found out, she pinched all my mum's paintbrushes and threw them away. Proper camel-hair they were, too. Then she threatened to smash all the patterns unless Mum made herself scarce." Marlene creased up with laughter. She didn't seem to notice the silence that greeted her remarks.

Josie was thinking that with a mother like that it

113

was no wonder that Marlene had no shame. Georgina was simply astounded at Marlene's acceptance of her mother's behaviour. To have an affair with a married man – that was a dreadful thing to do.

The band struck up another number, and then suddenly, to her absolute delight Georgina saw Dominic approaching. He *was* here!

"There you are," he said, with obvious relief. "I've been looking all over for you."

"Hello," Georgina smiled up into his eyes, before introducing him to the others. Josie smiled, but remained wary. But even she had to admit that he was incredibly good-looking.

When the band began to play 'Three Coins in A Fountain', Dominic turned to Georgina, who, without a word, followed him on to the dance floor. And this time it was perfect. As she moved into his arms, Dominic held her close, his hand firmly against her waist. With delight Georgina found that she was able to move in perfect rhythm. "I can see how you misspent your youth!" she teased, as they circled the floor.

"Hey, less of the past tense," he said. "But you're right – I've always liked dancing. I used to come here every week."

"It's my first time."

Dominic was surprised and looked down at her. How old was she? He decided to ask. "How old are you, then?"

"Sixteen," she said. "And you?"

"Twenty-three. Almost a sugar-daddy, as far as you're concerned," he said ruefully.

"I thought they were always bald, fat and fifty!"

"Don't you believe it!"

But when the music ended, Dominic showed no inclination to take her off the floor, and Georgina, her hand held loosely in his, turned happily into his arms as the band struck up again. This time it was a foxtrot, and the vocalist began to sing "Finger of Suspicion".

"Not as good as Dickie Valentine, is he?" Dominic murmured.

"Is anybody?"

"Oh, a fan, are you?"

"Sure am!" Dreamily, Georgina nestled closer. She glanced up, her eyes meeting and holding his, and Dominic smiled down at her, before they danced the rest of the number in silence. When, with a flourish of drums, the band stopped playing, Dominic said, "Let's go and find a table and talk, or would you rather . . ."

"No, that's fine with me," Georgina said. "I could do with a drink, though."

"I'll get you one. Lemon and lime okay?"

"Fine." As she settled at an empty table, Georgina watched him walk through the crowds to the bar, liking the way his height gave him prominence. Then, seeing that Josie was looking for her, Georgina waved across the ballroom, and pointed in the direction of the bar. Josie acknowledged she understood, and Georgina settled herself down to wait. The bar was crowded, and if it had been licensed she would have loved to try a Babycham. I'm sure I could pass for eighteen, she mused. Eventually, Dominic returned, handed her a brimming glass, and sat opposite.

"Now, tell me all about yourself."

"There's not a lot to say." She sipped the cool liquid. "My life's an open book so far. No scandalous past, not even an interesting present, unless you count the secretarial course."

Dominic gazed at her. She really was lovely; he'd never seen a girl with such classic bone structure. Unable to get her out of his mind, even though he'd fought against it, he had to come – had to see her again. Yet every instinct told him that, at this crucial time in his life, he couldn't afford any more complications.

"And you?" Georgina was saying. "How about your life?" But even as she spoke, she saw a bitterness enter his eyes. Dominic looked down and remained silent for so long that she felt embarrassed.

"I'm sorry," she said, "I didn't mean to sound nosy."

He looked up and put out his hand to lightly touch hers. "No, not at all," he reassured her. "I'm the one to apologise for making you feel awkward. It's just that . . ."

Perplexed, Georgina waited.

"Let's just say I'm a square peg in a round hole," he said eventually.

"With your job, you mean?" Georgina looked at the long, sensitive face before her, and murmured, "Is it that you've been pushed into the family business?"

116

"How did you guess?"

She smiled. "Let's just say that you look more like the creative type to me. Not that I'm any expert."

Dominic's eyes met and held her own for a moment, then he said, "That's very perceptive of you."

"I'm right then?"

He nodded. "I wanted to be an artist. Or at least to try and see if I could be. But that's not a proper job as far as my old man's concerned. He flatly refused to fund me through Art College. It was join the firm or I'd be letting the family down. You know the sort of thing, only son and all that."

"But if you're not happy . . ."

He gazed at her with sudden intensity. "Happy?" His face twisted. "I hate it!"

She looked at him with sympathy, seeing the strain in his eyes. "I think it's really important to enjoy what you do," Georgina said slowly, "and after all, it's your life, not your father's."

"You don't think it's selfish then, to want to choose your own career?"

She shook her head. "I think everyone should have that right."

"Oh, I can understand how he feels," Dominic admitted, "but if you only knew how much I've tried. I really have, Georgina . . ."

Distressed by the pain she saw in his eyes, she stretched out a hand.

"Can't you talk to him?" she asked. "Surely if he knew how you really feel . . ."

He shook his head and looked away. Georgina

waited, but then he turned to her and said, "I can't believe I'm burdening you with all this!" He ran a hand through his dark hair and exploded, "Oh, what the hell's the use!" Seeing her bewilderment, he got up abruptly. "Come on, enough of me and my problems, let's dance."

And that's what they did. Danced. Not only once, but all night. Georgina never did rejoin the other girls; by tacit consent she and Dominic remained together. Hands linked, they would stand and wait for the music to begin, dancing ever closer, cheek to cheek, or with Georgina's head nestling on Dominic's shoulder. Occasionally she would glimpse Josie swirling by with first one partner and then another, but Georgina was in another world. She was sublimely happy, loving the slightly rough feel of Dominic's sports jacket against her skin, the way his hand caressed her back. And his eyes told her that he felt the same way.

Dominic's feelings were chaotic. He just couldn't believe the attraction he felt for the young girl he was holding in his arms. And she was un-believably young – sixteen! He was being completely unfair to her, he knew that, for there was no pretence, no artifice about Georgina. Her expression was open and happy, her eyes soft and shining when she looked at him. And as the hours passed Dominic realised with despair that he was falling in love, *they* were falling in love. The tragedy was that only he knew the situation was absolutely hopeless.

Chapter 13

Josie, although she had the other girls to chat to in between dancing, couldn't help feeling resentful as the evening wore on. I might as well have come on my own, she thought, choosing to ignore that they had actually come as a group. Used as she was to Georgina's undivided attention, it irritated her to see her friend all 'gooey-eyed' over someone she'd only just met.

"I see you've had *your* nose put out of joint," Marlene taunted, rolling her eyes in Georgina's direction.

Josie ignored her.

"I'm going to powder *my* nose. Anyone coming?" Pauline stood up and paused by the table.

Josie joined her. "I will. It must be all these long drinks!"

Pauline grinned. "Glad to see you've not got too ladylike." As they walked around the edge of the floor, she nudged Josie. "Just look at those two! Talk about love's young dream!"

Josie turned to look. Like a few other couples, Georgina and Dominic were not so much dancing as 'smooching' in the middle of the floor.

The evening wasn't turning out at all as Josie'd expected – no giggling together, comparing notes on the talent, and sharing their enjoyment.

Pauline looked at her with sympathy. "This always happens, you know. But isn't that the main reason we all come to these things – to meet someone special?"

Josie looked at her, and realised suddenly that she was being childish. Suppose she'd met someone dishy? She'd be doing exactly the same as Georgina.

"You're right," she admitted. "And just look at that lot propping the bar up!" She nodded at the cluster of youths and young men. "Why do they bother coming if they don't go on the floor?"

"They're a load of big girls' blouses if you ask me," sniffed Pauline. "Probably too scared."

Georgina however, never gave Josie a thought, particularly during the last dance when the band played 'Goodnight Sweetheart'. "I can't believe it's almost time to go home," she murmured, but she was dreamily confident that although the evening might be ending, as far as they were concerned, it was only the beginning.

"I know," Dominic's voice was muffled against her hair. "I'll meet you outside, and walk you to the gate. How are you getting home?"

"My father's picking me up."

Dominic gazed down at her, and said softly, "I think you're the most beautiful girl I've ever seen. You've pole-axed me, do you know that?"

"I know exactly how you feel," Georgina smiled

120

up at him, liking his hazel eyes, loving the way he was looking at her. As the music stopped, she lifted her hand and touched him gently on the face, then with a last lingering glance, went off to find Josie.

Waiting outside the ballroom, Dominic fumbled in his pocket for a pack of Senior Service and, cupping his hand around a cigarette, flicked his silver lighter. Inhaling deeply he stood a little aside from the other young men, staring unseeingly into the darkness. Whatever had possessed him to come – tonight, of all nights? At the memory of the gentleness in Georgina's expression, her sheer loveliness, he almost groaned aloud. He'd never believed in love at first sight, would have sworn it didn't exist, but Dominic knew now that it did happen. She'd felt it too, he was sure of it. Yet to tell her how he felt, to raise her hopes of a future with him, would be not only selfish but cruel. She was young, she needed to be free. And what, if anything, could he offer her? Savagely, he drew on his cigarette, tossed it to the ground, and stubbed it out with the sole of his shoe. He'd have to tell her the truth, try to make her understand. And this was going to be the hardest task he'd ever faced in his life.

"He's waiting for me outside, to walk me to the gates," Georgina told Josie, as they stood in a queue to collect their coats.

Josie stared at her. "What if your father sees you?"

"He won't if you walk in front of us. There's bound to be lots of people going along – and it's dark. In any case," she shrugged her shoulders, "so what?"

"Yeah, so what?" Marlene was leaning against a wall, her face flushed, her eyes suspiciously bright. "My chap's waiting for me, as well."

Josie refrained from remarking that Marlene had only met him a few minutes ago, so he was hardly 'her chap'. She couldn't be bothered with Marlene, not after she'd disappeared in the interval on a 'pass out'. That meant she'd gone down to a local pub with a group of other rowdy types. Josie liked a bit of fun herself, but that didn't mean you had to make yourself cheap. She glanced at Pauline, who was hovering nearby. It seemed silly for her to catch the late bus home, when William Hawkins would be driving past her house. She nudged Georgina. "What do you think?" she said, keeping her voice low. "Would your father mind giving Pauline a lift home?"

Georgina wrenched her mind away from Dominic. Unsure of her father's reaction if he was treated like a taxi-driver, she shook her head. "Not a good idea," she muttered.

Josie turned away. She was the one who was going to have to walk along the drive with Pauline. It was going to be embarrassing to part at the gates, while the other girl went off to queue for the late bus. She was bound to realise there was a spare seat in the car. Not that she blamed Georgina, but fancy not feeling able to ask your dad a simple favour!

122

The other girls were already leaving, with many cries of, "See you on Monday," and, from Marlene, "Don't do anything I wouldn't do!" – a remark directed at Georgina.

"That gives you plenty of scope!" Josie said. "I'm not too happy about being associated with *her*, I don't know about you."

"Probably not," Georgina said, but she wasn't really paying attention. With relief she reached the head of the queue and handed in her cloakroom ticket. "Who will you walk along with?" she asked.

"Pauline," Josie said abruptly, as she reached out and took her own coat.

"Oh, of course. See you at the gates, then!" Hurriedly, Georgina headed for the main doors and, she hoped, Dominic.

He was there. He didn't see her at first. He was gazing out across the silver water of the lake, his profile outlined in the lights streaming from the windows. Georgina hesitated as she saw the sombre expression on his face, watched as he smote one hand against the other in a gesture of frustration and anger. Her step faltered, and then he turned and saw her. With a forced smile, he said, "There you are. I thought you'd got lost."

"There was a queue."

Dominic took her hand in his. "Isn't it a lovely night?"

"Blissful."

Slowly, their arms around each other, they walked along the tree-lined drive, while Dominic tried to find the right words. How on earth was he going to tell her? In desperation he tried to force himself to apply logic to the situation. He'd only just met the girl for heaven's sake – he knew hardly anything about her! With everything else that was happening in his life, one evening spent with her should hardly count at all. And he had to be practical, logical, remember what was at stake. Dominic could hardly believe he was even taking this seriously – it was crazy. Yet even as Georgina glanced up at him, he knew why. But she's only sixteen, he thought in desperation, and it could be years until . . . I can't spoil her young life, I can't! Damn, he cursed, damn fate for its idiotic timing!

They followed the crowds along the path, walking slowly, lingering, but all too soon the gates loomed ahead, and suddenly, Dominic took Georgina's hand and steered her away from the main drive, on to a path at the side. There, where they were hidden from view beneath a large tree, he gazed down into her eyes before taking her in his arms. Thrilled, Georgina raised her lips expectantly to his, and in the cold night air Dominic kissed her, tenderly at first and then again . . . only the second time his kiss was hard and desperate – so hard that when they drew apart, Georgina felt shaken.

"I'm sorry," he said, as he saw her put her hand to her mouth. "I didn't mean to . . ."

She looked up at him. This wasn't how she'd imagined it at all. He wasn't tender, happy, full of plans – he was full of anger! Bewildered, she took a step backwards.

Dominic swiftly drew her to him and kissed her again. Only now his mouth was gentle, searching, and then with his cheek against hers, he held her close for what he knew must be the last time. I must tell her, he thought, I must tell her now . . .

"*What the hell!!*" The thundering voice startled them both, and they sprang apart, to see William Hawkins, his face contorted with fury, glaring at them both.

"What's the meaning of this, miss?" he barked. "And as for you . . ." He moved threateningly forward, and Georgina, fear leaping into her throat, stepped back in panic.

Dominic, however, stood his ground. With a furious glance at Georgina's white face, he held out his hand. "My name's Dominic . . ."

But William cut across the rest of his words. "I don't care what your name is. Georgina . . . *home*, now!" He grasped her arm and pushed her back on to the drive, where, shaken, humiliated, and unable to escape his tight grip she found herself hustled along the short distance to the car. Josie, her face tense with anxiety, was already sitting in the back.

Within seconds, William had put the car in gear and begun to drive away, with Georgina, frantic for a last sight of Dominic, twisting around in the passenger seat. Wildly, her gaze searched the crowd around the gates, and then at last she saw his tall figure. He was standing on the kerb, his arm raised high in a farewell gesture.

Chapter 14

"But I couldn't stop him," Josie protested. "He was standing right in front of the gates, watching everyone come along. As soon as he saw you weren't with me . . ."

"Why couldn't he be like other fathers?" Georgina raged, pacing around the bedroom. "Why couldn't he wait in the car, or at least stand discreetly to one side! It's just typical. He has to spoil *everything*!"

The two girls had closeted themselves in Georgina's bedroom where, still angry and upset by the row the night before, she'd spent every possible moment since.

"He was furious, wasn't he?" Josie said, remembering that nightmare ride home. The atmosphere in the car had been thick with anger, as William had driven in icy silence. Josie, tense and anxious in the back, hadn't dared to speak.

"Furious wasn't the word," Georgina said, her face pale at the memory of her father's vitriolic attack the moment they were home.

"A daughter of mine," William had lashed out at her, "privately educated and picking up the

126

first boy she meets! Doing God knows what in the bushes! Well, you've cooked your goose, miss. It won't happen again; you won't get the chance!"

"It wasn't like that!" Georgina protested, hating him in that moment more than she'd ever done in her life.

"You would say that, wouldn't you!" Beside himself with fury, William forgot all his good intentions, and squared up to his daughter.

His expression was glowering, and Georgina's childhood terror, which she thought she'd conquered, threatened to re-surface. Determined to fight it, she managed to stare at her father with the contempt she thought he deserved.

"Well, it's obvious you think the worst of me, so there's no point in my saying anything!"

By now, Alice, woken by the noise, was hurrying downstairs.

"What's going on?" She tied the belt of her dressing-gown. "Has something happened?"

"You might well ask," William snapped. "Perhaps it's time you gave your daughter some moral guidance! Or," he twisted to face Georgina, "is it the company you're keeping?"

"If you mean Josie, it had nothing to do with her," Georgina shouted, tears again spilling down her cheeks. "And you've twisted everything! So, I met someone and he kissed me goodnight. Is that a crime?"

Alice looked from one to another. So that was it. He'd caught Georgina and some boy or other.

127

What did they call it these days? Oh yes – snogging. Such an ugly word.

To be honest, she hadn't thought her daughter had it in her. She'd always seemed too mealy-mouthed. Then Alice amended the word. No, not that, but colourless somehow. All those downcast glances and polite small talk. Maybe the old cliché was correct – the quietest were always the worst. William was obviously in a state, and she glanced sharply at the decanter on the sideboard, remembering he'd already had two large whiskies before she went to bed.

"Look, if Georgina says it was only a good-night kiss, I'm sure there's no harm done. But," she added quickly, as William began to bluster, "I'll certainly have words with her. You know," she said meaningfully, "just the two of us."

William glared at her, and then going over to the sideboard, poured another whisky and swallowed it in one gulp. "Do what you like!" he said through clenched teeth. "I'm going to bed." He went heavily out of the room.

Alice glanced at her daughter's tearstained, rebellious face, and stifled a yawn. As Georgina waited, obviously prepared to do battle, Alice decided she was just too tired for a confrontation in the middle of the night. She'd be better occupied calming William. "I think bed's the best place for all of us," she said, and picking up the long skirt of her dressing-gown, she followed her husband up the wide staircase, leaving Georgina to switch off the hall light, and follow.

Now, pale with lack of sleep, Georgina tried to blot the memory of the ugly scene from her mind.

"What did your mum say?" Josie said.

"Nothing."

The confrontation and lecture Georgina had been dreading didn't happen. In fact Alice hadn't uttered a word. Instead, as it was the first Sunday in the month, they had all attended the morning service at the local church. Sitting between her parents, she'd missed the whole of the vicar's rambling sermon, simply giving herself up to delicious daydreams about Dominic. Every word, every sensation, every gesture was etched indelibly on her mind, to be brought out and dwelled upon with delight. And sitting in the quiet pew had been the perfect opportunity. Later, as they ate their roast beef and Yorkshire pudding in the formal dining-room, Georgina had studiously avoided meeting her father's gaze. William still couldn't trust himself to speak to her, and the meal was eaten in silence, punctuated only by Alice's attempts at light conversation. Immediately afterwards, William isolated himself in his study, and half an hour later Alice went out, saying she was going to have tea with a friend. Happy families it was not, Georgina thought bitterly, but then, when had it ever been?

Now, she unburdened her feelings to Josie. "I felt so humiliated," she wailed. "Can you imagine? There we were, it was so romantic – and then *he* has to turn up."

"So," Josie said, "what are you going to do?"

"What can I do?" Georgina said in desperation. "At least until tomorrow. I'll have to try and explain – heaven knows what he thought!"

"He's bound to look for you at the café tomorrow lunch-time," Josie said. "And if it's any consolation, I think I was wrong about him. He's really dishy, despite his revolting occupation!" She gave a sly grin, hoping to lighten Georgina's mood.

"He hates it," she said. "He told me he wants to be an artist."

William was acutely conscious of the two girls' presence upstairs, and even more that they were probably talking about him. While he was still appalled that Georgina should be so free with what he thought of as 'her favours', his anger was now equally directed at himself. If only he hadn't had a couple of snifters before he went out, he would have handled the situation more calmly. Now, after all the effort he'd made over the past few months, his relationship with his daughter was as full of resentment as ever. Bridges will have to be built, he told himself. But that doesn't mean that she won't have to conduct herself with more decorum in the future!

Alice had decided not to mention the subject. Secretly, she was amused by William's outdated views on how his daughter should behave. But she supposed it was to be expected; after all, he was a different generation – even from his wife. And William had always been what she termed 'heavy'. Not at all like Neil, with his sense of fun and enjoyment of life. The fact that her lover took his pleasure with scant regard for his wife and family, she chose to ignore. As for Georgina, well, she'd do her growing up in the same way as everyone else, and make her own mistakes. There was certainly no need for Alice to intervene, not unless it caused disruption in the house. Her priority at the moment was her affair; she really couldn't be bothered with domestic issues.

On Monday morning, the two girls travelled in what was, for them, mostly silence. Georgina was still dreamy over the earlier part of Saturday evening, while Josie was becoming more and more worried that her friend might have taken Dominic's interest far too seriously. Okay, she'd danced and talked with him all night. Okay, he'd kissed her! But Georgina seemed convinced that this was the beginning of a great romance. Josie, who regarded herself as a realist, thought it likely that Dominic had just been having a bit of fun.

Their daily journey to the College was long and tedious, involving two buses. They always sat on the top deck – although both disliked the smoky atmosphere – and usually on the front seat, where they would test each other on their homework. But this morning as the bus trundled along the A50, past the grimy blank-windowed pottery factories lining the main road in Fenton, through the shopping centre of Hanley, and on to the mother town of Burslem, each was deep in her own thoughts.

And Georgina was quiet all morning, only thankful that the other girls, having gone ahead after the dance ended, were unaware of what had happened. She couldn't have borne Marlene's sarcastic comments. But when lunch-time arrived, and they all gathered around their customary table in the small café, Georgina felt suddenly shy. What should she do when Dominic came in? Should she get up and go and join him at his table? Would he think she was being forward? And then she chided herself for being silly. Of course he'd want her to go and sit with him. Oh, she couldn't wait to explain that her father's attitude made not the slightest difference. Each time the door opened, she turned eagerly, her face alight with anticipation, but there was no sign of him. As the minutes ticked by she checked her watch constantly, while Marlene and the others watched with amusement.

"Done a runner, has he?" Marlene quipped, and Josie glared at her. Insensitive cat!

"Oh, yeah," she said, "and when are *you* seeing lover boy again?"

Marlene tossed her head. "Dunno – around, I expect."

"Pot calling the kettle, then!"

But Georgina was oblivious. She could almost taste her bitter disappointment. She'd been so positive she'd see Dominic in the café, and it was with lethargy that she returned to face the afternoon's lessons. And he wasn't there the next day, or the one following. As time passed, she made excuses. He was ill. There was a rush job on at work. But by the time one week had ended and then another, bewildered and unhappy, Georgina had run out of excuses.

Devastated, she said in misery to Josie, "I don't understand it."

Josie looked at her with mixed sympathy. Now that she knew Dominic was twenty-three, she was sure Georgina had read far too much into the incident. "Are you positive you didn't tell him your surname?"

"No, we talked mainly about him. And he never mentioned his surname either."

"So," Josie pointed out, "as I said before, there's no way he could find out your phone number and ring you. I tell you what, why don't we go to Trentham again on Saturday – just the two of us. From what you tell me, he goes all the time. Maybe he was just expecting to see you there."

"Do you think so?" Georgina said, hope swiftly rising. Then she grimaced. "I don't think my parents would let me go. My father still hasn't forgiven me for last time."

"I'll put Mum on the case," Josie promised, with more confidence than she felt.

But Lily, once she'd been told the story, was intrigued enough to want to help in any way she could. Young love, she thought wistfully. She remembered when she'd been seventeen . . . Lily smiled to herself. Young people felt everything so intensely at that age. But it was a golden time, one to be spent in hope and discovery, not in feeling unhappy. "I'll do my best," she told Josie.

"They can't keep her penned up for ever – it isn't natural."

So, the following morning, Lily waited until her employer was relaxing after her coffee and then broached the subject. "Mrs Hawkins," she said tentatively, "Josie's wanting to go dancing at Trentham again. I was wondering . . ."

Damn, thought Alice. I might have known this would come up. And Josie had probably told her mother what had happened. Well, that could be used as a weapon. William hated anyone talking about his personal business, as she did herself. He'd been in a foul mood ever since that night, and she was fed up with it. Maybe it was time she sorted things out.

"Yes, of course you are, Mrs Ford," she said. "Leave it with me and I'll have a word with Georgina's father, and let you know."

But her tone was lacklustre, for Alice knew that only she could coax her husband into a better frame of mind. And the way to do it didn't appeal one little bit. Sex with William had always been a duty, although one with its reward, a lifestyle she relished. But since she'd met Neil and discovered what intimacy could really be like, "marital relations", as William called what took place on his visits to her bedroom, had become even more distasteful. The word marriage, she thought with bitterness, covers a multitude of sins.

A couple of days later, she told Lily that Georgina was allowed to go dancing at Trentham that weekend.

"We have to let the girls grow up, Mrs Ford, that's what I told my husband," she said. "By the way," she added, "could you change the beds today, instead of on Friday?"

Half an hour later, Lily, stripping the bed in the main bedroom, heard Alice leave the house. With a wry smile, she put the soiled sheets into the linen basket, and shook out fresh ones ready to spread on the bed. You know, she mused, I don't think I'd like other people to know what went on in my private life. But then, perhaps people like me don't count. Aren't the hired help supposed to be invisible? But the thought was transitory, for Lily had her own problems to think about. Only one more week, and Peter would be home on leave. And what was more, he was bringing a friend with him!

Chapter 15

"It's all right for you," Josie grumbled the following Saturday afternoon. The two girls were strolling around Queen's Park enjoying the early spring sunshine. Georgina paused by the aviary, admiring the colourful plumage of the exotic birds.

"Gosh, look at that little one in the corner, he's absolutely gorgeous."

"You're not listening, are you?"

"What?"

"I said, it's all right for you. You'd never have to give up your bedroom to two hairy sailors!"

Georgina giggled. "Chance would be a fine thing! Anyway, how do you know they're hairy?"

"Because our Peter was always showing off his hairy chest! When I was little, he used to pretend he was a monster just to scare me."

"So where are you going to sleep?"

"Where I did as a child – in the boxroom. It's about as big as your wardrobe," Josie complained. "The three boys used to share the bigger bedroom. Once Dennis and Peter left home, Mum asked John to change with me."

"Didn't he mind?"

Josie shook her head. "No, he was always good to me, was our John."

They headed for the lake, where they liked to watch the rowing boats. "There's something very relaxing about the rhythm of the oars, don't you think?" Georgina said.

"Do you fancy going on?"

"No, not today. I'm too worked up about going to Trentham tonight. What are you betting? Do you think Dominic will be there?"

Josie just shrugged. "We can only hope." She longed to point out that Georgina was kidding herself, that even if he was, there was no guarantee he was still interested. But instead she turned away to watch the activity on the water.

That evening, William drove the two girls in silence, although he glanced a few times at Georgina's set face. He was still regretting his outburst on the previous occasion, although considered he'd been right to be angry, to be shocked at his daughter's behaviour. But he should have controlled his temper, dealt with the matter in a more tactful way. Blame it on the whisky, he thought with bitterness. Well, he wouldn't make the same mistake this time. It was cups of tea only for the next few hours, although it was no way for a red-blooded man to spend his Saturday night! And thinking along those lines, William wondered briefly whether, as he got older, Alice minded that the intervals between their 'marital relations' were becoming increasingly longer. But then she'd never been what one would call a passionate woman.

Josie, sitting behind, was just thankful that at least there wasn't a dreadful atmosphere. She stared at the back of the mottled neck of William Hawkins. She still didn't feel comfortable with him; merely to be in his presence caused her to stiffen. He was a strange man, as far removed from Josie's own father as any man could be.

Georgina, in the front, was fully occupied trying to control the nervous fluttering in her stomach. She hardly knew whether she wanted Dominic to be there or not. Either could bring bitter disappointment. But half an hour later, she entered the crowded ballroom with a determined step. If he was in the room, she'd find him. And if he wasn't . . .

And so the evening wore on. What Georgina's partners thought, Josie couldn't imagine, as every time she danced past her friend, it was to see her paying them scant attention, as her gaze constantly roamed over the crowds.

"It's no use," she admitted at last. "He isn't here." The two girls were standing near the bar, both needing a cool drink.

Josie was about to sympathise, when, "Don't worry about him," a voice chaffed. "We're here, aren't we, Rob?"

They turned to see two young men grinning at them. They both had 'short back and sides' haircuts, and Josie guessed correctly that they were doing their National Service. "Oh, yes," she said, "for how long?"

One grinned ruefully, and ran a hand across his head. "A dead give-away, isn't it? We're both in the Army, based at Lichfield."

"My brother was there – it's Whittington Barracks, isn't it?"

Georgina looked at her friend, thinking how knowledgeable she was. Yet again, she wished she'd had brothers – she might have understood the male species better. She had to face it, Dominic wasn't coming. After all her hopes, the anti-climax was bitterly disappointing, and to her horror she had to struggle to blink away tears pricking at her eyelids.

"What's up with your friend?" asked Rob, speaking for the first time and Josie was surprised to hear a soft Scottish burr.

"Nothing, she was just hoping to see someone and he isn't here."

Georgina shot her a resentful glance. Did she have to tell everybody! She reached out to put her empty glass on the bar, and as the band struck up a quickstep, Rob turned to Josie.

"Would you care to . . ."

The other youth turned to Georgina, and she moved forward, then, "Sorry," she said in a strangled voice, "I've just got to . . ." Rushing out of the ballroom, past surprised couples, she burst into the cloakroom, struggling to control the tears welling up in her eyes. Thankful to find a cubicle empty, she shot the bolt, and then sank on the toilet seat, fishing in her bag for a hanky. She'd made a complete and utter fool of herself!

Not only wasn't Dominic here, she had to accept the unpalatable fact that he hadn't made the slightest effort to see her again or even to contact her. Those few hours, so precious to her, had obviously meant nothing to him at all. He probably just thought she was a silly young girl – which she obviously was! But it hurt – it really hurt! How could she have read so much into a few hours, into a couple of kisses? Eventually, conscious that there might be a queue waiting, she forced herself to get up and, with a final dab at her eyes, went out to try and repair the damage to her make-up.

Josie was enjoying herself. Rob was not only a good dancer, he was trying to teach her some fancy steps. Nimble on her feet, she twisted her slim hips in time to the music, and easily mastered a new routine. Rob laughed as she smiled up at him in triumph.

"What do you do?" he asked.

"I'm at college, doing a secretarial course – how about you? That's when you're not defending the country, of course!"

"I want to be a farmer, like my father. So, that's what I've been doing – working on the farm."

"Oh yes, and where's that? Scotland?"

"Clever puss, aren't you?" he murmured, and kept hold of her hand as the band changed to a different number. This time it was a waltz, and Josie, held firmly in the circle of his arms, was discovering that she liked this soft-spoken soldier, liked him very much indeed. Well, she wasn't going to be caught out like Georgina – at least she'd find out his full name!

"I'm Josie Ford, by the way," she said.

"Rob Graham." He smiled down at her, and Josie noticed his eyes were brown, soft and warm, just like his voice. They continued dancing until the band finished the sequence with a roll of drums. Then they wandered back, still holding hands, to where they'd left the others.

"I can't see your friend," Josie said.

"Doug? There he is!"

Doug came forward to join them. "Is your friend all right?" he said to Josie. "Only she rushed off looking upset. I only asked her to dance, honest!"

Concerned, Josie turned to go out to the cloakroom, only to see Georgina coming back, looking a bit embarrassed.

"Are you okay?" Josie said.

"I'm fine. Sorry about that," she said to Doug, "but if you still want that dance?"

He grinned. "Sure do."

"How about you?" Rob murmured to Josie. "Or would you rather sit the next one out?"

Josie nodded and, as they found a table at the side of the ballroom, she smiled to herself, thinking of her first visit to Trentham. Talk about role reversal! This time it was Georgina who was on her own, whereas she—

"Hey," Rob smiled at her. "Don't forget I'm here!"

"Oops, sorry!"

141

"I know it's a dreadful chat-up line – but do you come here often?"

"Only in the mating season," she quipped. Then added, "No, it's our second time. How about you?"

"Oh, we come over about once a month. There's a coach from Lichfield and we catch that. Go on, then, tell me about yourself – the full works – how old you are, any brothers or sisters, that sort of thing."

Josie told him she was seventeen. It sounded better than sixteen and her birthday was only a few weeks away. "I've got two brothers, one in the Navy, and one married. I did have three, but John died when he was twenty-three."

As Josie told him what had happened, Rob watched her expressive face – the way as she talked intently to him she ran her fingers through her dark curls. He began to feel edgy. She was gorgeous! And his feelings dismayed him. This girl was dangerous – for him anyway. So far, although he'd had a few girlfriends, it had all been light-hearted. He enjoyed flirting, but never went beyond that. He didn't want to get involved with anyone, not with his National Service coming to an end, and certainly not hundreds of miles from home.

As Josie finished speaking, Rob touched her hand gently. "I'm so sorry, that must have been awful for you."

Embarrassed, Josie turned her head away for a moment, and then said, "I thought soldiers were supposed to be tough, not sympathetic."

"Ah, you should see me on the parade ground," he laughed. "I'm a corporal, you know, a right bossy type."

"I can just imagine."

If Rob had but known, his own thoughts were echoed in the mind of the girl opposite. Josie, aware of how attracted she was to Rob, was subconsciously trying to rein in her emotions. Scornful of the way so many of her friends tied themselves down at an early age, she'd decided ages ago that this conventional path was not for her. She wanted to enjoy herself first. Not only that but she wanted to be independent, see how successful she could be. Josie never forgot her childhood vow. She had only to conjure up an image of the childish form of Georgina, her hands tucked cosily into the blue fur muff, for her resolution to harden. When she did get married, she'd choose not only the man but also the lifestyle.

What did Rob say he wanted to be – a farmer? Ugh, she could just imagine it. There was a farm not far from where she lived. Surrounded by rusting old farm implements, it was not only isolated, but she'd caught glimpses of the farmer's wife. Wearing a mackintosh and wellingtons, she seemed to have to work out of doors in all weathers. Not for me, Josie shuddered. Besides, she was scared of cows!

Rob, who had been wondering what she was thinking, decided not to ask. He'd changed his mind; he didn't want to know any more about her. No more confidences – it was safer. "Come on," he grinned, "I'll show you how to samba!"

"I might teach you a few things," Josie laughed.

Georgina, still dancing with Doug, was merely going through the motions. It wasn't that she disliked him, but her insides were filled with misery. She just wanted to go home, to the refuge of her bedroom, to come to terms with the fact that her dream was over.

And later, she did just that. Lying curled up in bed, Georgina tried to be logical, to think through the situation. If Dominic had wanted to see her again, had felt the same urgency as she had, it would have been easy for him to do so. After all, he worked in the same small area where she was studying. So she was left with two alternatives. Either he wasn't interested, or she hadn't given him enough time. Although the past three weeks had seemed an eternity to *her*, maybe he was more relaxed about such things. I'll give him another fortnight, she determined, turning over restlessly and pummelling her pillow into softness. Then I'll know.

Josie too was finding it difficult to sleep. Although they'd spent the rest of the evening together, the two young soldiers, saying goodnight at the end of the dance, hadn't offered to walk them to the gates, and perversely she felt piqued. Rob had liked her, more than liked her, she could tell, and although she definitely, definitely, didn't want to get involved, that didn't mean she wouldn't like a . . . she searched for a word and came up with one straight out of Jane Austen. 'Dalliance', that was it, a 'dalliance'. It described exactly how she felt.

Chapter 16

Lily had the whole house in uproar. It was an hour before Peter's expected arrival, and as Josie teased, "Woe betide any speck of dust that dares to linger!"

Sid tried to make himself inconspicuous behind his newspaper, already having had to change into his best trousers and a clean shirt.

"And you can take those slippers off," Lily told him. "They're past their best anyway. I'll get you another pair off the market next time I go."

Sid grunted and got up. He might as well, or he'd only get nagged. "I can't see why you're making such a fuss."

"Peter's bringing a guest, that's why!" Lily rolled her eyes heavenwards. Men! They'd got no idea! "Where's Josie?"

"Upstairs, taking her things out of the drawers. She says she's having no strange sailors nosying through her underwear!"

Lily, duster in hand, slumped into an armchair laughing. "Oh, it'll be good to see him though, Sid," she said. "Peter always seems to bring a breath of fresh air with him."

"It's because he's got no responsibilities."

"Well, he's only twenty-four – there's plenty of time for him to settle down."

"The trouble is," Sid grumbled, "if he leaves it too late, all the best girls will have been snapped up!"

"You were nearly thirty when I married you," she reminded him. "Cradle-snatching, some called it!"

"Aye, but I was a catch – that's why you chased me," he grinned.

"I never did any such thing!" Getting up, she playfully punched him in the shoulder, and he caught her hand.

"We haven't done so bad, have we?"

Lily pretended to consider, then smiled down at him. "Maybe I'll keep you!"

"I wish you would – I've always wanted to be a kept man!"

"Aw, go on with you!" Going into the hall, Lily called up the stairs, "Josie? You haven't forgotten about fetching the bread?"

"No, don't fuss, Mum. I'll be down in a minute."

"I wonder what he'll be like?" Lily said, as she went back into the sitting-room.

"Who?" Sid looked up from lacing his shoes.

"Peter's friend – Fergal."

"You ask the daftest questions, Lil. Now, how would I know that?"

"I was just wondering."

Georgina and Josie were also 'wondering'. After all, the impending arrival of a young sailor in a street where strangers were rare, was quite an event. But neither thought about it as much as they would have done a few weeks ago. Georgina was still desperately clinging to the hope that Dominic would suddenly turn up in her life again. Not only that, but he would have a perfect explanation for not having been in touch, would be equally as desperate as she had been these past few weeks. At least that was her emotional side. Her brain told her she was a fool.

Josie, to her annoyance, was finding her thoughts returning far too often to Rob. You're daft, she told herself. When he's demobbed, he'll return to Scotland, and the last thing she wanted was to get involved with someone living so far away. But he's gorgeous – you could just have a fling with him, a small voice whispered inside her mind. But Josie had seen too many girls begin with a flirtation, a bit of 'fun', only for it to turn into an early wedding, either voluntary or 'shot-gun'. Where would her ambitions be then? Turned into dust, before the altar of domesticity. Oh no, that was definitely not for Josie Ford!

When the great day arrived, the sound of Peter's key turning in the lock had Lily rushing to the front door to be swept into a bear hug by her tanned son. "Let me look at you," she said, blinking back happy tears. Her eyes feasted on his open features, his sun-bleached hair and easy smile. No longer did she feel hidden guilt that she favoured her daughter. Since losing one son, Lily's remaining ones had become equally precious.

147

"Put her down, lad," Sid said, hovering at her shoulder. "There's a queue waiting."

Peter laughed and shook his father's hand. "Dad! It's good to see you. And this glamorous minx can't be our young Josie!"

"Still the same old charmer," she grinned, as he kissed her cheek.

Peter moved aside, and ushered in a tall youth of about nineteen. "This is Fergal. He looks dangerous but I promise you he's perfectly harmless!"

The two young men, impressive in blue bell-bottoms and square collars with three white stripes, crowded into the narrow hall. "Come on in, Fergal," Lily smiled. "Dump your kitbags both of you, and come into the front room. I bet you're dying for a cup of tea."

Which means I'll have to make one, Josie thought wryly. She cast a curious glance at Peter's friend. What did Peter mean, dangerous? Then, as Fergal left the dim hall and moved into the light, she saw the scar. It ran from above his right ear in a diagonal puckered line across his cheek, cruelly distorting what was otherwise a strong, handsome face. Her eyes fleetingly met his, and she saw in them a painful awareness of the effect his appearance had on strangers.

Lily, whose eyes were also drawn to the disfigurement, felt her heart go out to the young lad. For that was all he was. She'd expected him to be older – after all Peter was now twenty-four and she'd have thought he'd prefer friends more his own age.

148

Having seen many a facial injury during the War, Sid's reaction was one mainly of curiosity. How had it happened – was it during a training exercise? Or had it been during a fight? But all that could come later – now he was eager to hear all the news, to talk men's talk, Navy talk. Although maybe they'd have to wait until they could get over to the pub for a few pints. Sid sat back in his chair. He'd let the women take over for now, let them fuss and provide food. What with another two men in the house, and their Dennis coming up later, this promised to be a grand day, and no mistake.

"He's got nobody, Mum," Peter explained, when Fergal had gone upstairs to unpack his kitbag. "That's why we take it in turns to invite him home on leave, otherwise he'd just drift around."

"That's a thoughtful thing to do," Lily said. They were now in the scullery, with Peter leaning against the sink. "No family, then?"

Peter shook his head. "Nope, not a soul. He was brought up in a children's home in Ireland. A pretty tough one too, from one or two things he's let drop. That's where he got . . ."

Lily stared at him aghast. "You don't mean they did *that* to him, to a defenceless child! Surely not!"

"No, not the staff – one of the boys – a nutcase by all accounts. He slashed Fergal across the face when he tried to stop him . . ." Peter hesitated, his eyes avoiding those of his mother "let's say 'bullying' another boy".

Maternal instincts now aroused, Lily could only think, 'What a rotten deal!' No proper home – and then the lad had to go through life with a face like that on him. Honestly, she fumed, as she began to open a tin of salmon, there's no justice in this world.

"Does he know anything about his real parents?" Josie asked. She'd been quietly listening as, making a tremendous effort to keep the slices thin and even, she cut a crusty loaf to make sandwiches.

"Not a thing. He was dumped on the parish priest's doorstep. They never did find out who the mother was."

"Well, I'm glad you've brought him," Lily declared. "He's more than welcome. It just makes you realise how lucky you are when you hear something like this."

"Thanks, Mum." Suddenly lightening the mood, Peter bent down and fingered the hair on the top of Lily's head. "A few more grey hairs, I see?"

"Well, what do you expect?" she smiled. "We're none of us getting any younger. And what do you think about your sister? She's at secretarial college now, you know."

"Yes, you wrote and told me." Peter put his head on one side and looked at Josie who, seeing his critical gaze sweep over her, stuck her tongue out at him.

He grinned. "Can't see anyone making a young lady of *her*. Too spunky by half."

"I needed to be with three brothers in the house," she snapped, and then bit her lip. What did she have to bring their John up for?

There was a moment's silence. "How's Dennis and the sprog?" Peter asked.

"The 'sprog' as you call him, has got a name," Lily said. "He was named after your brother, and no-one in this house needs to be afraid to use it! And hadn't you better go and see if Fergal's okay?"

"God, you're right – I'd forgotten all about him!"

"And don't blaspheme," she called after him.

Sid, busy marking out his Saturday bet, grinned. Did Lily think Peter was away on a Sunday school picnic? She'd have a fit if she could hear the strong language bandied about on board ship!

When Georgina heard the story of Fergal's tragic childhood, she was immediately filled with compassion. "Oh, how awful! Is it very bad – the scar, I mean?"

"I'm afraid so," Josie said.

"What's he like? His personality?"

Josie considered. "Difficult to say. He's that quiet you'd hardly know he was there. Mind you, as our Peter could talk the hind leg off a donkey, he doesn't get much chance! I haven't seen a lot of either of them really. Dad took them off down the pub last night, and Fergal went to Mass at St Gregory's in Longton this morning. Peter didn't get up until dinner-time."

"I wish I could come and see you all," Georgina

151

said wistfully. "I feel a bit like Rapunzel, shut away in her tower."

"I know. But it's not just your family, it's mine," grumbled Josie. "Don't ask me how their minds work."

"Snobbery and inverted snobbery, that's all it is. Still, I wouldn't want to cause awkwardness for anyone." Georgina picked up her Commerce book. "Come on, let's do some revision and get through these exams. I'm dying to get out in the real world." But in reality, she wanted to do something to blot out her constant anxiety about Dominic. One week of her self-imposed deadline had already passed – that left just one more!

Downstairs, Alice was reading the newspapers, while William snored gently in the armchair opposite. Sundays, she thought with resentment. I'm stuck in the kitchen all morning preparing lunch, then William has his nap, Josie comes round to see Georgina, and I read the papers. It's all so utterly predictable. She wondered what Neil was doing, and what his Sundays were like. To Alice, weekends had become an unwelcome interruption in the tempo of her life. Her 'fulfilled' life, she mentally amended. It was still a source of amazement to her that she had this high sex drive. And if she hadn't met Neil, she would never have known. I suppose, she mused as she gazed at the sleeping man opposite, it's because I'd only ever slept with William, and I never fancied him even at the beginning. Maybe if he'd had more finesse, something she now knew existed, her sexuality would have been awakened. I was like Sleeping Beauty, she thought, and pleased with the analogy, turned to the letters page and yawned. It would soon be time to get the tea. Honestly, Sundays were all about eating and lazing about – a waste of time really.

Chapter 17

There was a distinct atmosphere as the two girls climbed into William Hawkins' car the following Saturday evening, this time caused not only by anger but also embarrassment. The anger came from Josie, aware that her brother and Fergal could easily have squashed next to her on the back seat. Embarrassment from Georgina, who knew she should have had the guts to ask her father to give the two sailors a lift. William, ignorant of any of these things, wondered what on earth he'd done this time to justify the cold-shoulder treatment.

Josie had mixed feelings about going dancing at all. She begrudged the cost – her budget was tight, and she'd rather save her money to go when there was a chance Rob would be there. After all, Rob had said they only came over once a month.

But Peter had appealed to her. "I know exactly how it will be if you don't come. Fergal will sit in a corner and hide away. At least he'll have someone to talk to, while I'm, well, you know . . ."

"Off enjoying yourself?"

He'd grinned. "Got it in one!"

Georgina, of course, was just desperately hoping

that Dominic might be there. But as soon as they entered the ballroom, Josie was glad they'd decided to come. The band was playing the 'Woodchopper's Ball', the lively tempo immediately raising both their spirits, and it was with eagerness that Josie scanned the crowds for a sign of her brother.

"There he is!" With Georgina following, Josie began to hurry around the side of the milling crowd, to where Peter and Fergal were sitting at a side table some distance from the dance floor. Fergal, she noticed, had positioned himself in such a way that, unless he turned his head, the ugly scarring remained unseen.

"This is Georgina, you two. Now, she's my best friend, so I want you behaving yourselves, do you hear? We all know what sailors are!"

"Hey, I'm your brother, remember?" protested Peter.

"Exactly!" Josie grinned at him. "That's why I've got no illusions!"

"Hello, Peter," Georgina smiled at the tanned and muscular young man, and turned to the taller Fergal, who had no alternative but to face her.

"Nice to meet you," she began to say, but nothing had prepared her for the extent of his disfigurement. A scar, Josie had said. But what she hadn't described was the way it puckered the surrounding skin. All this she saw in the first second, then her gaze met his, holding it steadily, recognising the defensiveness behind the slate blue of his eyes. Georgina managed a casual friendly smile, before turning away and flopping into a chair. "Gosh, it's hot in here!"

"Well, don't take your stole off. Our Peter bays at the moon when he sees a pair of bare shoulders!" Josie teased.

"Aw, give it a rest, our kid, you're spoiling my image!"

"Which one's that then?"

"Fine and upstanding, as befits a member of Her Majesty's Navy. That's us, isn't it, Fergal?"

"Sure, and that's the truth," Fergal agreed. He'd grown used to the chaffing in the Ford household. He liked it. Bantering and teasing meant he could remain in the background. And that suited Fergal McKenna just fine. So this was Georgina Hawkins, he thought, the one who lived in what they called the Big House. He knew Peter had been surprised by the close friendship between his sister and this girl. Certainly they were different, not only in background but also in looks. Josie, with her dark curls and animation, and Georgina, with her fair, sleek hair, and rather pensive expression. A quiet girl, he guessed, and possibly a sensitive one. Fergal had seen enough expressions of shocked distaste to know she'd made an effort to spare his feelings.

"Right," Peter said, rubbing hands together, "let's have some drinks. I suppose this place still hasn't got a licence?"

"No," Josie said. "You'll have to get a pass-out in the interval if you want your tot of rum!"

"I might just do that," he grinned. "It all depends

on whether I can find a young lady to come with me, and I don't mean a schoolgirl!"

He dodged a mock blow from Josie, as she snapped, "Do you mind? We're at College, aren't we, Georgina? And she wouldn't be a 'lady' if she went with you, Peter Ford."

"Rubbish," he said easily. "You're behind the times, kid."

Georgina smiled at Fergal, who was watching the interchange with a slightly wistful look. "Are you thinking the same as me," she whispered. "Wishing you'd had brothers or sisters?"

He looked at her in surprise. "You too? But I thought . . ."

"Oh, I've got parents," she said, "but as an only child I always feel I missed out."

"Not as much as I did," Fergal said grimly, and as soon as he uttered the words, he regretted it. It was his absolute rule not to talk about his deprived childhood. Pity, he'd already received in abundance – he wanted no more.

But Georgina didn't, as he feared, pursue the subject, didn't probe or ask embarrassing questions. She just accepted his comment, while her eyes restlessly searched the room. Fergal was about to speak again, when a young man in a tight blue suit, his hair plastered to his scalp with Brylcreem, approached.

"Could I have this dance?" he asked in a falsetto voice, and with reluctance Georgina accepted. Peter and Josie spluttered with laughter, and even Fergal had to smile.

157

"She'll not enjoy that, I'm thinking."

Almost immediately, a rather good-looking youth gave a mock bow before Josie, and she allowed herself to be swept away in a quickstep.

As the evening wore on, Peter kept wandering off to find a partner, while Josie and Georgina tried hard to make sure that Fergal wasn't left alone at the table. And although Josie understood his reluctance to join the crowds on the dance floor, privately she thought he should just get out there and have a good time. Let people stare, she thought. If it was me, I'd just glare back at them! Scanning the room, she noticed that Peter was now dancing again and again with the same buxom blonde. He could at least take his turn at staying with Fergal, she thought crossly, and she watched as the couple gravitated towards the middle of the ballroom, to join a small group of 'smoochers'.

"Look at that," she nudged Georgina. "Call it dancing? He's all over her! It's disgusting!"

Georgina saw Fergal hide a grin, and when the band began to play 'Stranger in Paradise' and Josie was asked to dance, suddenly made a decision. The young sailor couldn't come to Trentham Gardens and just sit at a table all night. He was supposed to be on leave, for heaven's sake! She got up. "Fergal – what *is* your surname, by the way?"

"McKenna."

"Right, Fergal McKenna. May I have this dance, please?"

Fergal stared up at her. Was she mad? Expecting

him to join the crowds on the dance floor, to deliberately invite expressions of shock and revulsion? It wasn't so bad at sea, the crew was used to him. He'd only agreed to come tonight to please Peter, had always avoided dancing, knowing that people would not only stare at him, but also the girl he was with. Beauty and the Beast – that's what they'd think.

"No-one need see your face," Georgina persisted. "Look!" She lifted up a curtain of hair from her pageboy bob. "If we dance sort of cheek to cheek, your scarred side can rest against my hair. You won't look any different from anyone else!"

Startled, Fergal gazed up at her, and saw with dismay that she wouldn't take no for an answer.

"Come on!" Georgina moved towards the edge of the dancefloor and held out her hand. With obvious reluctance, Fergal got up to join her. "I'm not much good at it," he muttered. "Haven't had a lot of practice."

"It's easy," Georgina said, and putting one hand on his shoulder she leaned towards him. Tilting her head so that her hair swung between them, she hesitated, finding the whole thing more embarrassing than she'd expected. She pressed her head lightly against his face. "It's a slow foxtrot," she said. "We can just move around to the music for now. I'll teach you the steps later if you want. Just follow me."

And Fergal did. Awkwardly at first, bemused by the softness of her silky hair against his scarred cheek, but he then found that as Georgina moved backwards, he was able to follow her lead.

When eventually the music stopped, Georgina gripped his shoulder. "Don't pull away," she told him. "We'll just stand close together like this, lots of couples do."

Fergal held her loosely against him, and then saw Peter just ahead. He was still in a clinch with his blonde, who was giggling helplessly. Suddenly, Peter looked up and, at his astounded expression, Fergal gave a wide grin. Peter's hands moved behind his partner's bare back to give a triumphant 'thumbs-up' gesture, and then seconds later the band began to play a waltz. Once again, Fergal and Georgina moved slowly in time to the rhythm.

Meanwhile, Josie's partner had unceremoniously dumped her in the middle of the floor – after she'd threatened to 'knee' him if he didn't keep his hands to himself! Indignantly, she marched back to the table, prepared to complain, only to find it empty. Deciding Georgina was probably dancing, and Fergal at the men's cloakroom, she slumped disconsolately into a chair, and wished for the umpteenth time that Rob had come. Not one of the young men she'd met tonight could compare with him. Don't start 'mooning', she told herself sharply, and with irritation transferred her attention to Peter, still drooling over the blonde. Huh, she thought, he doesn't bring her over and introduce her, and I can just guess why! And then she saw them – Fergal and Georgina – both on the dance-floor, and of all things, they were dancing cheek to cheek, Fergal's dark head pressed against Georgina's fair hair! Josie stared in consternation. Georgina couldn't be interested in Fergal? He was a nice enough lad, and she felt desperately sorry for him – what with that awful scar and everything – but he was hardly in Georgina's class! Almost as soon as the phrase entered her mind, Josie felt ashamed of herself. How could she even think such a thing? Didn't she despise people who made such judgements? And then, following on the previous uneasy thought, came another. Surely Georgina couldn't be so fickle? What had happened to her 'great romance'? Had she so quickly forgotten Dominic?

But within minutes the young couple had returned to the table, stopping as they danced past to let Fergal sidle into his secluded seat.

Josie stared at them both. They seemed elated somehow. She glanced sharply at her friend. "You look like the cat who's swallowed the cream!"

Georgina grinned. "It can be your turn next – your hair's certainly long enough."

"What do you mean?"

"No," Fergal interrupted, "there's no need, honestly."

"Nonsense, the night's only half over." Georgina turned and smiled at him.

"I wish you'd tell me what you're talking about," Josie said crossly.

"It's simple. You make sure your hair is between your cheek and Fergal's. The perfect disguise."

For a moment Josie didn't understand, then light

dawned. "Oh, I see what you mean." That explained everything. It also meant she'd misinterpreted the whole scene!

"You know, that's a brilliant idea," she said. "Well done!"

"Perhaps I should change careers, and go into MI5," Georgina laughed, pleased that her plan had been so successful. And she'd been right – being concerned for someone else had helped to block her own heartache.

Josie sat in silence. It was a good plan, but she couldn't help thinking that what Fergal should really do was to brazen it out. It was all very well hiding away behind his fellow sailors, but he was going to have to make a life for himself sooner or later. And then, once again she felt ashamed. It was easy for her to think that way. Nobody knew what Fergal had gone through in that home; it was bound to have affected him.

Fergal was also the subject of discussion in the Ford household.

Sid brought up the subject first. Always slow to express an opinion, he'd been thinking about it ever since the two young sailors had arrived.

"Has Peter said anything? You know, about that lad's face?"

"How do you mean?" Lily tutted as she examined a hole in the toe of Sid's sock. "I wish you'd cut your toenails more often, Sid – it would save me a lot of darning!"

But her remark was wasted. Sid was single-

162

minded, and had no intention of being distracted from his subject. "That scar the lad's got. I mean, has he seen anyone about it? They can do wonders with plastic surgery these days. Look at those poor lads in the RAF during the war, how badly burned they were. There's a hospital down in London, isn't there, where they specialise in such things?"

Lily stared at him. People didn't give Sid enough credit for the brains he *had* got, in her opinion. It wasn't the first time he'd surprised her.

"You're right," she said. "I can't think of the name of it at the moment, but it would be easy to find out. There's that consultant up at the Infirmary as well – he does plastic surgery."

"There you are then." Sid took out a packet of Senior Service, lit a fag, and picked up the *Evening Sentinel.*

"But I can't believe they haven't gone into all this before," Lily commented. "I mean, surely the ship's doctor would have suggested it?"

"Maybe, maybe not. I'll ask Peter."

Meanwhile, as the dance drew to a close, Georgina, bitterly disappointed that Dominic wasn't there, had a problem. Since spending the evening with the two young men, she felt even more embarrassed that they would have to board the last bus, while she and Josie were driven home in style. When, after the last waltz, Peter came over to tell them that he was taking Sonia home, Georgina made a decision. Fergal was coming with *them,*

163

and if her father didn't like it, that was his hard luck!

"You don't mind giving Fergal a lift, father, do you?" she said, when they reached the car, already opening the back door for him to climb in. William, taken by surprise, had no choice but to reply, "Of course not."

Fergal, seated in the back, remained quiet. He'd seen Georgina's father's startled expression, and instinctively attributed it to the shock of seeing his scarred face. But in reality, due to the dusk, William hadn't even noticed. He was more interested in what he saw as his daughter's show of independence. She'd asked him a favour – could it be that she was offering an olive branch?

Chapter 18

It was a week later, the week she'd allowed herself, that Georgina made her decision. Still constantly on her mind, the whole issue of Dominic was preventing her from concentrating on revision for her exams. And she wanted to do well, not only since she needed the qualifications but because of the competitive spirit on the course. Both she and Josie were determined to outshine Marlene, for a start!

Georgina was miserably beginning to accept that she meant nothing to Dominic. As far as he was concerned, she was obviously just a girl he'd flirted with at a dance. But although her mind told her this, she couldn't erase a tiny but stubborn refusal to believe it. I'm not stupid, she thought. I know I'm young. I know I haven't had any experience of life. But there *was* something between us, something special. I'll have no peace until I know, and there's only one way to find out!

So that was why, one morning, when Josie came along to Rosemount, it was Alice who opened the door.

"Georgina won't be going to College today – she's not well."

Typical, Josie thought. No, 'Good morning Josie'! I bet she'd greet one of her own kind in a different manner!

"What's the matter with her?"

"Sore throat and temperature," Alice said.

It had been so easy, Georgina thought. There was no chance of her mother placing an anxious hand on her forehead, or looking down her throat. As she'd anticipated, Alice simply nodded, told her to stay in bed, and brought up a hot lemon drink with honey. "I've got a committee meeting at ten," she said, "and I'd planned to have lunch out before my hair appointment. If I leave you some soup in a flask – you'll be all right, won't you? I'll ask Mrs Ford not to disturb you."

"I'll be fine." Georgina had furtively checked Alice's diary the night before. "I'll probably sleep most of the time." She passed the hours by reading, until at last she heard Lily leave. Immediately, she flung back the bedclothes and hurried to the bathroom.

Then she brushed her hair until it shone, took especial care with her make-up, and put on a navy fitted suit. It was new, from Bratt & Dykes, an expensive department store in Hanley, and even Alice had commented that it made her look quite sophisticated. Picking up a pair of white gloves and a navy handbag, she went out into the sunshine, and walked quickly down to the bus stop. It seemed odd, travelling alone over the same route she normally shared with Josie, and the passengers were totally different. Gone were the schoolchildren in their uniforms, copying their neglected homework each time the bus stopped, the typists sitting upright, proud of their smart appearance, the shop assistants, the glum clerks. Now there was a more relaxed atmosphere, as housewives clambered on to banter with the conductor, and greet friends as they found a seat. A young mother boarded, carrying a baby, with a toddler clinging to her hand. Sitting in the seat in front of Georgina, the two-year-old, cherubic with ginger hair and freckles, turned and regarded her with an unwavering stare for at least three miles.

Georgina realised that she knew absolutely nothing about small children. I've never even held a baby, she thought, and was surprised how sad that made her feel. She tried to imagine what it would feel like, a small, soft body in her arms, the feeling of being needed, of another human being dependent on her.

Some day, she determined, some day I'll have a child of my own – no, definitely more than one child. And we'll be a real family, warm and loving, and there'll be laughter in the house, and . . . Suddenly she realised that in this fantasy world, the face of the children's father wasn't vague and cloudy; it was distinct. It was, of course, Dominic's. Well, she thought grimly, when the bus reached Burslem, this has got to end, and if all goes to plan, in the next couple of hours, I'll have my answer.

Head down, feeling like a truant schoolgirl,

Georgina hurried past the entrance to the College of Commerce in Queen Street. With a sigh of relief she passed out of what she thought of as the 'danger zone' and began to walk briskly along a busy main road. After several minutes, unsure of the way, she turned into a small oatcake shop. The wonderful oaty smell, and the sight of the freshly made pikelets laid out on racks to cool, reminded her that, to make her story of illness convincing, she'd skipped breakfast and hardly touched her soup. A middle-aged woman flipped over a row of oatcakes on the griddle, before turning to look curiously at the elegant young woman before her. They didn't see many dressed as expensively as that in this area! "Yes, luv?"

Georgina asked for directions and the woman jerked her head. "Yer turn right, then left, and then left again." Georgina resisted the temptation to buy a warm pikelet – it would only mess up her lipstick – and this was definitely a time when she needed to look her best.

It had been at Longton public library that Georgina found the information she wanted. She'd never been inside the building before, although she'd often passed it, and she looked around curiously. All these books – she could hardly believe it. Why had Alice always frowned on her request to join? It was ridiculous the reason she'd given:

"You don't know where those books have been. You could bring germs into the house. If you want a book, I'll buy it for you."

Now, seeing the hundreds of volumes to choose

from, Georgina realised what she'd been missing – all this enrichment, all this literature. Why, there were books here you would never find in a bookshop! But on this first visit, she had only one mission.

"Local information is at the bottom of the last aisle," the librarian told her, and conscious of the '*Silence*' signs, Georgina tiptoed along on the polished floor until she found the right section. Eagerly she scanned the shelves, and there it was: a directory of local companies. There was only one firm it could be. It was, judging from the number of abattoirs listed beneath its heading, a substantial business, with the head-office address in Burslem. The name of the firm was A Hargreaves & Son.

So, Georgina thought as she walked briskly along, her navy court shoes tapping on the pavement, for good or evil, now I'm about to find out!

The offices were in a square redbrick building set back from the road. From the front, it just looked like any other administrative centre, its blank windows facing on to a carpark, with no hint of what she regarded as its necessary but distasteful business. Squaring her shoulders, Georgina marched up to the front door and turned the brass handle. She found herself in a small entrance hall, with a closed door facing her. On it was a sign: *Enquiries*. For a moment she stood uncertainly. Was she sure she wanted to do this? She was acutely aware that it just wasn't done for a girl to chase after a young man. Was she cheapening herself? Would Dominic think even less of her, despise her for embarrassing him? And then she lifted her chin. So what! She needed to know. Only then could she get on with her life. It was the uncertainty that was unbearable.

So Georgina pushed open the door into a small office. There was a counter, and behind it sat a young woman of about twenty, tapping away on an Imperial typewriter. Dark-haired and pretty, she looked up with a friendly smile.

"Good morning, can I help you?"

Georgina looked at her, meeting open blue eyes, and immediately abandoned her original plan. Having expected to confront some old battle-axe, she'd been prepared to put on a display of poise and authority. But now, she decided a different approach was needed.

"I wondered whether I could have a word with Dominic?" she said, returning the friendly smile.

"Dominic?" The receptionist's eyes widened, then with blatant curiosity her glance swept over Georgina's face and hair.

"Yes. The owner's son?" Georgina didn't want to say Dominic Hargreaves, just in case it wasn't his surname. After all, she knew from her father that when some companies changed hands, they kept the original name to preserve any goodwill. She waited.

The receptionist became flustered. "I'm sorry, but he isn't here any more."

Georgina stared at her. "Isn't here? What do you mean?" Her mind went into a whirl. Had he had a row with his father? Had he left his job?

Again, the receptionist looked curiously at her. "Are you a friend of his?"

Georgina nodded.

The receptionist leaned forward, her eyes gleaming in anticipation. "So, he didn't tell you, either."

Georgina frowned. "Tell me what?" Her stomach began to churn with nerves.

"He's gone! Cleared off to Australia about a month ago."

"Australia?" Georgina stared at her wide-eyed.

"Just went off on one of these Assisted Passage Schemes! Never told any of us, not even his parents!"

Georgina swallowed, hardly able to believe what she was hearing. "Do you know the exact date on which he left?"

The receptionist rifled through the pages of her desk diary. "Sunday, the tenth, although I shouldn't need to check because it was the day before my birthday."

Sunday, the tenth – that was the day after the dance at Trentham. He'd known! Dominic had known all the time he was leaving the country – that she'd never see him again! He'd held her in his arms, kissed her, made her believe . . .

The receptionist, looking guiltily over her shoulder, was speaking again. "It really put the cat among the pigeons, I can tell you. He didn't even leave a forwarding address." She glanced with avid speculation up at Georgina. "Would you like to speak to Mr Hargreaves? He's in."

Georgina, already in shock, began to panic. The last thing she wanted was to be interrogated by Dominic's father.

"No! No, thank you, it's fine."

"Do you want to leave a name or anything?"

Georgina just wanted to get out of the building, away from the other girl's curious gaze. Australia! He'd gone to the other side of the world! "No, it's all right. Thank you for your help." She rallied enough to smile, and then turned and fled.

Automatically, almost in tears of humiliation, she made her way back to the centre of Burslem, to wait in despair at the bus stop. Sick with nervous reaction, yet hungry at the same time, she cursed that she'd walked blindly past the oatcake shop without buying anything. It was a long, monotonous bus journey home, and in misery she checked the time by her wristwatch. At least she'd arrive before her mother. Only there, alone in her bedroom, could she come to terms with the fact that Dominic had gone, gone forever out of her life.

That same evening, Josie was having an argument with Peter.

"You can't go out again," she hissed. They were upstairs, where she'd confronted him on the tiny landing. "What about Fergal? What's he supposed to do? Stay at home and watch *Dragnet* with Mum and Dad?"

"Go on, Josie," Peter pleaded. "Just this once.

It'll be the last time, honest! Can't you take him to the pictures or something?"

"Well, *you* can pay, and for the best seats!" Josie told him. "I suppose it's that blonde bit again – Sonia? The one you met at Trentham?"

"Yes. And I can't think why you're so horrible about her."

I bet you can't, thought Josie. What was it with men, were they blind or something? "I can't see Mum liking her," she said stubbornly.

Peter stared at her. "What makes you think she'll ever meet her? Grow up, Josie – it's only a bit of fun."

"Oh yeah, do you have a girl in every port, then?"

He grinned. "Something like that!"

So Josie and Fergal went to The Empire in Longton, originally a Victorian theatre but now con-verted to a cinema, to see *Rebel Without A Cause*. As they walked, Fergal kept his head bent, staring at the pavement, which irritated Josie. But once the film began, spellbound by James Dean, she almost forgot he was sitting next to her. However, once the lights came on at the end, after standing for the National Anthem, Fergal slumped down in his seat again, covering his scar with his hand.

Josie glanced at the queue of people ascending the stairs at the side of them. "Nobody's looking at you," she muttered. "You worry too much!"

"I suppose it wouldn't bother you!" Fergal looked at Josie's smooth complexion, her skin dewy with youthful good health.

"Of course it would!" she said. "I think it's dreadful what happened to you. But I can tell you one thing. You wouldn't find *me* skulking around, hiding from everyone. People would have to accept me as I was, and if they couldn't handle it, then that would be their lookout!" Josie spoke impulsively, using the same language she would use to her brothers. No-one stood on ceremony in the Ford household. If you had something to say, you said it. Too late, she realised that the young sailor next to her was not part of her family, and deserved more tact, more respect.

"Sorry," she said quickly. "I didn't mean to be rude or to upset you. I haven't, have I?"

Fergal didn't answer, just got up to leave as the queue for the exit diminished. They were following the other cinema-goers out into the dusk, when there was a call behind them.

"Josie? Oh, yeah, sitting up in the balcony with the nobs, eh?" It was Pauline. "Oh, sorry, I didn't realise you were with someone." She looked with undisguised curiosity at Fergal. "I've seen you around. You're Peter's friend, aren't you? My name's Pauline – I live in the same street." She turned to Josie. "Do you mind if I walk home with you? I'm not interrupting anything, am I?"

"No, of course not." Josie cast an uneasy glance at Fergal, but his face was impassive. The three of them began to walk along the pavement, down Commerce Street, and along Trentham Road. Fergal fell slightly behind the two girls.

"Do you fancy some chips on the way?" Pauline

nudged Josie. "You didn't tell me his name?"

"Oh, sorry, it's Fergal."

Pauline turned round. "How about stopping for some chips, Fergal? That okay with you?"

"Fine."

Pauline flashed a grin at him, then putting her head close to Josie's said, in what she thought was a low tone, "Hey, *he's* a bit of all right! Ever likely you've been keeping him to yourself!"

But Pauline had never been able to speak quietly, and Fergal, who'd closed the gap between them, heard her words. Almost against his will, a slow grin began to split his face. 'A bit of all right', eh?' Well, that was a first!

He looked again at the girl in front. He'd been so taken aback by Josie's words, that he hadn't really taken much notice of her. Nice hair, he thought, looking at the back of her head. An image of her glossy brown pageboy against his cheek as they danced came into his mind, and he dug his hands in his pockets in embarrassment. He'd been surprised, not only at how easy dancing was, but by his enjoyment of it. Could Josie be right? Was he his own worst enemy? Certainly, he tended not to go ashore with the rest of the crew, preferring to stay on board ship. And hadn't his mates told him exactly the same thing? Only they had put it even more bluntly. He had an ugly mug and he might as well get used to it, was their advice! But this girl, this Pauline, hadn't thought that. She'd seen beyond the scar, had thought he was 'a bit of all right'!

When Josie went to call for Georgina the following morning, she was relieved to see her coming down the drive to meet her.

"Are you better? It's nothing catching, I hope?"

Georgina shook her head. "Tell you later," she mouthed. "Once we're out of earshot."

Intrigued, Josie contained her impatience, with Georgina hardly speaking until they were on the bus. As always, they climbed the stairs hoping their usual front seat was vacant. It was, and with a quick glance over her shoulder to check that the seat behind was empty, Georgina began to explain. "For a start, I wasn't ill!" Swiftly, she detailed her actions the previous day, while Josie stared open-mouthed.

"Gosh, you've got a nerve! But why didn't you tell me?" she demanded.

"Because I felt a bit of a fool for doing it! Well, I got more than I bargained for." She looked away, but not before Josie had noticed the dark circles under her eyes.

"So, what happened? Did you see him? What did he say?"

Georgina repeated what she'd been told by the receptionist.

Josie could only stare at her. "He's emigrated, you mean?"

"I suppose he must have. I think they have to stay for two years anyway, and I don't suppose he'll come back!" Georgina's voice was flat, final. She stared blindly out of the window. It was a futile movement, as it was raining and they were

176

misted with condensation, but she felt so ashamed. It was humiliating to think that she'd been nothing but a distraction on Dominic's last night, a way of passing the time before he left the country. It was even more humiliating that she'd taken it all so seriously. And once again, the thought surfaced – how could I have been so wrong?

Josie was livid. It was the injustice of it that nettled her. Georgina had been upset for weeks about Dominic, and all the time . . .

She thought of Peter's words, and burst out, "You know they're all the same! It's all a bit of fun to them, they never think they leave a trail of heartbreak behind them. I'm going right off men, I can tell you!"

Georgina turned to her. "You haven't started with any yet!"

They stared at each other, and despite herself, Georgina couldn't help giggling.

"That's better," Josie said, rummaging in her bag for a packet of Murraymints. "Here, have one of these." Frowning, she looked at her friend with open curiosity. "But what were you going to say? I mean, if he'd been there?"

"I'd got it all planned. I was going to say that I happened to be passing and I'd got the chance of free tickets for the Theatre Royal."

"And had you?"

"No, of course not. But I could always have bought a couple."

Josie looked at her sideways. "You could have rung him, you know, once you'd found out the firm's number. You didn't have to go and see him."

"Yes, I did," Georgina said. "I wanted to see him face to face." And that, she thought with despair, is something you're unlikely to do ever again.

Chapter 19

Alice was completely unaware of her daughter's emotional upheaval. But then, she paid scant attention to Georgina anyway. Rosemount, she ran with her usual efficiency, and to William she was careful to present the image of the submissive wife that he had come to expect, but her thoughts, her hopes, her emotions, were all tied up with Neil.

Sometimes Alice was afraid that her lover was becoming like a drug. Could sex be addictive? She only knew that she was becoming desperate to see him, was inclined to take chances that even a few months ago would have horrified her. Neil, on the other hand, believed that an element of danger added spice to their affair. And it was certainly true that when he arranged for them to meet at a prominent city hotel, where they ran a risk of discovery, it gave an extra sexual *frisson* to their rendezvous.

Lily's life continued as usual. She cleaned the luxurious Big House, and then went home and cleaned her own modest one. And having two extra young men to look after had made her a lot of extra work. Nobody seems to realise, she would grumble to herself, what a difference it makes. The house was untidy. They were forever 'under her feet' so she couldn't get the vacuuming done. Then there was the extra shopping, cooking, and laundry. It was hectic, just like the days when all her sons were at home, and even as the thought entered her mind, Lily felt the sadness that never left her.

Sid, of course, was in his element. He was a man who liked male company, a 'man's man', and he was proud of it. Lily would scoff at the term, saying it was just an excuse for men to escape to the pub, but knew she had no real cause for complaint. And if she did sometimes wish he'd spend more time watching TV with her, she only had to remind herself that it was only because of Sid's drinking habits Josie was here at all. And thinking of Josie, Lily couldn't believe she would soon be leaving college. Even before the examination results were out, the girls were seeking positions. Lily smiled to herself, remembering how Josie had told her the word 'position' was old-fashioned.

"It makes us sound like servants," she complained. "Going cap in hand to the mistress. The word's 'job', Mum – you have to keep up with the times!"

And Lily did try to keep up with the times. Wasn't she one of the first in the street to have a twin-tub washing machine? Although it was on the 'never, never'. It had rankled though, when she'd gone to buy it. The shop wouldn't let her sign the Hire-Purchase Agreement, even though she told them she'd be the one paying the instalments. No, she'd had to bring the form home for Sid to sign, to prove she had his approval. Lily had been furious. Wasn't she a person in her own right? She'd told the shop assistant that she had a job, earned money of her own. But no, it was Head Office rules, he said. If she hadn't been so keen to have the washing machine, she'd have told him to forget it.

Sid had been unperturbed. "It's because some housewives would go and buy these things without telling their husbands. Then they wouldn't be able to keep up the payments, and where would that leave the shop?"

Lily stared at him. "Some housewives? What do you mean, some housewives? I'm a woman, not just a housewife!"

Josie butted in. She was sitting on the settee, applying bright pink nail varnish. "I'm never going to be called 'just a housewife'. I'm with you, Mum. I think it's a demeaning term."

"I didn't say that," Lily said sharply. "And I wish you wouldn't do that in here! It stinks the place out!" She got up, intending to put the kettle on.

"What I meant was, that I'm a housewife inside the house, but I'm an individual out of it. Why were we women given the vote if we're going to be treated as second-class citizens?"

Sid decided he'd had enough of Lily 'on her soapbox' and picked up his daily paper. "Are you making a cuppa? I'll have a biscuit with mine."

Josie glanced up at him. "What about the magic word?"

"Please!" Sid called through to the scullery, then pulled a face at his daughter, who grinned, saying, "It's soon gone, hasn't it? Peter's leave, I mean. I can't believe they're going back to their ship tomorrow."

"Aye." Sid glanced at her. "Has he ever said anything to you about Fergal? You know, about his scar?"

Josie frowned. "How do you mean?" She was fluttering her fingers to help the varnish to dry.

Sid returned to his paper. "Nothing. I'll have a word with him before he goes."

Later that evening, Sid seized an opportunity to raise the subject of Fergal with Peter, but was dismayed by his answer.

"Nothing doing, Dad. Not as far as the Navy is concerned. It might have been different if he'd been injured while in the Service. But a scar on his face doesn't interfere with his duties. Anything else is a personal matter."

"But they did wonders with such things after the War," Sid persisted. "Plastic surgery, it's called."

"I'm not saying something couldn't be done," Peter said. "But it was different then – the men would have received their injuries in action. No, it would be up to Fergal, and it would have to be when he comes out of the Navy."

"How long did he sign on for?"

"Four years, like I did. We were lucky," Peter grinned, "falling in for that short-term engagement they brought in after the War, particularly with the £125 bounty at the end. I've still got mine safe in the Post Office. Of course, that's finished now, the regular engagement is nine years, which as you know, I signed on again for."

Sid looked at his younger son. "Are you still glad you did?"

"Oh, yes," Peter said. "I like the Navy. The life suits me."

And so, the following day, the two young sailors prepared to leave. Just before they left, Peter went into the scullery and slipped several notes into Lily's hand. "Fergal feels a bit embarrassed to give it to you himself. But he likes to pay his way."

"He's a nice lad," Lily said, both touched and relieved by the gesture. "You're welcome to bring him any time."

"Thanks, Mum." Peter enfolded her in a bear hug, then stood back to gaze intently at her. "Take care now, and make sure our Josie behaves herself."

"Like you've been doing, I suppose!" Lily said tartly, but her eyes were smiling and Peter just grinned.

A few minutes later, with Fergal awkwardly expressing his thanks, they both hoisted their kitbags, and strode away. Lily, standing at the small front gate to wave them off, had mixed emotions. Her son was happy in the life he'd chosen, she knew that, but it was still hard to watch him go. I'm luckier than many mothers she tried to console herself. I still have Josie at home, and our Dennis not so far away.

It wasn't until a few days later, as they travelled home on the bus, that Georgina confessed to Josie that she was going to write to Fergal.

"How do you mean, write to him?" Josie was astounded. Had something been going on after all? Right under her nose?

"Oh, not like that," Georgina laughed. "As a sort of pen-friend, I mean." She became thoughtful. "He never gets any post, you know. Can you imagine what it must be like, having no-one, not a single person you can write to, or have a letter from?"

Josie thought for a moment. "You know, that's really sad. I feel awful not thinking of it myself. Mind you, he does have his shipmates."

"Yes, but it's not the same."

"Well, I think it's really nice of you," Josie said.

"Not really. I liked him." Georgina thought, I could add that I recognise loneliness when I see it. In that respect we're kindred spirits.

The two girls went dancing at Trentham every Saturday, and sometimes Pauline went with them. But although Josie always hoped to see Rob again, no matter how she searched the crowds, there was no sign of him.

I don't know why I'm bothering, she thought. I don't want to get involved, so what's the point? But that didn't prevent her from being disappointed.

It was Georgina who first spotted Doug, the young soldier who had been with Rob. "Doug's over there," she hissed. "Standing by the bar."

Josie turned, saw him, and immediately got up. "Come on. Let's go over."

"Are you sure?" Georgina felt embarrassed, remembering the fool she'd made of herself last time.

But Josie was already threading her way through the crowds, and Georgina had no alternative but to follow, hoping Doug wouldn't even remember them.

"Hello, soldier!" Josie, her vivid colouring shown off in a petrol-blue halter-neck dress, tapped him on the shoulder.

Doug turned round. "Oh, hello! I was hoping to bump into you two."

"We haven't seen you for ages," Josie said.

"I haven't been coming," he grinned.

Don't I know it, Josie thought. "Rob with you?" she asked, in what she hoped was a careless tone.

Her spirits plunged as he shook his head. "No. His father's ill, so he's been using his leaves to go up to Scotland. I've only come tonight because it'll be my last time." He grinned, "I'm being demobbed next week. It will be back to Nottingham for me, and I can't wait!"

Georgina, glancing at Josie's stunned expression asked, "What will you do?"

"Go back to Raleigh – you know, the bicycle firm," he said promptly. "I've worked there since leaving school."

"And Rob?" Josie said, yet somehow she knew what the answer would be.

"He's due to be demobbed too."

Josie looked away. She couldn't believe it! That was it, then. She'd never see Rob again. And the irony was that she had no-one to blame but herself. If she'd let him see how much she liked him, in other words had followed her heart instead of her head, then things might have been different. "Well, I hope all goes well for you, Doug. Tell Rob we wish him all the best, won't you?"

"Sure will."

Doug didn't offer to buy them a drink, and the two girls made their way to the cloakroom, where Josie took out a comb and savagely attacked her unruly hair.

"Hey, you're making it worse!"

"It's since I washed it," Josie grumbled, but she didn't fool her friend.

"You liked him, didn't you?" Georgina said. "More than you've let on."

Josie, moving away from the mirror as a group of laughing girls came in, just shrugged. "If I did, it's come to nothing. Maybe we're jinxed. It seems funny it should happen to both of us." They looked at each other for a moment, then with one accord turned to go back to the ballroom.

"Come on," Georgina said with a wry smile. "There's plenty more fish in the sea."

But Josie's spirits remained low, and by the time the band played the last waltz, she was more than ready to go home. Serves you right, she told herself crossly. Just because you thought he was a farmer and it didn't fit in with your master plan! She ignored the fact that Rob had made no attempt to arrange to see her again. She hadn't encouraged him, had she? Now she'd never know if anything might have come of it.

Chapter 20

Three weeks after her seventeenth birthday, and a week before the end of the secretarial course, Josie went for her first job interview. The morning was stiflingly hot, and she dithered for ages over what to wear. She didn't possess a suit, something she was determined to remedy once she got her first pay packet. Unfortunately, Georgina was taller, which meant Josie couldn't wear her clothes. She did, however, borrow a leather navy handbag.

"Accessories, my dear!" Georgina mimicked the voice of her form mistress at boarding school. "Never stint on the accessories! Good shoes and a good handbag can cover a multitude of sins."

Now, as she presented herself at the prestigious Royal Hotel in Hanley, wearing a white broderie anglaise blouse, pleated navy skirt and high heels, Josie felt both confident and full of excited anticipation. As soon as she'd seen the advertisement in the *Evening Sentinel,* she'd written her letter of application. She could learn so much in a job like this, would be able to mix with successful people, ones who knew the right way to talk, the correct way to behave.

The interview and test went well, Josie being confident of good results in the examinations she'd just taken. She liked the formality of the General Manager in his blue pinstriped suit. She noticed how his fingernails were clean and manicured. This was a world she longed to be part of, one of good manners and civilised behaviour. She was grateful that despite his air of authority, his attitude was friendly. There and then she knew that she desperately wanted the job. When, half an hour later, the post of shorthand typist was offered to her, Josie almost floated out of his office and into a room behind reception. While another member of staff telephoned the housekeeper to arrange for someone to show her the hotel, Josie gazed around her with avid curiosity.

It was then, glancing through the open door into reception, that she saw her. It was Alice Hawkins! But Alice Hawkins as she'd never seen her before, because she was wearing a silk head-scarf! It was soft blue paisley; Josie was always to remember it. Now women in the street wore head-scarves, the Queen wore a headscarf, but Georgina's mother – never! Afterwards Josie was to wonder what had made her hang back, why she hadn't attracted her attention, and smiled. Instead, withdrawing out of sight, she watched Alice leave the desk and walk briskly across the vestibule to begin to climb the stairs. There seemed something odd about her behaviour; she kept her head down, almost, Josie thought, as if she didn't want to be seen. But why on earth would that be?

Georgina was always saying that her mother went out for expensive lunches, and, Josie saw, checking her watch, it *was* lunch-time, and the hotel was certainly expensive. Then, to her amazement she saw Alice turn sharply as the receptionist called, "Mrs French?"

Alice retraced her steps.

Josie stood motionless, hardly able to believe what she was seeing. Self-consciously, she glanced over her shoulder, hoping she wasn't making herself conspicuous, but the clerk, with her back to her, had the phone to her ear while she doodled on a blotting-pad.

Josie strained her ears as the receptionist spoke to Alice. "I'm terribly sorry, madam, but I told you the wrong room. It's forty-five, not fifty-five."

"That's all right, thank you." Alice walked quickly back to the broad red-carpeted staircase. A few seconds later, she was out of sight.

Josie, in a state of shock, jumped as the clerk, a middle-aged woman with greying hair and spectacles said, "Mrs Massey says someone will be down in a minute. In the meantime, why don't you ask Pam in reception to show you the ropes – we all cover for each other at times."

She smiled at Josie, who, although automatically smiling back, could think of nothing except the significance of what she'd just seen. Georgina's mother, the superior Mrs Hawkins, was having an affair! She was here, posing as Mrs French, in this hotel, upstairs in a bedroom with her lover! She was actually committing *adultery*! No, Josie rejected the word, she couldn't be! Why, she went to church once a month, was on all those charity committees! But no matter how she tried, Josie knew there could be no other explanation.

As she went through to reception she tried to push the shocking image from her mind. She had to concentrate – first impressions were so important! But it was impossible. The hotel register acted like a magnet, and as soon as Pam wasn't looking, Josie scanned the entries. There it was! Mr and Mrs N French – booked in for one night. Josie frowned, she'd never known Alice to stay away overnight. Could she be wrong, could there be another reason Alice was here? But the doubt was fleeting. She'd booked in as this man's wife and that could only mean . . .

Upstairs, Alice was already undressing. Neil, lying back on the quilted eiderdown, was sipping a glass of whisky. He always brought a bottle with him in his suitcase.

"We have to make it look all above board," he'd explained to Alice, the first time. "Hotels always look out for luggage. And we have to book the room overnight. No decent hotel would let us use a room for a couple of hours."

"I couldn't possibly stay overnight," Alice had protested.

"No, but I can. I happen to have a few clients who live some distance away. You know, a bit old and decrepit? A couple of whom, in particular, are very demanding – always wanting to change their wills and so forth." He'd grinned. "Another one has a habit of getting into disputes about boundaries."

Alice had stared at him. "Are you making this up?"

"You'll never know, my love." Even as he spoke, Neil had been unbuttoning her blouse and sliding his hand inside to cup her breast. "It adds to my air of mystery and devastating attraction."

And Alice, already in a state of nervous arousal, feeling his thumb start to caress her, had to agree.

It was something else she liked about him, she thought now, as, her limbs heavy and relaxed, she lay once again curled up in his arms. Neil was so masterful – he just took care of everything.

Look at the way he had organised their affair. Most of the time, they used the flat of a friend of his, whose work often took him away, and Neil held a spare key as security. Whether this friend – Neil refused to tell her his name – knew that Neil used it as a 'love nest', Alice neither knew nor cared. But then there were periods when the flat wasn't available, and this was when things became even more exciting. Careful not to use the same hotel too often, Neil would write a false address in the register, using a different one each time. After their lovemaking, late in the afternoon, Alice would slip away, leaving Neil sleepily relaxing in the double bed. He never ate in the hotel dining-room, but would drive to an out-of-the-way restaurant. For breakfast he used room service, always ordering for two, with a few feminine garments – provided by Alice, scattered around. He always chose a large, busy hotel and he paid the bill with cash. The name French was a private joke, as he referred to Alice as his "French mistress", teasing that she must have been a courtesan at a Parisian court in a previous life.

Neil had, Alice thought drowsily, covered every eventuality.

Chapter 21

Much to her relief, Josie was going to have a respite before she saw Georgina again. As luck would have it, the interview had been held on the same Friday that Georgina was travelling up to Edinburgh to spend the weekend with her old school-friend, Fiona.

So, Josie thought grimly, as she walked home from the bus stop, at least I won't have to go to Rosemount on Sunday – she doubted whether she'd be able to look Alice Hawkins in the face! The sordid discovery had almost overshadowed her triumph in getting the job she wanted. And it had left her with an agonising moral dilemma. What should she do? She couldn't possibly tell Georgina such a terrible thing! It would destroy any remaining respect she had for her mother. For Josie was well aware that there was little affection in Rosemount. Georgina never complained, never said anything – she was far too loyal for that – but Josie had eyes and ears. The polite, cool relationship that existed between Alice Hawkins and her daughter mystified Josie. Some families in their street were close, others had terrible rows, but in her experience their houses, even if poorly furnished, were at least homes. Rosemount might be 'grand', but there was no warmth there, no affection. And now she knew that deceit lay beneath the civilised surface.

As soon as Lily heard the front door open, she rushed into the hall.

"Well? How did it go?"

"Brilliant!" Josie whirled her mother round. "I've got the job! Four guineas a week! Can you believe it? I start in a fortnight."

"Four guineas! That's a really good wage. Oh, well done, love! Come on, I'll make us a cup of tea, and you can tell me all about it." Still talking, Lily led the way to the scullery, with Josie following. "You know, I've never been inside a hotel, not a proper one. We stayed in a boarding house in Blackpool on our honeymoon, but a real hotel – well, only the rich could afford those."

"From what I've seen of the prices, nothing's changed!" Josie opened the clasp of Georgina's handbag and brought out a brochure and tariff. "Just look how much it costs to stay there!"

Lily studied the printed sheet and her eyes widened in shock. "What! For one night?"

"Yes, believe it or not!"

"People must have more money than sense!" Looking at the picture of the imposing hotel and elegant reception, Lily could only imagine how wonderful it must be to stay in such luxury and to be waited on.

"Oh, our Josie, what a lovely place to work!"

But Lily couldn't help a flash of envy. Girls

these days had so many opportunities. Still, she thought, as she ladled two teaspoons of tea into the pot, at least my girl will have a better chance than I had.

Josie wandered back into the front room. Unlike many of her neighbours, Lily had never liked the custom of keeping one room for 'best', only to be used for special occasions and at Christmas. They'd had to do so when the children were growing up, as they couldn't afford to heat two rooms, but once the family's budget eased, Lily had put her foot down. And so the back room was used for meals only, and when they had a television set, Lily insisted on waiting until they could afford a walnut console model. Set at an angle before the small bay window in the front room, it was, she informed Sid with pride, "Not only a television set but a nice piece of furniture," and on the top she could display her floral china ornaments.

Josie, her head still buzzing with the enormity of what she'd discovered, slumped on to the moquette settee. Absently, she straightened the lace-trimmed antimacassar that had fallen off the back. But it was no use trying to evade the issue. Part of her was dying to blurt out the scandalous news about Alice Hawkins to her mother, but another, more cautious part, was holding her back. Lily might not be a churchgoer, but every Sunday morning she would always listen to the Morning Service. Sid and Josie were resigned to the sound of hymns as Lily prepared the vegetables, and made a rice pudding. Working-class morality was instilled into the Ford household. "We may be poor, but we do have standards," was a saying Josie had heard all her life.

How would her mum feel, knowing she was working for someone who was 'carrying on' with another man, betraying her husband, and to some extent her daughter? She might even, Josie thought with dismay, decide she couldn't work for such a woman, and leave her job. And that would be a huge pity, because things had been so much easier since her mum had been working at Rosemount. Now, with Josie's wages also coming in, her parents would be able to treat themselves, might even go on a proper holiday, instead of just day trips. What would I achieve by telling her, Josie thought? I can't. I just can't. Although she was beginning to wonder whether, as Georgina's best friend, it would be disloyal *not* to confess what she'd discovered. But how on earth did you tell anyone something so awful about her mother? Then quickly followed another dilemma. As a future member of staff, wouldn't she be expected to treat what went on in the hotel as confidential? Certainly they'd been taught on their secretarial course that discretion was an important part of their job. Oh, damn Alice Hawkins, she thought in despair. This is all her fault!

When the two girls travelled on the bus on Monday morning, Georgina, while thrilled at Josie's news about her job, was full of the fantastic time she'd had. "We went to the theatre on Saturday night. It was music hall, and oh, Josie, you'd have loved it. And Fiona has a boyfriend! I didn't meet him, but she showed me a photo. He's a second-year medical student at St Andrew's University."

"A doctor?" Josie said. "Gosh, that sounds so romantic."

"She's mad about him. Will probably marry him, I should think. The family have known him for ages."

Georgina chattered on, and Josie listened, but beneath the surface she was still agonising over what she should do. She glanced at her friend's happy, animated face, and knew that if she told her about her mother, Georgina's life would never be the same again. Yet Josie still wasn't sure where her duty lay.

Meanwhile, at Rosemount, Monday morning began like any other. Then, shortly after Georgina left for college, Lily arrived. And within minutes, Alice's day turned into a nightmare.

"Our Josie's got herself a job," Lily announced, her face beaming with pride.

"Oh, yes?" Alice said. She was fiddling with the wireless, trying to change the station to the Light Programme.

"As a shorthand-typist at the Royal Hotel, in Hanley. She went for an interview on Friday." Lily looked in triumph at her employer. I bet she never thought a Ford would be working in a place like that!

But Alice wasn't capable of thinking anything. The words *Josie – interview – Friday – Royal Hotel*, had been like a series of physical blows. For a moment she couldn't even speak, then conscious that Lily was looking at her expectantly, managed, "That's wonderful news, Mrs Ford."

Lily stared at her. "Are you feeling all right?" I hope she's not getting this bug that's going about, she thought. That's the last thing I want.

"I'm fine." Alice struggled to regain her composure. "A bit of a headache, that's all." But she was horrified – what if Josie had been there at the same time as herself – what if she'd seen her?

Her voice sounded strange even to herself as she asked, "What time was her interview?"

Lily was filling the plastic bowl in the sink ready to wash the breakfast dishes. "Eleven fifteen," she said, swishing the hot water to make suds.

Alice felt her hands begin to shake. Oh, my God! Where were the interviews held? Where would the offices be? Behind reception, came the swift answer. Hadn't she seen desks with typewriters and accounting machines through the open door? She'd arrived to meet Neil at twelve! Josie definitely could have seen her! Why, the receptionist had even called her back because she'd given her the wrong room number! That meant that twice Alice had walked across the vestibule, twice she'd climbed those stairs. If panic had been present before, now it threatened to overwhelm her.

"Why?"

"Sorry?" Alice looked with confusion at Lily.

"Why did you want to know what time Josie's interview was?" Lily was scrubbing with a wire-wool pad at the frying pan.

Alice's brain scrabbled for a reason, then the words came out in a rush, "It's just that I went up to Hanley on Friday afternoon – if it had been then I could have given her a lift."

That would be a first, Lily thought, rinsing the pan and propping it on the dish-rack. "They gave her a test before she saw the general manager. He offered her the job, then she went into reception for a bit, was shown around, and was home by half past one. She brought me a hotel brochure – it doesn't half look posh!"

But Alice was no longer listening; she was already moving away, escaping from Lily's curious eyes. She needed privacy, to bury her face in her hands, try to stem the sheer terror within her. Because the odds were that Josie Ford had seen her at the Royal Hotel. And what if she had looked in the hotel register? Asked questions? There had been some bad moments in Alice's life, but never before had she experienced such dread, such apprehension. And yet it was out of her hands; there was nothing she could do except to wait.

Chapter 22

And so, over the next few days, Josie spent miserable hours wrestling with her dilemma, and eventually came to the uneasy conclusion that to remain silent was in everyone's interest. At first she tried to avoid going to visit Rosemount, but it was hopeless, the routine was too well established.

Josie knew that Alice had asked about the interview, because Lily had told her. "Quite interested she was," Lily said. "She even wanted to know what time you went for it."

I bet she did, Josie thought grimly. She knew Alice would be desperate to find out whether she was seen or not. And Josie was afraid that her face would give her away. She'd never been any good at covering things up. But she had to hide her knowledge, for it would never do for Mrs Hawkins to feel she was threatened in any way. She might decide that having Lily working for her was too risky. So, in her lunch-hour, Josie went into Woolworth's and bought the biggest pair of sunglasses she could find. If the expression in her eyes couldn't be seen, she might have a chance of getting away with it.

When Alice, who was leafing through *Vogue* in the sitting-room, heard the bell ring, every nerve was jarred. She glanced across at William who, immersed in the *Evening Sentinel,* didn't even look up. They both knew it would be Josie. Alice heard Georgina go to open the door, and then stood up. It was no use, she was going to have to confront the girl. She had to know – she hadn't had a decent night's sleep for days. Going into the oak-panelled hall, she paused by a vase of red roses on the half-moon table.

Josie stepped inside, and Alice, who was pretending to adjust the flowers, turned to face her. Eyes of guilt and desperation gazed into eyes concealed behind dark lenses. Josie, as usual muttered, "Hello, Mrs Hawkins," and, as she felt the heat rise to her cheeks, ran up the broad stair-case behind Georgina.

Alice, her heart thudding against her ribs, could only gaze after her. There had been nothing! Absolutely nothing! Of course the damn girl had been wearing sunglasses – but surely she'd have shown some sign? Her mother was behaving normally, and so was Georgina – surely if Josie *had* known she would have said something? So, it had been a nasty, but false alarm. Alice began, for the first time in days, to breathe more easily.

Georgina, for whom there was no hurry from a financial point of view, was also keen to get a job. Both of the girls felt they'd done well in their exams and their form tutor, Miss Jameson, had advised them only to take a job where the company would pay for day-release studies. "Increase your qualifications, and you increase your options," she told them, and Josie considered herself fortunate that the hotel manager had agreed to this. Miss Jameson had also had a private word with Georgina. "Just a bit of advice. I wanted to say that as far as a career is concerned, you should try to capitalise on your education and home background. And always remember that the world doesn't begin and end in the Potteries."

Home background! Georgina thought wryly. Having spent the weekend at Fiona's home, she was seeing the flaws in her own with increasing clarity.

As Georgina had planned to have a break after leaving college, William and Alice took her on holiday to the same luxury hotel in Bournemouth that they always used, but it was not a success. Much of the time she went off on her own, to walk along the wooded Chines, browse around the shops, and, when the sun shone, to swim in the sea. William and Alice rarely ventured on to the beach, so here she could relax in a deckchair and read, without having to make polite conversation.

Alice seemed strangely interested in Josie's job. "Does she say much, about what goes on at work?" she asked one morning. They were sitting in the hotel lounge having morning coffee, while rain spattered on the large windows.

"Not really. She tells me about the guests sometimes."

Alice frowned, reaching out for a biscuit. "Gossips about them, you mean?"

Georgina looked sharply at her. "No, not at all. She never refers to them by name or anything. Just if something funny happens, that's all."

Alice breathed a sigh of relief. She didn't know why she was asking really; it was obvious she'd had a lucky escape. But clearly she and Neil couldn't use the Royal Hotel again, which was a pity. She glanced at her watch. "I'd better be going for my hair appointment."

After she'd gone, William, who'd been immersed in the *Financial Times*, looked up and across at his daughter. "A bit quiet for you, isn't it – here, I mean? With just your mother and myself for company."

Georgina said in surprise, "It is a bit, yes."

"Aren't there any other young people in the hotel you liked the look of?"

Georgina stared at him. "You mean you wouldn't mind if I made friends with someone?"

"Why should I? You're old enough to choose your own friends now." William's beetle eyebrows drew together as he leaned forward to put a spoonful of brown sugar into his cup. As Georgina picked up the silver coffee pot, and began to pour the coffee, he added, "We're never too old to learn, Georgina. I want you to remember that."

She was speechless. Her father's words were the nearest to an apology she'd ever heard from him. So, he *did* realise how wrong he'd been that night at Trentham Gardens. Although now she was beginning to think that inadvertently he'd actually done her a good turn. After all, Dominic had hardly turned out to be trustworthy!

Realising he was waiting for her to show some reaction, she just said, "I will." But almost unwillingly, her eyes met his and, with consternation, for one fleeting moment, she thought she saw an appeal. She gave a slight smile, and then looked down in embarrassment. For that one instant, her father had almost appeared human, someone she could talk to, but Georgina couldn't forget her childhood misery, when the man opposite had filled her soul with terror. No, she thought, looking away, regret might be easy for him, but I'm the one who has to do the forgiving.

Once home, spurred on by Josie's success in getting a job, Georgina began to apply herself to scanning the advertisements in the *Evening Sentinel*. To her surprise, Alice took an interest in the project, anxiously waiting for the paper to be delivered, sometimes taking it before Georgina could, her pale hands hovering over the 'Situations Vacant' pages.

"We need to discuss it," she said, "before you decide to apply for anything." With her eyelids lowered, she asked, "Were you thinking of a hotel, like Josie?"

"Not necessarily," Georgina confessed. "To be honest, I rather fancy something in the public sector. Then I'd definitely be able to go to college on day-release. I want to get up to 140 wpm shorthand. That would really open doors for me."

Relieved, Alice considered her daughter's suggestion. The public sector. That could mean the Town Hall in Stoke, or at least a similarly respectable organisation. William would be pleased, for already he'd been expressing his opinion. But not to Georgina, Alice noticed – he waited until she was out of earshot.

"I'm not having her working in a factory, even if it is in the office," he warned. Alice credited her daughter with more sense than to think of it.

But Georgina had thought of it. She was conscious that although she was 'Potteries born and bred,' she was completely ignorant about the industry which had made the area famous throughout the world. Often, as she passed the factories lining the main A50 which linked the five towns, she would wonder what they were like inside. Fine china they had in abundance at Rosemount, and it seemed ludicrous that these beautiful objects were manufactured so near to where she lived, and yet she had never seen the inside of a potbank. But she was astute enough to know that her father would object and had decided it just wasn't worth the hassle.

It was William Hawkins who discovered the perfect job for his daughter. Or so he thought. It was while he was having lunch with his bank manager that the subject arose.

James Campbell listened, at first with polite boredom, and then with some interest, as one of

206

his most valued clients told him of his daughter's achievements. Until then, he'd hardly been aware of William's home life. The successful builder scorned many of the social niceties, and his single-mindedness seemed to have worked for him by the healthy balance sheets he'd studied that morning.

"What I want for her, James," William continued, "is a job in keeping with her private education, if you see what I mean."

"Actually, there is a job going at the bank."

"Really? She's very keen on a day-release course. Would that be available?"

"Certainly. We like to encourage our staff to gain more qualifications. Look, tell her to come and see me. Can't promise anything, but I'll certainly give her an interview."

William frowned. "It wouldn't mean her knowing all about my affairs, would it? A man likes to keep these things to himself."

"Of course not," James was quick to reassure him. "I handle your accounts personally. There would be no breach of confidentiality, I can promise."

But when, after dinner that evening, William in triumph announced his achievement, Georgina was not only without enthusiasm, but resentful.

"I can get my own job," she told him. "I don't need any 'old boys' network', thank you very much."

"But . . ." William began to bluster. Could he never do anything right in his daughter's eyes?

"And I don't want to work in a bank!" she

207

insisted, angry at what she saw as her father's attempt at control. He hasn't changed, she thought with bitterness. He still wants to dominate everyone and everything. It would just suit him fine, wouldn't it, to have me working for someone who could act as a spy for him!

"I think you're being childish!" Alice intervened, deferring as usual to her husband. William's temper, once provoked, could cast a pall over the household for hours.

Georgina flashed her a glance of contempt. She could count on one hand the times Alice had stood up for her. She got up and collected the dessert plates. "I'll make the coffee."

"Honestly," William exploded, after she'd left the room, "she's impossible!"

"You were only trying to help," Alice soothed.

"Fat lot of good it did me!"

But Georgina had her way, and a couple of weeks later, she told them she'd been offered, and had accepted, a job at the Town Hall.

"It's in the Lord Mayor's department," she said. "Quite socially acceptable, don't you think?"

But she wasn't just trying to please her parents. Although fiercely defensive of any hint of snobbery, Georgina was realistic. She knew that boarding school had given her an extra self-assurance, an extra polish, and had every intention of exploiting that advantage. This difference was the key to achieving her secret ambition, the one she hadn't told anyone, not even Josie.

Chapter 23

It was just before Christmas when the loud knock came at the Ford's front door. In the parlour, Josie, who had unwound a paper chain, was holding up one end, while Sid pinned the other in the centre of the ceiling. She glanced at her mother who was opening a packet of balloons. "Can you go, Mum?"

"Well, I hope it's not visitors – just look at the mess we're in!" Lily picked her way over the littered floor, stooping to pick up a half-open packet of tinsel. "This stuff gets everywhere!"

Pushing back her hair in an effort to tidy it, Lily opened the door. A chill wind swept into the hall, and before her stood a heavily built man with a young woman standing behind him. It was the man, wearing a tweed cap and with his coat collar turned up, who spoke.

"Mrs Ford?"

"Yes?"

"Is your husband in?"

Lily stared into bloodshot eyes above a bulbous nose. They were aggressive. There was also a whiff of beer on the man's breath.

"I'll call him." She left the door ajar and went into the front room.

"Sid?"

"Yes?" He stepped down from the hard chair, and looked critically at the paper chain.

"There's a man and a young woman at the door. He wants to see you!"

Sid glanced at her, hearing the anxiety in her voice. "Did he give a name?"

Lily shook her head.

"Right." Sid marched out of the room, while Lily shrugged her shoulders at the unspoken question in Josie's eyes. Both strained their ears, but all they could hear was the murmur of voices.

A couple of minutes later, Sid came back, bringing the two strangers with him. Lily took one look at his clenched jaw, and knew she'd been right. It was trouble!

"This is Mr Brown and his daughter, Sonia." He turned to the visitors and stiffly introduced Lily and Josie.

With a lurch of her stomach – she'd recognised Sonia immediately – Josie moved a pile of inflated balloons off the settee. Lily's gaze swept over the blonde girl, her brown tweed coat straining over her belly.

Sid cleared his throat. "Mr Brown tells me that his daughter's pregnant, and she says Peter's the father!"

Lily glanced sharply at the man now sitting on the edge of her settee, his head thrust truculently forward. "I see. How far gone is she?"

"I'm seven months and I can speak for meself,"

Sonia snapped. Her eyes darted to Josie, who gazed back unsmilingly.

"Seven months? If that's the case, I'm surprised you didn't come before now!" Lily snapped, suspicion rushing to block out the shock. She looked at Sonia. Bottle-bleached hair, thin pencilled eyebrows, bright red lipstick – common as muck! Not their Peter! Never!

"Aye," Mr Brown said, speaking for the first time, "you would think that. But she hid it well, didn't start to show until recently. Our Sonia's always been . . ."

"Well-developed," Josie finished the sentence for him. She hadn't liked Peter's choice of girl-friend from the start, but there was no doubt in her mind that the accusation was true. A vision flashed before her of the two of them entwined on the dancefloor, Peter's hands touching and stroking. They'd had no shame, the pair of them. If Sonia hadn't minded that in public . . .

Lily turned swiftly to face her daughter. "You know this girl?" she jerked her head at Sonia.

"He met her at Trentham." And hardly a girl, Josie thought.

Lily obviously had the same thought. "Do you mind my asking how old you are?"

Sonia, whose bulge drew Lily's eyes like a magnet, muttered, "Twenty-three."

Old enough to have more sense, Lily thought with disgust. Trollop!

Sid, his expression stony, said, "Make our visitors a cup of tea, will you, Josie?"

211

With reluctance, not wanting to miss anything, Josie left and went into the scullery, leaving both doors open.

"It was her mum who first sussed it out," Jim Brown told them. "I don't know how long she thought she was going to keep up the pretence. Then she wouldn't say at first who the father was."

Sonia's face was defiant. She opened the clasp of her handbag. "Okay if I smoke?" Without waiting for an answer, she took out a packet of cigarettes.

Josie, busy with the teacups, could just imagine her mum's expression. She didn't approve of women smoking, any more than she approved of them going into public houses.

There was silence in the room as Sonia lit up, and Lily silently passed her an ashtray. Sid stood on the hearthrug, blocking the warmth of the coal fire he'd lit earlier. He looked at the Browns, father and daughter, and didn't much like what he saw. The man was a drinker; he'd seen the type too many times not to recognise one. And as for his daughter! Had Peter been blind? Or, after months at sea, just looking for an easy lay? Lily wouldn't understand that, of course. But then, Lily hadn't served time in the Forces.

"So," Sid said quietly. "What do you want us to do?"

"I want Peter's address," Sonia told them.

"Aye," Jim Brown said. "He'll have to marry her. There's no question about it!"

212

Josie, bringing in the tray, paused in the doorway, horrified at the thought of Peter married to Sonia? That meant she'd be her sister-in-law!

Lily compressed her lips. "We'll need to write to him ourselves," she said, "so that we can hear his side of things. There'll be no decisions taken until then!"

Her voice was clear, decisive, and Josie felt a surge of pride. That's the spirit, she thought. The Fords don't get told what to do by anyone, let alone the likes of these! But then as she handed Sonia a cup and saucer, she looked up, and Josie saw the glisten of tears in her eyes. So, she wasn't as tough as she made out!

"I hope you're not calling my daughter a liar!" There was more than a hint of menace in Jim's voice.

"Of course not," Lily said briskly, "but it's best to get these things out into the open, isn't it? For everyone's sake."

There was a slight rattle as Sonia put her cup back on to her saucer, and for the first time Josie felt sympathy towards the girl her brother had "knocked up", as people called it. Peter could be charm itself, and she recalled how he'd gone out one night to meet Sonia wearing his navy uniform. All set for the big seduction, no doubt! And suddenly Josie wondered where it had happened. Peter didn't have a car so it couldn't have been on a back seat. Her parents must have gone out one night. From what she'd heard, quite a few babies were conceived in parents' front rooms! A

213

girl in every port, he'd boasted. Well, he'd got more than he bargained for this time!

By now Lily had been to the bureau which stood in one corner, and rummaged in the compartments for a writing pad. She copied out Peter's address and gave it to Sonia. "I'm surprised," she said tartly, "considering you were so 'close', that he didn't give it to you himself."

"He did," flashed Sonia, "but I lost it."

That's a lie for a start, Josie thought, but I can understand why she said it.

Jim Brown stood up, and brushed a strand of tinsel from his trousers. "Well, we won't take up any more of your time. You'd better have a note of our address," he told Lily, and, her hand now beginning to tremble, she wrote it down.

Minutes later, they were gone, and Sid returned to the room to find Lily's brave front already crumpling. He drew her into his arms, as she dabbed at her eyes with her hanky. "How could he be so stupid! And with a girl like that!"

"She might not be so bad, Mum," Josie said. "Peter must have seen something in her."

"Yes, and we all know what that was!"

Sid, whose face looked haggard, sat heavily in his armchair. "We'll just have to wait and see what he's got to say."

"I haven't even started the dinner," Lily said, glancing at the clock. "And look at all this!" Helplessly, she looked at the decorations strewn around the room. "I just haven't got the heart for it now."

"We'll close the door on it," Josie said. "We can go in the other room. And I'll fetch us some fish and chips. My treat!"

Lily managed a weak smile. "You're a good girl, our Josie."

Yes, and I'm going to remain one, thought Josie grimly. Her head bent against the icy wind, she walked down the hill into the comforting aromatic warmth of the chip shop. I'm never going to find myself in *that* situation, she thought, as ten minutes later she hurried home with the hot mouth-watering package clutched against her chest. There'll be nothing doing in that department until I've got a wedding ring on my finger! One thing's for sure though – this is going to put a downer on everyone's Christmas!

Once Peter admitted parentage, his fate was sealed. Sid was adamant. "If she's good enough for one thing, she's good enough for the other!" was his opinion.

And so Peter came home to get married.

"Just think," said Lily. "What would we have done if this had happened a few months ago, when the Suez crisis was on? There'd have been no chance of a wedding then – he'd never have got leave."

Then, to everyone's amazement, Sonia insisted on having a 'big do'.

"Has she got no shame?" Lily was indignant. "Let's just hope she doesn't have the cheek to wear white!"

215

But even Sonia balked at defying that convention, and chose a long, full-skirted dress in pale pink chiffon.

Josie, sitting in a front pew with her family, thought the bride, with her fluffy blonde hair, looked like a huge candyfloss, then chided herself for being catty. Lily was thankful that Sonia's bouquet, the largest she'd ever seen, helped to disguise her advanced pregnancy. There was a good chance that it wouldn't be obvious on the photographs. Sid was stiff-necked, although he couldn't help a sense of pride as he saw his two sons – for Dennis was best man – standing side by side at the front of the church. Georgina, although not an official guest, had slipped into the back of the church only to find Pauline already there, who whispered, "I thought Fergal was coming."

Georgina shook her head. "He couldn't get leave."

Josie had always expected to be a bridesmaid at Peter's wedding, but instead, Sonia had two small girls dressed in cream frills, one of whom was in tears because she'd lost her two front teeth that morning. There were some stern expressions of disapproval among the guests, but Peter, looking smart in his Naval uniform, appeared not to notice. At the reception in a room over the Co-op, Josie had to admit that his cheerful face did much to dispel any impression of a 'shotgun wedding'.

"Do you think they'll be happy?" murmured Lily to Sid. "It's not the best start to a marriage."

"We can only hope. Still, at least Peter didn't try to sidle out of it, I'll give him that."

Lily watched her son awkwardly slip an arm around his new wife's expansive waist. They were going to make their first home with Sonia's parents, at least until the baby was born. As he glanced across at her with a wry smile, Lily could only think: Well, my lad, you've made your bed, you must lie on it.

Chapter 24

Georgina continued to write regularly to Fergal. "He's a great reader," she told Josie. "So fortunately, we can discuss books. We're both reading *How Green Was My Valley* at the moment."

"I wondered what you found to write about! I think I'd be stuck for words."

Pauline, when Josie once mentioned it, agreed. "I'm not much of a letter writer. Mind you, I might have made an effort for Fergal." She glanced sideways at Josie. "They're just pen-friends, you say?"

"Oh yes, there's nothing in it," Josie said. "Hey, you've gone all pink! Don't tell me you liked him? You dark horse, Pauline Machin!"

"And why shouldn't I? If you mean because of that scar, well, I know what that's like. Having something wrong with your face, I mean. Remember my buck teeth as a kid?"

Josie was quick to reassure her. "They're fine now."

"Well, as good as they'll ever be. And then I had to wear those awful braces!" She looked down. "I just thought he had a lovely voice, that's all."

Josie grinned. "You're obviously a sucker for

the Irish lilt. Anyway, I thought you had a boyfriend."

"I have, but I don't think it's going anywhere. How about you?"

"Too busy," Josie said loftily. "Furthering my career!"

"Get you!"

The two girls laughed. They were walking back from Longton Indoor Market, where they'd been to buy some nylons, and to do a few errands for their mothers. The large market hall was situated behind the impressive Town Hall, which had been rebuilt in 1863, and there was one particular stall where Lily always bought her underwear. Josie hated shopping there! It was full of old men's long johns, and women's opera-top vests and volumin-ous cotton knickers. Suppose someone saw her, and thought she was buying the frumpy interlock underwear for herself? Josie liked a bit of glamour, and bought her own 'panties', from Dorothy Perkins in the High Street.

"I like cotton next to my skin," Lily insisted. "I don't hold with nylon underwear. It's not healthy."

"I bet she'd like silk, though," Georgina said, when Josie laughingly told her.

"Pigs would fly before she got the chance to try it," Josie retorted. "The same goes for me."

It seemed so unfair, Georgina thought. Here she was with money to spare – her father refused to let her pay anything towards household expenses. He seemed so much more generous lately – she even received a clothing allowance.

She could easily afford to buy Josie a present of pretty silk lingerie for her birthday or for Christmas, but of course it would never do. It would put her friend in an impossible position, because Georgina knew Josie would feel she had to buy an equally expensive present back. Pride, Georgina thought wryly, gets in the way of a lot of things.

A couple of months later, on the morning of her eighteenth birthday, Georgina came downstairs to breakfast in an anticipatory, if not exhilarated mood. Birthdays at Rosemount always followed the same routine. There would be a single present waiting for her at breakfast, and then the occasion wouldn't be mentioned again.

"Good morning." Alice was busy at the cooker, and didn't turn round. "Morning." Georgina paused; then, as her mother didn't say anything else, wandered into the dining-room. The table was already laid, but there was no wrapped parcel. So, no kiss, no birthday greeting, no present. They'd forgotten! Georgina stood for a moment, and despite the warmth of the June morning, felt a chill creep around her heart. Even this, the one day of the year when she was supposed to feel special, even this was denied her. It wasn't the lack of a gift, heaven knew she didn't lack anything material, it was the thoughtfulness she missed, some warmth, some emotion in that beautiful barren house.

She went back into the kitchen. "Father's late

this morning." Despite her efforts, her voice was tight with disappointment.

"He certainly is! Do you want a boiled egg?"

"Yes, please." Georgina helped herself to a bowl of cornflakes and, feeling disconsolate, went back into the dining-room.

Alice, wondering what on earth was taking William so long, put the eggs on to boil. She was staring blankly at the wall before her, when she recalled that it was Georgina's birthday. The reason she'd forgotten was because she hadn't had a present to wrap.

"I'll deal with it this year," William had told her. "Leave it to me."

Well, this will be a first, Alice thought, as she put bread under the grill to toast. He's never chosen a present for her in his life, or for me – I normally get a cheque. She frowned in exasperation. What on earth was he doing up there? His breakfast would be ruined at this rate.

William was standing at the front bedroom window, peering through the leaded panes, and getting more and more impatient as the minutes ticked by. Then at last he breathed a sigh of relief. It was about time!

Georgina heard him come down the stairs, his heavy tread quicker than usual, but instead of coming into the dining-room, he unlocked the front door and went out. She looked up, puzzled. That was strange; he hadn't had any breakfast! Then she shrugged and, having finished her cereal, stared blindly before her. At least Josie won't forget, she thought. And the postman hadn't been yet.

But almost immediately the front door was flung open and her father was striding across the hall and standing in the doorway before her. His heavy features were flushed, his tone peremptory.

"Come with me!"

Startled, Georgina obeyed in some bewilderment, while Alice, who had come out of the kitchen at the commotion, followed. William went out through the front door, then as his wife and daughter emerged stood to one side, his arm extended in an expansive gesture.

"Happy birthday!"

Georgina gasped as she saw the brand new Austin A35. Green and gleaming, it stood proudly on the drive, the driver's door invitingly open.

"Go on," urged William. "Get in. See how it feels!"

Tentatively, Georgina got into the driving seat, and placed her hands on the steering wheel. The car had a distinctive 'new' smell, and it felt exciting, full of the promise of adventure. She glanced at her parents – William's expression was triumphant, while Alice looked stupefied!

Turning her attention back to the car, Georgina touched the intriguing dashboard, ran her hand admiringly over the upholstery, and then swung out her long slim legs and stood before them, her face glowing.

William said gruffly, "There's a course of lessons booked for you at the British School of Motoring. Just fix up a convenient time."

Georgina looked again at the car. Her own car! Her father had given her the independence she'd always longed for! Thrilled, impulsively she flung her arms around him. "Thank you, oh, thank you! It's absolutely fabulous!"

William, with his daughter's arms clinging to him was almost unmanned. Overcome with emotion, he hesitated, then awkwardly hugged her to him. But the intimate moment was all too brief. Georgina, suddenly recovering herself, drew back in confusion and embarrassment. William nodded, and not trusting himself to speak, turned away. The gesture had been like a velvet sword – reminding him that not since his daughter was a baby, could he ever remember her showing him spontaneous affection. And that insight hurt!

Alice watched the scene with mystification. This was such unexpected extravagance! And why had William been so secretive about it? What was happening here? For one moment, watching her husband and daughter, she had felt excluded, of no consequence, and it was a sensation she didn't much care for.

After an intensive course, Georgina passed her driving test, and was determined that having a car would bring a new dimension not only to her life, but also to Josie's.

Their first step, she decided, should be to join a Tennis Club. The nearest was a few miles away in an area considered 'very residential', or as Lily would put it, 'posh'. The fees, naturally, reflected this. But Josie, horrified at the cost of a subscription, was adamant. "I can't possibly afford to pay that!"

"I never intended you to," Georgina told her. "I want to pay for both of us. I can easily afford it."

"Oh, no," Josie said. "No way!"

"Why not?"

"Because," Josie said stiffly, "I don't accept charity – even from you!"

It was Sunday afternoon, and they'd gone for a stroll around Queen's Park. Already, with September on the wane, there was a hint of autumn in the air, and soon the trees would be shedding their leaves. Georgina knew it wasn't the ideal time to join a Tennis Club. But, weather permitting, even in the winter games could be played, and there were bound to be social events. Now, Josie was putting obstacles in the way!

"This damned working-class pride!" Georgina exploded. "Don't you see how it holds people back! Why shouldn't I pay for you? You're my best friend, for heaven's sake!"

Josie stared grimly ahead. "I know. But I've never accepted money from you before, and I'm not going to start now!"

"Oh, rubbish!"

Georgina turned away in anger and began to walk faster. It was all very well going dancing and to the pictures, she fumed, but there was more to life than that. Now she had the car, they'd be able to have more fun. Maybe go to the Theatre Royal in Hanley, and to the Victoria Hall to listen to concerts. Because no longer could her father object to her travelling on public transport at night. And she really did want to join the Tennis Club!

Josie, hurrying to keep up with Georgina's long strides, pleaded, "Don't be angry. Look at it from my point of view!"

"And you look at it from mine!" Georgina flashed. "If you don't join, then neither shall I. Your pride is holding me back, as well as yourself!"

Josie was flabbergasted. She'd never seen the other girl so angry. She swallowed and dug her hands sulkily in her pockets. They walked along the tree-lined path in icy silence, which was broken only when a small Shetland sheepdog came running up and circled around them, barking.

"Hey!" Josie twisted to avoid its snapping jaws, then realising the dog was being playful, bent to pat it.

"Debbie! Come here!" Both girls glanced up to see a couple walking towards them. The man, wearing a green tweed hat, came forward, blustering and brandishing a lead, while the grey-haired woman, her legs bowed with arthritis, followed slowly.

"What an unusual colour!" Georgina said, as the dog's owner grabbed its scruff and clipped the lead on.

"Yes," the woman gave a gentle proud smile. "She's almost silver. People always comment on it."

The two girls turned and watched as they

walked slowly away, the little dog prancing beside them. The small encounter had helped to defuse their quarrel. "Don't let's fall out about it," Georgina said. "I don't mean to be patronising, you know."

"I know you don't," Josie admitted. She glanced sideways. "You think I'm being selfish, don't you?"

"I think you're looking at it from too narrow a viewpoint," Georgina evaded. "Go on, Josie. Live dangerously!"

Josie grinned. That was more like Georgina – she was always careful not to hurt anyone's feelings. "All right then," she capitulated. "But just between ourselves, mind? And," she added with some embarrassment, "thank you very much."

Georgina whirled round and hugged her. "Brilliant! We'll show them! Talk about Wimbledon – it'll be Althea Gibson and Little Mo all over again!"

Josie had no worries about her standard of tennis. Georgina had passed on her coaching tips and, being naturally good at sport, Josie was now an equally good player. And so the two girls joined the club. But although Josie enjoyed the social side, she found some aspects irritating. At the hotel she was used to the vagaries of the wealthy, but it was one thing to be talked down to when you were a mere member of staff, another when you were supposed to be on an equal footing. And some of the female members seemed unable to do anything else.

Georgina just laughed at them. "You don't have

to take any notice. It's not just you they're like that with, they're always the same. Some people seem to think they're superior to the rest of us on this planet."

But Josie couldn't help bridling. Their voices were so snooty, their tones so piercing it was almost painful to listen.

As Christmas drew near, not only did the Club hold their own 'bash', but the two girls, as Georgina had hoped, began to receive invitations to parties at the homes of other members.

"I'm going to have to buy some new clothes," grumbled Josie one Saturday night.

"Look on it as an investment," Georgina told her. "It's time you and I got ourselves boyfriends, and we're not having any luck here!"

They were sitting on the balcony at the King's Hall, a ballroom in Stoke Town Hall, listening to the male vocalist singing the latest hit, 'Young Love'.

"Very apt," Josie said, "I don't think! You're right, you know – we'll be getting left behind!"

"I heard the other day that Heather's already pregnant!"

"That didn't take long," Josie said, then grinned. "Remember how we used to tease her about him being slow?"

"Well, he obviously made up for it once they got married!"

"Rather her than me," Josie said. "I'm not ready for that yet."

"Do you ever hear anything about Marlene?"

"Oh, didn't I tell you? She's going out with a married man. Someone she met at work."

"Like mother like daughter then!"

They both laughed and then fell silent, Josie's thoughts turning uneasily to Alice Hawkins, as they so often did.

"Yes, we really will be left behind if we don't do something," said Georgina eventually.

"We're only eighteen," Josie pointed out.

"I know," Georgina looked down at the ball-room, "and we've been going to dances for eighteen months. In all that time, how many boys have we met we really liked?"

"Two," admitted Josie.

"Exactly. And that was one each – Dominic and Rob. I tell you what, let's have a wager. The first one to get a boyfriend before the New Year wins!"

"That's easy," protested Josie. "We both get asked out all the time!"

"I said a proper boyfriend, not a couple of dates!" Georgina giggled. "What do you think?"

"You're on!"

The two girls went back downstairs, where almost immediately a heavily perspiring youth with glistening Brylcreemed hair and drainpipe trousers appeared before them and jerked his head at Josie.

"I don't think this is him," whispered Georgina, and they struggled to control their laughter.

Then Josie apologised. "Private joke, sorry!" and to make amends got up to dance with him.

Georgina remained where she was, deep in

thought. Her suggestion might be a joke but it would be nice to have someone special. Sometimes she wondered whether she was destined always to carry within her a small cold cell of loneliness. No-one had touched her heart in the way that Dominic had. Even after all this time, the memory lingered, although she despised herself for allowing it to. After all, she wasn't sixteen any more, although she knew she was still an incurable romantic. And that mystified her. She would have thought that with her harsh upbringing she would be more of a realist.

Anyway, she thought, watching the dancers down in the ballroom, at least the wager will be a bit of fun! I wonder who will be the first – me or Josie?

Chapter 25

Lily seemed to spend much of her time worrying about their baby granddaughter. Sonia's baby, at almost ten months, was a beautiful child, with soft curly blonde hair, sky-blue eyes, and a smile that went straight to your heart. But Lily's concern was not that there was anything wrong with little Kay – it was her mother who was the problem.

"It's a good job our Peter's away at sea so much," Lily grumbled to Sid. "It's the only way he'll get fed properly. Sonia never cooks, just heats everything out of a tin. And what use is that to a growing child?"

"Kay looks all right," Sid pointed out.

"Maybe. But these early years lay the foundation to a good constitution. I tell you, Sid, that girl spends all her time smoking and reading trashy romances. You can write your name in the dust on her furniture!"

"At least they've got some now," he said, "even if it is second-hand."

"Yes, and you'd think she'd want to look after it!"

Once the baby was born, Peter, blessing his foresight in saving his lump sum from the Navy, had put down a deposit on a small terraced house in a street within walking distance of his parents'. It was Lily's firm opinion that he'd chosen the location so that someone could keep an eye on his flighty wife while he was away! She tried not to be the interfering mother-in-law but, as she told Sid, she only had to set foot in Sonia's house for her fingers to itch to do some cleaning.

"She's lazy, Sid, and that's the top and bottom of it," Lily complained.

But her husband wouldn't be drawn. "It's her home, love, and she has a right to live in it as she sees fit."

"But . . ."

On the receiving end of one of Sid's stern looks, Lily subsided.

Josie, slouched in an armchair reading *Woman's Own*, could see both points of view. But she hated the way women were judged purely by their housekeeping skills – and other women were the main culprits. Weren't women supposed to *have* brains? Glancing at her mother, she thought with a stab of guilt: we're not all content to spend our lives cleaning.

She adored little Kay, just as she did Dennis's son, Johnny. But Josie had seen how much work a family made. For now, she and Georgina were resolved to have some fun. This was a word that had only just crept into her vocabulary. The first time she'd used it, even her father had looked up from his paper.

"*Fun*," he mimicked. "What sort of word is that?"

Josie felt embarrassed. "I hear it all the time at the Tennis Club."

"The only time I've heard it used is to describe a funfair," Lily said tartly. She wasn't sure she liked her daughter acquiring 'airs and graces'.

"I suppose some of the expressions we use could be strange to other people," Josie pointed out.

Lily doubted it very much but wisely kept silent.

However, one expression – or rather a matter of pronunciation – Josie did find difficult to adopt. This was the use of the long 'a', the very one that Marlene had criticised in Georgina's speech. Josie was used to visitors using it at the hotel – after all many were from London or at least 'down south'. And of course to Georgina, educated privately, it came naturally. But with Josie, any attempt to change the way she spoke sounded false, and affected. And so she adamantly refused to change. It was her identity, after all. Had she but known it, this was one thing she had in common with William Hawkins, even though he'd recognised early in life that people judged you on your accent. As a matter of principle, he'd refused to change his pronunciation, much to the contempt of Alice whose own vowels, of course, were beyond reproach.

"I'm a Potteries man," he'd told her. "Why should I pretend to be someone else?"

Now it was Josie's turn to realise that her speech marked her out as being from a different social class. And this was cruelly brought home to her by an incident that happened at a party, just before Christmas. Leaving Georgina downstairs chatting to a rather dishy young man in a white polo-neck sweater, Josie slipped upstairs to the bedroom where all the coats were piled on to a bed. She'd left her hanky in her coat pocket, and to her embarrassment her nose was beginning to run. Great timing, she thought – very glamorous I must say!

As she walked along the landing, the bedroom door was ajar and suddenly she heard the carrying voice. "Of course, they're letting anyone join the Club, these days. Have you seen that girl with the bushy dark hair?"

"Josie, you mean?"

"Yes. Well, darling, she's all right, but as soon as she opens her mouth . . ."

The sentence remained unfinished, but Josie could just imagine the expressive shrug that followed it. At first humiliation and then anger swept over her and her impulse was to burst into the room but instead, with her nose now running freely, she had to rush to the bathroom.

"Useless stuff!" She screwed up a sheet of Bronco toilet paper, flung it down the lavatory and rooted under her skirt for the hem of her waist slip. It was a bit of a struggle, but eventually she managed to lift it high enough to wipe her running nose. If she'd faced those snobs in that state, it would only have given them something else to bitch about!

But Josie's dander was up and she flung open

the bathroom door and marched along the landing to the bedroom. She'd show them, show them up for what they were – supercilious, po-faced, spiteful cats! Every time she opened her mouth, eh? Well, she'd open it this time, and they'd get an earful! But when she flung open the bedroom door, the room was empty.

In a thoroughly bad mood, Josie stomped back down the stairs, squeezing uncaringly past a young man who was coming up. He turned and gazed after the girl with a face like a thundercloud. At least she seemed to have some life in her, unlike most of the girls here. Sometimes he thought that if he heard one more polite platitude, he'd die of boredom! And that magnificent hair!

Georgina was still talking to the 'polo-neck' bloke when Josie went back to the party. Most guests were crowded into the sitting-room, a lovely spacious room with a red and blue Axminster carpet. In the large bay window stood a Christmas tree, resplendent with silver, gold and red baubles. And the people giving the party were nice too; it was just a pity about some of their guests, she thought grimly. Her gaze scanned the room, resting on one or two women she thought might have been responsible for the insulting remarks. One caught her eye and gave a slight smile. She was blonde, heavily made up, with a long cigarette holder. Was it her? Josie gave a tight smile back – she couldn't be sure.

Not wanting to intrude on Georgina, Josie wandered over to where the food was laid out on a white cloth-covered table at one end of the room, and began to inspect what was left. Getting angry always made her ravenous. But even as she began to fill her plate, she was still smarting from the remarks she'd heard. *Every time she opens her mouth!* That hurt, it really hurt. Because she knew her grammar was all right. Since she'd been friends with Georgina, Josie had worked hard to improve herself. But there was one insurmountable problem. It was one thing to speak properly, another to sound what local people would call 'lah-de-dah'. She would be a laughing stock, and Josie knew it. In any case, she thought, why should I deny my roots? Intent on her musings, she turned away from the table, only to find herself facing a tall young man, whose eyes were glinting with amusement.

He smiled. "Hello, I don't think we've met."

Josie wondered what he found so funny. "No, I don't think we have," she said shortly.

"You look a bit happier now," he said, moving slightly and picking up a plate.

"Pardon?"

"I passed you on the stairs," he grinned. "I wouldn't like to be the one who'd upset you!"

Josie reddened. "Was it that obvious?"

"Well, perhaps the way you pushed past me as if I didn't exist was a clue!" But his smile took any sting from his words, and Josie smiled back.

"Can I get you a drink?" He indicated the bottles at the end of the table.

"Yes, please. A white wine would be nice." She

watched him select a couple of ham sandwiches and a slice of pork pie.

He handed her his plate. "If you can find somewhere to sit, I'll bring the drinks over."

Nicely manipulated, thought Josie with respect. I think I'm going to like this one. And her first impression remained as they sat companionably in a corner, Josie sitting in an armchair, the young man whose name she still didn't know perched on the arm.

"I'm Nick Hamilton, by the way."

"Josie Ford," she said, nibbling on chunks of cheese and pineapple. "I haven't seen you at the Tennis Club?"

"That's because I'm not a member," he said. "I'm here as a friend of the family." He bent forward, "I think they were short of eligible young men!"

Josie laughed.

"And what does Josie Ford do for a living?"

He listened while Josie told him about her job at the hotel.

"The Royal, eh – very salubrious! I've been to a few 'do's' there."

"I hope they were good."

"Excellent."

They were quiet for a moment while each enjoyed their food, then after a sip of wine, Josie said, "And what do you do?"

"Oh, a bit of this and a bit of that."

She cast a suspicious glance at him and he laughed.

"All legal and above board, I assure you." He didn't elaborate, and Josie didn't like to probe further. She cast a furtive glance at him. A strong face, she thought. Thin yes, with an aquiline nose, but his features were arranged in a way she found distinctly attractive.

"And how old is Josie Ford?"

"You ask a lot of questions," she said tartly. "I'm eighteen and a half."

Then she realised how childish that sounded. Only kids added halves to their age.

"Well, I'm twenty-four, so that's just about right!"

She laughed, and looking up at him her pulse quickened as his gaze met and held her own. The room was getting even more crowded, and they both leaned towards each other as people squeezed by.

"We're bound to get split up in a minute," Nick said. "I'd like to see you again. Would you like to go to a film or something?"

Josie would definitely like; she'd like that very much indeed. But instinctively she knew that this wouldn't be any casual date – already there was magnetism between them. I'm not ready for this, she thought in panic. I'm too young to get involved with someone, this isn't how I planned things. But then with the memory that she'd let her head rule her heart with Rob, only to regret it, she looked up at him and said, "I'd love to."

"Good. You took so long, I was beginning to

wonder!" But his lips were twitching, and she laughed with him.

They arranged to meet a couple of days later outside the Odeon in Hanley, and then seconds later their hostess bustled over.

"So there you are. Excuse us, won't you," she said to Josie. "It's just that there's someone I want to introduce Nick to."

Josie watched as Nick was dragged across the room to a pale but expensively dressed girl on the other side. You're too late, she thought in triumph. I got to him first!

As she drove them both home, Georgina, listening to Josie prattle on about Nick, felt a pang of jealousy. Not that she wanted Nick for herself – she hadn't even spoken to him – but she was jealous of the dreamy look on Josie's face. She remembered that feeling.

"It looks as though you'll be winning the bet!" she said.

"What about that bloke in the polo-neck? You seemed to be doing okay with him?"

"Yes, he was all right, I suppose," Georgina said. "He's asked me to go to another party with him."

"There you are, then! That's both of us fixed up."

Georgina glanced sideways at her, her lips twitching. "His name's Felix."

Josie spluttered. "Felix! Nobody's called *Felix*, unless they're a villain in a Victorian melodrama!

He hasn't got a thin moustache, has he?"

Georgina giggled. "No, he has not!" But, she thought ruefully, neither does he make my bones melt, like Dominic did.

Josie had decided not to tell her friend about what she'd overheard on the landing. At least Nick had liked her. Now *he* spoke beautifully, and he'd got a lovely voice – sort of gravelly. In fact, Nick Hamilton was pretty dishy all round!

Chapter 26

During the following month, both girls saw what they jokingly called their 'swains', on a regular basis. Georgina went out with Felix, and Josie with Nick. And then the two friends decided it was time to make up a foursome.

"They should have plenty in common," Georgina pointed out. "They both went to university, for one thing."

"Nick says he did. Mind you, he doesn't seem to have done much with it," Josie grumbled. "Why doesn't he get a proper job, instead of just buying and selling stuff."

"He's into pottery, you say?"

"Yeah. He picks up seconds, ends of ranges, in fact anything he thinks will sell. And he's branching out from pottery – he told me he'd bought a job lot of mirrors the other day."

"He seems to do all right out of it," Georgina said. "That's a nice car he's got. I saw you drive by the other day."

"Oh, that isn't his. It belongs to a friend. He borrows it sometimes. Usually he takes me out in a tatty old van." Josie cupped her chin in her hands as she watched Georgina tidy her make-up drawer. "I never know what to say when people ask me what he does."

"Say he's a market trader."

"That sounds as if he stands on the market!"

"How do you know he doesn't?"

"I don't," Josie said glumly. "And it wouldn't surprise me if he does!"

Georgina laughed. "You thought you'd only meet chinless wonders through the Tennis Club, didn't you? It just goes to show – you never can tell in this life."

"Absolutely. Mind you, he isn't a member, although I'm trying to persuade him. Of course, you would choose someone who's an estate agent!"

Georgina laughed and opened her dressing-table drawer. She took out a box. "Look, what do you think? It's a birthday present."

Josie stared at the silver cuff-links. "For Felix? Aren't you going to give him the wrong impression? After all, I thought you said it wasn't serious."

"It isn't," Georgina said. "At least I don't think so. But he's spent a lot of money on me, you know. We've been several times to the pictures, and then he took me to the Theatre Royal. He always buys the best tickets."

"How much *do* you like him?" Josie was curious. Georgina didn't talk much about this mysterious Felix whereas, as Lily said, it was 'Nick this and Nick that' with Josie.

There was a silence, then finally Georgina said, "I don't know, and that's the truth, Josie. I like being with him, but . . ."

241

"He's no Dominic."

Georgina nodded.

"It's no use, you know," Josie said gently. "You're going to have to forget him."

"I know. And I will – I've got to! Have your parents come round yet? You know, about Nick being six years older?"

Josie grinned. "They've had to. Once I'd pointed out that Dad's several years older than Mum, they hadn't a leg to stand on."

"Well, I'm warning you, if we do all meet up, he'll have to pass a stern test from me!"

"The same goes for this Felix," Josie retorted.

It was Nick who came up with the idea that they should all go to see the Illuminations at Blackpool.

"It'll be fun," he grinned. There he goes again with that word, Josie thought with amusement. The middle classes thought life was all about having fun, as they called it. I'd like them to try and live on a labourer's wage with four children, she thought. They wouldn't have much time or energy left for fun. Then she realised she was being unfair. After all, there had been plenty of laughter in her childhood, and wasn't that the same thing?

Georgina, however, was thrilled at the idea of Blackpool. She'd never been to the popular seaside resort, as William and Alice Hawkins considered it the playground of the workers. Bournemouth, they'd always told her, was far more 'select'.

"Can I have one of those 'Kiss Me Quick' hats,

like I've seen on the films?" she asked.

Josie laughed. "Only if you want every male you pass making you an offer! I think you'd better stay close to me, Georgina Hawkins."

"I'll have Felix to look after me!"

And so she did. But Felix, they all discovered, was more interested in the interior of Yates's Wine Lodge. Okay, Josie thought, it is winter, and it is bitterly cold. But we haven't come all this way just to spend our time drinking; he can do that at home, for heaven's sake!

"I had no idea he liked a drink," Georgina muttered. "At the theatre, he only had time for one during the interval. And funnily enough, I've never been to a pub with him. But I did wonder why his breath always smells of peppermints."

Josie glanced at Nick, who, tight-lipped, was watching Felix make his fourth trip to the bar. She studied Georgina's boyfriend. He was very good-looking and he certainly knew how to dress. Again, he was wearing a white polo-neck beneath a V-necked navy sweater and his trousers were beautifully tailored. A bit of a dandy, was Josie's opinion, and she didn't trust vain men.

"Are you nearly ready?" Nick said, when Felix returned. "It's getting late, and the girls want to see some more of the lights."

"Sure thing!" Felix drained his glass. "Come on, gorgeous." He held out his hand to Georgina, who, with an apologetic glance at the others, trailed behind him.

Nick and Josie joined them on the pavement

outside and they crossed the wide main road, then waited for a noisy tram to pass, before reaching the busy promenade on the other side.

But even Georgina couldn't remain downcast for long, as the two couples strolled hand-in-hand, enthralled by the sheer technical brilliance of the imaginative tableaux. There were cries of, "Oh, look at that one!" while both girls, entranced by one of an 80 ft *Swan Lake* ballet, stood listening with delight to the accompanying music as illuminated Giant Swans slowly revolved. Felix, however, preferred the Hula Hula dance display.

"That figures," muttered Josie, and Nick grinned, saying, "For my money, you can't beat the Queen of the Lights." They all turned and craned their necks upwards to look at the brilliant crown on the top of Blackpool Tower. But eventually, almost dizzy with the wonderful sights they'd seen, they neared Bispham, to realise they were not only chilled, but hungry, and turned to retrace their steps.

"How about a fish-and-chip supper?" Nick suggested, and laughed as he was almost deafened by a chorus of, *"Yesssssssssssssss!"*

But amidst the laughter, Josie was watching Felix. He certainly had charm and she could understand why Georgina had been attracted to him. But the drinking episode had disturbed her. She'd seen the misery a heavy drinker could cause. Not first-hand – Sid came home mellow rather than drunk, but more than one child in their street was terrified of their dad after he'd been 'down the pub'. And she didn't suppose it was any different which class you were born into. But she pushed such thoughts from her mind, joining in the merriment as the four of them turned and linked arms to walk back down the wide promenade. Nick began singing 'Oh, I Do Like To Be Beside The Seaside,' and their young, strong voices chorused out the words, prompting many a passing grin, some children joining in as they clung in excitement to their parents' hands.

"Just look at them," Georgina laughed. "I bet they've never been up so late. I wish I'd been brought here as a child – it must be like fairyland to them."

"You've had a deprived childhood," laughed Nick. "My parents often brought me. How about you two?" He turned to look first at Josie and then at Felix.

"I came once," offered Josie. "I was only little though. I just remember our Peter being seasick on the boats at the Pleasure Beach."

"And he ended up a sailor!" laughed Georgina.

"I never came," grumbled Felix. "But then I grew up in India. Mind you, there were lots of colourful festivals."

"I'd forgotten that," Josie said. "It must have been fascinating."

"Flaming hot, you mean!" By now Felix's mood was turning truculent, not helped by frequent swigs from a half-bottle of brandy he'd bought. Still clutching Georgina's hand, he staggered to sit on the low sea-wall, dragging her with him, and tried to pull her on to his lap. Georgina jerked away angrily, and stalked off, her face red with humiliation. He'd done nothing but show her up all day! Josie and Nick followed, leaving Felix to stumble after them.

Nick turned to Josie, and said quietly, "What do you think? Once we've had something to eat, shall we call it a day before he gets any worse?"

"Definitely. I don't fancy going to the Pleasure Beach with *him*!"

He squeezed her hand. "It's a pity Georgina had to work this morning, or we could have come earlier and gone there first. Never mind, I'll bring you another time – just the two of us."

Ten minutes later, Josie settled into the passenger seat of the borrowed blue Ford Zephyr, while Georgina, with an uneasy glance at Felix, sat beside him in the back. But within minutes of setting off, Nick began to exchange exasperated glances with Josie, as again and again, they heard Georgina hissing, "Don't, Felix. I've told you . . . stop it! Oh, for heaven's sake!"

There came the sound of struggling, then a sharp slap, at which Nick slammed on the brakes and the car came to an abrupt halt throwing them all forwards. He turned round, his face thunderous. "Pack it in, Felix, or you can make your own way home!"

Josie also twisted round and, dismayed to see Georgina's mussed-up hair and scarlet face, flung open the car door and got out. Angrily, she opened the rear door. "In the front!" Her voice cut like a knife, and with a bad-tempered shrug, Felix stumbled out and slumped into the passenger seat.

As the car sped away, Georgina, with a shame-faced glance at Josie, rearranged her clothing and smoothed down her hair.

"Sorry," she said through clenched teeth.

"Put it down to experience," Josie whispered.

"I'd like to break his bloody neck!" And, she thought, glaring at the back of Felix's head – those silver cuff-links are staying in my dressing-table drawer!

Chapter 27

And so Josie won the bet, because New Year came and passed, and at the beginning of spring she was still 'going out' with Nick. When she was with him even the sky seemed brighter. Yet part of her, a part she didn't like very much, fought against the way she felt. Although she wanted a boyfriend like the other girls, Josie had never anticipated feeling like this. Not when she was only eighteen. She was the one who'd always declared that she wanted to live a bit first. Yet now, thoughts of Nick consumed every minute of her life. Nick made her laugh, he made her wistful – he made her feel special. And Josie was discovering new things about herself, new feelings, new emotions. She winced at how contemptuous she'd been of other girls in the past. It had been Josie the virtuous, Josie the one who would always be in control. Now, she only had to feel Nick's arms around her, his lips on hers, to know that she hadn't had a clue what love was all about.

But what neither Josie nor Georgina had realised was how much a boyfriend on the scene would affect their friendship. Georgina would give Josie a lift to college one morning and one evening a week – a condition of their day-release course was that they gave up one evening a week of their own time. But no longer could they plan their Saturday nights out, although Josie always kept Sunday afternoons free.

As a result, Georgina was beginning to find herself increasingly at a loss. Sometimes, independent now in her 'Green Dragon' which was the name she'd christened her beloved car, she went dancing at Trentham. She could usually find someone she knew, often from the Town Hall where she worked, or occasionally one of the girls from college would be there. Sometimes she would see Josie and Nick, but she was always careful not to play 'gooseberry'. Pauline now had a boyfriend, although she said she wasn't actually 'courting'.

"He thinks we are," she told the other two girls. "I'm not so sure. He's a bit of a flirt, to tell you the truth, and as we work on the same potbank, I get to hear all that goes on!"

Georgina began to feel left out, although, as she told Josie, she'd rather be on her own than with 'that rat, Felix'. It wasn't that she was too choosy to go out on dates, but she'd discovered that an evening at the pictures usually meant being kissed and cuddled in the back row, and increasingly she just wasn't interested. If only she could meet someone who made her feel like Dominic had, she thought wistfully. Once she made the mistake of saying so to Josie, who was scathing in her disapproval.

"For heaven's sake, Georgina, it'll be three years

249

soon. You can't go on holding a torch for him all your life – it's barmy. He could be married for all you know!" She bent to adjust the footrest on Kay's pushchair. It was Sunday afternoon, and they were taking the toddler for an airing in Queen's Park.

"I know – you needn't rub it in!" Georgina smiled down at the little face staring up at her. "You're a poppet, aren't you? You know, Josie, I just can't believe we were there at the . . . well, not the conception obviously, but we were there when Peter and Sonia met. And now look at the result!"

"Mmm. If you say so."

"Are you still not keen on her – Sonia, I mean?"

"Oh, she's not so bad, and of course we wouldn't be without our little sweetheart. But, well, as you know, I think our Peter could have done a lot better for himself."

"Is he happy?"

"Seems to be. But then," Josie muttered darkly, "he's away a lot."

Georgina was silent for a bit, then said, "I heard from Fergal yesterday."

"You're always hearing from him."

"Yes, but this was different. He's coming to the end of his service." She glanced at Josie. "It's a big decision for him, whether to re-enlist or not."

"I thought the Navy was the only family he had?" Josie frowned. "And what would he do? In Civvie Street, I mean?"

Georgina shrugged. "He has no idea. But he says if he does decide to come out, he'd rather

250

like to settle around here – he really liked it when he came. He also says," she hesitated, "I don't know whether I should tell you this . . ."

"Hey, you've already started – you can't stop now!"

"Peter's thinking of asking Sonia whether she'd put Fergal up as a lodger. It would bring in extra money, he'd be company for her, and . . ." Georgina looked down in embarrassment.

"He wouldn't be any threat, because of his scar!" Josie finished the sentence for her. "It's not a bad idea, though," she said thoughtfully, "He was a nice lad. I liked him."

"So did I," Georgina said quietly.

Josie shot a suspicious glance at her, but Georgina's face was averted as she pointed out a squirrel to Kay. The toddler squealed with delight as she watched the little animal scamper up a tree trunk.

"Mum and Dad are beginning to make a fuss," Josie suddenly said.

"What about?"

"My not bringing Nick home."

Georgina looked at her. "Well, I am a bit surprised. You haven't met his parents either."

"I know. It's funny, isn't it? I mean that we both seem so reluctant."

"Does he talk about his family much?"

"Not a lot. I think I told you that his father died, and his mother married again. I get the impression he doesn't get on too well with his stepfather."

"Why *haven't* your parents met him? Any particular reason?" Georgina had wondered before, but hadn't liked to ask.

Josie hesitated. She felt too ashamed to confess even to Georgina the real reason.

"I just didn't want any pressure, that's all," she said lightly. "You know what families are like, wanting to know if you're serious and all that."

Georgina, who had no idea what a normal family was like, said, "And are you? Serious, I mean? Come on, Josie. We don't have secrets between us."

Josie turned the pushchair into the children's playground and began to unbuckle Kay's harness. To answer Georgina's question she would have to probe too deeply inside herself. "I think it's too early to know," she evaded and, picking up Kay, carried her over to the baby swings.

Georgina watched her for a moment and then, wheeling the pushchair, slowly followed. It was obvious that Josie was hiding something and equally obvious that she didn't want to tell her what it was.

Lily and Sid were, indeed, becoming increasingly mystified as to why their daughter didn't bring her 'young man' home.

"It makes you wonder what's wrong with him!" Lily snapped one evening. She was in a bad mood, after visiting Sonia earlier in the day.

Sid, who had just had an ear-bashing about the state of Sonia's kitchen sink, put down his paper with an air of exasperation. Why, he wondered, did his wife always think he could read her mind. She'd be thinking, and then just burst out with something or other, and half the time he hadn't a clue what she was talking about. "Who?"

"This Nick."

Sid glanced at her, and then reached down to the side of the hearth where he kept his pipe cleaners. He inserted one into the stem of his pipe and began to clean it. "Maybe," he said quietly, "Josie thinks there is something wrong with us."

Lily put her knitting down on to her lap, and stared at him. "Whatever do you mean?"

"She met him at that party she went to. Wasn't it some people from that posh Tennis Club? Stands to reason he doesn't come from a rented terraced house."

Lily looked around her cosy sitting-room. All right, so the cushion covers were made out of remnants off the market, and the armchairs had certainly seen better days, but she'd done her best to make it nice. And it was clean – which was more than she could say about her daughter-in-law's home! "We could all live in Buckingham Palace, if we had the money, Sid."

"Aye, we could," he agreed. "But Josie's young, Lil, and these girls get fanciful ideas."

"How would you know?" Lily looked at her husband in surprise.

"I hear the lasses talking on the potbank. Got their heads in the clouds, most of 'em. They soon come down to earth once they get married."

253

"You make it sound like a prison sentence," Lily retorted. "I don't think you've done so badly out of it!"

"Don't be daft. I didn't mean that." Sid got up in annoyance. "I think I'll go over for a pint."

"You might as well move your bed into that blasted pub," Lily muttered, but Sid ignored her. Lily always got like this when something was bothering her. He was best out of the way – he'd learned that by experience!

Once he'd gone, Lily, who was following a pattern for a white summer cardigan for Kay, picked up her knitting. The more her thoughts whirled, the faster she knitted and purled. Sid's words had shocked her. Could their Josie be ashamed of them? Of her home? Lily shook her head in disbelief. Never! The girl had more sense than that. Lily would lay money on it. No, it was something more, and before long Lily was determined to prise it out of her. "It's time," she said aloud in the empty room, "that you and I had a mother-and-daughter talk, young lady."

A week later, Josie snuggled down in the passenger seat of Nick's car in contentment. He was driving her home from the cinema, where they'd shared a double seat on the back row. Not that she'd seen that much of the film! Nick seemed a bit quiet, and she glanced at him, at his intent profile as he drew up at a set of traffic lights. She loved driving with Nick, there was something intimate about being enclosed with him in such a small space.

Nick however, was feeling far from relaxed. He'd felt in a quandary about his relationship with Josie for some time now. Ever since that split-second encounter on the staircase at the party, she'd rarely been out of his thoughts. Whenever he tried to analyse her attraction for him, he always came up with the same words – her vitality. He'd never met anyone who radiated energy in the same way that Josie did. Even her unruly dark hair seemed alive at times. "Why can't I have sleek, elegant hair like Georgina," she'd wail. But although Georgina was lovely, in a Grace Kelly sort of way, her cool, classical looks weren't for him. He preferred his colourful and fiery Josie any time. And that was Nick's problem. He wasn't sure that she *was* his Josie. When she was in his arms her kisses were as passionate as his own, and often they were both shaken by the intensity of their feelings. But, although at these times he whispered that he loved her, not once had he heard the words he longed for in reply. And so, when he drew the car to a halt at the end of Josie's street and turned off the ignition, he didn't move to kiss her goodnight immediately.

As Josie turned towards him, he looked at her for a moment, then said, "You never let me drive you to the house. Why?"

Josie said carelessly. "Oh, you know what people are like. I don't want all the lace curtains twitching."

"It's more than that though, isn't it, Josie?" Nick stretched out a hand and gently wound one of her curls around his finger. "Is it because then you might have to invite me in? You've never taken me home, you know."

"Neither have you!" Josie was flustered, defensive.

"Maybe I have a reason." Nick looked at her steadily, willing her to gaze at him. He loved this girl; her dark beauty stirred his senses as no-one else ever had. He loved her honesty, her fierce sense of justice, her exhilarating zest for life. And they were good together, right together, he was certain of it. But always he sensed within Josie a reserve, a holding back, and Nick found this disturbing.

Josie remained silent, waiting for him to elaborate, but when he didn't continue, she said, "And what reason's that then?"

Now it was Nick's turn to look away. But he'd begun this conversation, so he had no choice but to tell her the truth. "It's just that I wanted you to have time to get to know me before I exposed you to my home background."

Josie stared at him. "How do you mean?"

"Let's just say that the main entertainment in my home is character assassination – namely mine."

Josie felt horrified. "I don't understand, Nick. Why?"

He shrugged. "You'd have to meet my stepfather to know that."

"Well, he'll have met his match in me, I can tell you," Josie said in indignation. Then, seeing Nick's serious expression, she teased, "Unless he's going to tell me you're an axe-murderer?"

But Nick didn't laugh as she expected, he just said, "Oh, he won't go as far as that – he's far too clever." He took her hand and began to stroke the fingers, one by one. "I just wanted to be sure of our relationship, of our feelings, before I took things further. You must know I love you."

At the huskiness in his voice, Josie felt her eyelids prick with helpless tears. Why did she feel backed into a corner? A corner part of her desperately wanted to be in, and yet her mind kept erecting barriers. Remember the blue muff, it said, remember your grand plans, your determination to have a different life? This won't happen if you marry Nick – a man who buys and sells cheap pottery and gifts is never going to amount to anything. The voice was insidious, its poison instilling doubts that clouded her judgement. Why couldn't he have had a proper job, Josie thought in desperation – one with prospects and security? The Fords were great believers in security. Apart from during the War, Sid had worked on the same potbank ever since he'd left school.

Nick, whose gaze had never left her face, saw her hesitation, her uncertainty, and felt sick with disappointment. He wasn't sure what he'd expected, hoped for – a return declaration of her love for him maybe?

When Josie looked up into his eyes, he looked at her searchingly, saw confusion, bewilderment, and an expression he couldn't read. "Am I rushing you? I don't mean to."

"Perhaps," Josie said shakily.

With a sigh Nick drew her into his arms. "Don't worry about it," he said. "You've got all the time in the world."

Their goodnight kiss was poignant, and Josie thought with despair that she didn't deserve him. She stood and watched the car drive away, and then walked slowly along the street to her home.

Josie Ford, she thought, you've become mercenary. That's your trouble!

Lily was banking up the fire with coal slack in the back room when she heard Josie open the front door. She put the mesh guard in front of the fireplace, and straightened the black half-moon rug before the hearth.

She always liked to leave the room tidy before she went to bed. Not like Sid. If she went up to bed first, he just walked out and left everything, newspapers and all!

"Have a good time, love?" she said, as she went into the scullery to make Josie some cocoa.

"Yes. The film was great. You can't beat a Doris Day."

"I agree." Lily looked at her daughter shrewdly, noting the flush in her cheeks, the brightness of her eyes. Something had got Josie all fired up, that was for sure. Would this be a good time to talk to her? Lily glanced at her daughter, who was leaning against the doorframe, staring into space.

"Penny for 'em?"

"What? Oh, nothing."

Lily put three teaspoons of cocoa powder into an earthenware beaker, added sugar and a little milk and began to stir briskly. The rest of the milk was heating in a saucepan on the gas hob. "This Nick," she said quietly, "when are we going to meet him?"

"I've told you, Mum. Soon."

"That's what you always say." Lily watched the milk bubble, then finished making the cocoa. She handed the earthenware beaker to Josie.

"Come on through to the front room," she said. "The electric fire's been on, so it should still be warm in there."

With reluctance, Josie followed her mother and sat in an armchair. She knew that tone of voice: it meant her mum wanted 'a word' with her. And she had a pretty shrewd idea what it was all about. But Lily's next words both surprised and dismayed her.

"Is it that you're ashamed of us? Of this house?" Lily asked the question bluntly, her eyes fixed on her daughter's face. Josie's appalled expression gave her the answer she'd hoped for.

"Of course not. Surely you don't think that!"

"Your dad does."

Josie felt guilt-stricken. "I'm sorry, Mum – the thought never entered my head."

"Well, that's a blessing, anyway. I thought your dad was wrong, but it upset me a bit hearing him say it. We might not be rich, Josie, but we've always done our best to provide you with a nice home."

"I know you have, both of you. And it is – it always has been. Please, Mum, you must tell him that's not the reason at all."

Lily looked at her daughter's troubled expression. She didn't want to pry, didn't want Josie to think she was interfering, but . . .

"Do you want to talk about it?" she said.

Josie looked down, unable to meet her mother's eyes. "It's just that I feel . . . if I bring Nick home to meet everyone, we'll become more of a couple somehow. And then the questions will start. 'Is it serious?' 'When's the happy day?' You know the sort of thing."

"It's only people's humour, love."

"I know. But don't you see, it makes it almost an accepted fact before it's happened, so to speak."

"And you're not sure that's what you want?"

"I don't know what I want." Josie looked at her mother, at her plaid fur-trimmed slippers, at her careworn face, her greying hair. Hard work and Lily Ford had been bedfellows for as long as Josie could remember, but it wasn't just that. Josie didn't mind hard work. But the year she'd spent at the hotel had opened her eyes even more than visiting Rosemount. The women who stayed there seemed to live such civilised lives. Josie loved to see the hotel restaurant formally laid for meals, with the crisp white tablecloths, napkins, crystal and silver cutlery. She liked the chandeliers and the way the waiters moved discreetly among the tables. She longed to be part of that life, to be able to stay in luxurious hotels, to wear expensive clothes, to be with a man who knew how to order wine. Was that too much to ask for a girl from her background? But Josie also knew that she wanted love, a man she could trust and rely on. Surely that meant that she wasn't just mercenary? Or, in wanting both, was she just reaching for the moon?

Lily was watching the play of emotions on her daughter's face. You're growing up, my love, she thought, and finding like the rest of us that life can get complicated.

"Don't you think you're trying to make decisions too soon?" she said. "You've only known him about three months. And as for bringing him home, well, you're reading far too much into it. It's only natural that we want to meet your boyfriend, Josie. And any comments – well, it's just people's way."

But Josie remained silent, and looking at her downcast face, Lily said, "Is it Nick? Aren't you sure how you feel about him?"

Josie's answer was swift and vehement. "Oh, no, nothing like that. It's just . . ."

"Just what?" Lily said gently. "You can tell me, you know. It won't go any further."

Josie looked at her mum's concerned face and, although she knew that was true, she drained the last of her cocoa, and stood up.

"It's okay, Mum," she said. "It's nothing for you to worry about, I promise. And only I can sort it out." She bent and kissed Lily's cheek.

"I'll sleep on it. Isn't that what you always advise?"

"Aye, things often look better in the morning." But Lily's eyes were troubled as she watched her daughter leave the room. There was disappointment too that Josie hadn't confided in her. It's not easy being a mother, she thought, but then only a fool would expect it to be.

Chapter 28

Georgina, who thought her parents indifferent to what happened in her life, would have been deeply surprised if she'd known of William Hawkins' keen interest. When Alice had told him Georgina was seeing a lot of a young man called Felix, he'd waited impatiently, but silently, for her to bring him home. When this didn't happen, he had, with what he considered great restraint, said nothing. He'd even managed to hide his disapproval of her going off on a day trip to Blackpool. And it had paid off, because the so-called 'romance' came to nothing.

But it was obvious that his daughter was missing Josie Ford. Funny friendship, that, in his opinion. Who would have thought she'd have so much in common with their cleaner's girl? Not that he didn't like Josie – he did – but surely there must be other young ladies she could make friends with, if not at the Town Hall, then at the Tennis Club? Yet Georgina seemed to spend more and more time in her room. Sometimes, when she did go out, he would watch from the window as she drove away, wondering what was going on in that lovely head of hers.

Because she *was* lovely; yet he'd wasted so many years resenting her, overlooking her, and yes, he was forced to admit, even bullying the girl. Although that had been partly her own fault. If she'd stood up to him more, not been so easily cowed, then perhaps he'd have had more respect for her. William despised any form of weakness. He'd found out early in life that the man who forced his willpower on others was the man who got on. But now, seeing the slim, graceful girl who quietly lived in his house, he found it difficult to reconcile her with the timorous child who'd irritated him so much. He realised now it was because of the bitterness he'd allowed to fester within him, bitterness at being denied a son. But then his father had always told him he was pig-headed. Well, he was older and possibly wiser now. There was still time to make it up to Georgina, but for that he needed her to remain at Rosemount for as long as possible. That meant no emotional entanglements. He was very suspicious of those airmail envelopes from that Irish sailor. Who knew what they contained, even though Alice reassured him that Georgina only saw him as a pen-friend. Not that William thought much of any of the young men these days. In his opinion they'd had it too soft. It was hardship that shaped character, not education, the lack of which had never done him any harm.

Alice just thought it typical that Josie would have got herself a steady boyfriend at such an early age. Didn't all the girls in the area do so within a couple of years of leaving school? Most were married by the time they were twenty-one, and babies soon followed. She didn't want that for Georgina, and the fact that she felt such concern surprised her. She'd often wondered if women felt jealous of daughters as they grew up, with the contrast between their fresh young beauty and their own fading looks. But strangely, Alice, who'd thought she hadn't a maternal instinct in her body, was startled to discover feelings of not only pride, but also protectiveness. Georgina might be poised, she was undeniably attractive, but she was also hopelessly naïve and romantic. Alice guessed this by the never-ending stream of novels she borrowed from the public library. And romantics tended to get hurt. Maybe, Alice thought, as early one morning she watched Georgina leave for work, I'm being given a second chance. Ever since William's harsh rejection when Georgina was born, Alice had found it difficult to feel anything other than indifference towards the fretful baby who grew into what she considered an insipid young girl. It was unnatural, she knew, but she'd always accepted it. Now Alice was beginning to realise Georgina had not only become a person to her, but someone she actually cared about. And the discovery brought mixed emotions. Not ones of penitence for the past – Alice considered examining one's conscience a waste of time – but regret that she hadn't felt like this before. Being a mother would have been a much more enjoyable experience.

★

Over the next few months, as Josie's relationship with Nick became more intense, so did her guilt. She knew her lack of commitment was causing Nick pain and hated herself for what she thought of as her mercenary streak.

Georgina too was finding it difficult to understand Josie's reticence.

"My mother asked me this morning if it was serious between you and Nick," she said, one Sunday afternoon. The two girls had been playing tennis in the late May sunshine, and were sitting on the bench at the side of the court.

Josie shrugged. "Don't ask me."

Georgina said softly, "But I am asking you, Josie, and I've asked you before."

Josie remained silent. Although she longed to confide in Georgina, she felt too ashamed. Josie would have to describe how as a child full of envy of Georgina's blue muff, she'd shivered in the cold at the gates of Rosemount, and made a vow to climb up the social ladder. Maybe not in those words of course, she'd been too young, but that was the ugly truth. She would have to reveal that her friendship in those early days had been based on an ulterior motive, that in a way she'd used Georgina. And for Georgina to understand fully, Josie knew she'd have to confess all these things. Her friend, her dearest closest friend, would not only be deeply hurt, but the knowledge would sow a seed of doubt, would undermine their friendship. And that was too great a risk.

"Is it," Georgina probed, "because he's your first real boyfriend?"

Josie quickly seized on the suggestion. "Possibly," she said. "After all, I've no-one to compare Nick with." And that was true, she thought.

Georgina glanced at her, hesitated, then said, "I would have thought that if you really loved him, you wouldn't feel the need."

Josie looked down. But I do love him, she thought miserably – and that's my problem, because I wish I didn't.

Georgina, seeing her friend's strained expression, wondered exactly what was troubling her. There was definitely something, and Josie obviously couldn't talk about it. Was Nick pressuring her in any way? Georgina was well aware of Josie's views on sex before marriage; the two girls completely agreed that this was a 'no-go area'. Of course Josie never discussed her personal, intimate relationship with Nick. And Georgina wouldn't expect her to. But that didn't stop her being curious.

Just then Alice Hawkins came towards them, carrying a tray of iced lemonade. To both girls' surprise, after placing the tray on a small wooden table, she joined them on the bench. "Lovely to feel the sun after such a long winter," she said. "I suppose you two will be getting involved in league games this summer?"

Georgina looked at her in surprise. "I don't know. Maybe."

"How about you, Josie?" Alice turned to face her, and as always Josie tried to avoid meeting her eyes. Ever since that fateful day she'd seen Alice posing as Mrs French, Josie found it impossible to act naturally in her presence.

"I'm not sure," she said. "I'm trying to persuade Nick to join, but he's more interested in football."

"Does he play?"

"He's in a Sunday league."

Josie's voice was tense, and Georgina said quickly, "He's also a Stoke City supporter. He even took Josie once. He was really miffed when she said she used to like Basil Haywood!"

"Oh, why?"

"Because he plays for Port Vale, of course!" the girls chorused, and then both fell silent. Georgina was thinking how strange it felt to have her mother sitting and chatting, and even looking as though she was enjoying it.

Feeling uncomfortable, Josie said, "I think I'll be off. I'll see you at evening class, Georgina."

Georgina watched her go with misgivings. Damn, if her mother hadn't decided to be sociable for the first time in her life, Josie might have plucked up the courage to confide in her.

But apart from what she thought of as the Nick situation, Josie had something else preying on her mind. And she wanted to get it sorted out. Deep in thought, carrying her racquet in its press, she walked the short distance home, and came to a decision. I'll have it out with them, she thought

– this particular situation has gone on long enough.

"What's brought all this on?" Lily said, when Josie, now changed out of her tennis dress, faced both her parents in the front room.

"I just think it's ridiculous, that's all! Everyone round here knows Georgina and I are friends – they see me driving around in her car, for heaven's sake!"

"She's right, you know, Lil." Sid, who was suffering from a cold, fished in his pocket for a handkerchief to wipe his nose. "I never could see why the girl can't come here. After all, Josie's been to her house often enough over the years. You're being a bit daft about it, in my opinion."

Lily glared at him. "I wasn't aware I was asking, thank you very much!"

"Oh, go oh, Mum. You're only keeping snob-bery alive, you know. And if the neighbours are that petty, well, just let them get on with it. Why should we let them rule our lives?"

"Exactly," Sid agreed.

They both looked at Lily, who was sitting with the Sunday papers spread untidily over her lap. Her expression was one of annoyance, although Josie suspected she was still smarting from Sid's earlier comment. And she was proved right, when Lily said, "Daft, am I? Well, let me tell you, Sid Ford, it was a tricky road I had to walk, what with me working at Rosemount. And remember, at one time old Hawkins was all against his daughter mixing with the likes of us."

"Yes, but times change, Mum. He's fine about it now and we have to move on," Josie pleaded. "We're best friends, Georgina and I, and always will be. It's just not right that she's never been inside my home."

"Maybe not." Lily glanced sharply at her daughter. "And maybe it's not right that your boyfriend hasn't either? Have you thought about that, young lady? It's one excuse after another!" She paused, then said, "I'll tell you what, Josie. I'll lift the ban on Georgina *if* you bring Nick home to meet us."

"Exactly," Sid said.

"Are you an echo or what?" Lily shot a baleful glance at him before turning her attention to Josie. Got you, my girl, she thought in triumph.

As mature eyes challenged young resentful ones, Josie, realising her mother had outwitted her, capitulated. "All right then, it's a deal."

"Right. We'll expect him for tea next Sunday." Lily held up a hand to ward off Josie's protest. "You can still go along and see Georgina beforehand. So if that's settled, maybe you'll let me read the paper in peace."

Georgina, delighted by Josie's news, couldn't wait to go inside the house she'd passed nearly every day of her life. Although her father owned all the houses in the street, she'd never once seen inside one, and having listened for so long to Josie's accounts of her family life, Georgina was dying to see what her home background was actually like.

"We won't make a big thing of it," Josie told her. "Or I'll have Mum and Dad standing on ceremony and feeling awkward. When you drop me off after evening classes on Tuesday, I'll just ask you in. I'll say I want to lend you a book or something." She knew her mother. For Georgina's first visit she'd want the room to be pristine, and Sid to be in his best clothes. As a result the atmosphere would be stiff and polite. And that wasn't what Josie wanted at all. She wanted to show Georgina a typical Potteries home, cosy and informal. One where families could just be themselves, could argue, laugh, eat together, and above all, support each other – a home totally different to Rosemount.

Georgina was perfectly happy with Josie's suggestion. She didn't want to be a 'visitor' in Josie's home, someone they had to tidy up for. She longed to be someone they treated casually, included in their family circle. But she did feel slightly nervous. Not of Lily – she had always liked and got on well with Josie's mother. But there was Josie's father. Georgina wasn't at all sure what his reaction would be.

But Sid wasn't bothered at all when Josie brought Georgina into the front room where he and Lily were watching television. Sprawled in his armchair, wearing his comfy slippers, his shirt collar undone and in his braces, he glanced up from *The Arthur Haynes Show*.

"This is Georgina, Dad."

Sid stood up. "Glad to meet you, Georgina. You're welcome in this house any time."

"Thank you, Mr Ford." Georgina, smiling, shook his hand. Sid, who'd often seen her driving by, had expected old Hawkins' daughter to be a bit stand-offish, but instead recognised the open friendliness in her eyes. He'd always known he was considered not to be the brightest penny in the shilling, but Sid knew he was a sound judge of people. And his first impression was that he was going to like this friend of Josie's.

Lily, a bit flustered that she hadn't had more warning, began to get up, but Josie waved a hand at her. "It's all right, Mum. I'm just going to lend Georgina a book. She's not stopping."

Lily sank back into the chair, her gaze darting anxiously around the room. She hadn't dusted since Saturday, there was a bundle of socks on the floor by her chair, waiting to be darned, her husband was in his braces, and they'd had cabbage for dinner! Irritated, she could only wonder why on earth Josie hadn't given her some warning.

The room seemed terribly small to Georgina. She was trying desperately not to look 'nosy', but a quick glance took in the mottled tiled fireplace, the two-bar electric fire, the polished brass plaques on the wall above, the wooden arms of the two armchairs, and the small console television. There was patterned wallpaper too, cream with green trailing ivy, and a flight of china ducks on one wall.

"Are you sure you won't have a cup of tea?" Lily said.

"No, thank you, Mrs Ford. I'll be having some cocoa when I get home."

"Of course."

It was with relief that Georgina heard Josie come down the stairs, and she took the copy of Anya Seton's *Foxfire*, from her. "Thanks." She turned to go. "Goodnight. Nice to have met you, Mr Ford."

"And you, lass." Sid, who was chuckling at a comedy sketch, glanced up briefly from the screen.

Josie saw Georgina out and whispered. "There, I told you that was the best way. Now you've broken the ice, just come round any time you feel like it."

And that invitation, Georgina thought, as she closed the wrought-iron gates after parking Green Dragon, is the most welcome one I've ever received.

Chapter 29

Nick was delighted by the invitation to tea, and quietly congratulated himself on his patience. Because not once since that evening in the car when he'd sensed that Josie was feeling pressured, had he raised the subject of meeting her parents, nor of her meeting his own. But that didn't mean there had been any change in his feelings. Nick prided himself on being decisive, and there was no doubt in his mind that he wanted to marry Josie Ford. And he didn't want to wait years to do it, either. Wanting her was driving him insane. And he knew Josie felt the same. There were times when they both came near losing control, but Nick knew it would be disastrous for them to 'slip up'. He didn't want Josie to feel she was forced to marry him because he'd made her pregnant. And she'd left him in no doubt as to her views on sex before marriage. All very well in theory, sweetheart, he thought, but there are times when . . .

So Nick saw the invitation as one more step towards putting his relationship with Josie on a permanent footing. But he knew it was much too early to expect her to get engaged. Maybe at

Christmas; they would have known each other a year by then. For now, he planned to buy her a really special nineteenth birthday present. But first, he needed to make a good impression on her parents.

As Josie had foreseen, the Sunday when Nick was due to visit was not one for relaxation. Once they'd eaten their roast lamb followed by a rice pudding, Lily insisted on the washing-up being done immediately, Sid was sent off to get changed, and a great deal of cushion plumping and tidying away of newspapers went on.

Lily, at last satisfied with the appearance of the house, waited until Sid reappeared, and went upstairs to put on her make-up. Changing into the peacock-blue frock she'd worn for Peter's wedding, she fastened around her neck the strand of pearls that had been her twenty-first birthday present, and thought with satisfaction that she'd never looked smarter.

Josie, finding herself infected by the general air of anticipation, also changed her clothes. Deciding to wear a new coffee and cream check skirt, she pulled on a lightweight cream sweater, and changed her slippers for a pair of high heels. Right, Nick Hamilton, she thought, you're about to meet the Fords of Dreston!

But any worries she'd had were soon dispelled. Lily had taken to Nick immediately. From the first moment when he held out his hand and she looked directly into his eyes, she'd seen a man she could trust. And he was *so* good-looking! What's the matter with the girl, she wondered, watching him talking to Sid. Young men like this don't grow on trees, and I shall tell her so.

"So, how's business?" Sid was saying.

"Booming, to tell you the truth. Considering I've only been going a couple of years or so, it's building up nicely."

Sid nodded. "Aye, it must take time to get established. Still, you're working for yourself, and that's something most people can only dream of."

Josie listened with astonishment. When she'd told her parents that Nick bought pottery seconds and sold them to market traders, Lily's reaction had been similar to her own. "Not much security in that, I wouldn't think!" she'd said.

But Sid had merely commented, "Well, at least he isn't work-shy – there's plenty who are!" Now, her father was talking as though he admired Nick for what he was doing.

Josie, finding herself somewhat in the background, found it fascinating to see her boyfriend chatting so easily to her parents. Sid, forced to wear a tie, had already loosened his collar. And Lily's approval was confirmed when Nick asked for a second slice of her home-made fruit cake.

Nick liked Josie's parents immediately. He felt comfortable with them. "Salt of the earth," he could hear his stepfather saying. Only his patronising tone would belie his words.

Nick looked at the two wedding photographs displayed, another two of the grandchildren, and one of a dark, thin-faced young man. This, he guessed, would be the brother who'd died, John.

"Next time you come," Lily was saying, "it will be around Josie's birthday. You'll be able to meet the rest of the family, our Dennis, his wife Mavis and little Johnny. Then there'll be Sonia, our Peter's wife, and their baby. She's lovely, is little Kay."

Josie felt a bit annoyed. Surely it was up to her to decide if and when Nick came again? Already it was starting – assumptions were being made, just as she'd expected. But then, she thought wryly, I can hardly blame anyone. After all, we've been inseparable for over six months.

Eventually it was time for Nick to leave, and Josie went out to the car with him.

"Are you coming for a drink?" he said.

Josie hesitated, then said, "No, I'll skip it. I'll go and give Mum a hand with the clearing up."

"Had enough of me for one day, eh?" Nick looked at her and grinned, "Well, how did I do?"

"You were a resounding success, as you very well know, so stop fishing for compliments!"

"Oh, come here!" Nick pulled her to him and kissed her mouth.

"Hey, not in public!" Josie drew away in embarrassment.

Nick laughed, then unlocked the door of the car. "They're really nice people, your parents."

"I know, that's why I'm so fantastic!"

"And modest with it." He bent and kissed her swiftly. "I'll pick you up on Tuesday for the flicks.

277

I take it I'm allowed now to come and collect you at the door?"

Josie laughed. "Just as long as you behave yourself."

For Georgina, the fact that Josie had left Rosemount early that afternoon to prepare for Nick's visit, was highly significant. Things were changing in their lives – Georgina was only too aware of the light which came into her friend's eyes when talking about Nick, and knew there was a real danger that soon Josie's life might no longer run parallel with her own. It was to be expected of course. After all hadn't they both talked dreamily in the past of meeting their 'knight in shining armour'? She liked Nick Hamilton very much, and anyone could see he adored Josie.

The problem was that Georgina hadn't anticipated this happening so soon. She and Josie had pledged to have fun before they settled down, but Georgina now realised just how naïve they'd been. All it had taken was for someone like Nick Hamilton to appear on the scene. And of course, it would have been just the same if things had worked out differently with Dominic, she thought with her usual sense of loss. Then, there would have been no need for her secret ambition.

Georgina thought about all this, as she sat in the drawing-room later that Sunday evening. The television was on, and her parents were absorbed in *Armchair Theatre*. But although she gave every appearance of watching the programme, Georgina's mind was whirling with regrets and disappointment. She should have told Josie about her ambition for them both, instead of letting it burn silently inside her. But Georgina had always known that the timing would be crucial. She'd needed to wait until Josie was feeling stale, and unsettled in her job. Because Georgina's plan would involve leaving Stoke-on-Trent, moving away to embark on an adventure. Getting jobs in London or Edinburgh – sharing a flat, leading exciting, independent lives. And for Georgina, freedom from the stifling atmosphere of her home. It was with this goal in mind that she'd agreed to continue to accept the allowance from her father. But every penny had been deposited in the Trustees Savings Bank. This nest egg was to have been their security.

Would it have made any difference if she'd confided in Josie? But Georgina knew that Josie felt no desire to move away from her roots. She was happy at home, had a strong sense of family. Why should she want to lose all that to live among strangers in an unfamiliar city? She loved her job too. What Georgina had hoped for was to be able to make the suggestion at the right time, hoping that Josie's sense of adventure, her impulsiveness, would impel her to agree.

As the television programme credits came up on the screen, Georgina could only think in despair that this was now unlikely to happen. Josie might not want to admit how serious things were between herself and Nick, but Georgina intuitively felt that

Josie's future, one where her best friend would be unlikely to play a central part, was already settled.

But Nick, if he'd had a chance to see inside Georgina's mind, would not have agreed. Progress was certainly being made, and he still hoped that he and Josie would be engaged by Christmas. But that was all it was – hope. There was something his lovely girl was hiding from him, he was sure of it. Nebulous it might be, but there was an uncertainty there, and try as he might, Nick couldn't fathom the answer. And it was bothering him so much that he took an untoward step.

"Georgina?" Alice called up the stairs a few days later. "Telephone." Georgina ran down and picked up the receiver.

"Hello."

"Georgina, this is Nick. Look, I know you'll think this a bit odd, but do you think you could meet me for a drink, sometime?"

Surprised, Georgina said, "Yes, of course. When would you like . . ."

"As soon as possible, if that's all right."

After arranging a date and time, Georgina thoughtfully put down the telephone. Now this *was* intriguing.

Seeing the expression on her daughter's face, Alice, whose interest in Georgina was growing, wished she'd asked who it was. "Was that anyone important?" she said.

"No, just someone from the Town Hall." Georgina didn't know why she'd lied, but she just had a feeling that this meeting was 'off the record'. Why else would Nick say "this is a bit odd"?

She didn't have to wait long to find out. They'd arranged to meet the following evening at the Borough Arms, a pub in Newcastle-under-Lyme. This was not only convenient for Nick, but he also knew there was less chance of Josie seeing them.

"What's all the mystery?" Georgina said lightly, once they were settled with their drinks.

Nick took a draught of his beer. "It's about Josie," he said bluntly.

"I rather thought it might be." Georgina sipped her Dubonnet and lemonade and waited.

"I think you know how I feel about her," he said ruefully. "It's certainly no secret."

Georgina nodded, but eyed him warily, unsure of what was coming next.

"There's something, Georgina, something bothering her, holding her back, and I can't seem to get to the bottom of it." He looked up at her and she saw the uncertainty in his eyes. "I know she loves me. I'm sure of it."

Georgina remained silent. Did Josie love him? She'd never actually said as much. Yet it was written in her eyes, on her face. And she knew exactly what Nick meant. Hadn't she wondered about it herself, many times?

Nick gave a wry smile. "It's supposed to be the other way round, isn't it? Men are usually the ones who can't talk about their feelings." He looked across the table at Georgina. "I was hoping you

281

might be able to shed some light on the matter."

She shook her head. "I'm sorry, Nick, I can't. And I'm not just fobbing you off out of loyalty to Josie. I honestly don't know. I do think though that you're expecting too much too soon. I mean, what's all the hurry? You haven't even known each other a year yet."

She paused, and Nick said quickly, "Go on."

"Well," Georgina took another sip of her drink. "We both always said we'd like to have a bit of fun before we settled down. Maybe it's just that she's met you too soon." She glanced at him, "You'll have to give her time to readjust."

Nick looked glum. "I hadn't thought of that." No, he admitted silently, you've been too busy looking ahead, seeing your love for Josie as a beacon of light, a means of escape. Nick was well aware that he could leave home and find a bed-sit somewhere, but that would break his mother's heart. Now, if he were to move out because he was getting married – that would be a different matter entirely. He wondered whether subconsciously this dream had been driving him, had given him this sense of urgency. I've been totally self-absorbed, he thought with a pang. Six months is nothing, and Josie's so much younger. But Nick had no doubts about his own feelings; he wanted to marry Josie Ford, and if he had to wait a couple of years or so, then he would.

Georgina watched the fleeting expressions on Nick's face and wondered what he was thinking. "Have I been of any help?" she said quietly.

Nick smiled at her, and yet again Georgina thought how lucky Josie was.

"More than you know." He reached across the table and put his hand over hers. "Thank you. You're a good friend, do you know that?"

Pauline hadn't really wanted to go to the Borough Arms. "It seems a long way to go for a drink," she grumbled. "What's wrong with the Trentham Hotel? We'll be driving right past."

Alan, her boyfriend, didn't answer. He was struggling with the temperamental engine in his old Morris 10.

"What are you doing?"

"Double de-clutching," he muttered.

Pauline glanced at him in exasperation. Honestly, she didn't know why she bothered. Habit, probably. For weeks now, she'd been wondering whether she ought to finish with him. Alan Jones was a young man with a cheeky grin and an eye for the girls – Pauline had always known that. But he made her laugh, and it was a heady experience to be going out with the heart-throb of the potbank.

However, within minutes of entering the bar of the Borough Arms, Pauline knew exactly why they'd come. She was blonde, brassy and buxom, and her white lacy blouse was cut revealingly low. Not only that but, although she was serving another customer, she greeted Alan with a suggestive wink. That decided it for Pauline. Just you wait until you've taken me home, she thought grimly. Then, Alan Jones, it's curtains.

She turned to glance around the lounge bar. It was a nice pub, she'd grant that. Then within seconds she saw them: Josie's boyfriend and Georgina Hawkins, sitting at a secluded table in the corner! Neither looked her way, but Pauline's appalled gaze saw Nick lean across to hold Georgina's hand. Pauline's reaction was immediate. Swiftly she turned, grabbed Alan's arm and said, "We're getting out of here."

"But I was just about to order!"

"Forget it!" Pauline marched out, and Alan followed seconds later.

"What's got into you?" he demanded. "Have you gone mad?"

"I've never felt saner." Pauline went over to his car and stood by the passenger seat. "I just want to go, that's all. We can call for a drink somewhere on the way back."

"If you say so," he complained. "But I wish you'd tell me what all this is about."

Pauline didn't. But she did watch Alan's stupefied expression as, his beer glass halfway to his lips, she told him they were finished. The shocking scene she'd just witnessed, she kept to herself. But already concern and anxiety was growing within her. She couldn't ignore what she'd seen; the problem was, what was she going to do about it?

Chapter 30

Nick, to his discomfort, was being forced to make a decision. Now that Josie had invited him to her home, in the natural course of events he should invite her to his. And the prospect filled him with misgiving. Also, following his talk with Georgina, he couldn't help wondering whether Josie would see this as an added pressure. But eventually he accepted that he had no choice. Convention demanded it – he and Josie had been together for six months now, and he knew his mother was increasingly anxious to meet her. His stepfather he preferred not to think about.

However, Josie's reaction was not one of resenting the pressure but of avid curiosity. Nick hadn't told her much at all about his background, although she imagined it would be very different from her own. She loved his voice; he had neither a local accent, nor did he talk 'all five-pound notes', as Lily would put it. But then, she reasoned, as she sat in front of her dressing-table the following Sunday, surely his people can't be too posh, or he wouldn't be driving that rackety old van, and working the markets?

With her knees jammed against the drawers,

Josie spat on a block of mascara and leaned forward to peer in the mirror to carefully apply it. One day, she determined, I'll have a proper dressing-table, one with a kneehole, instead of this old thing. Utility, her mum called it, like most of the furniture in their house. Wasn't the word supposed to mean useful? Well, whoever designed dressing-tables like this certainly hadn't been a woman! She stood up and gazed at her reflection in the long mirror on the inside of her single wardrobe door. Georgina had advised her to wear something subdued, but Nick liked her in bright colours. Anyway, his parents might as well meet the real me, Josie thought, or I might feel I have to go on pretending. And so she'd decided on a new coral shirtwaist dress, with white revers and matching cuffs on the sleeves. With white court shoes and handbag, Josie felt satisfied, and presented herself for inspection downstairs.

Lily looked at her with ill-concealed pride. "You look a picture, love. Doesn't she, Sid?"

But for a moment Sid was unable to reply. He'd seen his daughter dressed up to go out before, but this time was different. It showed in the way she held herself, her head high, her eyes full of excited anticipation. It had happened too soon, this young man coming into her life. Sid wasn't ready to lose his daughter, not yet, but he was under no illusions. Nick Hamilton was serious. And Lily was right – she did look a picture. Sid coughed and said, "Yes, your mum's right. That frock suits you."

Pleased, Josie went to watch out for Nick through the front window, hoping he'd been able to borrow his friend's car – she wasn't always sure the seats were clean in the van he used for work. Brian lived next door to Nick and they'd grown up together. "I pay the insurance," Nick explained. "It helps us both out."

Lily, sitting in her armchair, her knitting idle on her lap, was watching her daughter. She and Sid were in full agreement about their approval of Nick, and Lily still couldn't understand why it had taken Josie so long to bring him home. Good-looking, nice manners, and no 'side' on him at all, was Lily's opinion! As she saw Josie drop the net curtain and move quickly away, Lily could only think that if his parents could find fault with her, they must be very difficult to please.

Nick was quiet as he drove Josie along the main road leading to Hartshill, an area between Stoke and Newcastle-under-Lyme. As they turned left to pass the North Staffordshire Royal Infirmary, Josie instinctively looked away. That was the hospital where they'd taken John after his accident – she didn't want to be reminded of that, not today. The roads they went along were tree-lined, the houses of varying sizes and types.

Then suddenly Nick drew to a halt outside a large Edwardian semi-detached house. Ivy grew up the side of one wall, and the arched porch had an elegant front door surrounded with stained-glass windows. Nick switched off the ignition and came round to open the passenger door.

"Here we are," he said, his face a mask of tension.

Josie, her heart beginning to thud with apprehension, got out and then waited as he inserted his key in the front door, and opened it to let her enter.

Josie stepped on to a gleaming red and black tiled floor. The hall was spacious with a high, deeply coved ceiling, flanked by a plate rack around the walls displaying an impressive collection of decorative china plates. As Nick closed the door behind them, his mother immediately came out of the sitting-room to meet them. She was a woman of medium build, with fair, rather fluffy hair. The sage-green jersey wool suit she was wearing was unobtrusive and in impeccable taste, and Josie, conscious of her own colourful dress, wondered in panic whether she should have listened to Georgina.

"Welcome, Josie," she said, and with a smile, leaned forward to kiss her lightly on the cheek. "Come along in – tea won't be long." She indicated a door on the left, and Josie went into a large room with a tall square bay window overlooking a lawned garden. Bookshelves lined both alcoves at the sides of the fireplace, but although the room was comfortably furnished, it seemed rather formal to Josie.

"Gerald will join us in a moment. Sit yourself down, Josie – no, sorry, not that chair, that's where he likes to sit."

Nick took Josie's elbow and guided her to the large brown leather sofa.

"How are your parents? Are they well?"

"They're fine, thank you."

Nick turned to Josie. "Mum belongs to a Luncheon Club. I keep telling her they should change their venue, and try your hotel."

"I've told you, Nick, Hanley isn't all that convenient for some of our members."

Nick persisted, "But you often say you aren't happy with the food where you go now."

"We do have a high reputation," Josie said. "I could always send you some details."

"Thank you, Josie, I'd like that."

There was silence for a few seconds, then Josie said, "This is a lovely house."

A smile of pleasure softened Nick's mother's carefully composed expression, and then she turned as the panelled door opened and a tall man with a distinct military bearing came in.

Nick rose and said stiffly, "This is Josie."

"I think I can work that one out!" Older than his wife, Nick's stepfather was extraordinarily handsome, his luxuriant grey hair tinged with silver, his complexion clear and full of health. Dressed in cavalry twill trousers with a knife-edge crease, a cream shirt and what Josie guessed was a regimental tie, his presence already dominated the room.

Josie stood up and held out her hand. "I'm very pleased to meet you, Mr Hamilton."

"Rhodes."

The tone was curt, and bewildered, Josie glanced at Nick, who was cursing himself for being a bloody fool! How could he have forgotten to tell Josie that his own surname of Hamilton was that of his natural father?

"It's my fault, Gerald. I didn't explain it." He turned to Josie, "I'm sorry. I never thought. My mother's married name is now Rhodes. But I've remained Hamilton."

"Oh, I see. So," Josie repeated, anxious to cover her mistake, "I'm pleased to meet you, Mr Rhodes."

Gerald gave a curt nod, then sat in the leather-winged chair by the bookshelves. "Have you offered our guest some tea yet, Mary?"

"No, I was waiting until you came."

Josie watched the colour rise to her hostess's cheeks, as she hurriedly got up and left the room.

"All I can say," Gerald said, "is that I'm glad Nick has, at last, done the right thing for once, and brought you to meet us." Josie noticed with surprise that his voice had hardened, become almost harsh. "I was beginning to wonder if you had two heads."

His eyes briefly met hers, and then his gaze deliberately roamed over her. Not an inch did he miss, from her unruly dark hair to her white court shoes. It was obvious he was summing her up, making a judgement, and Josie's resentment flared. Her own father, even with his lack of education, would never have been so blatantly ill-mannered.

Conscious of Nick's taut presence as he sat

beside her, Josie said in desperation, "I was saying to your wife, that this is a lovely house."

"It always was," Nick muttered, and immediately regretted his comment.

"Ah – he speaks. That is most unusual, Josie. Nick doesn't normally grace us with his conversation."

Nick remained with his head bent, knowing that to look up and react was exactly the confrontation that his stepfather hoped for.

"But I think," Gerald continued, languidly crossing his ankles, "what Nick is inferring is that this was his home, before *I* arrived on the scene."

"Inferring?" Josie frowned. "You mean it wasn't?"

Gerald became rather still, his grey eyes like flint. "My, we do have a literal turn of mind."

Nick and Josie turned as Mary came in pushing a wooden tea trolley. Resplendent on an embroidered cloth was a Wedgwood tea-service, flanked by a tiered cake-stand displaying home-made scones, a Victoria sponge, and two plates of sandwiches.

"Ham or cucumber," she said with a smile. "I'm sure we're all ready for some refreshment."

"That looks good, Mary."

She flashed a relieved smile at her husband.

Then Josie watched the man who had initially repelled her change into one of easy charm as he asked her questions about her job, enquired after her parents' health, and relaxed over the teacups. But although the scene gave every appearance of a pleasant family afternoon tea, Josie was acutely conscious of Nick's stiffness beside her. She noticed how quiet he became whenever his step-father spoke and began to feel uneasy. She'd read that you could tell what people were really like when you saw them in their home surroundings. *'That's when they lower their guard,'* the magazine article had advised. *'Always watch how the rest of their family interact with them.'*

And Josie saw a side of Nick she hadn't seen before: a tense young man, someone with constant resentment simmering beneath the surface.

"I think another pot of tea would be nice, dear," Gerald eventually suggested, and Mary rose and carried out the teapot.

As soon as she left, Gerald said to Josie. "It's so refreshing to see a smiling young face in this room. That's what youth does for us older people – it brings sunshine into our lives."

Josie smiled with pleasure, thinking what a lovely thing it was to say, then Gerald added, "Of course, that's what one normally expects, but . . ." His inference was clear as his gaze rested briefly on Nick.

Discomforted, Josie glanced at her boyfriend. Was Nick moody? She'd certainly never seen any sign of it before.

"I believe you went to secretarial college, Josie?" Gerald asked, his fingers drumming slightly on the arm of his chair.

"Yes, I went to the College of Commerce in Burslem."

"So I can take it that you think working for qualifications is important?"

"Yes, of course."

"Mmm." Again, Gerald's gaze rested on his silent stepson.

There was a short silence, then Nick said curtly, "What my stepfather is implying in his own unique way is that I don't."

Josie stared at him. "But you've got a degree."

"Is that what he told you?" Gerald said softly.

"Did I?" Nick said. "I don't think I did, Josie."

She stared at him in astonishment, then realised that Nick had never mentioned actually getting his degree. When they first met, she asked him about his schools, and he told her he'd gone to Newcastle High School, and then on to university. She'd just assumed that meant he had a degree – that was the main reason she'd never understood why he'd chosen the type of work that he did. So what did it mean? Had Nick been stupid enough to throw away his chance? Had he been one of those students who were too lazy to work? Or was it that he just hadn't been clever enough? But before she could say anything, Mary returned, and Gerald smiled, rubbing his hands together. "Ah, the cup that cheers! I hope when you decide to be more responsible, even get married, Nick, that you find a wife as wonderful as my own."

"Gerald," Mary chided. "You'll be embarrassing the young people."

"Surely not. I think Josie realises I'm only joking, don't you?"

293

"Of course." Josie, however, was feeling bewildered. What was happening here? Why did she feel her boyfriend had suddenly turned into a stranger? It was as though he'd become a different person since his stepfather entered the room. She felt enormously relieved when the time came for them to leave.

Mary kissed her lightly on the cheek. "I'm so glad Nick brought you. Do give my regards to your parents."

"Thank you, I will," Josie smiled at her, then turning was glad to see genuine warmth in Nick's eyes as he kissed his mother. "Thanks for the tea, Mum – it was lovely."

Josie turned to Gerald, who was standing behind his wife. "Goodbye, Josie," was all he said.

As the front door closed behind them, Josie glanced frowningly at Nick, but his expression was withdrawn. Silently, he opened the passenger door for her and she sank into the seat.

Glancing at the house next door, she said, "Is that where Brian lives?"

Nick nodded, then put the key into the ignition, revved up the engine, and drew away.

"Your mum's really nice," Josie said, as much to break the silence as anything else.

"Yes, she is." His jaw was tense. "But unfortunately, she worships the ground Gerald walks on."

"And you obviously don't."

"Got it in one!"

Josie turned to him as they drew up at a set of traffic lights. "Nick, why don't you tell me what's going on? I mean, I felt really stupid in there, not knowing you dropped out of university."

"Does that matter?"

"No, of course not. It's just that I thought you might have told me about it, that's all."

"Yes, well, perhaps I will, some time." His tone was curt, and Josie stared out of the window. But obviously not now, she thought grimly.

"What do you want to do tonight?" Nick said, once they were approaching Dreston. "We could go for a run in the country, if you like. Brian doesn't need the car until tomorrow."

"Sounds fine," Josie said.

But her voice was tight, and Nick knew she'd taken offence at his refusal to explain. He intended to, but at the moment his nerves were too raw. Every minute spent in Gerald Rhodes' company was one too many. When he did, at last, explain the truth to Josie, then he wanted to do it calmly, not when he was simmering with anger.

Chapter 31

"Well, what do you think?" William Hawkins stood facing his daughter in the drawing-room on a warm Sunday afternoon towards the end of May. He'd expected her to be surprised, but Georgina's reaction to his proposal was one of utter disbelief.

"You mean, a *free* holiday?"

"What do you take me for? I don't invite someone as a guest and expect them to pay for themselves!" William was affronted that his daughter could even ask the question. "But it's something you'd want to do?" he persisted. "Rather than it be just the three of us?"

"Oh yes, I think it's a brilliant idea. Was it yours or Mum's?"

"Well . . ."

"I bet you haven't mentioned it!" Georgina began to laugh, and startled, after a moment, William joined in. Then they both stopped and looked awkwardly at each other. "Shall I?" she offered.

William nodded, then watched her go out of the room. Alice could hardly object this way, and there was no doubt in his mind that the Ford girl would agree. Now hopefully, the two girls wouldn't have any daft ideas about going away independently. William wasn't at all sure about the morals of young men these days, what with Teddy Boys and rock and roll. At least if his daughter was with her parents, then she couldn't come to harm.

Josie was astounded. "Two weeks in Bournemouth with you and your parents – as their guest? Has your father been visited by aliens?" She clasped a hand over her mouth, horrified by her gaffe.

But Georgina giggled. "You might well ask. Anyway, what do you think? The hotel's fantastic – you'll love it."

Josie didn't even need to consider it. She'd never been away on a proper holiday, although she'd been saving up for one. Day trips had been the norm for the Ford family. "Yes, I'd love to come!"

"What about Nick? Won't you miss him?"

Josie looked away. Of course she'd miss him. But the holiday would give her a chance to do some serious thinking. She could hardly believe it – two whole weeks!

"Won't your parents have already booked?" she worried. "It's high season – they might not be able to get me in."

"No problem," Georgina said. "I've checked. The hotel would be quite happy to change my single room for a twin. Single rooms are always scarce. You don't mind sharing, do you?"

"Not a bit!" That would be a novelty in itself,

Josie thought. Unlike Georgina, who'd slept in a dormitory at school, Josie had never shared a room with anyone.

"Oh," she exclaimed laughing, "I can hardly wait. I'm so excited!"

"You don't think there'll be a problem getting time off work?" Georgina asked.

"I shouldn't think so. I haven't taken any of my holiday entitlement. Anyway, I can twist old Jenkinson round my little finger."

"Minx!" Georgina laughed. It was going to be great, having Josie with her in Bournemouth. She hadn't been looking forward to the holiday at all before, but now . . . She looked quizzically at her friend, "You haven't told me yet how the 'visitation' went!"

"Oh, all right, I suppose. Nick's mother's really nice. Not so sure about his stepfather, though."

"Oh, why?"

"Difficult to say. Just a feeling I've got. It was quite obvious that he and Nick don't get on."

"It must be difficult," Georgina said. "Seeing another man with your mother, so to speak."

"Dreadful, I should think." Josie yawned. "It's very quiet downstairs – did you say your mum had gone out?"

"Yes. I'm not sure where – she was meeting an old school-friend, I think. It's unusual for her to go anywhere on a Sunday."

'Old school-friend', Josie thought. That's a new name for it! But, of course, she had no idea whether Alice Hawkins was still involved in an affair. After all, it was two years ago that she'd seen her at the hotel. Did these things go on forever?

Alice was, in fact, asking herself a similar question. Lately, she'd felt a change in her relationship with Neil. She could sense a lessening of desire in him, a more casual attitude towards the frequency of their meetings. Alice was no fool. Her mirror told her every day of the passing years, and although she tried hard to maintain her trim figure, she couldn't deny that she'd gained a few extra pounds. Sometimes she would look at her reflection in despair. She was middle-aged, and it was beginning to show. Yet Neil only grew more attractive, in a sort of dissipated way. The silver threads at his temples simply made him look distinguished, and his slightly more corpulent body gave him an air of authority. Neil Maxwell still cut a dashing figure, and Alice, who had no illusions about him, was beginning to worry that the time might come when he would want a younger mistress. In the note he'd passed to her at a committee meeting, he'd suggested they meet for afternoon tea on Sunday afternoon at a small café in Market Drayton, a small market town on the border of Shropshire. Alice felt slightly apprehensive. What did he want to talk to her about? Because in a café, talk was all they would be able to do. And never before had Neil suggested meeting unless they could make love.

As she drove along the country roads, Alice was oblivious to the summer beauty of the hedgerows.

Apart from her anxiety about the coming meeting, she couldn't help thinking about the changed plans for the holiday in Bournemouth. She'd been astounded when Georgina told her of William's suggestion, and furious that he hadn't consulted her first. So, she'd been confronted with a *fait accompli*. Alice didn't feel easy around Josie Ford; she never had since that day at the hotel. Oh, the girl had given no sign of anything being wrong, but if Alice was honest, she could trace back the distance between them to that date.

Or was she being paranoid? After all, she had to admit that she'd never made much effort to be familiar with her cleaner's daughter until then. Perhaps Josie just saw her as her mother's employer and behaved accordingly. Alice could only fervently hope so.

But when she swung the car into a small car park outside the café, all thoughts of Rosemount and its problems were forgotten. Before her was Neil's Jaguar with its personalised number plate. Alice frowned. She'd always considered it a stupid vanity for Neil to have his car so easily recognised, particularly in view of his infidelity.

The café was small, a typical English teashop, and she saw him immediately, sitting in a corner, already with a pot of tea before him. He rose as she approached. "Hello, Alice. I hope you didn't mind my ordering, only I got here early."

"No, of course not." Alice smiled brightly. "How are you?"

"Quite well. And you?"

"I'm fine. A bit intrigued, perhaps."

"Mmm, yes, I thought you might be."

"It's not easy to get away on a Sunday, I've told you."

"Same for me." He turned as a waitress, her black dress and white cap and apron immaculate, paused by the table.

"Tea and scones, please," Alice said.

"Jam and cream, madam?"

"Yes, please." She looked enquiringly at Neil and he nodded. "For two." Once the waitress had removed Neil's used crockery and left, Alice sat back in her chair. She watched as Neil lit a cigarette.

"Is something wrong?" she said quietly.

"It's Jane."

Alice frowned. "How do you mean?"

"She's getting suspicious." Neil inhaled and looked directly at her. "Apparently, we were seen together."

Alice froze. Oh God no, not that! She couldn't afford the slightest whiff of scandal getting back to William.

"You mean . . ."

Neil shook his head. "Don't worry, you weren't mentioned by name or anything. But do you remember that hotel where there was a big charity lunch going on?"

"Yes, of course – The Golden Hind. I said at the time it was a bit risky. You never know who's at these things."

"Yes, well, I didn't know about it when I booked.

301

The problem is that Sally, that's Jane's closest friend, was there with her daughter."

Alice stared at him in horror. "What did you tell her?"

"That you were a client, of course. But to be honest, I'm not sure Jane believed me."

Alice regarded him steadily. Was his story true? Or was Neil looking for an easy way out? Either way, she would have to be careful how she responded. "Maybe," she suggested warily, "we should cool things for a bit, be more careful?"

"Yes," Neil's expression was one of relief, and then he paused as the waitress brought their order. "I don't think we have much choice."

Alice remained silent and, her eyes downcast, began to butter a scone.

"I've always been straight with you, Alice," he said. "I can't afford a scandal in my profession. I'm not saying that I don't want us to go on seeing each other – I do – but at the moment it's posing a threat."

Alice, playing for time, bit into her scone. Neil's words had reassured her, and what he said did make sense. In any case, she couldn't afford to take any risks either. She glanced across the table to see a rueful expression in Neil's eyes. "I shall miss it," he said, stretching a hand out to take hers. He turned the palm over and began to massage it with his thumb.

"It's been good, hasn't it?" she said.

"Bloody marvellous."

Hearing him say that made Alice feel silly for

doubting him. She really must rein in her imagination – she was in danger of becoming neurotic. I hope it's not the 'change', she suddenly thought with alarm, because she'd heard that women often lost their sexual drive after the menopause. For heaven's sake, she thought with despair, I hope *I* don't – I've only just found mine! That would be just typical!

"So," she said, "I take it you're suggesting that we keep our distance for a while?"

"I'm afraid so. It seems only sensible." Neil looked at her. "Jane's a possessive woman – I simply can't take the chance. Maybe once the dust has settled . . ."

Alice nodded. At all costs, she must act in a mature manner, make it easy for him. That had been their agreement, no emotional involvement. And she'd found that quite possible at first. The novelty and exhilaration of discovering her sensuality had been all that she needed, but gradually as the months turned into years, their relationship had come to mean more to her. Not that she loved Neil – Alice often wondered if she was capable of loving anyone – but it was impossible to share such intimacy over two years without forming some sort of attachment. Although Neil, apart from a few murmured words of flattery during their lovemaking, had never talked of his feelings for her, now Alice was beginning to realise just how much she would miss him.

Chapter 32

Nick, when Josie told him about the holiday in Bournemouth, had very mixed feelings. He was pleased for her, of course. After all she deserved a decent holiday, but he couldn't help wishing that he'd been the one to take her away to a luxury hotel. Although, he thought with a wry smile, her parents would have had something to say about that suggestion! But two weeks at a holiday resort in the company of Georgina? Naturally the two girls would want to go out and enjoy themselves. Just suppose, while things weren't quite right between them, Josie met someone else? And Nick was keenly aware that things weren't as they should be. Not only was there the small distance between them that he'd mentioned to Georgina, but since the day Josie had met his parents, that distance seemed to have lengthened. And for that, he thought grimly, I have to blame my sainted stepfather.

And so, Nick came to a decision. Before Josie went away, he was going to talk to her, really talk. Nick didn't find it easy to let his guard down, to talk about intensely personal matters. His style was the easy-going friendly bloke, the nice guy.

Not that he deliberately put on a front; he liked to think that was his natural personality. Except of course, when he was in the company of Gerald Rhodes.

When, a few days before her nineteenth birthday, Nick told her he wanted to take her out to dinner, Josie was delighted. She'd never been out for a 'posh' evening meal before. At least that's what she hoped it would be. Nick had refused to tell her where they were going, saying he wanted it to be a surprise.

Josie, wearing a vivid green cocktail dress bought with the approaching holiday in mind, was astonished when Nick drove up to Hanley and into the carpark of the prestigious Royal Hotel. "Hey, I've only just left here!"

He turned and smiled at her. "Ah, but that was as Cinderella! So, Cinders, do you want to go to the Ball?"

"You bet!" Josie laughed, and hand in hand they entered the rotating entrance doors into the impressive vestibule. They went into the bar for a preliminary drink, and then Nick ushered her into the large dining-room with its crystal candelabras, long blue velvet curtains and beautifully set tables. The head waiter, his composed expression lightening when he saw them, gave Josie a surreptitious wink before ushering them to a table set for two in a quiet corner. He drew back a chair with a flourish for Josie to sit, and she placed her silver evening bag on the floor beside her, and smiled up at him. "Thank you, Henry," she said, as he shook out her napkin and placed it on her lap.

He nodded gravely then turned to Nick. "The waiter will bring your menus in a moment, sir."

"Did I make the right choice?" Nick whispered, but he could already see the answer in her face. Josie's expression was alight with happiness. And Nick could only think, yet again, how much he loved her.

The waiter who brought the menus was a stranger. One of the evening and weekend staff, Josie thought. But she hardly needed to open them. Didn't she know every word? Hadn't she typed out the evening's table d'hôte menu that very morning? She remembered her mouth watering as it so often did at these times. And now here she was, for once in her life one of 'them' instead of one of 'us'.

"I know what I'm going to have!" she immediately announced.

"Glory! I'd expected you to take ages!"

"Ah, but I have advance information, don't I?" She laughed. "It's a game of mine. Every time I type out a menu, I choose a meal for myself. The trouble is I never get to taste it."

"Well, you will tonight." Nick smiled into her eyes, thinking how lovely she looked. The green dress, with its halter neck, revealed not only her bare shoulders but also a slight hint of cleavage, and he knew he wanted this girl more than anything in the world.

Josie told him her choice, and Nick said, "I was

going to have the sole, but if you're having Steak Diane, you'll need a red wine, not a white, so think I'll join you, and have the same." He ran his finger down the wine list and then looked up as the wine waiter approached. "A bottle of the Burgundy, please."

"A good choice, sir, if I may say so."

The waiter retreated, and Josie looked at Nick with new respect. "I didn't know you knew about wine."

"Oh, my father would often bring Mum and me out for a meal. I think he saw it as part of my education to know about wine. Not that I'm an expert, but I know enough to choose a decent vintage."

Josie looked at him. Nick had never talked of his father before. "You were what, twenty when he died?"

Nick nodded. "Yes, a few months after I finished my National Service. It was very sudden – a heart attack."

"It must have been awful."

"It was." A shadow flitted over his face, then Nick smiled at her.

"Are you sure the soup won't fill you up?"

"Not me," Josie grinned. "It's asparagus and I've always wanted to try it."

"I thought you'd have gone for a prawn cocktail."

"No, thanks! I tasted a prawn once at one of the Tennis Club parties and it was revolting. Anyway, they're too pink!"

Nick laughed, and when the wine arrived, Josie watched him swirl it around the glass, bend his nose to it, and then taste it. "Yes, that's fine," he said, and the waiter poured them a glass each.

"I'm learning new things about you all the time," she said, as she buttered a roll. She was ravenous. Josie glanced at her watch. Eight o'clock already – no wonder she was hungry! Normally Lily had her tea waiting when she got home from work.

"Yes," Nick said quietly, then drew back as his starter was placed before him. For a few moments they ate in silence, and Nick kept the conversation light, letting Josie talk about her plans for Bournemouth.

"You haven't got a suitcase I can borrow, have you? I know I could ask Georgina, but somehow to go with even my clothes packed in a Hawkins' case, seems a bit . . ."

Nick laughed. "I see what you mean. Yes, of course I have. I'll give it a sponge out first though."

"I should hope so," Josie told him. "I've got brothers – I know what sweaty socks smell like."

"That's what I love about you," Nick grinned. "You're so romantic!"

Josie looked down. Love, Nick had said it again. She was acutely aware that she'd never said those words to him. But she did love him, she loved him so much it hurt at times. She looked around the busy dining-room, at the expensively dressed women. Some of the men were even in dinner jackets. Wasn't this the world she wanted to be part of? And sitting opposite a man who knew

308

how to order wine? Josie looked up and saw the intensity of feeling in Nick's eyes, and every fibre of her wanted to say, "I love you, too, Nick," yet even now a part of her drew back. What about the niggling doubts she'd had since visiting Nick's home? The inference that Nick was irresponsible, was moody, was difficult to live with? Although she couldn't remember the words actually being said, she had felt uneasy ever since.

Nick wondered what Josie was thinking. What exactly did go on in that lovely head of hers? He only knew there was a shadow there, slight but persistent, and was even more determined that by the time the evening ended, everything would be out in the open between them, on his part anyway.

They ate their main course with quiet enjoyment, and by the time Josie's glass had been replenished a couple of times, she felt sublimely relaxed and happy.

"This is the life!" she said.

"I'll drink to that."

"Really," Josie asked him, "is this the sort of life you want?"

"Of course. At times anyway." He regarded her steadily. "But the life I want most of all is a happy family one. And money can't buy that. Still," he added, with a grin, "I don't see why you can't have both."

"Absolutely."

Nick reached in his pocket and took out a small leather box. "Happy birthday, darling."

Josie took the box from him and opened it. "It's

lovely," she said with delight, taking out the marcasite pendant.

"Like you," Nick smiled at her.

"Oh, Nick, thank you, I do . . ." the words, 'love you', almost stumbled out, and she stammered instead, "think you've got good taste."

When the waiter brought the sweet trolley, she took much longer to decide, choosing eventually a meringue and cream confection, while Nick opted for the cheese board.

"Will you require coffee, sir?"

Nick glanced at Josie and she nodded.

"Would you prefer it served in the lounge?"

Nick thought quickly. Here they were quiet and private, whereas the lounge might be crowded. "We'll have it here, please."

And it was after their coffee had been served, knowing they would now be free from interruption, that Nick raised the subject of Gerald Rhodes.

"Josie," he said quietly.

"Mmm?" She was admiring her pendant, holding it up for the light to catch it.

"I haven't told you, have I, why I came down from university?"

Despite the wine she'd drunk, Josie was immediately alert.

"No, you haven't. In fact, until—"

"My stepfather 'let the cat out of the bag', you didn't know?"

"Yes," she said slowly. "That's right."

"Only," Nick said, "he didn't just 'let the cat out of the bag' – he said it deliberately."

310

Josie frowned. "Why would he do that?"

"Because that's his way – a hint here, a word there. It's always the same, even with relatives. I'm sure most of Dad's family think I've turned into an irresponsible layabout since he died. Gerald is a master at dripping poison. He does it in such a way that afterwards you can't be sure exactly what he did say. You only know you're left with an uneasy feeling. I know all this, not only by what I've seen myself, but because Brian told me. He grew up with me, knows me inside out, so it doesn't wash with him. And, of course, Gerald never does it in Mum's presence."

Josie looked at him thoughtfully, trying to recall Gerald's words while she'd been there. "But you still haven't told me why he does it, or why you threw away your chance to get a degree."

Nick winced at the words 'threw away'. "When Dad died," he said, "Mum just went to pieces. They were terribly close, and I suppose it's true to say that she'd always leaned on him. I was away at university in London, just beginning my second term, and although I phoned and wrote and came home as often as I could, to be honest, Josie, she just wasn't coping, even with medication from the doctor. It was dreadful to see her. She lost all pride in her appearance; hadn't got any interest in life, became terribly depressed. Then she was persuaded to go to a friend's dinner party, and that's when she met Gerald. Good, strong, reliable Gerald, who'd just retired from the Army, and shortly afterwards lost all his money on the stock market – or so he said." Nick paused, and took a sip of his coffee. "Well, by the time I got on the scene, Mum was a different woman." He looked at Josie and she could see the hurt in his eyes. "Six months, that's all it took for her to put another man in Dad's place. I found that really hard, Josie."

Appalled, she reached out a hand to gently touch his. "I can imagine – it must have been awful for you."

She waited while he lit a cigarette before continuing.

"I didn't trust him then, and I still don't trust him. But what could I do? I tried to talk to Mum, advised her to be cautious, to wait, but she wouldn't listen. She just told me how lonely and unhappy she felt with me away in London. So, I packed in university and came home." He looked at Josie in appeal. "I thought I owed it to Dad. There I was seeing my mother making what I thought was a terrible mistake, being taken advantage of when she was at her most vulnerable. I reasoned that if I was at home, then at least loneliness wouldn't push her into it."

"But you were wrong," Josie said softly.

He nodded. "Six months afterwards, despite all my efforts, they got married, and Gerald moved into our home. He got himself a comfortable house and a wife who adored him. The only blot on his perfect life was myself."

"But surely she realises what's going on?"

He shook his head. "As I've told you, he's always

careful to be charming to me when she's around." He looked in despair at Josie. "She's changed since she married him. It's as though he's sapped her character, and she was never a strong person. The galling thing is that she seems happy with him. That's why I don't say anything to her, and I don't move out. I don't want to do anything to upset her, not after how ill she was with her nerves."

Josie looked at him thoughtfully. Surely anyone living in that house couldn't fail to be aware of the atmosphere between Nick and his stepfather. Mary probably did know – she was just too weak to do anything about it. Certainly she hadn't considered Nick's feelings when she'd decided to marry Gerald.

"Once all this had happened, couldn't you have gone back to university?"

He shook his head. "It doesn't work like that. They will only pay you a grant once."

"Oh, I see. And so you decided to work for yourself." Josie's fingers, which had been playing with her glass, suddenly became still, as she waited to hear Nick's answer.

Nick's whole expression lightened. "I came into it by accident really. When I left university, I didn't really know what I wanted to do, so at first I did a bit of driving for a taxi firm. I often picked up businessmen, and before going to the railway station, they would ask to be taken to one of the factory shops to buy pottery seconds. While I waited for them I used to browse around. That's how I got the idea that if I bought in bulk directly from the potbanks, then maybe there was a good profit margin." He looked at her, his eyes alight with enthusiasm. "I love buying and selling, Josie. And there's a huge potential for someone with an eye for the right product." He leaned forward, holding her gaze, his eyes intent. "I won't always be just a market trader, I can promise you that!"

And Josie believed him. Why hadn't he talked to her like this before? Let her see his enthusiasm, his ambition?

But now Nick was leaning back in his chair. "I seem to have done all the talking," he said wryly, "but I just wanted you to know how things were."

"I'm just glad you told me." She smiled across the table at him, thinking, you'll never know how much!

Later, they drove home in companionable silence, and when the car drew to a halt, she turned to him. "It's been a fabulous evening, thank you," she said.

He switched off the engine and drew her into his arms. "The first of many, I hope," he whispered, before he kissed her. It was a tender loving kiss, and was it his imagination or was there a difference in the way that Josie clung to him? Nick looked down into her eyes, which were soft and shining. "Good night, my love," he murmured, and waited until she was safely inside before driving away. Framed in the doorway, Josie watched him drive away, then suddenly drowsy after the wine and liqueurs, slowly climbed upstairs to bed. Tonight, she needed to sleep, but she knew that when she awoke the next morning there would be much to remember, to dwell upon. One thing she did know was that at that moment she was happier than she had ever been in her life.

Chapter 33

Both Sid and Lily were pleased about the holiday in Bournemouth, but although Lily's pleasure was wholehearted, Sid couldn't help resenting the fact that another man was paying for his daughter's accommodation and food.

"You're looking at it all wrong," Lily told him. "They're taking our Josie for Georgina's sake, not giving her charity."

"It still doesn't seem right."

"That's just stupid pride. Can you afford to pay for her at this fancy hotel? No, of course you can't." Lily softened as she looked at her husband's glum expression. "You know people like the Hawkins don't take someone to a posh hotel unless they're sure they won't get shown up. It's a compliment to Josie, and to us, that's what it is."

"If you say so."

In an effort to placate him, Lily said, "What we can do, is to make sure she's got enough spending money."

But when Sid offered, Josie was quick to refuse, saying, "No, it's all right, I've got a bit put aside. Although," she said, "I will be a bit short on clothes. If you could manage to lend me a bit, I'll pay you back, honest."

"Don't you worry about that! We'll see you all right, won't we, Lil?"

"Josie knows that." Lily leaned over to the coffee table to choose another Black Magic chocolate. "Just think – when you get back, Peter and Fergal will be here."

"I know, it's a pity I'll miss the first week of their leave," Josie grinned. "I'm dying to see how Sonia gets on with Fergal."

"We'll just have to keep our fingers crossed."

Peter's suggestion had been welcomed by all of them, especially Lily, who was hoping Fergal's Navy training would rub off on her daughter-in-law. Everyone knew that sailors were neat and tidy – they had to be in the confines of a ship.

"What happens if she doesn't take to him?" Josie asked.

"In that case, the deal's off. It's her home, and she's a right to say who lives in it," Sid said firmly.

Lily glanced at him in exasperation. Why did he always stand up for the girl! "Well, I can't see it being any problem. Fergal's no trouble at all."

"He's right though, Mum," Josie said. "After all, she's the one who'll be living with him – so to speak."

"Maybe Fergal won't like Sonia. Have you thought of that?" Sid said, leaning back in his chair.

"Of course, he will," Lily snapped. "He'll be glad of the home she's offering. Anyway, no-one could resist little Kay."

"That's true. Still," Sid grinned, "it'll be interesting, to say the least."

And so, on a warm August morning at the beginning of Wakes Week, when the potbanks closed down for their annual holiday, William drove out of the gates of Rosemount, along the street, and drew up outside the small gate to the Fords' house. He opened the boot and waited. Georgina hurriedly got out of the back of the car as Sid carried out Josie's case.

"This is Mr Ford, Dad," she said.

William shook the hand of the man who'd been his tenant for twenty-five years. Sid, feeling awkward, handed over the suitcase. Of all the people to be beholden to, he thought bitterly. Sid had heard many tales of William Hawkins' harshness in dealing with his workforce. A mean bugger, he was called, but then from what Sid had seen of the world, that was how the rich made their money – out of the sweat of other people.

Pauline, on her way to fetch a fresh loaf, paused to look at the scene. She knew, of course, about the holiday. And the news had come as a relief, because Pauline was still wrestling with her conscience. She hated what she called 'tittle-tattling' but after all Josie was a close friend, a childhood friend, and if Nick was two-timing her she deserved to know. But for it to be Georgina of all people! Pauline only knew that she was going to have to confront one of the two girls – she hadn't decided which yet – but not until they got back from Bournemouth. To say anything before would be spiteful. It would only ruin their holiday. As she walked down the hill, the car passed her and both girls waved goodbye. Pauline waved back, but not without a pang of envy. Ah well, she thought as she opened the door to the baker's, I'm off to Trentham tonight. There's always the chance something exciting could happen for me!

Josie sat enthralled as they journeyed south. Eager to see everything, she stared avidly out of the window at the passing scenery. As the hours went by, the countryside became softer, the hills gently undulating, the villages more picturesque. When they arrived, and she saw the impressive façade of their hotel, she felt a moment of sheer panic, then reminded herself that her job should give her the confidence to follow the Hawkins inside as if she'd stayed in such luxury surroundings all her life.

Georgina, who'd had her own anxieties about the holiday, was relieved to find that her parents both made an effort to be friendly to Josie. However, neither seemed able to be fully at ease with her. Georgina wished they'd be more relaxed about it all, like Mr and Mrs Ford. She loved to go along to Josie's home, where she now felt supremely comfortable. Lily even told her it was her turn to make the tea. And every time Georgina went into the tiny scullery, she could only marvel how Lily had managed to bring up four children in such cramped surroundings. And yet, there was such a happy atmosphere in the house. Once again, Georgina realised that money could bring comfort, but people generated happiness.

And eventually the holiday went well, with the two girls dutifully eating their meals with Georgina's parents. Recognising that Alice was trying to make her feel welcome, Josie managed to put the name 'Mrs French' and the incident at the hotel firmly out of her mind.

William showed her the burial place of Mary Shelley, where Josie stared in awe.

"What an interesting life! Not only married to a poet, but writing a novel such as *Frankenstein*. She must have had a wonderful imagination."

But most of the time, the two girls went off by themselves. The weather smiled on them, and every day they strolled through the Lower Gardens, watching the squirrels scampering among the pine trees. Sunbathing on the beach in between swimming in the sea, they both began to acquire a golden tan. At least, as Josie grumbled, Georgina did. Her own complexion was more like a brown nut.

And she loved the shops. They spent ages exploring the small boutiques. Josie bought souvenirs for her parents, sticks of rock for little Johnny and Kay, and a striped tie for Nick.

They bought and shared books and magazines to read, but by the end of the first week, with one accord they decided relaxation wasn't enough – they needed a bit of fun. William and Alice had taken them to a Symphony Concert at the Winter

Gardens, but what the girls really wanted to do was to go dancing at the Pavilion.

"Although," warned Josie, "I've no intention of cheating on Nick."

"Of course not. In any case, I can't really have a holiday romance either, or what would you do all next week!"

"Chance would be a fine thing," Josie laughed. "You're too choosy."

But their good intentions didn't stop them from flirting outrageously, safe in the knowledge that at the end of the week they would be going back home.

"I'd forgotten how much I enjoyed it," Josie laughed.

And it was true, although when she thought about Nick, she did feel a slight pang of guilt. But when one amorous young man – the spitting image of Elvis Presley – tried to kiss her, Josie pulled away. Flirting was just a bit of fun, but anything else was definitely out of bounds. The holiday had made her realise just how much she missed being with Nick. So many times she longed to share her happiness with him, her delight in being at the seaside. Often she would look wistfully at young couples, strolling around hand in hand, and wish he was here with her. Maybe, she thought one warm evening after dinner, when she'd wandered out on to the deserted hotel terrace, one day they could come here for their honeymoon, and as the unexpected word slipped into her mind, her eyes widened in shock. It's the wine I had with dinner, she thought in panic. It must be! A honeymoon meant marriage, and she certainly wasn't ready for that! Yet even as she tried to dismiss such a foolish notion, Josie could only feel a thrill at the image of belonging completely to each other, sleeping together, waking up in Nick's arms. On these warm summer nights her body ached for him. As she heard the hum of voices coming towards her, she walked swiftly away, down the flower-bordered stone steps into the landscaped hotel gardens. She needed to be alone, needed time to sort out her confused emotions. Could this be the turning point in her life? Had she, after all her resistance, at last come to terms with the truth?

"Where's Josie?" Alice asked idly, as she sat in the lounge watching the other guests. It was the only exciting thing to do here, she thought, to look at other people. Not only to judge the women's clothes and hairstyles – she had devised a game of her own. While her expression was one of polite interest, she was in reality assessing each male guest as a potential lover, visualising him in an intimate situation. Not this one, she would decide, he had too large a paunch – that would turn her off, that one was bald and ugly, this one looked like a dried prune. But there was one man in a blazer and flannels who she wouldn't mind getting to know better! Seated next to her husband, knowing he was ignorant of the erotic images passing through her mind, gave Alice a delicious sense of illicit pleasure. It also proved to her that she could be attracted to men other than Neil. And if he wasn't going to be available . . .

Georgina answered her question. "She went out on to the terrace. Said she felt like a breath of fresh air."

William was sitting in a leather club chair, feeling well fed and complacent. It had been his idea to invite Josie along, and the holiday was undoubtedly a success. Georgina, instead of the self-effacing companion she'd always been, was brimming with vitality, and as William watched the two girls together, laughing and joking, yet again he wondered why she had for so many years concealed her real personality. Why was it that only outside her own home, the house upon which he'd lavished such expense, she could display such high spirits? William had long managed to quieten his conscience about his own role in her childhood. It was no use regretting the past; it was the present and future that mattered. And Georgina was definitely softening, becoming more sociable with him. That was another of his inspirations, buying her that car.

After a while, Georgina got up and went to look for Josie. She scanned the throng of guests on the terrace, then in the balmy evening air went down the steps into the garden. She found her friend sitting alone on a secluded seat, staring out over the ocean. "Are you okay?"

"Fine." Josie moved along so that Georgina could join her. "Lovely view, isn't it?"

"Perfect." Georgina glanced sideways at her. "Are you sure you're all right?"

"Of course I am, honestly," Josie reassured her. "I'm having a wonderful time." She hesitated. "To tell you the truth I was thinking about Nick. It's just that coming here has made me realise how much he means to me."

"I'm glad," Georgina said softly. "I think you're made for each other."

"Really?"

"Absolutely."

"I think it's serious," Josie said suddenly. She turned to Georgina. "I just wish I'd met him later. You know how we always said we wouldn't get married too young?"

Georgina stared at her in astonishment. "You didn't tell me Nick had proposed!"

"He hasn't, but I know he will." A soft smile played around Josie's lips, and Georgina thought how wonderful it must feel to be so confident of someone's love for you. She couldn't help a pang of envy as she looked at Josie, at the light in her eyes. Dominic made me feel like that, she thought, but it's never happened since.

Josie swung round to face her. "What do you think?" she said. "Would I be stupid to get engaged so young, maybe at Christmas?"

The two girls stared at each other, and Georgina said thoughtfully, "Well, you will be twenty the following June. After all, it's not the same as going down the aisle at seventeen!"

"I suppose not."

Georgina hesitated. "I've always been a bit puzzled about you and Nick. I mean, it was obvious he was crazy about you, but I sensed there was something holding you back. Was that what it was – wishing you hadn't met him so soon?"

For a moment Josie didn't answer, then she said, "Partly."

Realising her friend wasn't telling her the whole truth, Georgina frowned. "It's a big decision Josie – you have to be sure."

But Josie's smile was full of confidence. "Oh, I am, Georgina. I've never been more sure of anything in my life."

"Then that's wonderful!" Georgina hugged her, laughing. "I'm really, really happy for you! Hey, you'll have to practise your acceptance speech!"

Josie struck the modest pose of a Jane Austen heroine. "I am honoured by your proposal, sir . . ."

Georgina giggled. "Do you think he'll go down on one knee?"

"He'd jolly well better!" Josie gazed happily at the ocean, where a ship, remote and mysterious, was just visible on the horizon. She knew she would always remember this night, when everything had become clear to her. The relief of having all that angst removed from her mind, to know for certain where her future lay! Faintly, drifting from the hotel lounge, she could hear a female vocalist singing the Ronnie Hilton hit, 'No Other Love Have I', and she thought, I've been so stupid. How could I have let myself be influenced by childish dreams? Nick had ambition, so had she, and together there was no limit to what they could achieve. Suddenly Josie was impatient to go home. The holiday had been wonderful, but her place was with Nick, and now she just couldn't wait to see him again.

Beside her, Georgina too was looking at the tranquil view and listening to the song. She could still remember Dominic's every feature, the way his hair had fallen on his forehead, how he'd smiled at her. I hope the words of the song aren't going to be true in my life, she thought in despair. She was thrilled for Josie, of course she was. But what had *she* got to look forward to when they returned to Stoke-on-Trent? Just more of the same job, which was becoming increasingly boring. Even the day-release course, which she and Josie had attended together was finished, in fact the exam-ination results would be out when they got back. Georgina hadn't really made any other close friends – not in the way that she and Josie were close. And once Josie was engaged, then naturally she and Nick would become even more involved with each other. I need to make changes in my life, Georgina thought. Perhaps the summer of 1958 is going to be auspicious for both of us.

Exactly what her own plans were going to be she wasn't sure, but what Georgina did know was that once she got home she had some serious thinking to do about her future.

Chapter 34

"Come on in, love. My, you do look well!" Lily, hearing Josie's key in the door, came hurrying forward to kiss her cheek. "We haven't half missed you."

Josie dumped her suitcase, and looked around. The hall seemed pokier than ever after the spacious rooms at the hotel, although she would have thought she was used to the difference, working as she did at one. But of course, it wasn't the same as being a guest. Most of the time she was stuck in a cramped office.

"Hey, is that the gadabout?" Peter came into the hall, holding Kay in his arms. "Look, here's your Auntie Josie back home!"

"Come here, sweetheart. Let's have a hug." Josie took Peter's baby daughter from him and carried her into the sitting-room. "Hello, Sonia, I didn't expect to see you here." She turned as Fergal got up from his chair. "Fergal, how are you?"

"I'm fine, Josie, thanks. That's quite a tan you've got."

"Yes, I look a bit like a gypsy," she laughed. "Whereas Georgina, of course, is flatteringly golden."

"How is she?"

Josie smiled at him. "She's fine, and looking forward to you two meeting up."

"Me too."

Sonia looked at Josie with undisguised jealousy. "You're a lucky devil, Josie, being taken away like that."

"Yes, I know," Josie said quietly. She had a civil if not too friendly relationship with her sister-in-law.

"Right, I'll put the kettle on," Lily said briskly.

"Where's Dad?"

"Gone up to the park for a game of bowls. He said it was a match and he couldn't let the others down, otherwise he would have been here."

"Dad's really taken to bowls lately, hasn't he?" Peter said. "And, of course, those crown bowling greens are really good."

"I go and watch him sometimes if the weather's nice," Lily said. "There's nearly always another bowls-widow I can have a chat with. Anyway, Josie, come in the scullery while I make the tea – I'm dying to hear all about it."

Fergal crouched down on the floor to tickle Kay, while Peter cast an uneasy glance at his wife. Although he'd warned Sonia about Fergal's scarred face, she seemed unable to ignore it. Either she would stare with blatant curiosity, or avoid looking at him completely.

"He's got a face on him, hasn't he?" she said, the first night when Peter climbed into bed beside her. "Fancy looking at *that* first thing in the morning!"

328

Peter, who had a soft spot for 'young Fergal', as he was known on board ship, had no intention of leaving his friend in a house where he felt uncomfortable.

"I'm not sure it's going to work," he told Lily, when he went round a couple of days later. "If she keeps on like this she's going to make him go back in his shell again."

"I suppose," Lily said, trying to be fair, "we've had more time to get used to his appearance. Let me think about it – I might come up with something."

And she did. When Peter and his family had arrived that afternoon, Lily had a word with her son in private. "You've got to give her an incentive," she said. "Now, do you need Fergal's rent to make ends meet?"

"No, of course not. We're not flush or anything, but we're all right."

"Good. So, tell Sonia she can have Fergal's rent to spend, with no strings attached. I don't think she'd fritter it." Even Lily had to admit that Sonia could make a pound go a long way.

Now, Peter was just hoping his mother's suggestion would prove to be the solution.

The following evening, Josie was in an agony of impatience as she waited for Nick's car to pull up outside the house.

"Will you come and sit down," Lily said sharply. "You're making me feel dizzy."

"Well, I haven't seen him for two weeks!"

"Women during the War sometimes didn't see their men for years," Sid told her. "You're too soft, your generation."

"Now you wouldn't wish a war on the girl, surely," Lily commented. She shot a considering glance at her daughter. Maybe the old saying was right: absence did make the heart grow fonder.

"He's here now. 'Bye!" In a flash, Josie was out of the door and Nick got out of the car to meet her.

"Never mind the neighbours, come here!" He held his arms wide and Josie went into them. As Nick felt her hold him tightly, he realised that all his fears that she would 'cool off' while away, were unfounded. "God, I've missed you," he said huskily, pulling away to look at her. "And look at you, brown as a berry!"

"I know," she laughed. "The weather was gorgeous."

Nick opened the passenger door, and Josie slid in her tanned legs. "I'm taking you for a run in the country," he said, as he started up the engine. "Although what I really want is to find a nice secluded spot – guess what for?"

"I can't imagine," she laughed, while her gaze lingered on his thin handsome face. Why, there wasn't a single man in Bournemouth to compare with her Nick! And that was what he was going to be from now on. Just you try and demean him to me again, Gerald Rhodes, she thought. You'll find you've met your match!

But Nick's stepfather was far from her mind

once Nick turned into a deserted lane and pulled into a farm gateway. As he turned to take her into his arms, Josie kissed him with all the love in her heart, and it was Nick who drew away first, looking wonderingly down at her. "I believe you really have missed me," he murmured, as he twisted a curl of her hair in his fingers. "You'll have to go away again!"

"Only if you come with me," she whispered. She looked up at him, and at the softness in her eyes, he caught his breath. "I love you, Nick," she said, and joy flooded through him at the words he'd waited so long to hear. Nick kissed her again, even more passionately. As he lowered his lips to her throat, and to the soft swell of her breasts, Josie held him close to her, her hand on his dark head, feeling the warmth of his breath on her bare skin. I love you, love you, love you, she thought with delight.

As though he'd heard her, Nick raised his head and gazed deeply into her eyes. "I've loved you, my darling, ever since we first met. We belong together. You know that, don't you?"

Josie gazed down at him and smiled. "Yes, I do."

"Then I can only say, God bless Bournemouth!"

She laughed. "I'm so happy to see you! You can't imagine how much."

"Oh, I think I can," Nick said softly, and then cursed as a tractor chugged up the lane and indicated its intention to turn. "Damn, we'll have to move."

331

"Perhaps it's just as well," Josie said with an arch glance.

"You wait, Josie Ford," he muttered with a grin, as he began to reverse the car. "I'll have my wicked way with you yet!"

Not until I've a wedding ring on my finger, Josie thought complacently, as they drove back to Dreston. Although, she was beginning to realise, her determined vow wasn't going to be as easy to keep as she'd thought.

Lily's suggestion, much to Peter's relief, seemed to have the desired result. Instead of merely tolerating her guest, Sonia began to fuss around Fergal, trying to make sure he felt at ease in her home. She even, Peter noticed with amusement, dusted the sideboard. Fergal took it all in good part, offering to help with the washing-up, and acting as baby-sitter while Peter and Sonia went out. Little Kay found his scar fascinating, and would stroke his face with wonderment, but her engaging smile merely made Fergal laugh.

"You know, she's good for him," Peter said one afternoon, as he went into the kitchen, having left the tall young sailor reading aloud nursery rhymes to his baby daughter.

"Isn't she, and he's very good with her."

"So, it's okay then? For him to move in after the summer?"

"It's fine. And you didn't need to bribe me, either!"

Peter kissed her cheek. "Maybe, but you deserve

a few treats, what with me being away all the time."

"Are you sure you want to re-enlist?"

Peter looked down at the bottle-blonde head of his wife. "Oh, yes," he said, "I'm sure." His marriage worked for one reason only, and that was because most of the time he was away at sea. He missed his child, but Sonia was a good mother, and in Peter's eyes this was the best way he could give Kay stability. He still worried about the risks in leaving his voluptuous young wife alone so much – which was where Fergal was going to be useful. However, that arrangement wouldn't last forever. Maybe, Peter thought as he watched his wife warm up two tins of Irish stew for their lunch, it's time that Kay had a little brother or sister. Another baby would settle Sonia down even more.

Georgina, looking forward to seeing Fergal again, arranged to pick him up on Tuesday evening, and as she drew up outside Peter's home, Fergal, who had been waiting at the window, came out immediately.

"Fergal," Georgina said, getting out of the car and smiling at him, "how lovely to see you again. How are you?"

"Fine," he grinned.

They stood looking at each other for a moment, then Georgina laughed and leaning forward gave him a quick hug. Fergal returned it awkwardly, then drew back with both pleasure and embarrassment.

"You've changed," she said. And it was true – Fergal seemed to have grown from a youth into a broad-shouldered young man.

"You haven't," he grinned. "You're just as lovely as ever."

"Ah, you Irish with your blarney," she laughed. "Come on, let's go and have a drink."

It was a lovely summer evening, the air warm with just a slight hint of a breeze, and Georgina drove with the windows down, through Lightwood, and out to Moddershall, a tiny village where there was a popular country pub in an idyllic setting.

Fergal went to get their drinks, and Georgina settled herself at a cosy table in the corner. "Now," she said, when he returned, "tell me all your news. How are you getting on at Sonia's?"

He shrugged. "I wasn't sure at first, but I think it's going to be okay."

"At least it will give you a base. And if it doesn't work out, you can always find somewhere else."

"Yes, I know. Mind you, I hope it does, after all the trouble Peter's gone to."

Georgina took a sip of her Dubonnet and lemonade. "In your last letter you said you might try to get work on one of the potbanks."

"I know." Fergal looked at her. "I can say this to you, Georgina, but I'm not looking forward to working with a lot of strange people."

Georgina deliberately let her gaze linger on his features, staring at his scar. Fergal didn't flinch. "Now that," she said, "was very rude of me, and

I wouldn't have dreamed of doing it when you were last here. But you didn't mind too much, did you?"

He reddened. "No, but that was because it was you. It's just that since all the letters . . ."

She put out her hand to touch his sleeve. "We've become close, haven't we? In the way good friends should be. "

He nodded, then lifted his glass of beer to his lips, and, to give himself time, glanced around the room. Good friends! How stupid he'd been, all these months, lying in his hammock, reading Georgina's letters and dreaming. How could he have forgotten just how elegant and glamorous she was? No man could fail to be attracted to her. But if Fergal's harsh childhood had taught him anything, it had taught him to be a realist. For heaven's sake, he didn't even have a decent education!

Georgina, noticing the change in Fergal's expression, wondered if she'd said something wrong, but then he turned back to her and smiled.

"Amazing, isn't it, how you can get to know someone just by writing to them."

"I'll drink to that!" She raised her glass in a toast. "To you, my Irish pen-friend. Loads of success!"

Fergal laughed, but could only think – that's all you are, my lad, her Irish pen-friend, and don't you forget it!

Chapter 35

It was several days after the two girls returned from Bournemouth, before Pauline plucked up the courage to walk along to Rosemount. As she passed Josie's home she glanced curiously at the front windows, wondering whether Fergal was visiting, but could see no sign of movement. It would be a pity, Pauline thought, if she didn't get a chance to see him during his leave. She carried on walking, and although she was sure she had made the right decision, that didn't stop her heart thudding with apprehension. But she had to act; the image of Georgina and Nick together was constantly preying on her mind. Pauline had eventually decided that rather than tell Josie what she had seen, it was only fair to confront Georgina, to give her a chance to defend herself. And, Pauline thought grimly, it had better be convincing!

When she reached Rosemount's double gates, she hesitated. So many times as a child she'd admired the gold-painted tips of the wrought iron and the golden balls on the posts. But never would she have had the nerve to turn the handle. Even now, at twenty years old, she had to force herself to walk through them and up to the imposing front door.

When the doorbell pealed, it was William Hawkins, on his way to have a pre-dinner drink in his study, who was nearest to the door. With an exclamation of annoyance at being interrupted, he went to answer it. The young woman before him stepped back nervously, and he glanced sharply at her, thinking she seemed vaguely familiar.

"Yes?"

"Is Georgina in?"

William frowned at the blunt question. His gaze ran swiftly over her clothes. Cheap stuff, probably off the market, and his lips tightened.

"One moment."

As the door closed in her face, Pauline reddened. Nobody in her house would be so ill-mannered. They would at least leave the door ajar!

Georgina was lying on her bed, staring at the ceiling and thinking about her future, when she heard her father call. With reluctance she went out to the landing.

"There's a girl here, asking for you!" His tone was irate, and even from that distance she could see the frown on his face.

"Oh?" Georgina ran down the stairs. "Where is she?"

William jerked his head. "Outside!"

With a sharp glance at him, Georgina opened the door. "Pauline! This is a surprise. Come in. Please!" She stood aside as Pauline entered the large oak-panelled hall, and stood awkwardly. "This is Pauline, father. She lives down the street."

William gave a dismissive nod, then, outrage in his every movement, retreated to his study. Down the street! Did his daughter think his home was a public thoroughfare? It was bad enough that their cleaner's girl had the run of the place! He poured himself a dry sherry and slumped angrily into his leather wing chair. Surely a man in his position was entitled to some privacy in his own home!

Georgina, who, had William known it, was well aware of what was going through her father's mind, took her visitor into the spacious sitting-room. Pauline, in awe of her luxurious surroundings, immediately felt shabby. Thankful that at least she'd thought to change after getting home from work, she wished she'd taken more care in choosing what to wear. Although she doubted whether even her Sunday best would be good enough for this!

Georgina, intrigued as to why Pauline had come, sat on an armchair and waved her hand. "Take a seat," she said and, seeing the other girl was ill at ease, gave a smile of encouragement.

Pauline perched on the edge of the large sofa. "I expect you're wondering why I've come."

"I am a bit. Not," Georgina added hastily, "that it isn't lovely to see you, but I think this is the first time you've been here, isn't it?"

Pauline nodded. She remained for a moment looking down at the expensive carpet. This was

338

going to be both unpleasant and embarrassing, but it had to be done so she might as well get on with it.

"It's about Josie," she said abruptly.

"Josie? Is she all right?" Georgina was immediately alarmed. Had Josie been hurt? Was she ill?

"She's fine. At least," Pauline gazed steadily at the other girl, who looked so right in that elegant room, "she is now. How she is in the future rather depends on what you have to say."

Georgina frowned. "I'm sorry, Pauline, I don't understand."

"Perhaps if I tell you that I was in the Borough Arms a few weeks ago?"

"You mean in Newcastle-under-Lyme?"

"That's right. I'd gone there for a drink with Alan. We were still going out, then. You were there."

"I didn't see you."

"No, I made sure you didn't!" Pauline paused, and narrowed her eyes to watch Georgina's reaction. "Neither you, nor Nick!"

Georgina stared at her. What did she mean *'neither you, nor Nick?'*

Then, suddenly, to her horror she realised what Pauline was implying! "What are you talking about? You can't think . . ."

"I only know what I saw!"

"You didn't *see* anything!" Georgina said in disbelief. "For heaven's sake, Pauline, what sort of girl do you think I am?"

"That's what I've been wondering!"

Georgina was bewildered. "I wish you'd stop

339

talking in riddles and spit it out! That's obviously what you've come here for!"

Pauline lifted her head. "I saw you and Nick holding hands. You were in a pub miles away from Dreston, sitting alone in a secluded corner. Now, you tell me, what would you think?"

Georgina was speechless. Holding hands – she and Nick? What on earth was the girl talking about?

"I've known Josie since I was a kid," Pauline continued doggedly. "We were in the same class at school. You're lucky I didn't tell her! And if I don't get a satisfactory answer, that's exactly what I will do!"

Georgina was stupefied. Surely Josie wouldn't believe such lies, couldn't believe them! But what if she did and then accused Nick? He'd be devastated if he thought she didn't trust him!

"How dare you come here with your insinuations!" she flared. "You've either got a very vivid imagination, or you must have a suspicious, twisted mind. If you think I would ever cheat on Josie, then you don't know me at all!"

"I'm not making this up, Georgina!" Stung by the harsh words, Pauline was even more determined to get a satisfactory answer. And I'm not leaving until I do, she thought grimly. Not sure whether the two red patches on Georgina's normally pale cheeks were caused by anger or guilt, she could only think, well, *I'm* angry! In fact I'm bloody livid. I can think of better ways of spending an evening after a hard day's work than coming along here to be told I'm a liar! "You admit," she said in a tight voice, "that you were there – in the Borough Arms – with Nick?"

"Yes, of course, but—"

"And," Pauline went on relentlessly, "did Josie know about this meeting?"

"No, but . . ." Suddenly, an image flashed into Georgina's mind of Nick leaning over and putting his hand over hers! It had been when he'd said that she was a good friend. *That* must have been what Pauline saw!

"It's not how it seemed, Pauline," she said quickly.

"Ah, you remember all of a sudden! Because I might as well tell you that I'm not going to stand by and see Josie tie herself up with some bloke who can't be trusted!"

"Of course, Nick can be trusted, and so can I! Look, you've got it all wrong! I can see how it looked, but Nick wanted to talk to me – about him and Josie. He's crazy about her, Pauline – he's not interested in me, or anyone else!"

Pauline looked at her suspiciously. "How do you mean, he wanted to talk to you about her?"

Georgina hesitated. She hated betraying Nick's confidence, but decided that in the circumstances, she had no choice. "It was just that he wasn't sure how Josie felt, and was hoping that as we're so close she might have confided in me."

"Oh yeah? And he had to hold your hand to do it?" Pauline said with sarcasm.

"No, of course not!" Georgina snapped. "You are *so* wrong. Nick simply touched my hand when

341

he thanked me. That's what you saw, nothing else!" Helplessly, she stared at the other girl. "You do believe me? I'm not in the habit of telling lies, Pauline. And as for thinking I would cheat on my best friend . . ."

Pauline looked down. She wanted to believe her, but . . .

Georgina waited, and when Pauline didn't say anything, began to feel panicky. "You've got to believe me, Pauline. If you say anything to Josie, it could ruin everything."

"I suppose," Pauline admitted with reluctance, "I could just have come in at the wrong time."

"That's exactly what happened."

"I could only go on what I saw," Pauline said defensively.

"Well, now you know the truth!"

Pauline looked at the other girl. "All right, I believe you," she said abruptly. "But I hope you understand why I had to come."

Suddenly, despite her resentment, Georgina realised that it had taken enormous courage for Pauline to come to Rosemount with her accusation. "Yes, I do. You're a nice girl, Pauline," she said abruptly. "A good friend."

"I try to be."

For a moment, neither girl spoke, and silence hung heavily in the room, then Georgina said, "That was horrible! I feel all hot and bothered, I don't know about you. Would you like a cup of tea?"

Pauline nodded, and once Georgina left the

room tried to calm her jangled nerves. That was one scene she wouldn't like to go through again! But at least she knew the truth now. She'd been dreading the prospect of confronting Josie.

Pauline looked around the impressive room, absorbing the atmosphere, the silence and solid comfort. What a difference, she thought wryly, comparing it to the cluttered shabbiness of the house she'd grown up in. But she wouldn't want to change places; she found the large house with all its oak panelling oppressive. No, Pauline decided, although she had to share it with her noisy brothers and sisters, or maybe even because of that; given the choice, she'd opt for her own home every time.

Once Pauline had left, Georgina, still churned up by the unpleasantness of the last hour, wandered back into the sitting-room, collected the used cups and saucers and took them into the kitchen to rinse. She felt restless, unsettled, and suddenly decided to go for a walk in the park. It would help to clear her head, enable her to think more clearly. In the late summer evening there were several people in Queen's Park, some walking their dogs along the tree-lined paths, others just enjoying being out in the open air. Although several of the houses in the area had gardens, many only had small backyards, often joined by what the local people called 'backs', cobbled and often moss-covered, which ran along the rear of the houses. The nearby park, was, for them, a godsend, and became for their children almost a second home.

Georgina wandered through the rose gardens, and down to the bowling greens. She saw Josie's father, a familiar figure now on the crown greens, and gave him a friendly wave, before going down to the lake, attracted as always by the silver water. She watched the people feeding the ducks. But after a while, she went to find a secluded bench where she could sit and think. It was time, more than time, that she made some decisions. First of all, she was determined to change her job. It was time to move on, to find a post that offered her a more stimulating life. The experience she'd gained at the Town Hall had given her a solid background in office procedures, but Georgina now held an RSA certificate for 140 wpm shorthand, and wanted to be able to use her high speed. The man she worked for only dictated at a slow pace, and she knew that the maxim, 'Use it or lose it', concerning her skill, was only too true. But where did she want to work? Once again, the vague thought that had been lingering in the back of her mind re-surfaced. The restlessness within her was becoming constant. Maybe her idea *was* a good one. After all, it didn't have to be forever – perhaps a year or two. She could maybe find a more glamorous job, experience a different social life. And it wasn't as if she hadn't a friend there. Could she do it? Was she brave enough? Suddenly, the name Edinburgh, bringing with it a vivid image of the imposing Castle, and wide and busy Princes Street, seemed a Mecca. Why not, she thought? I'll write to Fiona tonight, and see what she thinks.

Chapter 36

It was with her customary emotional upheaval that Lily said goodbye to Peter. But at least this was a temporary farewell, not like the loss she'd suffered when John died. She would miss her laughing son, although the leave had gone well, with Peter delighting in his baby daughter, while Fergal, due to be demobbed after Christmas, was settled in his plans to come and live in the Potteries.

With a sigh Lily closed the door behind the two young sailors, and Sid put his arm around her shoulders. "He'll be back, love."

"I know."

They went into the sitting-room.

"I hope Fergal gets a job all right when he comes," Lily said.

"I don't see why he shouldn't." Josie was manicuring her nails. "But it's no use looking until he gets here."

"No, I suppose you're right." Lily sat in the armchair and yawned. "Gosh, I'm tired."

"Do you want a cup of tea?" Josie put down her nail file.

"I'll make it," Sid offered, and getting up went out of the room.

The two women raised their eyebrows. "It must be our lucky day!" Lily said, and Josie laughed.

"Did Pauline come along while I was away?"

"No, I haven't seen her for a bit. Why?"

"Nothing really. Well, I could be wrong, but I got the impression last time he was here, that she quite liked Fergal."

"Really?" Lily thought for a moment. "You know, he could do a lot worse."

"That's what I think." But, Josie thought, as she filed her nails, if I'm not mistaken, I think Fergal's eyes might be straying in another direction!

It was two months later before Georgina finalised her plans. Fiona had written back full of enthusiasm.

We've got loads of room in this rambling house, and it would be great to have you here. My parents are all in favour, and you'd have no problem getting a good job. Come on, girl, get a bit of culture! And there's nothing like a man in a kilt to set your heart fluttering! Anyway, with Alistair swotting for his exams, I could do with the company.

And so Georgina, without saying a word to anyone, gave one month's notice at the Town Hall. She reasoned that once it was a *fait accompli*, there would be less likelihood of her resolve weakening. In a way, she was surprised just how steadfast that resolve had become, and it was with quiet determination that one evening after dinner she told her parents.

"Edinburgh!" William put down his cup so

abruptly that the coffee spilled into the saucer. "What on earth do you want to go and live in Edinburgh for?"

"I just do," Georgina said and, looking from her father's shocked expression to Alice's astonished one, realised that perhaps her parents did care in their own way. Could it be that they might even miss her? "Maybe," she tried to explain, "it's because I never went to university. Most young people like to spread their wings a bit, experience a different way of life."

"Most girls," Alice said, "unless they go to university or college, remain living at home until they get married." She frowned. First Neil disappearing from her life, then Georgina! Life promised to be very boring with just William for company! And this *would* happen when she was at last beginning to like having a daughter in the house.

"I didn't say I was going permanently," Georgina said. "I'm just restless, that's all."

William, still reeling from the news, remained silent. It was possible she could get involved with someone up there, maybe even marry a Scot! Whichever way you looked at it, this was a parting of the ways, an end to an era. He looked at Georgina, hearing the enthusiasm in her voice, seeing the light in her eyes. She wanted to move away, that was painfully obvious. Yet during the last two years, she'd seemed happier, more content at home.

Georgina, glancing at her father, realised to her

amazement that he was actually upset. Suddenly she realised that at one time she'd have been trembling at the prospect of confronting him with news like this, or indeed news about anything. He would have shouted, blustered, reduced her to a quivering mass of nerves. How things have changed, she thought. How he's mellowed, at least towards me.

"It's not that I'm unhappy at home," she said quickly, mentally adding, at least not now, and saw a flash of relief in his eyes. "I just want to taste a bit of independence."

Alice sighed and looked across at William. "I suppose we must be thankful she'll be staying with people of some standing. It's not as if she's going off down to London, trying to exist on her own."

"That's true," William conceded. "We can't say anything to change your mind?"

Georgina shook her head.

"I suppose you'll take the car?" he said with resignation.

She nodded. "I shall need it. Fiona lives a little way out of the city."

"It's a long way to drive," Alice frowned.

"I'll take my time. Perhaps break the journey on the way."

William nodded. "Very sensible. Well," he stood up. "I'll have a fresh cup of coffee, Alice – in my study."

They both watched him go heavily out of the room, and Georgina said, "I'll do it." She got up and at the door glanced back at her mother, but

Alice, who was busy lighting a cigarette, didn't look up.

Josie was dumbfounded. "But you can't!" she wailed. "You can't go and live in Scotland! It's miles away, for heaven's sake!"

"I'll come back often, I promise."

"But why? What's brought all this on?"

"It's been a gradual thing," Georgina explained. "I'm bored at work for one thing. I haven't even got a boyfriend. And," she looked sheepishly at Josie, "you're going to be more and more tied up with Nick, particularly if you get engaged. I just feel it's the right thing for me to do. I need some excitement in my life, Josie. I'm in a rut!"

"I know what you mean, but I won't half miss you. Still, you've always got on well with Fiona."

Georgina nodded. "She keeps in touch with June as well, and says she might come up for a weekend." She grinned. "The three of us together again – it will be just like old times."

"Yes." Josie's tone was wistful, and Georgina was quick to reassure her. "There's no-one like you, Josie. You know that."

Josie managed a smile. "It's the same for me." But she was not only feeling a pang of jealousy, she was still trying to take in the fact that her best friend would no longer be living just along the street. Weeks and perhaps months would go by without them seeing each other! Josie turned away, not wanting Georgina to see her distress.

★

When Josie told Nick that Georgina was moving away, he was genuinely concerned. "I can't imagine your life without her," he said. "I've never known two such close friends."

"I know," she said. "We're going to write, but it won't be the same."

"Never mind, sweetheart." Nick drew her even closer. They were sitting in the back seat of Brian's car, drawn up on the secluded tree-lined road outside Queen's Park. "You'll just have to spend more time with me, that's all."

"What! I couldn't bear it!" Josie leaned back in mock horror.

"Then why do you keep coming back for more," he murmured. Josie ran her finger over his lips. "Hey, stop that, you minx, you're only trying to get me to kiss you."

"Then, why don't you?"

Nick obliged, and Josie snuggled contentedly into his encircling arm.

"It's nice sitting here," she said. Although it was dusk, some people hadn't yet drawn their curtains, and when she glanced across to the opposite side of the road, she could catch glimpses of the spacious rooms inside the imposing houses facing the park. Josie had always admired them. Built mainly in the Edwardian and Victorian style for master potters and other prominent members of the community, they had always seemed to represent influence, security and wealth.

"You know, Queen's Park and all this area have played such a big part in my life," she told Nick.

He looked down at her dark curly head, which fitted so well into his shoulder. "You mean you feel sentimental about it?"

"I think I always will."

For a few moments Nick remained silent, then he gently removed his arm and, opening the car door, began to get out.

Josie stared at him. "Where are you going?"

"*I'm* not – *we* are."

"But it's cold!"

"Not that cold!"

Mystified, she waited while he came round to open the passenger door, and then joined him on the pavement. Nick took her hand and they walked a few yards down the pavement, before he came to a halt at a spot where an overhead street lamp shed a soft glow. "I've never been a conventional bloke, as you know," he said. "But while the place I've chosen might not have soft lights and sweet music, even I know I've got to conform in one way."

Astonished, Josie stood in the lamplight as Nick went down on one knee.

In a theatrical gesture, he placed one hand on his heart and, declared, "Josie Ford, who I love more than life itself, I ask you this question in the idyllic setting of your youth. Would you do me, as Jane Austen would say, the considerable honour of becoming my wife?"

Josie began to laugh, then suddenly found it difficult to speak, her heart was so full of love and happiness. With misty eyes she gazed down at him, wanting to imprint this moment forever in her memory.

Nick, seeing the response he'd dreamed of in her eyes, began to grumble. "I wish you'd hurry up and give me an answer – this hard pavement's killing me!"

Josie laughed. "Get up, you idiot! Yes, of course I'll marry you!"

Scrambling to his feet, Nick picked her up in a bear hug and swung her round in circles until they were both breathless. "What do you think? Christmas for the engagement?"

Josie nodded. "It will give me time to choose a really expensive ring!" Nick laughed. "As long as I won't have to take out a mortgage!"

They got back into the car and huddled together to keep warm. "You don't mind, do you?" Nick said. "That I didn't choose a romantic restaurant or something?"

Josie shook her head. "Lots of girls have that. This was unique, just for me. I'll never forget it. You're a genius, Nick Hamilton."

"That's why I chose you," he murmured. He squeezed Josie's hand, started up the car, and drove further out into the country. It was, he planned, going to be much later that evening before he took his future wife back to her home.

Chapter 37

Lily and Sid received the news of Josie's impending engagement with both delight and anxiety. But the latter was slight, and only because of her young years. As Lily said, "You only have to look at the pair of them, to know this is a match made in heaven."

Sid smiled at his wife's romantic words. Nick Hamilton was a son-in-law to be proud of. He was intelligent, well-mannered, and easy to get on with. What more could a father want? Nick had the approval of the rest of the family too, as both Dennis and Peter, protective towards their younger sister, had already expressed their opinion.

However, Nick kept prevaricating about telling his mother and Gerald, until, as Josie pointed out, if they wanted to have an engagement party, then it was no use waiting until Christmas was upon them. And so, a month after Nick's proposal, just before Georgina left for Edinburgh, he took Josie home for Sunday tea.

They'd agreed not to make their announcement until after the social niceties were exchanged, and Josie was leaving it to Nick to choose the right moment. But on this second visit, she was wary.

Her eyes watchful, she tensed when shortly after they arrived, Mary left the room to make the tea before wheeling in the tea trolley. Just let Gerald try, she thought, just let him. . .

She didn't have long to wait, because Gerald began as soon as the sitting-room door closed behind his wife.

"Well," he said, "you're a stayer, Josie, I'll grant you that!" His lips were smiling, but Josie saw the coldness in his eyes.

"In what way," she asked, casually crossing her legs. She was wearing a red tartan skirt and white polo-neck sweater, and regretted the latter when she noticed how Gerald's eyes lingered on her breasts.

"Still with young Nick here! Not exactly in accord with his usual record, I must say."

"And what record is that?" she said coolly.

Gerald glanced sharply at her. "You must know what young men are like these days."

"Not really," she said. "Tell me."

Gerald's lips tightened, and she could see that he was annoyed. "Well, if you're as naïve as that, then maybe it explains a lot."

Nick, tense and angry beside Josie, struggled to control his temper, knowing that Gerald's intention was to provoke an ugly scene. A row in Josie's presence would embarrass his mother terribly, one more indication that her son was a trouble-maker.

Josie simply met Gerald's gaze and held it, making it obvious she wasn't going to be drawn.

354

Just then, Mary came back into the room. "Here we are," she said brightly. "I hope everyone's hungry."

"It looks lovely, Mrs Rhodes." And it did, Josie thought, seeing the home-made Dundee cake, and dainty bridge rolls.

"Do tuck in, Josie. Please don't stand on ceremony," Mary said.

Again, as before, Gerald played the part of the indulgent host, and Josie watched as he and Mary exchanged fond glances. There was even laughter at times, although Josie was acutely aware that Nick, sitting beside her on the sofa, remained quiet. It was appalling, she thought, that he should feel so uncomfortable in his own home, and even more disgraceful that his mother chose to close her eyes to it. She wasn't very impressed with Mary Rhodes. She might have poise and perfect vowels, but she hadn't nearly the strength of character of Lily. Her gaze wandered to the framed photograph of Nick's father, which stood on one of the bookshelves. He looked upstanding, that was the word, and with a similar long thin face and dark hair Nick bore a distinct resemblance to him. Josie knew, because Nick had told her, that Gerald had moved the photograph to a less conspicuous place shortly after he moved in, but Nick had simply replaced it whenever he came home from work, and eventually Gerald must have realised it was one battle he wasn't going to win.

"A small victory," Nick had said, "but a satisfying one."

Again, after a while, Gerald asked his wife to make another pot of tea, but this time, instead of remaining in the room, Nick got up. "Excuse me," he said, and followed her.

There was a short silence with Josie, although gazing steadily down at the patterned Axminster carpet, conscious of Gerald's eyes upon her. He won't be able to resist, she thought. And she was right.

"How long have you known Nick now?" he asked, his tone gentle and concerned.

"Nearly a year," she said.

"I thought so. Don't you think it's rather strange that this is only the second time he's invited you to his home?"

Keeping her tone non-committal, Josie said, "Not really."

"You're a nice girl, Josie – I wouldn't like to see you get hurt."

"I don't think there's much danger of that, Mr Rhodes," she paused, "at least not by Nick." Her eyes challenged his, and she saw his own narrow, but at that moment the door re-opened and Mary, ushered in by Nick, held out her arms.

"Josie, congratulations! This is wonderful news!" Josie went to be hugged, then Mary turned to her husband. "Nick's just told me they're getting engaged at Christmas!"

Gerald stared at them both. "Engaged! What are you thinking of, Nick? I keep telling you, Mary, he's got no sense of responsibility!"

"And why would it be irresponsible?" Nick's tone was icy.

"Oh Gerald, they're in love. Anyone can see that," Mary said.

"I'm still waiting for you to answer my question!" Nick, struggling to keep his temper, glared at his stepfather.

"Because you're taking advantage of the girl's age, that's why! How can she make such an important decision, when she's had no experience of life?"

"The girl, as you call her, has a name," Josie countered. "And, Mr Rhodes, you're wrong about Nick. He's the most responsible young man I've ever met." She turned to Mary. "I'm glad you're happy for us, Mrs Rhodes."

"Of course I am. And," she said with a placating look at Gerald, "my husband only has both your best interests at heart. I think we should have a party for them, dear," she said, turning to him.

"Of course," Gerald said, and added stiffly, "I offer my congratulations too."

Later, when they were driving home, Josie felt mystified by Gerald's attitude. If he simply wanted Nick out of the house, then she would have thought he'd have welcomed the engagement.

"What is it with Gerald?" she asked. "Have you fathomed out what's behind it all?"

"Oh yes, I've fathomed it out all right," Nick said, his expression bleak. "It took me a while, but I got there. In my opinion, and I'm sure I'm right, his plan is to convince my weak, and at times foolish, mother, that I'm some sort of wastrel. You heard him – I lack responsibility."

"Rubbish," Josie said. "But why?"

"So that she'll change her will."

Josie drew a sharp intake of breath. "How do you know she's made one?" She didn't think such a thought would ever enter her parents' minds!

"Because when dad died so unexpectedly, she told me he'd left everything to her. That when his will was drawn up, I was still a child." He glanced sideways at her. "I think formal will readings must only take place on the films, or if you're filthy rich. She never actually showed it to me, but she did say that the solicitor insisted she made a new one."

"And that was before she met Gerald?"

He nodded. "I don't know what's in it. Mum's a bit secretive about financial stuff." He gave a wry smile. "I don't think she's realised yet that I'm an adult!"

"But how do you know . . ."

"That she hasn't changed it since – in his favour? Because despite all her faults, I know she'd tell me first. She wouldn't just go and do it behind my back."

"But surely she wouldn't do it anyway. That would mean him inheriting everything your father worked for!"

Nick shrugged. "I know. It's not just the house – Mum's got money of her own, shares and invest-ments. It worries me sometimes, the influence Gerald seems to have over her."

"Well, I think it's awful, the whole thing!"

So do I, my love, Nick thought. So do I.

★

Georgina, who had ordered *The Edinburgh Evening News* on a regular basis, was concentrating on searching its pages for a suitable job. As she intended to move up to Scotland as soon as her month's notice was over, it was crucial that she had at least a couple of interviews lined up. Although she'd never experienced any lack of money in her life, Georgina's upbringing had made her very conscious of the importance of it. She had no intention of eating into her capital by being unemployed, even for a short time.

Two posts which were advertised especially appealed. One was in a barrister's office, and specified a high shorthand speed as being essential. Now that, she decided, would not only be fascinating, it would be a further step in her career. The other, as secretary to a professor at Edinburgh University, had the advantage of being a research post lasting twelve months. Enough time, she thought, for me to know whether I want to stay in Scotland or not. Maybe by then I'll be ready to come home.

Deciding that her parents might like to be involved in her plans, Georgina showed them the newspaper. William, gratified to be consulted, scanned not only both relevant advertisements, but also all the others.

"You've chosen well," he said, and looked at Georgina with new respect. For one fleeting moment he wondered whether he should have encouraged her to take more interest in the family business. But the thought soon passed. William didn't believe that women should take part in management. They had their uses in offices, of course, but running a company was a man's job, always would be.

Alice also approved, and so Georgina applied for the two posts, and within ten days had received offers of interviews. The dates and times fitted in ideally with her planned schedule.

"Almost," she told Josie, "as if it was fate."

"Which one do you fancy most?"

"I'm not sure. Possibly the twelve-month contract is the more practical. But I'll play it by ear, see how I like the people."

"You will be coming home for Christmas?"

Georgina laughed. "I don't think I'd dare stay away. I can't miss your engagement party!"

"You hadn't better!" But Josie was finding the arrangements for the party a bit of a headache. Lily and Sid wanted them to get engaged as part of the normal Christmas festivities.

"Boxing Day," Lily suggested. "We always have a bit of a do in the afternoon."

That sounded fine, but Josie simply couldn't imagine Gerald and Mary Rhodes fitting in with the casual, family chaos which was the normal state of affairs in the Ford home. The small house was always lavishly decorated with traditional streamers, balloons and tinsel, but it presented a far different appearance from the elegant silver and gold arrangements that Josie saw at the hotel, and suspected Mary would opt for. Dennis would be bringing his wife, Mavis, and their lively Johnny,

Sonia would be chain-smoking in a corner, little Kay running around sticky-faced, and Sid despite his best intentions always got a bit tipsy.

Now I can just imagine what it would be like if we held it at Nick's house, Josie thought. An elegant cocktail party, with people standing about with nibbles, and talking loudly about the latest book they'd read. How would her family fit in there?

"Why does life have to be so difficult?" she grumbled to Nick.

"What we could do is to just merge in with Christmas," he suggested. "You come to our house when guests come, and I'll come to yours when all your family are there." He grinned. "Then we'd have two lots of champagne."

"You won't get champagne at our house!"

"So what? I'm sure there'll be some beer."

Josie grinned. "You can bet on it. Although I think we might run to a bottle of sparkling wine!"

Both sets of parents were in agreement, although, as Lily said, "We're going to have to meet Mr and Mrs Rhodes at some point, Josie. I don't want it to be the first time at the wedding!"

"Oh, that's way in the future," Josie said.

But Nick glanced at her, thinking, not too far in the future, I hope. Josie turned and met his gaze, her cheeks reddening. I can read your mind, Nick Hamilton, she thought, but she was guiltily aware that his sensual thoughts simply matched her own.

Chapter 38

The morning Georgina set off for Edinburgh was cold, but at least the roads were clear of frost. She'd been ready to go for a couple of days, but William had insisted she waited until weather conditions were at their safest.

"You're going north, remember. And you've never driven this far before. It's going to take you at least six hours. The last thing you want is to have to worry about bad weather."

So Georgina drove at a steady pace, and with relief stopped for lunch at Kendal, where seeing its many limestone buildings with their slate roofs, she could understand why it was called the "Auld Grey Town". Later, glad to have the drive over Shap behind her, she had a mug of hot chocolate in Carlisle, then continued on her journey through the Scottish borders to stop for tea and scones in Dalkeith. Right, she thought, as she came out of the teashop, Edinburgh here I come!

William was relieved when she rang from Fiona's home to say she'd arrived safely. "I'm very tired," she said, "but I made it."

"Well done," he told her. "I'm proud of you."

If only, she thought with bitterness, as she

362

replaced the receiver, he could have said that when I was little! What *was* it that had changed him? But once she went into the high-ceilinged dining-room to join Fiona's family for dinner, all thoughts of Rosemount and its problems were forgotten.

Georgina, after her interviews, was offered both jobs, and was tempted by the prospect of attending court to take notes. But Fiona, whose father was a lawyer, told her she was more likely to listen to rulings on the percentage of meat in sausages, than to juicy murders or divorce cases.

"It's not as glamorous as it sounds," he warned. And so, after changing her mind at least three times, Georgina settled on the university, the one-year contract being the deciding factor.

Josie laughed aloud when she read her first letter from Scotland.

I'm surrounded, Georgina wrote, *by the most amazing array of talent you've ever seen. Handsome, clever young men, studious ones, shy ones; we've got them all. I'm going to have a ball!*

"I just hope," Josie told her parents, "that she does meet someone."

"Well," Lily said, as she turned a collar on one of Sid's shirts, "maybe that's why she had to go there. I'm a great believer in fate."

"You women do talk a load of rubbish," Sid grumbled. "What's on the telly, Lil?"

"I don't know. Have a look in the *Radio Times!*" she snapped. Rubbish, indeed! And that from a man who could talk for hours about a few men kicking a ball around a field! Not that Sid often went down to the Victoria Ground to actually watch Stoke City – he left that to Dennis – but he followed the Club's progress avidly.

Josie was holding out her left hand, trying to imagine an engagement ring on the third finger. She spent every lunch-hour browsing around the jewellers' shops in Hanley, trying to decide whether she wanted a solitaire diamond, a hoop, or perhaps an emerald.

"Go for diamonds," was Lily's advice. "It's more traditional."

Josie wasn't sure she wanted to be traditional, but diamonds were supposed to be a girl's best friend, at least according to Marilyn Monroe!

"But how," she asked Nick, "will I be able to know which one I can have? Suppose I choose one that's too expensive?"

"You'll know, my sweet, because," he told her, "once you've told me which jeweller's you want to go to, and when, then I'll go in beforehand and arrange for them to only show us certain trays."

"Oh," she exclaimed with relief, "thank goodness for that!"

He laughed. "You are a goose, at times."

And so the choice was made. A square solitaire, and despite Josie's protests, Nick tucked the blue leather box firmly into his pocket as they left the shop, saying, "Not a peep again until Christmas!"

And before they knew it, the festive season was upon them, with Josie searching the shops not only for presents, but also for something to wear when she went to the Rhodes' party. Elegant, she decided – that's what I'll be. And restrained. I'm not going to give them even an inch they can criticise, even if I am from the 'wrong side of the tracks', as the Americans call it.

She chose an angora dress in a pale camel shade. It had a mandarin collar, fitted waist with a matching belt, and slightly flared skirt, showing off her slim figure perfectly, and, as the rather superior assistant said, was 'classy'.

Lily could only look in wonder when Josie shook out her purchase from its surrounding tissue paper. "That must have cost a fortune!"

"More than I've ever paid for anything," Josie confessed. "But I needed to, Mum. I want to wear something that gives me confidence."

Lily glanced shrewdly at her. "You're not worried about mixing with the nobs, are you?" It was obvious that Nick came from a different background, even though he never 'put on any side'.

"A bit."

"Well, don't!" Lily told her. "Working in that posh hotel has taught you a lot."

"I know. Right, I'll try it on and you can tell me what you think."

Josie put on the dress and a pair of high heels, tidied her hair and turned to face her mother.

With a catch in her voice, Lily said, "You look like a million dollars!"

"Thanks, Mum!"

"But don't wear pink nail varnish with it –

you'll need a coral one," Lily called back, as she went down the stairs.

Josie grinned. That was rich, coming from someone who had never painted her nails in her life! She glanced down at her left hand, imagining the sparkling diamond ring. Sometimes she wondered whether she'd ever be as happy as she was now. Josie wasn't at all religious, but the prayer that came into her thoughts was instinctive. *Please, God, let me and Nick have a good life!*

While the Fords held their engagement party first, on Boxing Day, a chaotic, noisy family affair, Gerald and Mary Rhodes had invited their guests for drinks on the morning of New Year's Day. So Josie had already been wearing her ring for a week by the time she was 'paraded' before what felt like an inspection committee.

It was the first time she had met any of Nick's relatives, and it was with relief that she found that not all of them were 'stuck up'. Several were warm and friendly, although Josie did get fed up with hearing the same comment: "I'm so glad Nick is settling down at last." This seemed to be the prevailing opinion, and Josie couldn't help directing sharp angry glances at Gerald Rhodes, urbane and pleasant, as he moved around the room offering to replenish drinks. But after all, what could she say? She didn't know these people well enough to defend Nick, to accuse Gerald. Some of the guests, particularly the women, reminded her of the two snobs who had so upset her at the

366

Tennis Club party where she'd first met Nick. Even over the clamour of voices, she could hear the same nasal tones, and tortured vowels. It's as though they're part of a clan, a closed circle, she thought. I'll never be able to fit in with them, nor would I want to. However, when, after a champagne toast, she and Nick accepted people's congratulations, she began to relax and enjoy herself. And on this occasion, Gerald didn't shoot any of his subtle barbs – at least none that Josie overheard.

As always, January seemed an anti-climax after the festivities, with the house seeming bare without the decorations, the days short and the skies overcast and grey. It was now that Josie really began to miss Georgina, who had come down by train from Scotland to stay for a few days over Christmas, but had gone back early to spend New Year with Fiona's family.

"I can't miss 'first-footing'," she laughed. "Apparently they make more of New Year up there than they do of Christmas!"

But there was Fergal's demob to look forward to, and when he arrived in the middle of January he went straight to Sonia's house to get settled in. Lily invited them to tea on the following day, when the conversation centred mainly on the problem of where he should apply for a job.

Fergal, still amazed at how comfortable he felt with Peter's family, told them, "I want to find a job where I can get on. The trouble is, I haven't got any qualifications. We kids from the children's home weren't exactly encouraged to take exams, although I think it was partly my own fault. All I wanted to do was to keep a low profile. And to be honest, being treated like the dregs of society didn't do much for your aspirations."

Josie glanced at him. Using a word like 'aspirations' didn't sound to her as if he lacked education. But then he can't be stupid, she thought, or Georgina wouldn't have been able to write to him and discuss books and things.

"I've learned more by reading," Fergal added, "than anything I learned at school."

Lily looked at him thoughtfully. It was no use suggesting that he try and work in a shop; he needed to be with fellow workers who were used to him, not gawped at by the general public!

"Maybe Georgina could have a word with Mr Hawkins," she suggested.

Josie saw Fergal's expression stiffen.

"Oh, come on, Mum," she said, "Fergal and Georgina are friends, they've been writing to each other for ages. He's hardly going to want to become one of her father's employees. You know what a snob old Hawkins is!"

"There's the potbanks – he could try one of those," Sonia said, who was sitting slumped in an armchair. Now four months pregnant, she was looking distinctly peaky.

Josie agreed. "I was thinking the same thing. We could get Dennis to ask for him."

Fergal frowned, and she said quickly, "Don't

worry. It wouldn't be a special favour. That's how most people get their jobs on the potbanks."

Sid, who was quietly helping Kay with her alphabet, looked up. "For that matter, I could ask at our place." He went on to explain, "I work at Portland's in Longton. It's a colour mill – we supply glazes to the pottery factories."

He turned to Lily. "You know, that might not be a bad idea. The gaffer's quite keen on giving a likely lad a chance. Fergal could even end up working in the laboratories."

"What would he be taken on as?" Josie asked.

"Oh, it would just be labouring, in some form or other, like me. Mind you, a labourer is how I've ended up. But then," he added with a self-deprecating smile, "I was never going to be a brain surgeon."

"You're one of the best, Sid Ford, and don't you forget it!" Lily was quick to leap to his defence. "Never a day have you been out of work, and there's not many can say that!"

Fergal could only sit and listen, dumbfounded that these friendly people should take such an interest in him, were actually keen to help, genuinely wanted him to have a chance. It was my lucky day when I met Peter, he thought. I'd have been adrift without him, and would prob-ably have signed on again in the Navy. He's been the best mate anyone could have.

"Do you want me to have a word with Les, that's our glaze foreman?"

"Thanks, Sid, I'd be grateful."

And so after an interview with Percy Gallimore, the works manager, Fergal was taken on as a labourer. Under the supervision of a charge-hand, his job was to load glaze cylinders with raw materials, then add water so they could be run overnight ready for the following morning. To protect his clothing he was supplied with a white boiler suit, and wellingtons, but told that the men liked to provide their own hats. As soon as they saw Fergal's and realised he'd just come out of the Navy, they immediately dubbed him, 'Sailor'.

"Count yourself lucky," Sid grinned. "We all have nicknames, and mine's 'Soapy'."

"Why's that?"

"Think about it. You know how often we have to wash our hands because the white glaze gets stuck in our fingernails. Well, I went a bit over-board when I started, so . . ."

"Soapy Sid," Fergal laughed. But as had been expected, Fergal's appearance came in for some ribald comments.

"Hey," Sid heard someone say on the first morning, "we've got the Phantom of the Opera working upstairs!"

"Aye, I've seen him. He's still better lookin' than you!"

That was typical of the men's reaction, and Fergal did as he had on board ship, and retaliated in the same vein. "I might have an ugly mug," he'd say, "but at least they can't call me Schnozzle Durante like some I could mention!"

370

And there was camaraderie too, which he hadn't expected to find off ship.

At lunch-times, the men would take their break in a small room called the 'cabin', where they would eat their sandwiches or fetch chips in, and afterwards play darts or cards. The first time, Fergal got ribbed for not washing his hands properly and getting slip on his mug. "There's many a slip between cup and lip!" was the pun, with a few knowing grins. After work some would call for a drink at a nearby pub called The Portland, and eventually Fergal, with Sid's encouragement, began to join them.

"It always helps to be one of the lads," Sid told him. "By the time I retire, you should be well dug in."

Sid's coming retirement was a subject often on Lily's mind. "How I'll cope, having him under my feet all the time, I just can't think," she told Josie.

"But you get on all right."

"That's as maybe. But it's well known that you can't have a tidy house when there's a man about all day!"

But all the Fords were pleased at the difference in Fergal since he spent that first leave with them. No longer did he walk with his head down, but stared rigidly ahead, determined not to notice horrified stares and averted eyes.

"I still think," Sid said one day, "that he ought to go and see about that scar."

"I think so too," Lily said, "but let him get settled in before you say anything."

And Fergal *was* settling in. Sonia fulfilled her part of the bargain, and there was always a hot meal waiting for him when he got home from work. It might be 'makeshift' but to Fergal, who'd been brought up on institutional fare, it was more than welcome.

Dennis, soon after his arrival, hoping he'd take an interest in Stoke City, had taken him to one of their home games. "You can borrow my scarf if you're bothered about your face," he offered, and Lily winced. Dennis had always been a plain speaker.

But Fergal just said, "Thanks, I might do that." And after that first exhilarating match, when Stoke City beat Swansea Town, 4-2, Fergal went with Dennis on a regular basis.

"Why don't you go with them?" Lily asked Sid one evening.

"No sense in my standing in the cold and wet at my age," he said. "Anyway, I'd rather listen to the game on the wireless, same as I've always done."

"You're getting to be a stick-in-the mud, Sid Ford."

"Always have been," he said complacently, and it was true, Lily thought, as she plumped up the cushions before going to bed. But then so was she; they'd never been an adventurous couple. Climbing the steep stairs, she shivered, hoping that Sid had taken up a hot-water bottle. I wonder how Georgina's getting on in Scotland, she thought – I bet it's even colder up there!

Chapter 39

Georgina was enjoying herself. Fiona's parents, both professional people, were busy with their own lives, and apart from asking whether she was comfortable, left her to her own devices. And so, she realised she was lucky enough to have the best of both worlds. Somewhere safe and luxurious to live, and complete independence. She and Fiona had lots to catch up on, and they were both looking forward to June's visit that weekend. She'd written to say she was driving herself up from Leeds, and it was with relief that they saw her small red car pull into the drive.

"Come on," Fiona said later, once June had unpacked. "I've raided the cellar and put a bottle of wine in the fridge. The parents are out, our Jamie's away at school, so we've got the place to ourselves!"

"How old is your brother now?" June asked.

"Seventeen. He'll be doing his A levels this year."

Georgina was staring at June with admiration. "I just can't get over the difference in you!" June's ample curves had refined into a very sexy figure.

"It was bloody hard work," June complained.

"Here you see before you someone who never touches chocolate, cakes, biscuits or even crisps."

"What, never?" Fiona stopped pouring the wine and looked at her in amazement.

"Well, almost never!" June grinned. "But not tonight. Bring out the booze and food – this is a special occasion!"

"What gave you the incentive?" Georgina took a glass of chilled white wine from Fiona, and sipped it. "Mmn, that's lovely!"

"It should be!" Fiona laughed. "It's one of Dad's finest."

"Won't he mind?"

She shook her head. "Probably won't even notice."

"My incentive," June told them, "was a certain person called Duncan."

"You dark horse! Come on, give!"

Georgina sat back as the two girls talked incessantly about their boyfriends. Fiona, of course, was already engaged, and due to marry as soon as her fiancé qualified as a doctor. June, it turned out, was confident of a proposal within the next month. "He's just soulful," she said, her face becoming pink even at the thought of him, "and he's filthy rich. His grandfather owned a couple of coal mines."

"So it looks as though both of you will be married by the time you're twenty-one!" With a wry smile, Georgina drained her glass. "I'm getting left behind."

"Aye," Fiona said, "you'll end up an old maid,

particularly with a face like yours!" The three girls laughed.

"My mother believes in girls getting married young," June told them. "She says it's better to have your children before you're thirty. Then when they're grown up, you're still young enough to enjoy yourself."

"More like she hopes that way, she can keep you a virgin until you walk down the aisle!" Fiona teased, and she and June exchanged meaningful glances.

"It's really hard, isn't it?" June said, then realising what she'd just said, blushed scarlet, while the other two girls collapsed in giggles.

"Close your ears, Georgina," Fiona gasped. "You're much too innocent for all this."

"That's what you think," she told them. "I've had to fight off one or two blokes myself!" And she told them about Felix. "Talk about wandering hands!"

"You won't mind so much when you meet the right one," Fiona said.

Georgina looked at them both. Should she tell them about Dominic? But it all sounded so trite, so childish, to keep a flame burning for someone she'd only spent a few hours with. And it *was* almost four years ago!

But after Fiona had opened another bottle of wine, Georgina found the words spilling out to her old school-friends, as though the years since they'd met had never been.

"Oh, it's so romantic," breathed June. "Just like on the films. A tragic, lovelorn heroine!"

"Ah, but was Dominic a hero or a heel?" Fiona pointed out. "I can understand him falling for our gorgeous friend here, but he could have told her he was clearing off to the ends of the earth!"

"I think he might have done," Georgina said, "only my father didn't give him the chance!"

"Still the same old idealist!" Fiona poured herself another glass of wine. "And if you go on thinking like that, you'll never get over him."

"I agree." June was now lounging on the sofa, her eyes suspiciously bright, her words slightly slurred. "Go out and play the field, that's what I say."

"Absolutely." Fiona, who was holding her alcohol better than her friends, turned to Georgina. "How long did you say your job at the university was for?"

"Twelve months."

"Right. My advice is to work hard and play hard. And by play, I mean go out on lots of dates. After all, you're working at the university – just think of all those handsome undergraduates – it's a single girl's heaven!" Fiona drained her glass, and looked at her friends. "I can tell you pair don't imbibe very much," she said in disgust. "You're both nearly blotto!"

"I just want to go to sleep," murmured June, with a beatific smile.

"Then you'd better go to bed," Fiona said, holding out a hand to pull her up, "before the parents get back!"

"Me, too," yawned Georgina.

"I'll give you both a glass of water – and make sure you drink it!" Fiona, glancing at her watch, hurriedly began to clear away the debris and empty wine bottles.

The next morning, just in case Georgina had forgotten, Fiona reminded her about the agreed master plan. "Don't forget! You've got twelve months to find your ideal man . . ."

"I remember," Georgina said, with her head in her hands. "But remind me never to drink so much again! I feel dreadful!"

"Och, you get used to it!" Fiona grinned. "You should see my Alistair knock back the whiskies."

"You'll end up a pair of alcoholics," June said, who was unable to face any breakfast.

"Don't be daft, we know better than that! Life is for the living, you two! I tell you what," she nudged June. "Take a bottle of champagne to bed on your wedding night – it'll make all the difference!"

"You know that from experience, do you?"

Georgina looked up and saw that June's accusation had hit home. Shocked, she could only think that Fiona must really love Alistair to risk getting pregnant. But then, Fiona had always been daring, even at school. While I, she thought sadly, seem to lead a completely uneventful life.

"How is she?" Lily asked Josie, as she saw her put down Georgina's letter. "Is she coming home for her birthday?"

"It doesn't look like it." Josie's expression was

one of disappointment, and Lily tried to console her.

"Well, it's not as if it's her twenty-first. And it is a long journey, you know."

"Yes, but she's been up there six months now, and she's only been home twice. Once at Christmas, and once at Easter."

"You'll have to get used to it, love. She's made a new life for herself up there."

You can say that again, Josie thought. If she told her mum how many so-called boyfriends Georgina had been out with, she'd have a fit! Yet Georgina wrote, "*I've met some really attractive young men, yet when I spend time with them there's always something missing. I ask myself whether I'm looking for the gold that doesn't exist, but then I only have to think of you and Nick to know it does. I want what you've got, Josie.*"

Josie smiled. Well, according to her letters, Georgina had only got another six months to find it!

And then one day she got home from work to find Lily in a rare state of excitement. "I've just heard there's a chance of a house in the next street," she told Josie. "Edie Baker told me that they're moving to Rhyl to be near their son. Spotlessly clean she is, and her husband's a painter and decorator, so it should be well looked after."

Josie stared at her. "You mean for me and Nick?"

Lily nodded. "I know you've made no plans yet, but privately rented houses are like gold dust. Besides you've always liked it round here."

Josie, hot after her journey home on the bus, took off her jacket, and hung it on the peg in the hall. Following her mother into the front room, she sat facing her on an armchair.

"You'd need to act quickly," Lily told her. "Why don't you go and have a look? I'm sure Edie won't mind."

Infected by her mother's excitement, Josie tried to think clearly. She knew that Nick wanted to buy rather than rent, but that meant them waiting, possibly for another two years. His business was doing well, and needing more space he'd just taken on a lock-up unit to store his stock. Also he needed a larger van. "I've got to plough all my profits back for the time being," he said. "It will mean waiting, sweetheart, but these early days are crucial."

Josie understood that, but she was becoming worried. Their lovemaking was becoming increasingly risky, and although she hadn't yet taken that final step, Josie knew it was only the deterrent of her parents' shame that stopped her from risking pregnancy. Although Nick never pressured her, she was unsure how much longer they could remain in control. Josie wanted to belong completely to Nick, wanted them to be able to express their love with abandon. It seemed so unnatural always to draw back at the last minute.

She looked thoughtfully at Lily, who was watching her expectantly.

"I suppose we could rent for the first two or three years. I know Nick wants to buy eventually."

"Of course he does. That seems to be the way things are going now with you young people. And good luck to you, I say. After all, rent is like throwing money down the drain. But me and your dad never had any choice."

"I know. I think your generation had it really tough, what with the War and everything."

"So," Lily demanded, "what do you think?"

"I'll have a word with Nick," Josie told her. "I'm seeing him tonight."

"Remember," Lily warned, as Josie went upstairs to change, "don't hang about or you'll miss it!"

Chapter 40

Nick, when Josie told him about the house, could only feel a huge sense of relief. This was their answer, to move into a home of their own, even if it was only rented, at least for the first few years. He hadn't said anything to Josie, but the situation at home was becoming more intolerable with every day that passed. Nick found it an enormous strain to live in the same house as Gerald Rhodes, one in which he'd shared such a happy relationship with his real father. Not only was it galling to see his mother taken in by Gerald's false charm, but the fact that she allowed him to manipulate her, to poison her mind against her only son, was one he found deeply hurtful. Well, he'd done his best to protect her. He hadn't moved out despite Gerald's provocation. But it would be different if he was leaving to get married. But without his constant presence, could Gerald persuade her to do something foolish? Nick decided to have a word with their solicitor. Neil Maxwell had been a close friend of Nick's father, and he wasn't anyone's fool.

"Right," he said, turning to Josie. "Let's go and see it."

"I'll get Mum to fix it up. But it would mean getting married quite quickly."

"No problem!" They were walking along a high path in Queen's Park, known locally as 'Lover's Lane', and Nick drew Josie to him and held her close. "It can't come quickly enough as far as I'm concerned."

"Me too." For several minutes, they remained locked in an embrace and then, with arms entwined, continued walking, while Josie's mind ran ahead with excitement.

The house was perfect! Beautifully decorated, in pristine condition, and it even had a new sink unit. Josie exchanged one glance with Nick, and just knew it was meant for them.

"I'll have a word with Mrs Hawkins, first thing in the morning," Lily promised, when they went back for a cup of tea.

But when Lily approached Alice Hawkins, she was flabbergasted when her employer shook her head.

"Oh dear," Alice said. "I'm not sure, Mrs Ford. My husband's planning to sell off the houses, either offering them to sitting tenants, or when they become vacant, putting them on the market."

Dismayed, Lily said, "Oh, I see. But, Mrs Hawkins, couldn't you ask him if he'd make an exception in our Josie's case?"

"I don't mind asking him, but I doubt if he will." Alice looked at her cleaner and felt a flash of sympathy. After all it was the first time Mrs Ford had asked a favour in all the years she had worked at Rosemount, but Alice knew her husband. Where business was concerned, William Hawkins had always refused to consider sentiment. Not only that, but he prided himself on never going back on a decision. He might have mellowed in some ways, particularly towards Georgina, but generosity towards other people had never been part of his character.

However, after dinner she told him of Lily's request.

William frowned. "But I told you, I'm going to run down the tenancies, sell off the properties – at least where I can."

"Not all the tenants will want to buy," Alice pointed out.

"That's as may be. And there's nothing I can do about that. But it's a business decision, Alice. It's just unfortunate that this particular house, which will be the first to be sold, happens to be one that Josie's interested in."

"I just thought that as we've known her for so long . . ."

He shook his head. "Look at it from my point of view. I've already set things in motion and my staff have been told about the new policy. In fact the letters are being typed this week. Now if I make an exception for Josie, it will be the thin edge of the wedge. Word will get round, and next it will be someone with a disabled child or a sick granny. You know how these things develop. I'm sorry, Alice, but the answer is no."

When, the following morning, Lily was told of

383

the refusal, she was sick with disappointment. Not only that but she was furious. It wouldn't have hurt him to say yes, she raged, as she rubbed furiously at the brass fender. After all these years, she'd have thought she deserved more consideration. But then William Hawkins never did think of anyone but himself!

Even by the time Sid arrived home from work, Lily still hadn't calmed down. As soon as he came through the door he could hear her slamming saucepans around in the scullery. "I don't need to ask what the answer was, then?"

She told him what had happened. "He says if he makes an exception for Josie, he'll have all sorts asking him." Lily turned to face him. "Did you know before? That he was going to sell the houses, I mean?"

Sid shook his head. "No, never heard a dickie-bird. Not that it will affect us. Even if he offered us a good price as sitting tenants, we don't want to go taking on debts at our time of life."

"It'll floor her, this will. She'd set her heart on that house! Oh, my God, she's here now!" Hearing the front door close, Lily wiped her hands on a tea towel. She'd been dreading this moment all day.

"What did she say?" Josie came straight through to the scullery, her eyes alight with expectation. But one look at their faces and she didn't need an answer. "You're not going to tell me he said no!"

Lily could only nod, and repeat what she'd told Sid. "I'm so sorry, love."

"He can't do this to me! That house is perfect for us!"

Sid could only watch helplessly as tears welled up in his daughter's eyes.

"Now don't go upsetting yourself!" Lily put an arm around her daughter's shoulders. "Come on, I've made a meat and potato pie. You'll cope better with a good hot meal inside you."

But for once, Josie's healthy appetite deserted her, and an hour later, wanting to be alone, she went miserably upstairs to her room. It wasn't fair, she thought in despair. It's not right that someone else can make a decision that could affect the rest of your life. She wasn't asking for money or anything – just the chance to rent one of his blasted houses! Her misery gave way to growing anger, as she thought about Nick, desperately unhappy, living in the same house as Gerald Rhodes, of the wedding she was already planning, of how they longed to be together day and night. This was to have been their first home! Now it would all have to be abandoned. I'd have thought, she fumed, that as Georgina's best friend, he would have treated me differently from a complete stranger! Well, now I know better. I'm still not one of them. I never will be, and I might as well accept it. She thought again of the house, of how wonderful it would have been to live there with Nick.

Her dreams in tatters, Josie, shocked and horrified, dismissed the startling idea that slid into her mind. But the more she tried to push it away, the more insidious it became, feeding her frustration, her outrage at what she saw as injustice. But slowly, Josie's struggle with her conscience began to weaken. It wasn't as though she would actually *do* anything, after all! And what did people say? The end justified the means? She slumped on her bed, her mind racing, still unable to let go of her rage. Then impulsively, before she could change her mind, she ran downstairs and reached for her jacket.

"Where are you going?" Lily came into the hall, looking with concern at Josie's heightened colour.

"Along to Rosemount. I'm going to see if I can get him to change his mind!"

"Oh, love, you're just storing up more disappointment!" Lily hated to think of her daughter going begging.

"I don't care. I'm going!"

Lily went into the front room to Sid, who'd heard the conversation. "She'll only be humiliating herself for nothing, you mark my words."

Sid just grunted, and buried himself in the *Evening Sentinel.* There was nothing he could do. He'd learned years ago that men like William Hawkins would always do what was in their own interest. He admired Josie's pluck, but like Lily, he didn't hold out much hope.

A few minutes later, Josie closed the gates of Rosemount firmly behind her. Her throat was tight with nerves, but her determination never faltered as she walked quickly along the gravel drive. As she pressed the bell and heard it ring, she knew this was going to be one of the most difficult things she'd ever had to do. But William Hawkins wasn't the only one who could make decisions. Josie had made hers. She wasn't prepared to give in without a fight!

It was Alice who opened the door. "Josie!" She stepped aside for Josie to enter into the hall. "I think I can guess why you've come. But Mr Hawkins isn't in, I'm afraid."

"That's fine," Josie said. In fact, she thought with relief, it was perfect! "Actually, it's you I wanted to see."

"Oh?" Alice led the way into the sitting-room. "Do sit down. But I'm afraid if you've come to ask me about the house, there's nothing I can do. It's a business decision, you see."

Josie remained silent for a few moments. "I'm really disappointed," she said. "We'd even set a date for the wedding."

"I'm sorry," Alice said awkwardly. "Look, would you like a cup of tea, or maybe a glass of sherry?"

"A glass of sherry would be nice, thank you." Josie watched her go to the sideboard, lift a decanter and pour them both a drink.

"Have you heard from Georgina?" Alice asked, as she handed Josie her glass.

"Yes, she seems very happy up there. She says she's made lots of friends."

"It's good, isn't it? Of course the job is only for twelve months, so who knows, she might come back after that."

387

"I hope so, I miss her."

"So do we."

Well, that's a surprise admission, Josie thought.

"Anyway, as I've said, I'm sorry about the refusal, but you know what Mr Hawkins is like. Once he's made up his mind about something . . ."

Josie took a sip of the golden liquid, feeling its warmth fortifying her. She gazed steadily at Alice. "I thought maybe you could try again – you must have some influence over him."

Alice shook her head. "You overestimate me. I promised your mother I'd put a word in for you, and I did. But he was adamant. I'm sorry, Josie, but I'm afraid you'll just have to accept it. Of course, if you and your boyfriend were in a position to buy, that would be different."

"We can't afford to yet," Josie told her. "Not until Nick's business is off the ground. Of course, that's our intention in the future."

Yes, Alice thought. And if you decided to buy the house you were already renting, that would mean that as a sitting tenant you wouldn't have to pay the full asking price. That wouldn't suit William at all!

"And you're sure there isn't anything you could say to persuade him?" Josie said, trying to give her one last chance.

Alice shook her head. "I'm afraid not."

Josie looked down at the luxurious carpet. Her mouth felt dry, and she had to battle a sudden urge to get up and leave. Do it, she told herself.

Don't be a coward! You've rehearsed the words, go on!

She looked up. "Did you know," she said slowly, "that I'm intending to take up *French* cooking?"

For a split second, Alice was puzzled. What on earth had put that in the girl's head? This was Dreston, for heaven's sake. She wouldn't have thought Josie had ever tasted French cuisine. Then suddenly she realised the way Josie had empha-sised the word, '*French*'. She looked up, and in that one split second, she saw the truth blazing at her. Josie Ford *knew* – she had seen her that day at the Royal Hotel – she had always known! Alice felt perspiration break out on her forehead, as panic, embarrassment and fear threatened to over-whelm her. All these years . . . She couldn't speak, could hardly breathe, could only watch Josie rise to her feet and move away, turning only when she reached the sitting-room door.

"Thank you for the sherry, Mrs Hawkins. It's all right, I can see myself out." Seconds later, she was gone.

Alice collapsed against the cushions. She couldn't believe it! Just a few moments ago, her life was normal, uneventful, now she felt as if her world was caving in around her. Josie Ford, the girl who'd been on holiday with them, Georgina's best friend, *knew*! Oh, my God, and now her hand went to her mouth with horror at the thought. Has she told Georgina? And then came another unspeakable dread – does her mother know? Had Mrs Ford been sniggering behind her back all the time she'd been here at Rosemount, ironing and polishing? Alice felt sick with humiliation at the possibility. Get a grip on yourself, she thought wildly – William will be home soon! And at the image of her husband, Alice blanched. She had to think! It didn't take Einstein to work out why Josie had come. Why she'd chosen this particular moment to come and attempt blackmail. Although she'd been clever, Alice would grant her that, the devious little madam! The words she'd used had been so innocent, only Alice, with her guilt, would have known the message they contained. But what if William had been at home, would Josie still have made that comment? With a sick feeling in the pit of her stomach, Alice knew that she would have done, had been prepared to do so. When Josie rang the doorbell, she would have expected them both to be at home. Alice got unsteadily to her feet. Move about, she told herself, regain your composure. And just be thankful that William *wasn't* here. She went into the kitchen, deciding that what she needed was a coffee, a shot of brandy and a cigarette. I've got to think how to handle this, she thought in desperation, and failure isn't an option.

When William let himself in an hour later, Alice came into the hall to meet him. "I'm glad you're back," she said, reaching up to kiss his cheek. "The house has felt empty without you."

Surprised but pleased by the warmth of her welcome, William followed her into the sitting-room.

"Was it a good meeting?"

"Very profitable." He rubbed his hands together. "I could do with a brandy, though. Chadwick's a Methodist, so I only ever have one drink. Don't want to give him the wrong impression."

"Of course not." Alice poured him a generous measure of Remy Martin, and sat opposite. She'd hurriedly put on fresh make-up and changed into one of his favourite dresses, a soft rose pink, where the skirt clung to her still shapely legs.

"You're looking very attractive," he observed.

Alice smiled at him. "I hope I always do."

"And what have you been doing with yourself – watching TV?"

She shook her head. "No. Actually, William, I've been thinking."

William waited for her continue, while he took another sip of brandy, appreciating the feeling of warmth and ease it gave him.

"It's about that house and Josie Ford."

"I've told you, it's not negotiable."

"But have you thought," she said persuasively, "about another aspect of it, besides good business sense? How is this going to look to Georgina? Mrs Ford tells me that Josie is dreadfully upset – she's even going to have to cancel the wedding. And Georgina was to be chief bridesmaid!"

William's eyes narrowed.

"Josie's bound to write and tell her the reason." Alice looked appealingly at him. "I don't know about you, but I had felt lately that Georgina was drawing closer to us. I think we both know that hasn't always been the case. I'd hate her to blame us for spoiling things." Don't say too much, she warned herself. Let him come to the conclusion himself.

After a few moments, William said, "Cancel the wedding, you say?"

Alice nodded. "She's devastated, apparently. They'd been to see the house, and had set their hearts on it." She sipped her own brandy, and warily watched his brooding expression. "Mind you, I don't suppose they'd stay long. Nick's quite ambitious, so Georgina told me. He'd probably want to move on to a bigger place. So, when they did, you'd still be able to get a good price for the house."

"You mean all they're after is a start?"

She nodded. "What do you think? Shall we help them out, give them a chance? I know it would please Georgina."

William was deep in thought. He hadn't realised that his refusal would mean a cancelled wedding. Word would soon get about, and the last thing he wanted was resentment among his tenants, not when he was about to put his new plan into practice. But what had really hit home, was Alice's reference to Georgina. William was damned if he was going to take the risk of her blaming him for ruining Josie's plans. His relationship with his daughter, although much improved, was still too fragile.

He drained the rest of his brandy and looked

across at Alice. "I take your point," he said. "You can tell Mrs Ford in the morning that I've reversed my decision. Lay it on thick, mind. You must make sure she knows it's a special favour! And tell her not to broadcast it. With a bit of luck, people will think they were just lucky with the timing."

As relief, glorious, blessed relief, flooded through her, Alice had to wait until she could control her voice, before she said, "I'll do that, William. I'm sure you're doing the right thing."

William felt expansive, generous even. It was a novel feeling, rather a good one, and seeing that Alice was in such an approachable mood, he got up and poured himself another drink. "Do you fancy an early night?" Knowing the meaning behind his words, Alice forced a smile. "Good idea. I'll go ahead, while you lock up."

Later, lying awake while William slept heavily beside her, Alice was beginning to feel calmer. At least she was safe now. Or was she? She tried to force her thoughts into some sort of rational order. The Ford girl had kept her secret all this time. Now that she'd got what she wanted, what would she gain by causing a scandal that would hurt Georgina? It was the early hours of the morning before Alice felt able to sleep. And her last thought was that the close friendship between the two girls, so unlikely in the beginning, might prove to be her salvation.

Chapter 41

"He won't regret it, Mrs Hawkins!" Lily's face was alight with joy by the time Alice finished telling her the news. "Our Josie will be that pleased!"

"Maybe you'd like to ring her," Alice suggested.

"Could I? Oh, that is kind of you!" Full of excitement, Lily followed Alice into the hall. "I don't know the number, though."

"That's all right. I'll look it up for you." Alice had decided that the sooner Josie knew of William's decision, the better. She handed the receiver to Lily, and went into the sitting-room, leaving open the door.

Nervously, Lily dialled the number of the Royal Hotel. Normally, she wouldn't have dreamed of ringing Josie at work. Apart from reluctantly answering the telephone at Rosemount, when her employer was out, she'd never actually rung anyone!

Josie's voice, once Lily had been put through to her extension, came over full of anxiety. "Mum? What's wrong?"

"Nothing, love!" Lily took a deep breath. "I've got some good news for you. Mr Hawkins has

changed his mind – you can have the house!"
There was silence, and Lily raised her voice. "Josie?
Are you there? Did you hear what I said? You can
have the house after all!"

Her daughter's voice came back. "That's brilliant, Mum. But I can't talk now. Will you thank
Mrs Hawkins for me?"

Slightly deflated, Lily put down the receiver.
She'd expected more excitement from her
daughter, but consoled herself that Josie's boss
must have been in the room.

But she was wrong. Josie was alone in her small
office. Alone with her triumph, with the euphoria
which swept over her, and alone with the guilt
which shadowed it. She'd hardly slept all night,
haunted by the enormity of what she'd done.
How *could* she have gone along to Rosemount
and, sitting right opposite Georgina's mother,
blatantly said those awful words! Josie knew she'd
never be able to forget the horrified expression
on Alice Hawkins' face when she suddenly realised
their significance. It had been a despicable,
shameful thing to do, and Josie wasn't sure
whether she'd ever be able to forgive herself. With
her joy at the news tainted, she could only think,
that was just typical of how impulsive I am! I
never could stand injustice; I always waded in,
even in the playground. But she had been so hurt
and bitterly disappointed. After the holiday in
Bournemouth, Josie had thought she meant more
to Georgina's parents than just some girl from
down the street. I should have known, she thought

wryly, that where the middle classes are concerned, business and income always come first. But that was no excuse to try and blackmail someone. Josie buried her face in her hands; she wanted desperately to let her joy at the news flood into her mind, but she had to clear her head, to appease her conscience. She would *never* have betrayed Mrs Hawkins. Even if Georgina's mother had still refused to reconsider, Josie knew she wouldn't have said anything. I only wanted her to know that I *knew,* she thought miserably. I just thought it might make her try to change his mind. And her plan had worked! Fleetingly, Josie wondered just what had been said to persuade him. Not that it mattered. For the first time in her life, Josie had to come to terms with the fact that she'd done something she was ashamed of. Something she never wanted Nick, Georgina or her family ever to know about. Serves you right, she thought bitterly. You were always the one to take the moral high ground. Well, now you know what you are capable of. You might have won, Josie Ford, but at the moment it seems a very hollow victory.

Nick had known nothing about the threat to their plans. Josie, having at last come to terms with her guilt, told him that after an initial refusal, she'd simply gone along to Rosemount and appealed to Georgina's mother.

"You always were a persuasive little minx," he told her.

"We women have to be," she said. "Otherwise men would have it all their own way."

"Oh yes?" he pulled her on to his knee. "So you're not going to let me have mine, when we're married!"

"Ours will be an equal partnership, Nick," she said firmly. "It'll be the 1960's soon, and things are going to change for women. You'll see!"

"I'm shaking in my shoes," he grinned.

"Come on, we'd better get going." She kissed him and got up, smoothing down her skirt. It was Saturday night, and Nick had come for his tea before they went dancing at the King's Hall, in Stoke. Ted Heath was playing, and Fergal had agreed to go with them. Josie had discreetly found out that Pauline was also planning on going.

"I still don't understand why we can't give her a lift as well as Fergal," Nick grumbled, as they got into the car.

"That's because you're a man," Josie told him. "It will make the whole thing seem contrived, whereas if they sort of bump into each other, that's different."

"I'm not sure if matchmaking's a good idea," he said. "From what you tell me, Fergal's not keen on coming in the first place."

It had taken all Josie's wheedling to get Fergal to accept her invitation. "Look," she'd said to him, "you're fine at work, everything else is going well – what you need now is a social life. Just because Georgina isn't here to dance with, doesn't mean you have to become a hermit!"

Luckily, Josie spotted Pauline fairly early in the evening, and invited her over to join them. Nick immediately went to get her a drink, while Josie deliberately kept the conversation light and friendly. After a while, she looked critically at Pauline.

"What's the matter?" Pauline's hand went automatically to smooth her hair.

"I was just thinking. You could do the same as Georgina and I did – dance with Fergal so that your hair hides his scar!"

"Josie!" Fergal protested. "Don't embarrass the girl!"

"I'm not. Am I, Pauline?"

Pauline looked at Fergal and smiled. "No, of course not. I'd love to dance with you, Fergal. As long as you don't want me to do an Irish jig!"

He laughed, and looked closely at this dark-haired girl, the one who'd said he was 'a bit of all right'. He'd hardly seen her since then – somehow their paths had never crossed. She had an expressive, pretty face, and her blue eyes were open and friendly. A nice girl, he decided, and getting up said in an exaggerated Irish blarney, "Sure and begorrah, colleen, would you be giving me the pleasure, now?"

Pauline laughed and, following Fergal on to the dance floor, positioned her hair perfectly. Josie watched with satisfaction as the couple moved off to "That Old Black Magic".

"Clever puss," murmured Nick, who'd returned and watched the whole scene with amusement.

"Oh Nick," Josie turned to him. "I can't believe it – only three weeks now until the wedding!"

And it was. All the arrangements were going brilliantly, and in a way Josie thought it was even more exciting that everything was happening so quickly. She and Lily had gone shopping for a wedding dress, and in Lewis's department store in Hanley, had found the perfect one almost immediately. White, of course, with long lacy sleeves, a fitted waist and full skirt edged with Nottingham lace. Josie had chosen a mother-of-pearl tiara to hold her veil, and her bouquet was to be a mixture of pink carnations, and stephanotis. Georgina, of course, was to be chief brides-maid, accompanied by Pauline. Mavis had kindly offered to make their dresses, and Dennis was adamant. "Definitely not," he said firmly, when Lily offered to pay for her time. "You just provide the materials – she's only too pleased to do it."

Their son Johnny was going to be a pageboy, and little Kay, hugely excited,wanted to wear her favourite colour of pink. "And can I have frills, Auntie Josie," she'd asked, "and a little basket with flower petals in?"

"You can have anything you like, poppet!" Josie had picked her up and danced around with her. "You just promise to be good, and not make a noise in church."

Lily looked on proudly. She was thrilled with her own outfit of a lilac dress and jacket from C & A, and had seen a pretty white hat on a stall in Longton Market, which would just finish it off.

The wedding was to be held at Nick's local church; Josie, like the rest of her family, had never been one for church-going, Lily being of the opinion that it was mainly for the middle-classes. The reception was to be at the adjacent Church Hall, and this had been the only area where Mary and Gerald Rhodes had intervened.

With reluctance they'd had to accept that Nick would be wearing a lounge suit, instead of the morning suit they'd hoped for. On this point, Josie was adamant. "My family would just be embarrassed," Josie told Nick. "I mean, can you see Dad and Dennis in top hats? Peter, of course, will wear his naval uniform – at least he will when I tell him to!"

Nick didn't think it mattered. All he wanted was for Josie to have the perfect day, and if she wanted lounge suits, then that was enough for him. The important thing as far as he was concerned was that at last they'd be man and wife.

But his mother had insisted that she and Gerald should provide the catering at the reception. "It's bad enough," she told Gerald, "that my son is having it at a Church Hall, instead of a decent hotel. At least if we provide the buffet, we won't be embarrassed among our friends."

And Lily and Sid had accepted the offer with relief. "I'm not proud, Lil," Sid said. "We're paying for the dresses and the flowers, and for the hire of the hall. And let's face it, they can afford to put on a better spread than we can."

So, as far as Josie was concerned, everything

was falling into place. And at last she had managed to push the 'incident', as she thought of it, firmly to the back of her mind. One chance meeting had helped. It had been a day when she was shopping in Hanley one lunch-hour. Normally, she wouldn't have gone into Huntbach's department store, knowing that the prices were more than she could afford. But she was looking for something really special to wear on her wedding night, and it was in the lingerie department that she suddenly came face to face with Alice Hawkins.

Alice gave a tight smile. "Hello, Josie."

"Hello, Mrs Hawkins."

As Alice began to move away, Josie said quickly, "Thank you so much for all you've done."

Alice paused.

Josie said in desperation, "I'll have to tell Georgina we bumped into each other. I'm still wondering what colour she should wear as bridesmaid. I'll have to have the dresses made, of course, with her being so far away." Conscious that she was gabbling, she added, "Have you got any ideas?"

Taken aback, Alice tried to think. "She always looks good in blue . . ."

"Yes, she does, doesn't she? I'd been thinking that myself. And blue would suit Pauline as well."

"Well," Alice said, beginning once again to move away. "I hope you find what you want."

"Thank you. And Mrs Hawkins?"

"Yes?"

"I hope we'll see you both at the wedding."

401

Alice forced a smile. "Yes, of course."

Josie watched her walk towards the lifts, hoping that her clumsy attempt at normal conversation would have reassured Georgina's mother. Josie just wanted to put the whole distasteful issue behind her, behind both of them.

Alice, as she entered the lift, was thinking the same. The girl had obviously made an effort to convey that there would be no further threats.

Maybe, she mused as she lingered in haberdashery, just maybe I can relax now.

Ten minutes later, Josie stepped out of the doors of the store into the warm sunshine, exhilarated by her find of the perfect nightdress. She already had a demure white one that Lily had seen and approved. But this one – black, daring and silky – was definitely for Nick's eyes only.

Chapter 42

"*I can't tell you how excited I am about it all,*" *Josie wrote.* "*I just wish you were here to share it with me. We've definitely made the right decision to get married immediately. When you're in love, <u>waiting</u> isn't easy!!!*"

Georgina gave a wry smile at the underscored word. She was beginning to wonder if she'd ever find out! Although she'd followed Fiona's advice, and gone out on dates with several undergraduates, and even one lecturer, she hadn't really been physically attracted to them. Even that awful Felix stirred my senses more, she thought with despair. Maybe, I'm going to be one of those women who fall for the wrong type! Although she still struggled to accept that Dominic fell into that category.

There was a letter from Fergal too, and she slit open the envelope. But it held little news, apart from the fact that he regularly visited Longton library, and was enjoying his job. Georgina wondered once again whether he was going to do anything about his scar. It was such a pity that a handsome face like his should be marred. He doesn't mention whether he's made any friends, she thought. I must remember to ask Josie. Then, glancing at her watch and realising that her coffee break was over, she put the letters in her handbag, and returned to deciphering her shorthand notes.

It was later that morning when her boss, the vague but likeable Professor McKellar, came into the room. "Ah, Georgina," he said, and turned to indicate the tall young man who'd followed him in, "I'd like you to meet Angus Blair. As part of his Ph.D, he's going to be assisting me for the next six weeks."

Georgina looked up into appraising blue eyes. Gosh, she thought, he looks just like Van Johnson! And it was true, Angus had the same sandy hair, open freckled face and engaging smile. He looked around the room. "I suppose I'll be over there?" He pointed at a small desk tucked into a dark corner.

"I'm afraid so," she smiled, conscious that her own desk was larger and situated before a sunny window, "but at least you'll have no distractions."

"Oh, I don't know about that," he murmured, as the Professor left the room. He grinned at her. "You're a definite bonus! I thought this job was going to be dry as dust."

She laughed, liking the young Scot immediately. "It's not at all. In fact I find the research fascinating."

"You're interested in social mobility, then?"

"I think the country's definitely changing," she said. "People aren't satisfied any more with the same standard of living as their parents, and seem prepared to move away to achieve it."

"Mmn, and that could splinter the traditional family grouping." He leaned over her desk. "How about continuing this fascinating conversation over a meal after work?"

She laughed. "You're a fast worker, I'll say that for you!"

"Well, I've only got six weeks! I take it the answer's yes, then?"

"You're on!"

Angus grinned and moved away to get settled at his desk, while Georgina tried to concentrate on her typing. Six whole weeks! And he'd be working in the same office! Could it be that her luck was changing at last?

Angus took her for a fish-and-chip supper in a local fish bar. "I'm on a grant, remember," he pointed out, then grinned. "I'd have preferred a dish of haggis, myself, but seeing that you're an ignorant Sassenach . . ."

Georgina laughed. And she laughed a lot that evening, which set a pattern that remained over the next few weeks, as she and Angus worked together and went out together. At weekends they wandered around the leafy squares, through the parks, and along the Water of Leith to watch the anglers. As Angus had moved down from the Highlands, Georgina, who had already explored the city, was able to show him around, and they toured the historic Castle, and walked the length of the Royal Mile to see the Palace of Holyrood

House. In fact, they were inseparable.

"So," Fiona said one evening. "You've settled on one at last! I must say you've been very hard to please!"

Georgina laughed. "The best things are always worth waiting for."

"Aye, well it was about time. Remember what we agreed? How long have you got left – about four months? Anyway, you've not said much about him. Come on, I want to know every intimate detail!"

Georgina laughed. "There's none to tell. Not that I would if there was! I've told you, he looks like Van Johnson. He makes me laugh, and he's," she floundered, not knowing exactly how to describe him, "Angus is, well, he's a really nice person!"

"Nice! What sort of word is that to describe a man? What I want to know is, does he make you go weak at the knees?" Fiona glanced in triumph at Georgina's startled expression. "There, I was right! He doesn't, does he?"

"He's very attractive," defended Georgina. "In any case, he's only here for another three weeks."

"Plenty of time to profess his undying love. Or at least proposition you!"

Georgina laughed. "Come on Fiona. Don't judge everyone by yourself!"

"A hot bit of stuff, you mean?" Fiona grinned. "All I'm saying, George, is don't settle for second best, no matter how nice he is."

"Don't call me George!"

Fiona laughed. "I knew that would wind you up."

But her friend's words lingered in Georgina's mind, and the following morning at work, she found it impossible to concentrate. Her gaze kept wandering over to Angus, whose sandy head was bent in concentration over some statistics. Naturally he'd kissed her, light affectionate kisses, and she'd enjoyed the touch of his firm lips on hers. But their relationship was more of good friends, or, as the Americans would call it, 'kissing cousins'. But then, she reassured herself, it was only three weeks! What did she expect, a grand passion?

"Don't forget I'm off to Josie's wedding this weekend," she said.

Angus looked up. "Ah yes, you told me about it. How do you feel about being a bridesmaid?"

"I'm really looking forward to it. It will be lovely to see everyone again."

"Anyone in particular?" Angus looked quizzically at her.

She shook her head. "No, nothing like that."

"Good." He held her gaze for a moment, then returned to his work. Georgina inserted another sheet of paper into her typewriter. No matter what Fiona said, the word 'nice' really did describe him. She enjoyed being with Angus; his sense of fun appealed to her. I need someone like that, she told herself. I've always been far too serious. As for the 'in love' bit. Well, she'd had that with Dominic, and it had brought nothing except heartache. I'll be back in a few days, she thought. Then we'll see what happens in the next three weeks. And at least I know in advance that this one's going to leave.

Pauline too, was looking forward to the wedding. She loved her long taffeta dress in cornflower blue, but above all she was hoping to impress Fergal. Sometimes she wondered what it was about the tall young Irishman that drew her to him. It wasn't just that his disfigurement brought out the maternal instinct in her. She'd liked him from the first moment she'd seen him at the cinema with Josie, when turning round, her eyes had first met his, seen the wariness in them, the loneliness. And on that night at Trentham, it had felt so *right* to be held in his arms when they were dancing. They'd been easy and companionable together, but since then Pauline had waited in vain for Fergal to ask her out. A wedding is so romantic, she thought. Maybe he'll look at me with new eyes when I'm in my finery. It was a pity that Georgina would be wearing the same lovely dress. Pauline was under no illusions about her own looks. She might be attractive, but she couldn't compete with Georgina Hawkins. She was not only beautiful; she had the poise and assurance that only a privileged background could bring. Pauline could only console herself that it was unlikely she would be interested in someone with Fergal's background! But, she thought sadly, whether Fergal realised that was another matter.

Chapter 43

The same week that the Ford family was making last-minute arrangements for the wedding, a funeral was taking place at the other end of the city. Sombre businessmen and their wives, together with the deceased's relatives and friends, crowded into the parish church in Endon to pay their last respects to Arthur Hargreaves. In the front pew, his only son supported his mother, pale and wan in her black suit and a hat with a tiny veil. Much respected for his business dealings, Arthur had also been a strict, but fair employer, and there were many moist eyes among his employees in the congregation, many of whom had a black armband sewn on to their sleeves.

Tall and tanned, Dominic's appearance that day drew many eyes. But he was oblivious as he gazed in grief at the flower-bedecked coffin of his father – the man whose pride and personal ambition had blinded him to the unhappiness of his son. And as the cortege left the church, not a few in the congregation wondered what would happen now. Would the son and heir come back to the Potteries where he belonged and knuckle down to the family business? Only the privileged few were aware of the full story, and even they had no idea what Arthur's widow planned to do.

After a few days, those plans, which had to be discussed, became, for Dominic and his mother, one of the main topics of conversation.

"I don't know what to do," Enid mused. "Your father always said that if anything happened to him, not to do anything drastic for at least twelve months. I've no head for business, as you know, but we'll need to appoint someone in overall charge. Maybe you could help me with that before you go back?"

"Of course, I will. I just wish I could stay longer, but with the exhibition coming up . . ."

"I shall come out, of course." She looked away. "Maybe it will help, you know, be a distraction. I wouldn't travel all that way on my own, of course. Perhaps your Auntie Dora would come with me."

Dominic warned, "Now, don't go expecting too much. It's only a small gallery in Perth you know, not the Tate!"

"And the day job?"

Dominic nodded. "That's fine. I like teaching Art and Design. And we have to be realistic. Very few artists earn enough to support themselves by their paintings alone."

"You will," Enid said. "It's early days yet." She looked at her handsome son. "I'm so proud of you. You're very talented, Dominic. Even I, with my limited knowledge of art, can see that."

Dominic gave a wry shrug. "There were faults on both sides. I was stupid to go off the way I did, hurting you both so much. Thank goodness when it was time for your birthday, that I came to my senses." He smiled gently at her. "I just couldn't not send you a birthday card, now could I?"

Enid blinked back tears. "Sorry," she said, "my emotions are so near the surface at the moment. I was just remembering the overwhelming relief when we saw there was an address."

"You certainly didn't waste much time in getting in touch," he said. "Just one letter, and then you were both on your way out to Australia!"

Enid's expression became serious. "We couldn't have estrangement between us, Dominic. We never wanted that."

"Do you think I was wrong to go?" Dominic watched his mother give consideration to his words. That was one thing he'd always respected about her. Even as a child, every question had been taken seriously, and answered in the same vein. Slight of build she might be, and certainly there were silver threads in her hair, but Enid Hargreaves, in her own quiet way, had influenced him greatly. However, like so many women of her generation, she had often deferred to her husband, and Dominic wondered whether, in his particular case, she had ever regretted it.

Almost as if she read his mind, Enid said, "I feel it was a great pity you felt the need to. In some ways I blame myself. I should have stood up for you more when you wanted to go to Art College." She looked sadly at him. "It was wrong of him to push you into the business, but that was always his dream you see, to found a sort of family dynasty."

"I know. That's why I went along with it at first. But at least he came to accept that my path lay in a different direction." Dominic looked sadly at his mother, "I wish it could have been different, but . . ."

"Don't worry about it, darling. It's water under the bridge." Enid looked curiously at the tall young man sitting opposite. "I don't mean to pry, but I'd have thought, being in a strange country on your own, that you'd have found yourself a regular girlfriend by now. Are you sure there's no-one special?"

Dominic shook his head. "No-one. Don't worry. I promise you'll be the first to know."

Enid smiled, then stifled a yawn. "I'm awfully tired. I think I'll go and have a nap."

Dominic watched his mother go, and then leaned back in the leather armchair. But it wasn't long before, as so often happened, one name, one image filled his mind. During his stay in England, Dominic was determined to try and find the girl he'd met all those years ago. The girl for whom he had only a Christian name and the recollection that she lived in an area of the Potteries he was unfamiliar with: Dreston. He had never forgotten her. He'd been out with other girls, of course, but not one had touched his heart in the way that Georgina had. She'd been so lovely, so gentle and understanding.

412

Knowing that time was short, the day after the funeral he'd gone to the College of Commerce, in Burslem. But it seemed hopeless. The woman in the office had flatly refused to divulge any personal details of a past student. Because Georgina had told him nothing of her family, he had no clues, no idea how to find her. Once, out of respect, he'd allowed a further week to pass, he planned to go to Trentham Ballroom on the slim chance she might be there. And in the meantime he was prepared to go and knock on every door in Dreston. Surely someone would know of her? After all Georgina was an unusual name. Restless and dispirited, he reached down and took some magazines from the rack. He thumbed through *Country Life,* discarded it, and then began to look through an old copy of *Staffordshire Life.* But he didn't feel in the mood to read, and just idly scanned the pages of society photographs, wondering whether he would spot any of his old school-friends.

A few seconds later the world stood still. Because there she was, smiling out at him! No longer an unsure young girl, but a poised and beautiful young woman. Avidly Dominic gazed at the lovely image that had haunted him for so long, his eyes searching her hair, her eyes, her every feature. The heading at the top of the page was *The Federation of Master Builders' Annual Dinner,* and the caption below the glossy photograph read *Mr William Hawkins, and Miss Georgina Hawkins.* Many times Dominic had recalled the fleshy face of William

413

Hawkins, remembering his glowering fury as he'd grabbed his daughter's arm and dragged her away. One more second, and Dominic would have told her of his feelings, confessed that he was leaving the following day for Australia. So many times afterwards he'd agonised that if only he'd told her earlier, their lives might have taken a different course. He remembered how he'd stood smoking outside the ballroom, waiting for Georgina to join him, agonising over his dilemma. But his resolve, that it would be unfair to tie down such a young girl to a man on the other side of the world, had melted once he held her in his arms, felt the warmth and sweetness of her lips against his. If only her damn father hadn't appeared! How many times had he cursed that intervention! But could it be that now he was to be granted a second chance? Full of exhilaration, Dominic flung aside the magazine, leapt to his feet and went to search for the telephone directory.

On the morning of the wedding, Josie opened her eyes and smiled with relief at the sunlight streaming through the thin cotton curtains. Yawning, she lifted her left hand to look at her diamond engagement ring, trying to imagine it nestling against the plain gold band she'd chosen with Nick. However, she wasn't left in solitude for long. Soon, with a light tap on the door, Lily came in carrying a tray. "Good morning. Breakfast in bed for the bride! Isn't it a lovely day?"

"Wonderful!" Josie took the tray from her,

feeling a lump in her throat as she saw the single rose in a slender vase. "Where did you get that from?"

Lily reddened. "I snipped it off a bush at Rosemount when I left yesterday, but don't you dare tell Georgina!"

Josie giggled. "Ooh, you criminal!"

"Yes, well don't take too long, there's lots to do. You've got to get your hair done at half past nine, remember."

"I know."

After giving a parting tweak to the white wedding dress hanging outside the wardrobe, Lily left. Josie smiled as she noticed her mum had brought her childhood favourite of boiled egg and toasted soldiers, then she sipped her tea, and thought of the day's plans. Pauline was coming here to get ready, and so was young Kay. But as that meant Sonia fussing around as well, it had been decided it would be better if Georgina got dressed at Rosemount. The wedding car was to collect her on the way to the church. Everything was organised, Josie thought with satisfaction. The day was going to be absolutely perfect.

"Josie?" Lily's voice floated up the stairs.

"All right, I'm coming!" She swung her legs out of bed and looked with nostalgia around the small bedroom. Goodbye, she murmured, but refused to feel even a fleeting sadness. It was time to grow up, to move on and begin her life with Nick. Their three-night honeymoon was to be spent in Bournemouth, at the same luxury hotel where she had first realised how much she loved him. I'm so lucky, she thought, so very lucky.

Half an hour after the gleaming wedding limousine pulled away from Rosemount, a smaller car cruised along the street and drew to a slow halt outside the black wrought-iron gates. Dominic switched off the engine of his mother's Morris Minor, and looked at the so English setting of the mellow house with its rose gardens, trying to imagine it as the background to Georgina's childhood. Yet now he had actually reached this point, he felt reluctant, even fearful, to get out of the car. After a four-year absence, it seemed a colossal conceit to think that Georgina would remember him! Last night, the temptation to ring, to hear her voice, had been almost overpowering. But he'd forced himself to be patient, to wait, and for Dominic, that night was one of the longest in his life. Unable to sleep, he knew it would be a devastating blow if she stared at him without recollection. Humiliation he could bear; it was a risk he had to take, but only he knew how bitter his disappointment would be, how often her image had filled his thoughts. Was he being stupid, vain, to hope that those few hours had meant equally as much to her?

He'd been told that shortly after he'd left for Australia, a girl had come to the main offices looking for him. She hadn't left her name, but from the description it *could* have been Georgina. Was it possible that she'd fallen as deeply in love

416

with him as he had with her? It was crazy, he knew, after such a short time, but it *hadn't* been infatuation; his inability to form a relationship with anyone else proved that. And if she did remember, had felt the same, then she must have been terribly hurt at his disappearance. All these questions whirled in Dominic's mind, as at last he opened the gates, closed them behind him, and walked tensely up to the front door. After a moment's hesitation, he rang the bell and heard it echo inside the house. There was no answer. He rang again, twice, hoping to hear signs of movement, but it was no use. The house remained silent. In desperation he stepped back to stare in vain at the blank latticed windows. Eventually he had to accept that there was nobody in. The anticlimax was like a physical pain, and he was about to turn despondently away, when he paused. Surely he could hear something?

Almost immediately, the squeaking of his wheelbarrow preceding him, an elderly man came round the corner of the house and seeing Dominic lowered the handles. Taking off his sun hat, he mopped his brow. "I'll have to get this blasted thing oiled," he grumbled, squinting in the sunlight. "Who did yer want?"

Dominic hesitated. "I was looking for Georgina? Miss Georgina Hawkins?"

"Aw, yer too late, lad. Yer've missed her. It's the wedding today, yer see. I watched her leave in the car. Looked lovely she did, in her long dress. A proper picture!"

Wedding? What did he mean – *wedding?* Then, *'Looked lovely she did, in her long dress'.* The full significance of the words hit Dominic like a blow between the eyes. Oh my God, it couldn't be! He refused to believe it – it *couldn't* be Georgina's wedding day – not on the very morning he'd come back to find her! Dominic could only stare at the old gardener in profound and painful shock. At first he was unable to move, even to speak, then managed to mutter, "Thanks," before walking unsteadily away in a fog of despair. Fumbling with the lock of the car door, he opened it to slump on to the driver's seat. He was too late! He was too bloody late! Dominic smote the steering wheel with his fist. What a fool he'd been, right from the beginning! If he hadn't been so fiercely independent, so stupidly determined to finance his studies himself, he could have come back earlier, not waited until bereavement forced him into it! At least if he'd met Georgina again, and had explained, he might have had a chance. Now he'd lost her forever! Dominic tortured himself with an image of her as a bride, standing at an altar, pledging her love to another man, and could have wept with frustration and searing jealousy. If only he'd got here sooner, if only . . . But as he stared unseeingly through the windscreen, Dominic knew it was hopeless, that he had to accept defeat. There was absolutely nothing he could do. With one last despairing glance at Rosemount, he switched on the ignition, put the car into gear, and slowly drew away from the scene of his shattered dreams.

Chapter 44

Nick's local parish church was an ancient one – the sun filtered through the stained-glass windows to illuminate the polished oak pews, and the festive clothes of the congregation. Mary had done a wonderful job with the flowers, Lily thought with grudging admiration. She was sitting at the front, having, as the bride's mother, only just arrived. She looked down at her outfit with satisfaction. You don't have to spend a fortune to look smart was her maxim, and Lily felt she could hold up her head in any company. She glanced round to smile at Dennis and Mavis, and at Peter, who, in obedience to Josie's wishes, was wearing his naval uniform. Sonia was resplendent in pink, and between them was a carrycot containing their new baby, Paul. Next to Peter sat Fergal, stiff and smart in a blue suit.

William and Alice Hawkins were sitting in the pew behind – William complacent in his role of benefactor, and Alice elegant in a cream suit. She glanced up as a couple arrived to sit across the aisle on the bridegroom's side and, to her shock and consternation, stared straight into the startled gaze of Neil Maxwell! He gave an embarrassed nod of acknowledgement, which, with heightened colour, she returned. Oblivious now to her surroundings, Alice felt panic wash over her. What on earth was *he* doing here? Leaning slightly forward, she turned her head to steal a glance at the woman sitting next to him. So, that was Jane! Alice dismissed her as pretty but insipid. It was no wonder he sought passion outside his marriage. And then suddenly she was full of adrenalin. Alice glanced down at her legs in their sheer nylons and high-heeled shoes with satisfaction. Never had she looked better! And surely enough time had passed to allay Jane's suspicions. Alice's only thought was, as she stood up for the bride's arrival, that she was going to find it impossible to concentrate on the wedding service.

Sid, standing at the open door of the church, Josie on his arm, thought he must be the proudest man in the Potteries. When the organ began to play its opening fanfare, they began to move slowly forward, with Georgina and Pauline, both graceful and lovely in their long blue dresses, followed by Johnny, in velvet long trousers and waistcoat, and Kay, with her small basket of flower petals, walking behind. There were audible sighs of admiration as heads turned to watch the procession, and Nick, waiting at the front, turned to face his lovely bride as she lifted her veil. Radiant, Josie smiled happily up at him, then the young couple faced the vicar, ready at last to be joined together as man and wife.

★

"We could never have afforded to put a spread like this on!" Lily whispered to Sid, as later the guests sat down to a three-course meal. Mary had chosen outside caterers who specialised in wedding receptions, and the long tables looked impressive with their white cloths and fresh flowers. Dominating the top table was Lily's masterpiece, a three-tiered wedding cake that she had made and a neighbour had iced with delicate trellises. A miniature bride and groom on top even bore a faint likeness to Josie and Nick. The whole day was perfect, thought Josie dreamily, as she sat in splendour next to her new husband.

Georgina, who as chief bridesmaid was seated next to the best man, was enjoying herself enormously. Brian, whose studious looks belied an outrageous sense of humour, both flirted with her and reduced her to giggles.

"I can't wait to hear your speech," she told him. "But I warn you, Josie won't take kindly to any smutty jokes!"

"Now, would I do a thing like that?"

"I'm not sure," she said, laughing.

But, as Nick had expected, Brian's speech was faultless, not containing a single word that Gerald Rhodes could exploit or gloat over.

It was later, once the dancing began, that Pauline made her way to where Fergal was sitting quietly in a corner. He smiled up at her. "You look fantastic!" And she did, he thought. In fact, in her own way, Pauline was just as attractive as either Josie and Georgina. And that thought startled him.

421

"Thank you, kind sir. You're not dancing?" He shook his head, and she saw his gaze momentarily flit to where Georgina was dancing with Brian.

"Well, we can't have a bridesmaid being a wall-flower," she smiled, and held out her hand. Getting up to join her, Fergal felt Pauline's cool, firm clasp lead him on to the small dance-floor, where to his relief she positioned her hair to cover the scarred side of his face. Although grateful for the invitation to the wedding, he was finding being in the midst of so many strangers a bit of an ordeal. He'd got used to going to the pub with his work mates, any strangers there were mainly men who would just glance and look away. But women were different; they didn't seem able to stop staring, even if it was with concern and pity.

Fergal looked down at Pauline.

After that night at Trentham, he'd thought once or twice of asking her out, remembering her laughing comment the first time they'd met. But there had always been the lingering hope that, unrealistic though it was, Georgina might turn to him, that their friendship might develop into something deeper. But he knew now that would never happen. Wasn't there someone called Angus on the scene with a university degree? He could never compete with someone like that. Fergal knew he just had to accept that Georgina was, as people would put it, out of his league. And he was so lucky he thought, looking down at the attractive girl in his arms. Not many girls would look twice at him, and yet Fergal knew instinctively that

Pauline liked him, more than liked him. You've been a fool, he told himself. Those letters that meant so much on board ship have blinded you to real life.

Pauline had noticed the stir Fergal's appearance had made, had heard comments of, "Oh, what a shame!" and "that poor lad". Now, held close in his arms, she realised just how much she cared for him. When the dance ended, Pauline plucked up her courage. Still holding his hand, she led the way to a quiet corner.

"It used to happen to me, just the same," she told him.

Puzzled, Fergal looked down at her. "Sorry?"

"People staring at you. I used to look a real fright – enough to scare the horses! Honest! You should have seen me!"

He frowned. "You've lost me, Pauline."

"You can ask anyone. I had the worst, most protruding buck teeth in the world. I'd show you the photographs, but you'd probably go off me."

He grinned. "And what makes you think I'm interested now?"

Pauline looked steadily at him, holding his gaze. "Aren't you?"

Fergal saw not only the challenge in her eyes, but also the gentleness in her expression, and could only nod, "Sure, you must be able to read my mind."

"Right," Pauline said in relief. "That was an ordeal, I can tell you."

"What was?"

"Trying to get you to admit it! Having to reveal my shameful secret!"

He looked down at her. "But you've got a lovely smile."

"Well, it's not perfect. There's still a slight hint there. But it's only because I did something about it. I wore the most hideous braces for years to achieve this!"

Fergal stared at her, and said slowly, "Are you trying to tell me something?"

"What have you got to lose?" she said. "We've got a good plastic surgeon up at the Infirmary, Fergal. At least you can go and see your doctor and see what he says. It's only a suggestion, mind. It doesn't matter to me – I think you're a—"

"Bit of all right!" Fergal grinned, and Pauline leaned up to kiss his cheek. "So you heard! Well, as long as you know." She moved away as someone called her name, leaving Fergal to gaze after her thoughtfully.

Josie, standing on the other side of the room, nudged Georgina. "Did you see that?"

She smiled. "I most certainly did. Hey, Fergal and Pauline – now wouldn't that be something? I most definitely approve."

Josie glanced at her. "You've never thought of him in that way yourself, then?"

"Good heavens no," Georgina said. "We're just friends, that's all."

And maybe, thought Josie, Fergal has, at last, come to the same conclusion.

★

Alice spent most of her time at the reception covertly watching Neil. Seeing him again had alerted her every nerve-end to his attraction, which was as potent as ever. But she looked in vain for some sign, even a raised eyebrow, which would indicate a desire to renew their affair. So far, the two couples hadn't met, which she suspected was by avoidance on Neil's part, but as the number of guests wasn't large, Alice knew it was only a matter of time. And eventually, the moment came.

It was Gerald Rhodes who brought Neil and Jane over to introduce them. He was talking earnestly to Neil as they approached, and Alice saw Neil glance sharply at him and frown. She and William, had, of course, met Nick's parents at the reception line-up and Alice had been amused to see Gerald's gaze flicker appraisingly over her expensive outfit. Now, urbane and gracious, he murmured, "Mr and Mrs Hawkins, isn't it? I thought you might like to meet Neil and Jane Maxwell. Neil's my wife's solicitor."

"Oh, Neil and I already know each other," Alice smiled, amazed at how easy she was able to put on an act. "We used to sit on the same charity committee, until he had to resign due to pressure of business. How are you, Neil?"

"I'm fine thank you, Alice. And you?" Neil's eyes bored into hers, and she found his expression impossible to read.

"I can't complain. May I introduce my husband, William?"

William shook Neil's hand and nodded. "I take

it this lovely lady is your wife?" he said, with his customary heavy humour.

Jane smiled. "Yes. It's nice to meet you both. I asked Gerald to introduce us, William, because a friend of mine is interested in the properties you're building at the Westlands. Just one question – and I apologise for talking shop. Will there be any bungalows?"

"Yes, I'm planning a small cul-de-sac of detached ones with three bedrooms," William told her.

Gerald rubbed his hands together. "Good, good. I hope you're both enjoying yourselves?"

"Oh, yes, everything's been perfect," Alice said, and with a smile Gerald moved away.

Neil watched him with an inscrutable expression on his face, frowned, then turned his attention to William.

"So, I take it you're friends of the bride? Do you know her well?"

"We've known her since she was a child," William said gruffly. "Hold her in very high regard, don't we, Alice?"

She glanced at Neil, feeling uneasy. She knew that expression on his face, that intensity in his voice. This was no casual question.

"We most certainly do," she said.

"So *you* would say that Nick's a lucky young man?"

To Alice's amazement, William leapt to Josie's defence. "Josie would make any man a good wife. Got pluck and determination. Integrity too, if I'm any judge of character, and I flatter myself that I am. It's one of my houses that the young couple are renting. Actually, I'd decided to sell them off as they become vacant, but, as it was Josie, I made an exception."

"Well done," Jane said, smiling at them both. She turned as someone called her name. "Sorry, I must just . . ." She began to move away, and Alice frantically tried to catch Neil's eye, to flash a signal to him, an invitation, but he carefully avoided her gaze. She watched in humiliation as, with a polite smile, he followed his wife to speak to an elderly man and his wheelchair-bound wife. Was it just that Jane was present and he was being ultra-careful, or . . .

"Pleasant couple," William said. "And knowing a solicitor is always useful. Would you like another drink?"

Alice nodded, and watched him amble off to find a waitress. Seeing the two men together had sharpened cruelly the contrast between them. William looked what he was, a bluff self-made man, while Neil . . . Alice glanced again at him, devouring his handsome features, his assurance, knowing that her own husband would never have that polish. Also William, so much older than her, was beginning to look his age, while Neil . . .

But an hour later as the festivities were coming to an end, all her hopes of renewing illicit meetings and passionate afternoons were shattered. Alice, her gaze roaming around the room, froze as she saw Neil closeted in a corner with Georgina.

Mesmerised, Alice could only watch as she saw her young innocent daughter smile up at her mother's lover – saw him smiling down at her with practised charm, reaching out a hand to lightly touch the flowers in her hair. Georgina drew back slightly, but Neil leaned closer, and at the sight of that dark, handsome head so close to her daughter's fair one, Alice felt a revulsion so fierce she was hardly conscious of moving forward. Swiftly she wended her way through the crowd to where the couple were standing.

"Hello, Neil."

"Alice!" Neil swung round in surprise.

"You know each other, then?" Georgina said, feeling relieved at her mother's interruption. This man was far older than he'd initially appeared, and his attentions were beginning to make her feel uncomfortable.

"I think you could say that," Alice said sweetly. "And you, Neil, how long have you known my daughter?"

With a piercing sense of satisfaction, Alice saw a look of sheer horror pass over Neil's face. "I didn't realise she was . . ."

"Didn't you? Yes, this is my lovely Georgina. Josie is her closest friend."

Georgina stared at her mother, wondering whether she'd had too much to drink, and seized her chance to escape. "I must go and help Josie with her going-away outfit," she muttered, and Alice watched her go before turning her attention back to Neil.

"So, you didn't know?" she said. "Well, I suppose that's something at least!"

"I was only saying what a lovely bridesmaid she was," he protested.

"I know exactly what you were doing, Neil," she said softly. "And why! There's a name for men who go after young girls, you know. I wouldn't like to think you were going down that road."

"Alice, for heaven's sake, I was only being sociable."

But only once Jane was out of the way! And it certainly wasn't with me, Alice thought grimly! "Ah," she said, in a tone heavy with sarcasm, "here comes your little wife looking for you again. What a pity! You could have tried your luck with the other bridesmaid. Not that it would have got you anywhere! Grow up, Neil. It's pathetic in a man of your age!"

"Alice, honestly . . ."

"Forget it, Neil. Just forget everything!"

"I was going to ring you," he protested.

"Don't bother!" Alice turned as Jane approached.

"Hello again, Jane," she smiled. "Neil and I were just talking about my daughter. She's the chief bridesmaid, the fair one."

Alice saw a look of relief pass over Jane's face. "She's a beautiful girl."

"*Neil* certainly thought so. Didn't you, Neil?" Alice said, and, glancing at Jane knew that her words had hit home. "Well, I'd better go and look for William!"

Alice walked away, a grim smile playing around her mouth. I hope she gives him hell, she thought. And as for beginning our affair again, I crawl after no man!

Georgina was helping Lily to hang up Josie's wedding dress and veil.

The small room at the back of the church hall was far from ideal to use as a dressing-room, but Mary had thoughtfully provided a full-length mirror, and in the cramped space, Josie surveyed herself in her going-away outfit of peacock blue. With her vivid colouring she looked so striking that Lily had to fight back tears of pride.

Georgina looked at her friend, at her glowing face, and impulsively went to hug her. "You look fabulous!"

"Hey, watch out. You'll crease my jacket," Josie protested, but she was laughing, and yet again Lily marvelled at their unlikely friendship. Her original fear that Georgina would dump Josie when she found richer friends had long disappeared.

"Give my love to Bournemouth," Georgina said, and after a glance at mother and daughter, left them alone.

"I think this is where you're supposed to tell me about the birds and the bees!" Josie said, then seeing Lily's embarrassment, laughed. "I'm only joking, Mum!" She picked up her bouquet. "It's time I went. I just wanted to say, well . . ."

"Oh, come here," Lily said, and held out her arms. "Be happy," she whispered.

"I will. And Mum?"

"Yes, love?"

"I won't be living far away . . ."

"I know," Lily brushed away a tear. "Go on. Off you go."

Nick, waiting impatiently to leave, watched his young wife walk towards him with pride. Amidst murmurs of admiration for her outfit, Josie threw her bouquet to where Georgina and Pauline were standing, little Kay between them, and there was a burst of laughter as the small child jumped up and clumsily caught it.

"We were a bit slow, Pauline," Georgina laughed.

But now Nick and Josie were leaving, and guests surging forward to wave goodbye. Dennis gave her an awkward hug, while Brian and Peter were waiting outside the hall, one shielding the tin cans tied to the bumper of Nick's car, the other hiding the *"Just Married"* banner on the back. The young couple ran out laughing, braving a shower of confetti and then suddenly they were gone.

Sid placed an arm around Lily's shoulders, while Mary stood alone, Gerald having already gone back inside. The two mothers, both slightly tearful, exchanged quiet smiles.

"She's all right," Lily whispered to Sid a few minutes later, "but that Gerald's a right smarmy devil!"

Gerald, however, was the last person on Josie's mind. Sitting by Nick as he drove competently to their destination, she dreamily relived the day's

431

events, and kept glancing down at the plain gold band on her finger. From now on, and for the rest of her life, she would be Mrs Josie Hamilton. And, she thought happily, there isn't anyone in the world I would rather be.

Chapter 45

It was three weeks after the wedding, on his way home from work that Fergal eventually went to register with a local doctor.

"Do you need to see Dr Ferguson now?" the receptionist asked briskly.

Fergal looked down at his working clothes in embarrassment. "What time do you close?"

"Depends on how many are waiting," she said. "But you should be all right until about half past seven."

Later, having washed and changed, he sat on a black horsehair bench in the stuffy waiting-room. Before him in the queue, were two men who, from the sound of their coughs, had bronchitis, an elderly woman with a stiff white collar around her neck, and a young woman in an advanced stage of pregnancy. When his turn eventually came, he went nervously along a short corridor, and tapped on the partly open door.

Dr Ferguson, a middle-aged man with a tired face and greying hair, looked up automatically, and then, seeing Fergal's face, his eyes narrowed. He motioned to a chair. "I see you're a new patient."

"Yes, doctor. I've just registered, after leaving the Navy."

"Well, we'll have to get your medical records, of course, but in the meantime, what can I do for you?"

Fergal hesitated. "It's this!" He touched the scar. "I wondered whether anything could be done?"

The doctor frowned, peered at the disfigurement, then got up from his chair. "Just raise your chin for a moment." With a magnifying glass, he carefully studied the scar, then with two fingers gently stretched the surrounding tissue. "How did this happen?"

Haltingly, Fergal told him and didn't gloss over the reason he'd gone to the other boy's rescue.

The doctor's jaw tightened, "And you are how old now?"

"Twenty-two."

"Mmn. Well, I'll certainly refer you to a specialist. We're lucky enough to have an excellent man up at the Infirmary." Dr Ferguson smiled. "If he thinks it's possible, you couldn't be in better hands. Although I must warn you that skin grafts can be a very lengthy procedure."

Pauline, when Fergal told her, was optimistic. "I'm sure he'll be able to do something. Not that it matters to me, mind," she added, anxious to reassure him. "I love you, anyway."

"I know you do." He smiled down at her, remembering the first moment he'd felt the warmth of her lips on his. It was the only time in

434

his life he'd ever felt cherished, needed. It had been, for Fergal, a turning point. Now he couldn't understand why he'd hesitated, why he'd allowed a foolish dream to blind him to the beauty of the girl who was smiling up at him.

"I love you, too," he said, and it was in complete contentment that Pauline snuggled up to him on the sofa in her parents' front room. She might even, she mused, become a Catholic like Fergal. Mixed marriages could cause problems. Maybe she'd ask him to take her with him the next time he went to church. With memories of Josie's lovely wedding fresh in her mind, Pauline was already making plans. She smiled to herself. Fergal had probably never given marriage a thought, but she knew it was only a question of time.

Pauline however, misjudged Fergal, because he had already begun to look to the future. What he really needed was to make progress at the Glaze Mill. He was enjoying the work and lately, part of his duties had been to take X batch samples of glazes manufactured the day before, into the laboratories where they would be subjected to a test of 'old and new' trials. He'd once heard the senior chemist comment, "He seems a smart lad. We could use him in here," and knew there could be an opening for him.

But although tempted, Fergal knew his best chance of earning extra money was to remain in his present job. The Mill had to be run on a seven-day basis, so he decided to apply for weekend work, asking the foreman, Les, to teach him how to make phosphor bronze lawns. These were sieves of different-size mesh, used both in the Mill and sold externally. In this way, he would not only be paid at a time-and-a-half rate, but also for each individual lawn he made.

Fergal only knew that he had waited all his life for a home of his own. Now he'd found someone to share it, he didn't intend to waste any more time.

That same weekend, Georgina went to Edinburgh station to wave goodbye to Angus.

"It's been great," he said, smiling down at her. "I'll write. I promise." He bent and kissed her – a light affectionate kiss. It was not the kiss of a man in love. But hadn't she known that ever since the day she returned from the wedding? Seeing Nick and Josie again, their transparent love for each other had made Georgina realise that what she felt for Angus was a very pale shadow. There was no passion between them, no vital spark. And on the night before, when Angus had, as usual, kissed her lightly on the lips, then said hesitantly, "Georgina, I wouldn't like you to think . . ." she'd been able to say honestly, "Don't worry. It's the same for me. But it's been great fun, hasn't it?"

"Absolutely," he smiled and she could only wish it had been different, that they really had fallen in love.

Now, she watched him get into the railway carriage and heave his suitcase on to the luggage rack, before opening the window to lean out. "You must come up to the Highlands, some time!"

"I'd love to," she called, as the train began to move. But Georgina knew it would never happen, that he was only being polite. Maybe a couple of letters or postcards, she thought, as she made her way out of the station, and then eventually I'll be just another name on his Christmas card list.

And so Georgina continued as before, although it seemed strange now to be on her own in the office without Angus. But she was interested in the work, and the Professor's dictation, being rapid and erratic, provided a constant challenge.

As the weeks passed, and Christmas approached, she threw herself into the university's social whirl, and going to parties with Fiona and her fiancé. There was one medical student with laughing green eyes, who definitely made her heart beat faster, but it was soon apparent that he was an incorrigible flirt. "Some girl's nightmare waiting to happen," was Fiona's opinion, and reluctantly Georgina had to agree.

"I think I'm destined to remain a spinster, at least for the foreseeable future," she complained.

Fiona grinned. "Don't knock it! If I hadn't met Alistair, I'd probably be like you, single and free as air."

Georgina looked anxiously at her. "You are sure, aren't you?"

"About Alistair? Oh yes," Fiona's eyes softened. "He's the one for me. I've always known that."

Then gradually, Georgina began to count the

days until she could return to Stoke-on-Trent. She'd enjoyed her time in Scotland, but she missed Josie, and the secure parochial atmosphere of where they lived. She missed Rosemount, and also, to her surprise, her parents. I suppose one's roots are always a pull, she thought, and with reluctance had to acknowledge that her father had tried to make amends for those early bullying years. She was still wary of him, but knew now that in his own way, he did care for her. And lately she'd realised that her mother was simply a woman with little maternal instinct. Yet even she seemed to be less distant lately. But if I ever have children it will be different, Georgina thought grimly. I'm going to shower them with love and affection. No child of mine will ever suffer the loneliness that I did.

Josie, of course, was overjoyed when her best friend returned home.

"I've really missed you," she said, as she rummaged in a cupboard for a packet of biscuits. Struggling to open it she swore as crumbs and broken bits littered the small kitchen table.

"I think I'd better buy you a biscuit barrel," Georgina laughed.

"We could certainly do with one; but then we could do with a lot of things!" Josie looked ruefully around her.

"I think you've done marvels," Georgina protested.

"Well, considering it's been on a shoe-string.

438

Nick's picking up a sofa for us today – second-hand, of course."

"You'll get there," Georgina said comfortably.

Josie gave a wry smile, knowing that 'making-do' was a problem her friend would never have to face. Not that she'd change places. Josie was happier than she'd ever been in her life, although she did find having a full-time job and running the house quite tiring at times. Nick helped when he could, but he was working long hours.

"These are the years when we need to build up the business," he told her. "We'll benefit in the long run, I promise."

"What are you going to do about a job?" Josie asked, as she poured out the tea.

Georgina shrugged. "I'm just waiting until after the New Year, then there's bound to be something." She wandered restlessly, staring out of the kitchen window at the small, narrow backyard. "I want something interesting, not just a normal office job. I really enjoyed the research in Scotland."

"Try Keele University," Josie suggested.

"I might just do that. Thanks," Georgina took the proffered cup and saucer, helped herself to a digestive biscuit, and sat awkwardly at the small table squashed against the kitchen wall. "How about you? Still the blushing bride?"

Josie laughed. "If you're fishing, I'm not telling you anything. You can wait and find out for yourself!"

"You'd recommend it, though?"

"What do you think?" Josie laughed. "Your turn will come, my friend!"

Maybe, Georgina thought, biting into her biscuit, but when?

Chapter 46

Eighteen months later, Dominic stood with his back to the bar at Trentham. The ballroom was crowded, but although he'd already danced with a few girls, he was restless, distracted by his thoughts, his memories. Yet again, he glanced across to the table where he'd sat with Georgina five years ago, then with a resigned shrug, turned to replace his empty glass on the counter.

The next moment he was transfixed. The girl framed in the entrance to the ballroom – looking fabulous in a shimmering blue cocktail dress? It couldn't be! Surely that was Georgina? Dominic could only gaze at her in fascination, feeling again the same overwhelming attraction. She was with a tall, good-looking guy, who must be her husband, and then Dominic saw another girl with dark unruly curls join them. Shaken, he watched the small group remain talking for a moment before making their way to a quiet table. Consumed with jealousy and a renewed painful sense of loss, he moved away from the bar to a position at the side of a pillar, where he wouldn't easily be seen. He just wanted to look at her. After five long years, she was lovelier than ever. The vocalist was singing

441

"Too Young", and Dominic's lips twisted. If only Georgina had been older, then their lives might have been completely different. He would have told her how he felt, wouldn't have worried about her youth. He might even, he thought with despair, have been the lucky man sitting beside her. At the end of the number, the band began to play lively rock and roll, and Dominic saw the dark-haired girl, whose name he recalled was Josie, shake her head and laugh. Then Georgina was up, moving on to the dance-floor with her husband, beginning to twist and twirl, her long slim legs moving in perfect time to the beat. Dominic stood watching, but then realised he was simply torturing himself. This was unbearable! Suddenly, all he wanted to do was to leave, to get out of the ballroom. It had been a mistake to come – the whole scene, even before Georgina had arrived, had been too emotive. Another time, he thought grimly, if I want to go dancing, I'll make sure I go to the Kings Hall or to the Crystal.

But even as he walked away, Dominic couldn't resist one last lingering glance. The young couple had moved nearer to him where there was more space on the dance-floor, and as he paused, in that one instant, Georgina lifted her hand to push back a strand of hair. Dominic halted. Surely he must have been mistaken? He moved forward, regardless now of the risk of being noticed, and frantically tried to see Georgina's hands as she was dancing. But there was no mistake! *The third finger on her left hand was bare!* Swiftly he turned so that his back was to the dance floor, trying to sort out his stunned, yet chaotic thoughts. So, she wasn't wearing a wedding ring? It could mean it had gone to be altered! It could mean anything! But the wild, unbelievable hope that sprang up wouldn't be calmed. He had to know! Dominic began to thread his way through the crowds towards the table where Josie was sitting. To the table to which, as the music ended, Georgina and her partner were already coming back! Then he paused in bewilderment as he saw the man he'd thought was married to Georgina, lean over to kiss Josie gently on the lips as he murmured something to her. Dominic's eyes urgently sought her left hand. She was wearing both an engagement and a wedding ring. Could it be possible – *was* it possible – that the man he'd thought was Georgina's husband, was instead married to Josie?

Just then the band struck up "Blue Moon", and Dominic moved forward, his heart hammering in his chest, as he hoped with desperation that the girl he'd last seen five years ago would remember him.

Georgina glanced up, and as he saw the shock of recognition in her eyes, his name form soundlessly on her lips, Dominic's spirits soared.

He said simply, "Would you care to dance?"

Stunned, Georgina could only gaze in wonderment at the tanned young man standing before her.

"Dominic?" Her voice came out in a whisper of disbelief.

443

"Please dance with me?"

Unsteadily, Georgina rose and taking his outstretched hand joined him on the dance floor. Dominic held out his arms, and she melted into them with a feeling so exquisite it almost hurt.

"Georgina?" Dominic's cheek was against her hair, his voice urgent. "Please – I have to know! Are you married?"

Startled, she whispered, "No, of course not!"

His arms tightened around her but, as they danced to the romantic music, neither spoke. Georgina didn't want to talk, not yet. She was still in shock. To look up and see him before her – the fulfilment of all her dreams! The sheer joy of being close to him was overwhelming. She'd shed so many tears, had dreamed so many times of a scene like this. Was he just over on a visit? She hardly dared to hope . . . But all that could come later, for now she was just content to dance, Dominic's cheek resting against hers, feeling his skin, his warmth. Amazingly, it was as though the long, intervening years had never existed.

When the number eventually came to an end, Dominic drew back slightly. He looked down at her and smiled – that special smile which had haunted her for so long. "Shall we find somewhere quiet and talk?"

She nodded, and Dominic, still holding her hand, led the way to the far side of the ballroom.

"This is the same table we were at before," he said, as they sat down. "Do you remember?"

"Yes, I do." Georgina gazed across at him, her

eyes searching his face. "You haven't changed. A little older, of course!"

Dominic smiled at her. "You've grown even more beautiful."

They were silent for a moment, then he asked, "You're not with anyone? You know, about to get engaged or anything?"

"No," she said quietly. "There's no-one. How about you?"

He shook his head. "It's the same for me. I was afraid you wouldn't recognise me. After all, it's been five years."

Not recognise him? If only he knew, Georgina thought. "Are you over on a trip, or . . ."

"No, I'm back in England for good."

At those words, Georgina's life took on a new meaning.

Dominic leaned forward. "Georgina, this is going to sound crazy. I know we only met for a few hours, but if only you knew how often I've thought of you!"

"It's been the same for me," she said with a catch in her voice.

"It was all my fault!" he said abruptly. "I knew damn well I was emigrating to Australia the next day. I should have told you. But you were so young! I thought you needed to be free, to meet other people."

"You should have let me decide that," she said sadly.

"I changed my mind, you know! I was about to tell you, when your father appeared on the scene,

445

and we both know what happened then!"

Georgina gazed at him, seeing the sincerity in his eyes, the desperation in his voice, and knew she loved him more than ever.

"I must have hurt you badly," Dominic said. "I really am sorry."

"At least you're here now," she said shakily. "But I did try to find you. I went to the offices."

He nodded. "Someone told me when I came over for my father's funeral. I thought it must have been you."

"I'm so sorry, I didn't know. When did he die?"

"About eighteen months ago," he told her. "That's when I tried to find *you*. I even went to the college, but they wouldn't tell me your surname. Then by chance, I was browsing through an old copy of *Staffordshire Life*, and saw your photograph at some dinner or other. I found out where you lived and came to your house."

Dumbfounded, Georgina stared at him. Dominic had been to Rosemount?

Why had no one told her? "I never knew that? Did you leave your name?"

He shook his head. "There was no-one in. And once I'd heard what the gardener told me, there didn't seem any point. God, when I think how devastated I was. I was absolutely gutted!" Seeing Georgina's bewilderment, Dominic told her of the gardener's fateful words. "Can you imagine how I felt, discovering that on the very day I'd come to find you, that you were marrying someone else?"

"But it was Josie's wedding! I was a bridesmaid,

not a bride!" And that, Georgina realised, would be why Josie didn't see the notice of his father's death in the paper. She'd been too busy!

"I was so stupid! Why didn't I check, why didn't I make sure? When I think of all the time I've wasted!" He leaned over, covering her hand with his own. "I've never forgotten you, Georgina, not for a single moment."

She looked down at his hand touching hers, at the light dusting of hairs, the tanned skin. This was what had lingered in her memory, this intense feeling of rightness.

"You know I fell in love with you," Dominic grinned, "in that café, when you were eating an Eccles cake and trying not to get crumbs all over your mouth!"

Georgina, her heart singing at his words, laughed. "Fancy you remembering that!"

"I remember everything. Do you?" he asked, his voice suddenly tight with anxiety.

"Oh yes," she said softly, "I remember everything." Seeing the soft light in her eyes, that was, for Dominic, the defining moment. He didn't deserve it, but this lovely girl still cared for him.

"But" Georgina continued, "you haven't told me yet about your life over there? Did you manage to study Art?"

He nodded, and Georgina listened while he told her about Australia.

"My exhibition did quite well," he said, "but then a year after Dad died, my mother decided to sell the business. She came to see me in

447

Australia, saying she intended to invest in an art gallery in Staffordshire. It was an outright bribe, of course, to tempt me to come back to England." He grinned at her. "I'd have been a fool to refuse. So, the name of Dominic Hargreaves is going to be over a small gallery in Newcastle-under-Lyme. I shall be involved in the running of it, of course, but not full-time. The plan is to exhibit my paintings and some local artists, as well as some well-known ones. It has to be a paying concern – I'm determined to make a financial success of it."

"They forgave you, then? Your parents, I mean. I know you left without leaving a forwarding address."

He nodded. "Yes, it was rotten of me, but I got in touch a few months after I went out. Anyway, that's enough about me. What's been happening in your life?"

"What do you think he's saying?" Josie hissed, looking anxiously across at the table where Georgina and Dominic were sitting.

Nick laughed. "Well, they have got five years to catch up on."

"I know. I'm still flabbergasted! Just fancy, Dominic just turning up like that out of the blue!"

"So you've said, sweetheart. At least four times."

Josie looked across the table at him. "Oh Nick, I do hope he isn't going to disappear again! It would break her heart." Then she had a horrifying thought. "You don't think he'd take her back to Australia with him? I'd never see her again!"

"Why don't you just wait and see?" he said, and then caught at her hand. "Listen! They're playing our tune. Come on, Mrs Hamilton!"

Josie laughed. She'd told Nick about her 'moment of truth' in Bournemouth, with the refrain of "No Other Love" drifting from the hotel lounge. I only hope, she thought, as they danced dreamily together, that Georgina finds as much happiness as I have.

Chapter 47

Four years later, just as the autumn tints were fading, and the trees in Queen's Park were beginning to shed their leaves, a little girl ran laughing along the path at the side of the lake.

"Don't go near the edge!" Josie called.

Georgina, walking by her side, was pushing a navy Silver Cross pram, and bending, tucked a white satin-edged blanket around her small baby. "How are things going?"

"Fine. We've got our moving date now," Josie told her. "We should be nicely settled in for Christmas."

"It'll be wonderful having you live near us."

Josie smiled. "The fact that you and Dominic were living in Barlaston was a big attraction. Although it's a lovely area, what with the Downs and everything."

"Nick's done well, hasn't he?" Georgina said. "I mean, from supplying market stalls, to a whole-sale fancy goods business, is a big achievement."

"He just seems to have an eye for the right thing that sells."

"I think they call it being an entrepreneur," Georgina grinned.

"Well, his success has definitely been one in the eye for his stepfather!" Josie said with satisfaction.

"Are things no better between them?"

Josie shook her head. "No, but we try to keep the peace for the sake of his mother." And, she thought, now that her solicitor has talked some sense into her, Gerald Rhodes no longer poses a threat. She looked at her friend.

"How are things at Rosemount?" Josie knew things hadn't been easy since William Hawkins had suffered a stroke.

"Not too bad, although I don't think my mother's enjoying looking after an invalid. But he refuses to have anyone else in. The problem is she's been so used to being able to go off to her meetings and lunches. It's a big change for her."

Josie thought, I bet it is! But she simply asked, "So, they're not thinking of retiring to Bournemouth any more?"

Georgina shook her head. "No, although I think that was mainly her idea. My father was never that keen."

"I don't think my parents would ever move away from the Potteries," Josie said. "Their roots are here. Besides, they wouldn't want to leave their grandchildren."

"Have you seen Pauline and Fergal lately?"

"Yes, they're fine. No sign of any babies yet, but they're hoping. Fergal, of course, is looking better all the time."

"Well, the doctors did say it would be a long job."

They walked slowly for a while in companionable silence, and then Georgina said, "Oh, I didn't tell you – Dominic sold one of his paintings to a collector in London."

"That's brilliant!"

Georgina laughed, and glanced at her. "Funny, isn't it, how life turns out? It's really all chance."

"I know," Josie said. "That and timing." She glanced at her friend. "If Dominic had never come back, I wonder who you would have married?"

"I'd probably be a sort of maiden aunt to all your children."

"Hang on, I've only got one, so far!"

"Yes, but you've another on the way," Georgina laughed. "Perhaps it will be another girl, then she could be best friends with this one." She wheeled the pram round. "I think we'd better be getting back. It's turning chilly."

Josie nodded. "Come on, sweetheart! It's time to go home," she called.

And as the small girl turned away from feeding the ducks, Georgina said, "She loves that muff you had made for her, doesn't she? I've been thinking – I'm sure I had one just like that when I was young."

Both mothers watched Josie's daughter slip her cold hands into the cosy blue velvet.

"You were lucky," Josie said softly. "I never did."

THE END

'Ms Kaine's refreshingly simple prose is perfect'
Ireland on Sunday

A Girl Of Her Time

MARGARET KAINE

Vibrant Maureen Matthews has always dreamt of a life beyond the Potteries. Then, just like a scene from one of her beloved movies, she meets handsome, charming Trevor Mountford. He seems to be everything Maureen ever hoped for and when he asks her to marry him, she has no hesitation in saying yes.

But married life isn't what Maureen thought it would be, and she quickly starts to question both her life and her love. Then she meets Greg. He's completely different from what she thought she wanted – but could he be everything she's ever needed?

Available in paperback and ebook

HODDER

'It's an absorbing read, so well crafted that your heart
will beat just a little faster as you're drawn into the
riveting battle between heartbreak and hope'
Daily Record

Rosemary

MARGARET KAINE

**One girl's loneliness. One woman's emptiness.
One phone call that will change both
their lives forever.**

When her mother dies in a tragic accident, Rosemary
thinks life couldn't get any worse. Penniless and
alone, she is betrayed by the one man she thought
she could trust. Then her whole world changes
when she finds out that she's adopted.

Beth has spent a lifetime regretting giving up her only
daughter. Surrounded by the riches of the Rushtons,
she's determined that one day she'll find the child she
lost and reunite her with her true family.

And when that vital first connection is made, neither
of their lives will ever be the same again . . .

Available in paperback and ebook

HODDER